THE
EXILE

Books by Andrew Britton

THE
EXILE

ANDREW BRITTON

PINNACLE BOOKS
Kensington Publishing Corp.
www.kensingtonbooks.com

PINACLE BOOKS are published by

Kensington Publishing Corp.
119 West 40th Street
New York, NY 10018.

All Kensington titles, imprints and distributed lines are available at special quantity discounts for bulk purchases for sales promotion, premiums, fund-raising, educational or institutional use. Special book excerpts or customized printings can also be created to fit specific needs. For details, write or phone the office of the Kensington Special Sales Manager: Kensington Publishing Corp., 119 West 40th Street, New York, NY 10018. Attn. Special Sales Department. Phone: 1-800-221-2647.

ISBN-13: 978-0-7680-2256-4
ISBN-10: 0-7680-2256-6

First Printing: July 2010
First Paperback Printing: June 2011

10 9 8 7 6 5 4 3 2 1

Printed in the United States of America

For Valerie

ACKNOWLEDGMENTS

Thanks to all my readers, I hope I never disappoint.

And continued thanks to everyone at Kensington, especially Steven Zacharius, Laurie Parkin, Michaela Hamilton, Doug Mendini and Meryl Earl.

To my editor Audrey LaFehr, for her continued enthusiasm, encouragement and exceptional patience. You're a wonder.

And to my agent, Nancy Coffey, for her unwavering support and encouragement. I couldn't have done it without you.

AUTHOR'S NOTE

Readers familiar with the international security firm called Blackwater Worldwide may know it has been officially renamed Xe Services. This reportedly resulted from its association with United States military operations in Iraq, which continue to be opposed by many of Blackwater's client governments in Africa and the Middle East.

While Blackwater's name change did indeed occur, the journalists that covered the story were obviously unaware of Ryan Kealey's pivotal role in forcing the issue—as the following pages will reveal.

CHAPTER 1

CAMP HADITH, WEST DARFUR
APRIL

To the untrained eye, the inhabitants of Camp Hadith might have seemed like any group of refugees the world over—a cluster of lost souls bound by poverty, persecution, and a complete lack of hope. To the untrained eye, they might have seemed tragically the same. But in reality their squalid existence was one of the few things they had in common.

They comprised a strange demographic made up of black Christians from the south, African Muslims from the north, and poor Arabs from the slums outside Khartoum. They came from a multitude of tribes, which was arguably more important than their religious differences given the lack of a single national identity in Africa's largest country. They were Dinka, Masalit, and Fur. They were Berti, Bargo, and Beni Jarrar. But while sharing only the terrible circumstances that had thrust them together, they could all agree on this: were it not for the woman—the American nurse—their life in the camp would have been a living hell.

As it stood, they endured a daily struggle for survival despite the woman's devotion to them and their unrelenting plight, which was apparent to all. Situated one kilometer east of the paved road from Al-Geneina to Nyala—the capital city of South Darfur—the temporary settlement consisted of nothing more than three hundred hastily constructed shelters. Most were crudely composed of clothes, rugs, and plastic trash bags draped over a rough framework of interwoven branches. A few lucky families—those who had arrived in the early stages of the camp's development—had access to sturdy canvas tents supplied by USAID, also known as the United States Agency for International Development; UNICEF; or Médicins Sans Frontières, the Paris-based organization better known as Doctors Without Borders.

Surrounding the entire camp was a two-and-a-half-meter fence as crude and impermanent as the tents it was meant to secure. Covered by black tarpaulin sheets, its wooden poles were spaced at three-meter intervals and thrust two meters into the sodden earth to provide a reasonably stable frame for the makeshift barrier. The fence, in turn, was topped by a single strand of barbed wire that ran the length of the perimeter. Beyond it there was nothing but the road and the sun-scrubbed landscape, which stretched for miles in every direction.

The hospital, the only permanent structure to be found within the flimsy tarpaulin fence, rose like an island from the sweeping sea of tents. It was a sprawling, one-story structure of reddish brown mud bricks, each of which had been forged by a careful pair of hands before being laid out to bake in the harsh African sun. The humble building was topped by a roof of corrugated tin, its windows sealed with clear plastic, which provided some protection against the tiny winged predators whose flights could be as lethal as that of any stealth assassins in that part of the world.

Both the flies and the mosquitoes could kill a healthy aid worker with a single bite or sting, especially when the rains came in late July. For the vast majority of Camp Hadith's residents, the risk was far greater. Unless caught at an early stage, malaria was a virtual death sentence in the internally displaced persons camps—the young and the very old being at highest risk. African trypanosomiasis, or sleeping sickness, could be added to the long list of rampant scourges that included measles, tuberculosis, and the worst killer of all, the HIV retrovirus, which had held the continent in its iron grip for decades.

And, of course, there was the poverty and ignorance. The terrible, persistent unavailability of basic health care, education, and nutrition, which flung open the doors to every opportunistic strain of disease emerging from the steppes and woodlands to the north.

Never far from the nurse's mind, the many dangers that plagued the camp accounted for her sense of profound sorrow as she quietly made her way down the narrow aisle separating the hospital's forty beds. She always felt this way when she stopped to consider the magnitude of what the African people had suffered. Of what they *still* suffered on an hourly and daily basis. Lily Durant had been in West Darfur for just six months, but during that time she had come to see the true depth of hardship that her patients endured. Not to understand it, but to *see* it in front of her, around her, everywhere.

For Lily, that was an important distinction. She wanted to help these people, but she didn't claim to identify with them. Nor did she pretend to understand what they were going through. Her refusal to do so wasn't a matter of Western arrogance—in fact, it was the complete opposite. In Lily's eyes, the situation was simple. She was there to help. Not to judge, not to empathize, not to intellectualize. But to help. Nothing more, nothing less.

Reaching the end of the aisle now, she heard a small noise to her right. As she turned toward the sound to check it out, she moved quickly to the side of the bed and knelt by the hard mattress. Her calves and thighs immediately screamed out in protest, as if to remind her that she'd been on her feet for the past twenty hours. But Lily ignored the pain and focused on the patient lying before her.

She leaned forward, her fingers brushing against the mosquito net that covered the squirming figure.

"Hello, Limya. *Badai lo cadai?*" she whispered, asking the sick girl if she needed anything in the Zaghawa tribal dialect. It was one of many local phrases Lily had made it a personal imperative to master. While it was nearly impossible to absorb all the languages of the camp, she had found that even a few key phrases could help bridge the cultural and linguistic divide.

Do you need anything? And they all did. More than any one person could give. But nothing was worse than nothing, and that was the sum total of indifference.

Lily felt she'd waited a long time before the patient replied. Then, without warning, the girl let out a short, high-pitched squeal that sent a shiver of alarm through Lily's body. She grasped blindly for the girl's fragile hand through the mosquito netting. When she found it, she squeezed it gently in an attempt to reassure her. Only then did Lily realize that the girl was dreaming, caught up in the tangled web of her own terrible past.

She continued to squirm and cry out for a few minutes longer. After what seemed like an eternity, the moaning began to subside. Then it stopped altogether.

Once Lily was finally sure that the girl was asleep, she closed her eyes and permitted herself a deep, weary sigh. She was mentally and physically exhausted and knew that the strain was starting to show. Even as she acknowledged the truth of this, though, she silently rebuked herself for being so weak. What business did she have complaining about her minor aches and pains when the people in this very room had lost so much? The sleeping girl whose hand she even now continued to hold was a perfect example of the terrible things taking place in the region.

Only sixteen, Limya Sanoasi had lost her mother, father, and two younger brothers one week earlier, when their village was razed by the government-backed Janjaweed militiamen who terrorized the non-Arab population of Darfur. Their methods were notorious. Rape, torture, and murder were all considered acceptable tools of war—and since they had the support of the country's ruling party, they were virtually unstoppable.

Lily freed her hand carefully, doing her best not to wake the girl. Then she got to her feet and started back down the aisle in her foam-bottomed clogs, heading for the building's single entrance. As she passed each bed—all of them were occupied—Lily silently thanked God for the relative security of the camp and its perimeter fence, however symbolic the protection offered by the thin tarpaulin walls might be. The Janjaweed had attacked the IDP camps before, but such incidents were rare, as they typically resulted in a diplomatic outcry against the regime of Omar al-Bashir, the Sudanese president. Even al-Bashir—a man who topped *Parade* magazine's annual list of the world's ten worst dictators in 2006 and three years later was charged with crimes against humanity by the International Criminal Court—

had little interest in stirring up serious trouble with the UN or the United States.

At least, that was the general assumption. Personally, Lily wasn't so sure. Less than a month earlier, the United States had levied harsh sanctions against the North African country, adding to the heavy restrictions already in place as a result of the ICC's indictment. The punitive measures had touched the highest levels of the Sudanese government, most noticeably in the case of the defense minister, whose U.S. accounts had been frozen.

Al-Bashir had responded to the ICC arrest warrant through polite, if evasive, diplomatic channels—a public fight with its 109 member nations was the furthest thing from what he wanted or needed. But the United States, a nonmember still trying to dig its way out from the global ill will generated by its Iraqi conflict, was another story . . . and a convenient target for his chest-thumping wrath.

Months after the new sanctions were imposed, he'd given a fiery speech condemning them. And while he'd stopped short of threatening outright retribution, there was no doubt in anyone's mind that he was on the verge of striking back at the world's lone superpower and sending out an indirect, albeit powerful, message to the ICC—namely, his intention of submitting to foreign justice was nil. He was not going down without a fight and had cast himself in the convenient, familiar role of a victim forced to retaliate against the imperial American bully.

The question, in the big picture, was how, and when, the first blow would come.

Lily Durant's recent experiences at Camp Hadith, however, had given her a more close-up perspective.

For Lily the focus narrowed down to a little refugee camp in the middle of an African nowhere, a teenage girl caught in the throes of her fever dreams, and her fear that the inexorable madness of attack and reprisal would come, rolling them into the ground.

The cold air of the desert night seeped in through the open door and clawed at the exposed flesh of the commander's face and throat. He stood inside the darkened compound and watched as his men gathered on the hard-packed dirt of the parade ground in front of his office. The building was pitch-black, but the lights of the compound were ablaze, rendering him invisible to those milling about in the open area. They were laughing, joking, and slapping each other's shoulders. They were full of *life*, and watching them, the commander could not help but smile himself. He could feel their excitement, and it reminded him of the first time he had embarked on a similar venture—the first time he had successfully probed the fragile constraints of his own moral character.

He could not fully relate to these men, as they were not real soldiers in his mind, but a disparate collection of animals bound loosely by the promise of separate rewards.

Now he watched as they checked and rechecked their weapons, an assortment of small arms procured from every possible source: Kalashnikovs from Ukraine, PP-19 submachine guns taken out of Afghanistan, and Belgian-made FAL rifles left over from the bloody civil wars in Liberia and Mozambique. A few carried AR-15s, the civilian version of the U.S. Army's M16. Their favored tools, however, were not the battered firearms they carried, but the knives, hatchets, and machetes that hung from their belt loops.

Just as they carried a variety of arms, the men wore a wide range of clothing. A few had desert fatigues of the sort used by the U.S. military, a uniform that carried a certain level of prestige in the mixed unit. The rest wore police uniforms, tracksuits, or T-shirts and jeans. Like the inhabitants of the camp they were planning to strike, they were bound only by exigencies. His mercenaries, with their uneven training and wild temperament, accepting a slight degree of discipline in exchange for the promise of combat and treasure. The dedicated and more practiced mujahideen sharing their desire for earthly plunder, but seeking to pad their material bounty with the eternal gratifications of Heaven.

A patchwork force, yes. Still, the commander knew how to keep them primed and motivated as they prepared for action, knew what heady elixir was drunk by his ragtag coalition of zealots, godless infidels, and outlaws, whose dutiful prayers were only to assure they reaped the rewards of the destruction they were about to deal out. He'd savored its taste many times—and welcomed it.

They were bound now by anticipation. Anticipation for the work they would soon carry out with brutal, unrelenting purpose. Anticipation for the job he had given them, for the blood they were about to spill . . . and for the rewards that were sure to follow.

Their raucous laughter poured into the night and over the dark buildings like a rippling black tide.

The commander did his best to maintain a stoic bearing as he watched them, although he shared their contagious enthusiasm. The façade was necessary to preserve the fragile balance of power that existed in the small garrison. He held control over life and death in his hands, and there were few limits to what he could do. In the space of a five-minute telephone call, he could seal the fate of 100 Masalit villagers. With nothing more than a polite suggestion, a whispered word to the major in charge in Nyala, he could condemn a dozen Dinka children to death by fire. It was the ultimate authority, and he had never used it sparingly. In that respect, at least, this night's work would be no different from all the rest.

A sudden noise pierced the commander's thoughts, and he stepped through the open door into the cold night air, where the sound of approaching diesel engines was more pronounced. He shivered as he waited impatiently, his broad face twisting into a frown. As bad as it was during the day, the desert was even less accommodating at night.

Fortunately, he did not have to wait long. Less than a minute after he stepped out of the building, the trucks rolled into view and stopped next to the parade ground, a cloud of dust rising into the air, mixing with the stench of diesel fumes, cigarette smoke, and unwashed bodies. There was a loud babble of voices, and the keyed-up men began moving toward the vehicles.

The commander's car, a borrowed white Mercedes-Benz, was already waiting in front of his office. The driver was behind the wheel, his engine idling. The commander walked over, opened the door, and slid into the rear seat. He shut the door and shivered with pleasure when he felt the warm air churning out of the vents. He gave a signal to his driver, and the car rolled forward, the trucks following in convoy.

As the small line of vehicles left the main gate forty seconds later, the commander pulled a satellite phone from the deep right pocket of his field jacket, dialed a number from memory, and lifted the phone to his ear. Two rings later a man answered.

"We're on the move. Turn off the phones, and send the plane."

At first, Lily didn't understand why she was awake. She lay still for a long moment, wondering what could have possibly roused her from her much-needed sleep. She was conscious of the frigid air on her face, the warmth of her sleeping bag, and the mosquito netting that was draped less than a foot over her head. The camp was surprisingly quiet, except for the distant sound of an infant's cries. Everything was just as it should be, yet *something* had pulled her from the deepest sleep she'd had in a month . . . and that itself was unusual.

She lay there for several minutes, listening in her stillness. But while she heard nothing out of the ordinary, she could not shake the sense of lingering dread.

She tugged her arms out of her sleeping bag, flopped onto her left side, and pressed a button on her wristwatch—a sturdy Alpina her uncle had given her as a going-away present. The LED display told her it was just after 4:00 a.m., which meant she had been out for three hours. After making her rounds in the hospital, she'd walked straight back to her tent, which was located less than 100 feet from the building's main entrance. She could have had a bed inside the hospital, like the camp's doctor and the two other nurses, but had chosen instead to sleep in a tent, not wanting to take away from the refugees the already scant space inside the building.

Lily turned onto her stomach, covered her head with

her pillow, and tried to drown out the thoughts buzzing through her mind. Literally buzzing like a hornet's nest. There was so much to worry about. As always, the chronic lack of food and supplies, and now the troubling height and weight data from the feeding center. Earlier that evening she had learned that Faisel, a one-year-old boy from the nearby village of Sirba, was still losing weight despite extra rations of milk and close personal attention from the camp's medical staff. Given his current rate of decline, Lily feared he would not see the end of the week, and she still didn't know how she would explain his death to his parents. Two weeks earlier they'd lost his older sister, their only daughter, to dysentery. How were they supposed to understand it? What words of comfort would she find? Did a vocabulary even *exist* that could mitigate the sort of pain and grief she believed was in store for them?

These were the types of thoughts she could not block out no matter how hard she tried. And meanwhile the buzzing in her ears wouldn't stop, making her back so stiff, it ached from tension . . . keeping her awake, wide awake, on her narrow, springy cot inside the darkened tent.

And then, suddenly, she realized that the buzzing wasn't some kind of weird internal manifestation of nerves and fatigue, after all. When the awareness hit her, she instinctively rejected it, as the alternative just wasn't possible. The camps were supposed to be safe ground. She had been told as much the day she arrived. But the noise didn't fade. Instead, it grew steadily louder.

Struggling to suppress her rising unease, Lily climbed out of her sleeping bag, pulled on a pair of flannel pajama bottoms and a thick woolen sweater, and threw back the flaps of her tent. Easing her way through the narrow opening, she got to her feet and looked around in disbelief. She immediately realized that her earlier dread was completely justified. Dozens of refugees were struggling out of their makeshift shelters, and they were all staring upward, eyes wide with fear.

She tracked her own gaze in the direction they were looking and saw the plane at once, a black, slow-moving fleck against the starlit sky. For a second, she allowed herself to believe it was just a transport plane—a small Cessna ferrying aid workers back to Abéché, perhaps. Or a medical-supply flight making the daily run to Al-Geneina. Even as she considered these possibilities, though, she could hear—and sense—the panic rising around her.

The refugees had no room in their psyches for denial. It had been scoured from their inner landscapes by hard experience, leaving them with a keen, stark acceptance of reality. They knew what kind of plane this was. More to the point, they knew what was coming, and they had reacted with incredible speed. Hundreds were pouring out of their makeshift shelters, and some were already running toward the rear of the camp, their children and a few meager possessions caught up in their arms.

Frozen with dread and horror, Lily saw Beckett, the camp's doctor, stumble out of the building, a backpack slung over his right shoulder. As he looked up at the plane circling overhead, he did a slow, strange kind of pirouette, his mouth agape. Then his eyes came back to ground level, and he looked around wildly. For a second Lily didn't understand what he was doing. Then, as she looked on in sheer disbelief, he took off running, sprinting ahead of the steady stream of people running for the back side of the camp. The two nurses were just a few steps behind him.

"Hey!" she screamed, fighting to be heard over the general panic. "Hey, where are you going?"

She chased after the three fleeing aid workers, but there were too many people moving in the same direction, and she couldn't break through the crowd. The screams were deafening: parents shouting for their children to hurry, children howling for parents they had lost in the crowd, and Lily's own cries of outrage, all directed at the fleeing Americans. "Where are you going?" she shouted again. "Where are you . . . What are you doing? Come back!"

But she was wasting her breath—they had already moved out of earshot. Lily swore in an undertone, then turned and started toward the hospital, dodging the few people in her way. No one was moving in this direction. She could not believe what she had just seen. Beckett and the two nurses had abandoned their patients without a moment's hesitation. The full measure of their cowardice was staggering, but the worst part was that they *knew* the consequences of their actions. By running, they were leaving the refugees behind to be slaughtered.

The first bomb hit when she was 10 feet from the building's entrance. Even though she had been waiting for it, the impact still came as a shock and nearly threw her off her feet. A cloud of flames erupted somewhere off to her left, and she turned in time to see a pair of bodies hurled into the air. The sound came a split second later, a hollow boom that reverberated in her chest, and she heard the screams rise into the smoke-filled air as she sprinted the last few feet, flinging herself through the open door and into the hospital.

Once inside, she steadied herself and looked around desperately, trying to impose a measure of sense on the chaotic scene. Some of the patients had tried to flee, but most did not have the strength. The moment they'd climbed out of bed, they had collapsed to the floor . . . and that was where they were lying now. A number of them were completely motionless, while others were writhing around and crying out for help.

She went to the nearest, an elderly Fur man trying to claw his way free of the mosquito netting wrapped round his body. She quickly pulled it away from his flailing limbs, murmuring words of reassurance the whole time. Then she lifted him off the floor, shocked as always by how easy it was. All skin and bones, he couldn't have weighed more than 80 pounds.

Gently getting him onto the empty bed, Lily moved on to the next person. As she attended to each patient, she was all too aware of the terrible, earsplitting sounds outside—the crump of the falling bombs was loud enough to cover the screams of the wounded, but she could still hear their cries in the short, ominous gaps between concussive blasts. And despite the horror of the aerial assault, she knew that the worst was yet to come. When the bombs stopped falling, the Janjaweed would move in, burning everything in their path, killing anyone left alive.

Part of her knew that her efforts were futile—that everything she was doing to help these people would be wasted in the end. But even as these thoughts entered her mind, she kept working steadily. She didn't know for how long. Five minutes, ten, time was a measureless thing for her, distilled to a charged, frantic *now.*

Lost as she was in what she was doing, it took Lily a while to realize that something had changed. She stopped and looked up, listening hard. A quiet, quavering voice to her left startled her back to an awareness of her situation, and she turned to the person who'd spoken the words.

Limya Sanoasi was sitting upright in her bed, her small hands folded in her lap. Her broken left leg, one of the many injuries she'd sustained in the recent raid on her village, was hidden beneath a threadbare blanket. The blanket was still smooth and tucked in at the corners. Lily was struck by the fact that she hadn't even tried to run.

"It's the bombs," Limya repeated in English. Her solemn face was unnaturally calm; only her voice hinted at the true level of fear she was feeling. "That is what you are listening for."

"They've stopped," Lily whispered.

"Yes. The plane is gone, but the men will follow. You must go now."

Lily stared back at the girl for a long moment, intensely aware of the sounds outside the building. She could hear the militiamen's laughter and occasional bursts of gunfire mingled with the blood-curdling screams of the refugees who hadn't escaped in time.

"I'm not going anywhere," she finally said. She did her best to sound calm and assured, but her eyes slipped away when she spoke again. "Al-Bashir is afraid of my country, Limya. He is afraid of our army. They won't hurt you if I stand in their way, I promise. They wouldn't dare to—"

"You're wrong," the girl said. Her voice was quiet but certain, and Lily felt a sudden tremor of doubt. "They will kill you. They will kill everyone, and there is nothing more you can do. You should leave now."

Lily didn't shift her gaze from the girl, but her eyes glazed over as she struggled to take sane, logical stock of her choices—or some approximation of it amid the fundamentally *insane* circumstances confronting her. On one level, she felt a primitive, almost overpowering urge to run, and she hated herself for it. At the same time, what more could she do?

Fair enough question, she thought. She had stayed behind at this crucial moment, stayed true to her principles, and she had tried to help them. Wasn't that enough? Could she really stop what was going to happen here? Even delay it? Or would she just be another lamb to the slaughter?

Limya seemed to sense what was running through her head. "Go," she repeated. Her voice was little more than a whisper, her brown eyes damp, wide, and imploring. *"Please."*

Lily Durant cast one last desperate glance at the door, but she had already made her decision.

"I can't," she said quietly. She locked eyes with the girl again, and this time her gaze was steady. "I won't leave you."

A look of profound sadness crossed the teenager's face. She closed her eyes, lowered her head, and murmured a few words in Zaghawa. At that moment the first of several figures appeared in the door, blocking the last remaining route of escape. When she heard them enter, Lily took a deep breath, stood, and turned to face them. She had just set her feet when the first one reached her on the run.

She didn't see the punch coming. It simply *arrived,* landing high on her right cheek, splitting the skin to the bone. Stunned by the sheer force of the blow, she stumbled back and raised her hands in self-defense. But it was no use; they were just too strong.

The beating that followed was both methodical and completely merciless. They slapped her face, pulled her hair, and tore the clothes from her body. She felt a pair of hands groping her bare breasts and pried them loose with all her strength, or tried getting them off her, crying out in rage and revulsion. Then they wrestled her to the floor—five of them, six, maybe more than that crowding over and around her, *mobbing* her, too many of them to fight. Somewhere in the distance she could hear Limya and a few others begging them to stop, but the assault continued, their fists raining down from above, their boots pounding relentlessly into her ribs. Even as the world seemed to fade around her, she forced herself to stay conscious. For what, she didn't know. But some stubborn inner voice told her to keep fighting.

She turned onto her right side and tightened into a ball, trying to make herself a smaller target. That only seemed to enrage them further. A particularly vicious kick to the base of her spine caused her back to arch, and her arms and legs sprung open, as if of their own accord. Her assailants were quick to take advantage. One man dropped down on top of her, pinning her splayed arms and legs to the floor, and the others moved in on either side to await their turn.

At that moment a single shot penetrated the chaos. The hands moved away, and the men holding her down jumped up and stepped aside. They backed off slowly, and she managed to scramble away in turn, her feet kicking wildly at empty air, splinters from the rough wooden floor digging into the heels of her hands. She slid back until she hit a wall, but it wasn't far enough, and she kept pushing against it like a trapped, helpless creature surrounded by a feral pack, irrationally willing her body to sink into the solid material.

It took her a moment to realize that someone had followed the militiamen into the hospital. He was standing before her now, and even through the swelling around her eyes, she could recognize that his uniform was that of a lieutenant colonel in the Sudanese army.

He murmured something over his right shoulder, and another man stepped forward, lifted a digital camera to eye level, and pointed the lens down at her face. When he was satisfied that it was recording properly, he said a few words in Arabic to the officer, who replied with a grunt.

Lily had folded her arms over her exposed breasts the instant she saw the camera, but the officer didn't seem to notice. He was holding a small square of glossy paper in his right hand. He stared at the paper for a long moment, as if committing its contents to memory. As her mind slowly adjusted to the unexpected turn of events, Lily realized he was looking at a photograph. His eyes moved to her battered, tear-streaked face, and he studied her carefully.

"You are Lilith Durant?"

She was still struggling to catch her breath. When she could speak, she said, "Yes."

"The niece of the American president?"

For a second Lily did not think she had heard correctly. But then the full weight of the words hit her, and in that instant she knew why they had attacked the camp.

Somehow, they had learned who she really was. She had done everything in her power to keep a low profile, but it was now clear that somewhere along the line, she—or somebody close to her—had made a critical mistake. It was the only possible explanation, and the officer's words were enough to verify her worst fears. They had come for her, and in doing so, they had been willing to destroy anything and everyone that stood in their way.

Everything that had just happened to the camp, the destruction that swept over it, killing so many of the refugees, leaving those innocent men, women, and children *massacred* . . . she had brought it all down on them.

All of it, *all* of it, was her damned fault.

She closed her eyes in anguish, crushed by her sudden revelation. She felt dizzy, sick with guilt, but she couldn't change what had happened, and it wouldn't help to dwell on it. The only thing she could do now was try to save as many lives as possible, starting with the people in the surrounding beds.

She took a second to collect herself and then opened her eyes. The commander was watching her closely.

"Please," she whispered through bloodied lips. "Let it end here. With me."

The commander didn't react, but he had spoken in fluent English before, and Lily knew he could understand.

"You don't have to do this," she pressed. "These people are not a threat to you. The camp is destroyed, and the people who ran will not come back. You've made your point—"

"And what do you believe that to be?" His eyes were fixed on her. "Look at me carefully, Ms. Durant. Is mine the face of a master or follower?"

Lily stared in confused silence, her mind groping for a response. When it didn't find one, she simply shook her head in futility. "You've got what you came for. You have me. Please, just let the rest of them live. *Please.*"

The colonel seemed to consider her request for a long moment, and Lily felt a tiny spark of hope.

"I'm afraid I can't do that." The colonel held out his hand, palm up, and Lily watched in despair as a second man stepped forward to hand over a large black pistol. The colonel hefted it in his hand as he smiled down at her. "But don't worry. Those you came to help won't be without you for long."

He extended the pistol at arm's length, and Lily closed her eyes, found herself counting down. She didn't know why, maybe just to give herself something to focus on besides the pounding of her heart.

The last thing Lily Durant heard was a young girl's scream of rage and despair. Then her world ceased to exist.

CHAPTER 2

CAMP DAVID, MARYLAND

The sky was still dark over central Maryland as the Bell 206B Jet-Ranger cut a fast, steady path north, sweeping over the gentle rise of the Blue Ridge Mountains. Although the helicopter had room for four passengers, just one was on board for the short hop from Langley, Virginia, to Camp David, in the northernmost reaches of Catoctin Mountain Park. He had buckled in just twenty minutes earlier, but checking his watch, the sole passenger saw that he was already close to his final destination. The private retreat of every U.S. president since Franklin Delano Roosevelt was just 70 miles from the White House, and not much farther from the passenger's point of embarkation. When he realized how close they were to touching down, he swore softly under his breath. Everything was moving too fast, and the worst was still to come.

Normally, he would have been gratified by the short travel time, as it wasn't the usual state of things. As the deputy director of the Central Intelligence Agency, Jonathan Harper was used to working on the fly, whether it was in the backseat of a government car or in the air, on one of the Agency's executive jets. On this occasion, however, he could not bring himself to focus on the upcoming meeting. It wasn't even the lack of useful information on hand, although that certainly wasn't helping matters. Simply stated, he was still trying to wrap his mind around the news he had been given just one hour earlier.

The call had come in on his secure telephone at two minutes past midnight. Fifteen minutes later he had stumbled out of his three-story town house on Embassy Row to meet the black Lincoln Town Car that was already idling at the curb. His driver had taken him straight to Agency headquarters outside Langley, where the Jet-Ranger's twin rotors were already turning. In his hurry to get in the air, Harper had not had the opportunity to fully absorb what he'd been told by the night duty officer trotting along with him on the tarmac.

The news could not have been worse. The refugee camp at which the president's niece had been working in Darfur had been burned to the ground, a fact that satellite imagery had confirmed just five minutes earlier. They had heard from at least one reliable witness that Lily Durant had been killed in the attack. That particular fact had yet to be verified, though there was little doubt in Harper's mind that it was true.

The deputy director of operations at Langley had called Harper personally to relay the first piece of information—and although it wasn't much, Harper was grateful for it. The SATINT seemed only to confirm their worst fears, but at least it was something to work with. More to the point, it was hard intel. Harper couldn't abide conjecture for one simple reason. . . . He couldn't afford to. The nation's intelligence apparatus was fueled by information, and given the stakes, that information had to be rock solid each and every time. That partly accounted for Harper's dread of the upcoming meeting. He had almost no information to work with, which meant he was about to be put in the uncomfortable position of being briefed by his own superiors.

His own personal ignorance, however, wasn't Harper's primary concern. What really worried him was the emotional element involved in this particular situation. He had served the current president for nearly six years, and Harper knew him to be a smart, careful, methodical man. A man who had never let his power—or his anger—influence his ability to analyze and solve a given problem. He didn't always come up with the right answers, but to his credit he never lost sight of the overall picture, or the core awareness that millions of people were affected by every decision he made. Still, Harper couldn't help but wonder if the president would be able to maintain that sense of proportion given the tragic circumstances, and felt uneasy when he considered the possible consequences if he could not.

A voice in his ear jolted Jonathan Harper back to the present. It was the pilot informing him that they were three minutes out. Harper keyed his mic and acknowledged the words, then settled back in his seat. He closed his eyes and took a few deep breaths, trying in vain to clear his mind, knowing that he would need a clear head for the upcoming meeting.

A few minutes later the helicopter touched down with a slight jolt, the skids settling onto the rain-drenched tarmac. Harper waited until the pilot gave him the all clear. Then he unbuckled his harness, removed his headset, and reached for the door.

It was a short ride from the helipad to Aspen Lodge, the presidential cabin on the east side of the compound. As the black Tahoe threaded its way along the steep mountain road, a Secret Service agent behind the wheel, Harper stared out the rain-streaked window. This was his first time visiting the presidential retreat, and despite the troubling thoughts swirling through his mind, he found himself absorbed in the passing scenery. He had always been interested in history. In fact, he had minored in that particular subject at Boston College some twenty-two years earlier, and it was hard not to feel the weight of it here.

After passing the camp commander's quarters, they turned onto a secondary road and immediately hit a checkpoint. Harper displayed his ID to the marine sergeant standing post, and the sentry proceeded to call in the information. They were cleared through a moment later.

Without being asked, the driver hit a button and the window whirred up. Then the Tahoe lurched forward, the tires slipping for a moment on the damp road. A mile or so later the road curved gently to the left, and Aspen Lodge came into view.

Harper's first thought was that the presidential cabin didn't look like much. The brightly-lit exterior was constructed of rough-hewn planks painted a monotonous shade of gray. A single fieldstone chimney jutted from the black shingle roof, and the building itself was dwarfed by the surrounding oak, maple, and hickory

trees. In front of the cabin, a grassy slope led down to a
modest pond fringed by cattails and irises. On the
whole, the building looked like it could belong to anyone with a little money and a need to get away from it
all. The only sign that it might be something more was
the Secret Service agents posted in front of the two
main entrances, as well as the dark shapes Harper had
seen moving through the trees on the approach to the
building.

Harper knew that the retreat was guarded year-
round by approximately 100 soldiers and sailors, the
bulk of whom were drawn from the ranks of the navy
and the marines. As he opened the door and stepped
out of the vehicle, he found himself wondering if they
knew what had transpired in Darfur less than eight
hours earlier. Looking up at the members of the president's detail, he took note of the hard edge to their
usual fixed expressions and decided that these individuals, at least, had been made aware of the situation.
Even from 30 feet away, Harper could sense their anger
and frustration. A person close to the president had
died on their watch, and they had been unable to stop
it from happening. Of course, it was absurd to think
they could have prevented it, and on some level, they
would know that as well. At the same time, Harper was
quietly impressed by their demeanor. In his eyes, the
fact that they were taking it so personally was a testa-
ment to their commitment and professionalism.

A tall figure was coming down the steps at a brisk
pace, his features blotted out by the light at his back. As
he drew closer, his face came into focus, and Harper
recognized him at once. Joshua McCabe was the assistant director of the Office of Protective Research, one
of the senior figures in the U.S. Secret Service. Harper

had worked with him several years earlier to prevent an attempt on the president's life. The CIA—and one man in particular—had been instrumental in preventing the assassination, and to his credit, McCabe had never forgotten the Agency's crucial role in averting that near catastrophe. Thanks to him, Harper had more access to the president than most of the cabinet. More importantly, McCabe was able to provide insight as to the president's general mood, as well as his stance on various issues. Harper supposed that accounted for why he felt relieved beyond measure to see him coming down the steps.

"Josh, it's good to see you." Harper extended a hand. "I just wish it was under different circumstances."

"Same here," McCabe replied as they shook. "We need to get inside. They're waiting."

Normally, Harper would have been taken aback by the assistant director's curt tone. Looking at the other man's face, though, he could see that McCabe was merely trying to tell him something. He realized that his fears regarding the president's mind-set were probably completely justified. That was about the only thing that could have shaken McCabe to this extent.

"Who's in there?" he asked.

"Andrews and Stralen are meeting with the POTUS right now. Thayer was—"

"Stralen?" Harper frowned. Joel Stralen was the recently appointed director of the Defense Intelligence Agency and a close personal friend of the president. He was also a very vocal opponent of the CIA, which he considered to be a rival agency. Harper could almost understand the man's mind-set, as to some extent, every government agency was in constant competition for a larger chunk of the federal budget, but that didn't make his animosity any less tiresome or easier to bear. "Where did he land from?"

"I have no idea. He arrived fifteen minutes ago, and he went straight in." They were 20 feet from the main entrance and walking as slowly as they possibly could. "Are you aware of the timeline?"

Harper nodded, but in truth, he hadn't really considered it until now. The attack on the camp in West Darfur had taken place eight hours earlier, at 2:00 a.m. Darfur time. Sudan was eight hours ahead of Washington. The first report hadn't come into the U.S. embassy in Khartoum until six o'clock in the morning local time, and it had taken another forty minutes for someone to verify that the president's niece was, indeed, based at the camp that had been targeted. Harper checked his watch and saw that it was half past one. That meant that the president had heard the news less than . . .

Jesus. Harper shook his head as the time frame came together in his mind. The president had known for just over an hour. Not much longer than he had known himself. No wonder McCabe was worried.

"Yeah," Harper said. "I know the timeline." They were 15 feet from the main entrance, and he made an effort to slow his pace even more. "Any word on Lily Durant?"

McCabe shook his head slowly. "Nothing new. You know how we found out, right?"

Harper nodded. He had been brought up to speed by the night duty officer out at Langley even as they'd raced toward the airstrip. It had started, he knew, with a panicked call from Greg Beckett, the UNICEF doctor assigned to Camp Hadith, to the U.S. embassy in Khartoum. Harper had yet to see the transcript, but he knew most of what had been said between Beckett and the chief of mission, who had taken the call personally. Beckett had run when the attack began, but he had seen the entire thing unfold from a distance. About an hour after the raiders had left, he had ventured back into the camp with two other aid workers.

Inside the hospital, they had discovered the remains of 40 people, including Lily Durant. It had taken an hour from that point for the phones to come back on, at which time Beckett had placed his frantic call to the embassy.

"Have we been able to verify what Beckett said? I mean, has anyone actually seen her body?"

"Not yet. It's going to take a few hours to get people out to the scene, but we have no reason to doubt what he told us."

Harper took a second to think that over. "Does the president know? I mean, does he *really* know?"

McCabe suddenly stopped walking. Harper was caught off guard, but he stopped, turned, and stepped back to face the assistant director.

"I think he does," McCabe said. He seemed to hesitate, but he had already said too much, and there was no point in stopping now. "He's not taking it well, John. They were very close."

Harper took a moment to absorb this unwelcome news. It was just as he'd feared, and he only hoped he wasn't too late to reverse the slide. The world was a complicated place, and it was hard enough for a president to calmly process those complexities when weighing a response to brute aggression. When emotion entered the equation, it inevitably blew the whole damn thing to pieces. And Harper did not want to be in the position of having to stop President David Brenneman from making a potentially catastrophic decision based on nothing more than the rawest of passions.

"How did they find her?" he mused aloud. Whoever the hell *they* might be. "Did the leak spring from her end, or ours?"

McCabe shrugged uneasily. "That is obviously what we need to figure out. When Lily decided to go over there, the president tried to talk her out of it. And when he couldn't, he made an effort to distance himself so there wouldn't be tracks anyone could follow. I guess he was trying to protect her . . . and to be fair, it worked for a long time."

"Until now," Harper murmured.

"Right," McCabe said. "Until now."

His voice was strained, but Harper thought it was something more than the normal stress of the situation. Was it possible he had known Durant personally? It would certainly explain the casual way in which he had used her first name.

"Maybe it was intentional, and maybe it wasn't," McCabe was saying, "but someone gave her away, and the regime in Khartoum took advantage—"

Harper interrupted. "How do we know that?"

"I didn't say we know anything. But someone sent armed units in after her, and al-Bashir has been waving his sword for months. There's no doubt he's capable."

"Capable isn't the same as responsible. What I'm hearing is speculation, Josh, and that's fine as a springboard. But it's way too soon to draw conclusions. We need to take a step back and—"

"Hey," McCabe broke in, spreading his arms wide, "you'll get no argument from me. I agree with you, and I am not the man you need to convince." He lowered his voice and took a step forward. "POTUS needs to hear it from you, and he needs to hear it now. He's too close to the whole thing, and Stralen isn't helping matters at all. He's been adding fuel to the fire ever since he arrived."

Harper nodded slowly. "Where are they?"

McCabe shook his head grimly as they started to climb the steps. Clearly, he wasn't anxious to go back in there. "I'll show you," he said.

Harper followed the assistant director through the front door, ignoring the two agents sheltering beneath the eaves. The entrance hall was dark, as though the building itself were in mourning, but Harper still managed to catch sight of his reflection in a circular, gilt-framed mirror hanging over a mahogany side table. Fortunately, McCabe took that moment to confer with an agent standing nearby, and Harper turned to the mirror to check his appearance more thoroughly. His navy Brooks Brothers suit was slightly rumpled and damp at the shoulders; his tie poorly knotted. His graying brown hair was plastered to his head, and there was a slight nick on his throat where he had cut himself shaving. Minor imperfections, he decided. For the most part, he looked as respectable as anyone could at half past one in the morning.

McCabe waved him forward, and they continued down a long, dimly lit hall leading to a single door at the end. An uncomfortable-looking agent stood outside the living room, and as they approached, Harper could hear elevated voices beyond the plain wooden door.

They stopped just short of the door, and once again McCabe murmured something to the man standing post. Turning back to Harper, the assistant director grimaced and lifted his eyebrows in a silent question.

Harper straightened his tie and nodded once, indicating that he was ready.

McCabe leaned forward and tapped on the door. There was a brief silence, and then a voice called out for Harper to enter.

CHAPTER 3

CAMP DAVID

Like the rest of the building, the living room was draped in shadow. Harper thought that during the day, the picture windows on the east wall would have provided a spectacular view of the Monocacy Valley. Now, at this early hour, they offered nothing more than a hazy reflection of the room itself. A large fieldstone fireplace dominated the southwest corner of the room, the chimney towering up to the open second floor, and framed photographs of former presidents occupied every inch of the beige walls. The carpet was government issue, gray and sturdy, and the mismatched furniture looked as if it might have been purchased at a yard sale.

Harper was dimly aware of all of this, but for the most part, his attention was fixed on the three other men in the room—and on one man in particular.

Robert Andrews, the director of Central Intelligence and Harper's immediate boss, was seated on a red leather love seat facing the fireplace. He was a heavyset man with dark, curly hair, dressed in his standard Ralph Lauren suit. He nodded curtly as his deputy crossed the room toward the seating area. The man seated to his left, Harper saw, was General Joel Stralen. In his early fifties, the director of the Defense Intelligence Agency was wiry and tan, with a sparse fringe of iron gray hair, thin lips, and deep-set eyes. He was wearing his customary blue USAF service dress uniform, though his jacket was slung over the back of his chair. Harper returned Andrews's strained, silent greeting but ignored Stralen, who was staring at him with undisguised contempt. Instead, he began moving toward the man standing in front of the large windows.

On any given day David Brenneman looked at least a decade younger than his fifty-five years. However, the news he had just received had aged him in a way the rigors of the office had never managed to do. His silver-brown hair was disheveled, his eyes were red rimmed and bloodshot, and his mouth had set in a tight, angry line.

As Harper approached, he was acutely aware of the president's stance. Dressed in a navy tracksuit bearing the insignia of his alma mater, Georgetown University, he stood with his feet apart and his hands curled into useless fists by his sides, like a fighter who'd been sucker punched bracing for a second blow.

Harper could only imagine what he was feeling at that moment. David Brenneman was arguably the single most powerful person in the world, and yet, for all that, he had just taken a hit to the gut from which he would probably never recover. Worse still, there was nothing he could do to make it right, despite the enormous resources at his disposal. Harper couldn't have articulated why, but the tracksuit made him look all the more exposed. Brenneman was the president, yes. But this morning he was first and foremost a man reeling from grief.

Harper stopped a few feet away and forced himself to meet Brenneman's eyes.

"Sir," he began awkwardly, "I'm truly sorry for your loss. Believe me, we will do everything in our power to find the people who are responsible, and when we do, there is nothing to stop us from—"

"What the *hell* are you talking about?"

At first Harper didn't know where the words had come from. Then he turned to face the man who had snapped out the question. Stralen had jumped out of his chair and was staring at him with a mixed expression of irritation and disbelief.

"Excuse me?" Harper said.

"You heard. What are you talking about?" said Stralen. "We already know who did the deed. It was one man, and we know exactly where to find him. The only question is what we're going to do about it."

Harper let his gaze drift from Stralen to his immediate superior. Andrews was shaking his head slowly, almost imperceptibly, his gaze fixed on some distant corner of the room. Clearly, he wasn't about to stand up to his counterpart at the DIA. Harper wondered how long he had been able to withstand the blunt force of the general's rhetoric, or if he had even tried.

"Sir, with all due respect, it's too early to draw any conclusions about—"

"That's bullshit," Stralen said. "You know damn well that Bashir was behind this. It's payback for the sanctions we slapped on them last month. What else could it be?"

Harper frowned. "I don't think that's likely. Bashir may be dangerous, but he isn't certifiably insane. Why would he do this? What could he possibly hope to gain?"

Stralen was already shaking his head. "Who knows?" he snapped. "A world court's issued a warrant for him—and backed him into a corner. When he tried to attend Zuma's swearing-in conference as president of South Africa, Bashir was warned to stay home. Even those corrupt bastards in Uganda reluctantly washed their hands of him through diplomatic channels. As signatories to the ICC they'd have had to arrest him if he showed at their regional conference."

"How's any of that lead him to an act of retribution against us?" Harper asked.

"I don't know how his mind connects the dots. Or even what dots they connect. But it's a moot point, anyway. There are *witnesses*." Stralen pounded his right hand into his left to emphasize the point. "The camp's doctor, Beckett, the man who reported the attack in the first place. He ran when the bombs started to fall, but he didn't run far. He saw the whole thing from a distance, and he swears that he saw a man in army uniform getting out of a white Mercedes. Besides, there was a plane. If there was no government authorization, where did the plane come from?"

"I don't know," Harper said carefully.

Stralen narrowed his eyes. "Are you telling me you don't think the Sudanese government has a hand in this?"

"I think it might bear some level of culpability."

Stralen narrowed his eyes. "What does that mean, 'some level'?"

"I mean Bashir provides funds and training for the Janjaweed through the army," Harper explained. "But he does not direct ongoing operations in Darfur. He leaves that to his generals. There is a good chance he wasn't even aware of this particular attack, much less who was stationed at the camp."

"You can't be serious." Stralen looked at Andrews, then back to Harper, as though searching for an explanation. "Do you really expect us to believe that this was a mistake? Some kind of coincidence?"

"No, of course not. That is not what I'm implying. I'm simply saying that Bashir might not have authorized it," Harper asserted.

"And what about the plane? Let's not forget that bombs were dropped," said Stralen.

"I haven't." Harper sighed. "But a lot of ordnance and combat equipment is floating around out there on the black market. And across the region. Tanks, attack boats—"

"I repeat, Harper. This was a *bomber.* An F-7N, according to our real-time infrared satellite data. What does that tell you?"

Harper didn't answer. Acquired from Iran back in the late nineties, the Chinese-built warplanes were known to have been used in Sudan's bombing campaigns against rebel ground troops during its last civil war. Which in his mind still proved nothing.

He turned toward the president; the last thing he wanted here was a spitting contest. "Sir, I know it must seem pretty clear-cut from where you're standing. But I don't think there's sufficient evidence Omar al-Bashir ordered the attack, and I don't think we've established motive. He knows the consequences for himself and his government. To go after you personally, and in this way, would be an incredibly stupid thing to do at a time when he's already under siege. Bashir is a lot of things, but he isn't stupid. It would be an act of sheer lunacy for him to authorize your niece's murder."

Harper paused, painfully aware that it was the first time those words had been spoken aloud. For a long moment the president didn't respond, his red eyes fixed on some random point on the far wall. When he spoke, his voice was dangerously low.

"There's that plane, John. Let's not dance around it. And those men were wearing army uniforms," he said. "Bashir *controls* the army. It's one thing for them to raid a local village with impunity. But they're still undeniably on a leash . . . a long one, maybe, but a leash nonetheless. Say what you will, they don't lift a finger against us unless he tells them to."

Harper was momentarily shaken by the quiet rage he heard in the president's voice—as well as the utter conviction. But he did his best to set it aside, knowing that he couldn't stop now. Someone had to bring the man back from the brink, and it was clear that he was the only person still willing to try.

"Yes, but that just supports my point, sir. Even if they destroyed the whole camp, some of the refugees were bound to escape. There were going to be witnesses either way, so why would Bashir make the government's role in the attack so blatantly evident? Why would he allow the trail to lead right back to his doorstep?"

"To send a message," Stralen said. "Isn't that obvious? He claimed he was going to do as much when the State Department issued the sanctions last month."

"It wouldn't be the first time he spouted inflammatory rhetoric," Harper pointed out, "and not once in twenty years has he lifted a finger to do even half of what he threatens. What would make things different this time?" The deputy director shook his head and looked back at the president. "Sir, again, I'm not saying Bashir didn't have a hand in this. Plain and simple, I'm trying to point out that we need to have all the facts, look into every possibility, before you decide on a course of action."

"And what happens in the meantime?" Stralen asked quietly.

Harper reluctantly turned his attention back to the air force general.

"You want us to sit on our hands while Bashir sits in Khartoum, laughing about what he's done?" Stralen said, not giving an inch. "About what he's gotten away with? Is that what you're suggesting?"

"What are *you* suggesting?" Harper asked, meeting the other man's cold blue eyes. He knew he had crossed a line, but he couldn't back down. Andrews had already done that, and someone had to stop this conversation before it escalated to a far more dangerous level. "What do you propose we do instead, General?"

"What I propose," Stralen growled, "is that we send in a two- or three-man Delta team to verify his position, and then we drop a JDAM right on top of the bastard's head. What I *suggest* is that we take him out, once and for all."

There was complete silence in the room. Harper stared at the newly appointed head of the DIA for a long moment and couldn't help but wonder if the man understood the full gravity of what he was saying. Then he turned to look at the president. "Sir, please tell me you are not seriously considering this."

Brenneman had turned to face the window, but his shoulders were tense, his hands still curled into fists at his sides. He did not respond, giving Harper no idea what he was thinking. "Sir," Harper said, trying again, "I implore you to look at the larger picture. Omar al-Bashir may be a ruthless dictator, but he is still a head of state, the president of the largest country in Africa."

"He's also a wanted man according to the ICC," Brenneman said.

"And we've consistently opposed the court's author-

ity on the basis of its determinations shackling our political and military policies . . . and creating a global
standard of justice that may conflict with our own. It
would be hypocritical to use the indictment as an excuse to go after Bashir." Harper gave that a moment to
sink in. "We all need to remember that while Bashir
stays within his own sovereign borders, he has practical
immunity from any indictment. We can't legally send
forces across those borders to arrest him. And we can't
just assassinate him."

"So he gets away with it," Brenneman murmured. He
was still facing the window. "Is that right? Is that what
you're proposing?"

For a few seconds Harper wasn't sure how to respond. It was suddenly apparent that the president hadn't
really heard a word he'd said, and for one simple reason—he didn't want to. He was lost in his own private
world of pain and grief, and for the time being, he was
looking for one thing alone . . . a way to lash out. In
that respect, Stralen was giving him exactly what he
wanted, someone to blame and punish for his niece's
death.

Harper could see the appeal. Any human being with
a beating heart would be tempted by the lure of immediate vengeance. But that didn't make it sane or right.

"Mr. President." It was Andrews who had spoken
now, and Harper turned toward him in mild surprise.
This was the first time the director had made his presence known since his deputy had entered the room.
"With all due respect, Jonathan is right. We can decide
Bashir is accountable, but we can't take him out. The
international community would never stand for it."

"Who cares what they're willing to stand for?" Stralen
said. He fixed his counterpart at the CIA with an angry,
accusing stare. "That isn't the issue here, and for a

change our primary concern shouldn't be world opinion." He shifted his attention to Harper. "As for your remarks about the ICC . . . I don't give a damn about that organization. The indictment is fine with me but should have no bearing on our actions one way or another."

"Okay, forget the ICC," Harper said. "With all due respect, General Stralen . . . are you aware Sudan has an estimated oil reserve of two hundred billion barrels in its very large chunk of the Muglad Basin? And that Russia has made monumental financial and material investments in the Sudanese oil industry? The deals Putin has cut with Khartoum . . . specifically exercising his political clout through Slavneft—"

Stralen speared him with his gaze. "Don't lecture me. I know all about Slavneft."

Harper looked back at Stralen without blinking and went on with slow deliberation. "Then I assume you're aware it is not only Russia's seventh or eighth largest oil firm but is wholly state owned," he said. "I'm sure you also realize the Russians, via Slavneft, have spent something in excess of two hundred million dollars to develop the Abyei petroleum fields in south-central Sudan as part of an umbrella trade agreement—I think it's fair to use the term *alliance*—that requires Sudan to subsidize a large chunk of that investment with the purchase of Russian military hardware. Given what you know, I probably don't have to add that Sudan set an earlier precedent for this relationship with China, which now drills as much of a sixth to a quarter of its total oil supply from fields in the western part of the country. That's about two hundred thousand barrels every day of the week. The exchange there has involved weapons, too. Primarily small arms, though there were separate arrangements for the sale of Chinese attack aircraft and pilot training to Sudan. And assurances that Beijing would massage the United Nations Security Council in all matters relating to Bashir's regime, including his genocidal slaughter of the Dinka tribe—"

"Enough." Brenneman had turned away from the window without warning. "That's enough. I don't want to hear any more."

Everyone in the room fell silent. His anguish was plain for all to see. If Harper had to guess, he would have said that the president's grief was surpassed only by his barely suppressed rage.

"Sir, I understand that you're upset," Harper continued quickly. All he could think about was cutting off Stralen before he could do any more damage. "My apologies if this is repetitious . . . but going after Bashir directly would be a huge mistake. There's no stressing that enough. It is not a viable or responsible course of—"

"Upset?" The president stared at him with a blank, uncomprehending gaze. The deputy director instantly realized that he had missed something in Brenneman's tone of voice moments ago and, in doing so, had made a monumental error in judgment. Before he could take it back, though, Brenneman continued in a voice tinged with the wrong kind of amusement. "My niece has just been murdered by a pack of savages in a third-world country, and you think I'm *upset?* That's very perceptive of you, John. Thank you for shedding some light on the situation."

"Sir, I . . ."

The president held up a hand to stop him, then shifted his gaze to a far corner of the room, his face fixed in a tight expression of barely suppressed fury.

"That will be all for now, John. Would you step outside, please? Josh will come and find you if we need anything else."

Harper opened his mouth to respond, hoping to repair the damage, but nothing came out, and he could see that Brenneman would not tolerate any further argument. He shot a quick glance at his boss and saw that Andrews was studying him with a mixed expression of frustration, sympathy . . . and, perhaps worst of all, futility. He didn't have to look at Stralen to know he would see something very contrary to that in the general's eyes.

Harper knew when he was beaten. With a sinking feeling, he acknowledged the president's order in silence. Then he turned and walked out of the room, closing the door gently behind him.

It was still raining when Jonathan Harper stepped outside a few moments later—a warm, soft rain that seemed to drift out of nowhere. He walked past the agents standing post, down the steps, and continued on the drive, unconsciously trying to put some distance between himself and the president's cabin. Tilting his head back, he looked up at the empty black sky and closed his eyes. His head was buzzing, and he was completely unaware of the inclement weather, even though the rain was dripping down his face and his suit coat was already soaked through.

Harper was stunned to the core by what had just taken place. He had been advising David Brenneman for nearly six years, and in all that time he had never seen the man behave in such an irrational way. *That's very perceptive of you, John. Thank you for shedding some light on the situation.* Harper regretted his verbal miscue, but it probably hadn't worsened matters so much as exposed their already dire nature. Brenneman was allowing his grief and anger to cloud his judgment, and Stralen's provocative statements—none of which were based on confirmed facts—were only making things worse.

Harper had lost track of how long he had been standing there when he heard voices behind him. He turned to see Director Andrews walking down the steps, followed closely by Joshua McCabe. The two men paused at the top of the drive to shake hands, and even from a distance, Harper could see that they were both subdued, their shoulders slumped beneath a shared, invisible burden. As he looked on, McCabe turned to go back into the cabin. Then the director lifted a hand in his deputy's direction and pointed toward the Tahoe parked nearby. A minute later they were both seated inside the large truck.

Harper was tempted to apologize for the damage he had caused, but decided it would be better to let the other man breach the awkward silence.

The director pulled a linen handkerchief from his inner jacket pocket and used it to methodically wipe the rain from his face. When he finally spoke, he did so quietly and without turning to face his subordinate.

"You didn't help us in there, John," he said. "You didn't help us at all. You did your homework, and I thought it might have been enough to get through to Brenneman. But it would've been better if you'd quit while you were ahead and given him some time to mull things over. By pushing it, you went and played right into Stralen's hands. Made him seem almost reasonable. Now, thanks to you, we're on the defensive."

Harper bit his tongue, though he was sorely tempted to remind the other man of his own meager contribution to the heated argument inside the building. Instead, he simply agreed quietly.

Andrews acknowledged the words with a short nod, though judging by the testy look on his face, he could tell that his deputy's apology was less than sincere. "Look, I think I managed to talk him down a bit," he continued. "At least for the time being. Of course, Stralen is a problem for us, and he's not going away. He's probably still in there trying to undo everything I just said."

"He doesn't have any idea what he's talking about," Harper snapped, his demeanor of feigned calm slipping away with the mere mention of the other man. "I can't believe he doesn't understand the consequences that come with killing a head of state, especially when you don't have ironclad proof to justify direct action. In this day and age, it just isn't done."

Andrews shook his head wearily. "Don't sell Stralen short, John. He's a very smart man who understands more than you might think. And he has a great deal of power at his fingertips. You would be wise to remember that. More to the point, he has the president's ear. He can't be discounted simply because you don't like or agree with him."

"That isn't the issue, Bob. The man is beyond dangerous. You heard what he was saying in there. I send out a warning flare about getting into a pissing contest with Russia and China, and he does his best to shoot it right down." Harper shook his head. "Normally, the president would never consider something so crazy. He just doesn't want to listen to reason right now. . . . He's too wrapped up in what happened to his niece. Too emotionally invested."

The director didn't seem to hear. His mouth was

pursed into a sullen frown; his dark eyes locked on the seat in front of him.

"What is it?" Harper said. "Jesus Christ, you weren't even paying attention."

Andrews shook his head. "Wrong," he said. "I've registered every word out of your mouth."

"Then you're keeping something from me, Bob, because you normally don't go blank like you did a minute ago."

Andrews sat in silence for a long moment, that expression of brooding dismay again dropping over his features like a curtain. Finally he let out a deep, heavy sigh.

"The secretary of state is *this* close to jumping on board with Stralen," he said, holding his thumb and forefinger slightly apart.

Harper stared at him, incredulous. "Brynn Fitzgerald?" he said. "Do you know this for a fact?"

"It's my informed read," Andrews said. "I spoke with her before heading over here. Actually, she called me after speaking to the president."

"You've got to be mistaken. She's one of the most reasonable people in Washington. How could she suddenly be that knee-jerk?"

"I don't know," Andrews said. "Loyalty to the president? Or maybe the residual effect of having been taken hostage in Pakistan . . . and watching one of her good friends cold-bloodedly shot to death in the process. Whatever explains it, we're seeing a lot of clouded judgment around us." He shrugged his shoulders. "Let's take this thing a step at a time, John. It isn't as if we have a choice, anyway. You have to remember that the president's had only an hour or so to soak it all in. Besides, I think I managed to talk some sense into him. At least for now. Needless to say, we're going to have to watch this closely. If he decides to do something drastic, it's going to come back on us, whether we were involved or not. That is just the way it goes, and I have no intention of letting the Agency take the fall for something Stralen talked him into doing."

"I'm glad to hear it," Harper replied, relieved to see that Andrews had recovered some of his mettle. He was going to need it if the general wasn't content to let things lie, and Harper had a bad feeling that the director was right. Stralen was probably still in there pleading his case to the president. "So how do you want to handle this?"

The director thought for a moment. "In my opinion, the best way to defuse the situation is to give Brenneman the man who carried out the actual attack. An eye for an eye, so to speak."

"I agree. And given his current pickle with the World Court, I feel pretty confident that Bashir will hand him over without too much of a fight. After all, that would be the best way to prove that he had nothing to do with the raid . . . and a chance for a little diplomatic quid pro quo."

"You think he'd push for us to make overtures to the ICC?"

"Bashir would want something in return for his co-operation." Harper shrugged. "I'm sure he'd have no shortage of bargaining chips."

Andrews looked skeptical. "Do you really believe that he's innocent of this? Because I have to say, John, it doesn't seem likely, and you didn't exactly convince the president, either."

"I just don't see how doing something this brutal and direct would benefit the regime in Khartoum," Harper reasoned. "Bashir wouldn't see it, either. He knows how to work the international community. Remember his pilgrimage to Mecca? This is with the ICC warrant pinned to his back. And if that wasn't defiant enough, he attends the Arab Union summit in Qatar after saying his devout prayers. Complains that the ICC's decisions are biased against Africans. I mean, can you picture it? He's a fugitive from justice, and there you have Kaddafi holding his hand in a gesture of brotherhood, calling the ICC a terrorist body. Meanwhile, the UN secretary-general's squirming with embarrassment at the dais."

Andrews sighed. "I remember that junket. He can be like Saddam in his heyday."

"That's exactly my point, Bob. He knows what he can get away with, and the murder of the president's niece does not fall into that category. Of course, he'll deny it, anyway—I'm surprised he hasn't done so already. But Bashir will have to understand he needs to deliver the goods . . . the man who actually carried out the attack. That is the person we need to get our hands on. That is the person who can stop this from going any further than it already has."

"And what if you're wrong?" Andrews asked quietly. "Or if Bashir decides not to play along for some reason? What then?"

Harper mused over the questions for a moment, but the answers were already clear. "If it gets to that stage, we'll have no choice but to find the man ourselves. Otherwise, Stralen will have exactly what he needs to pressure the president into making a bad decision. Omar al-Bashir may be a devil, but he's the devil we know, and we have no idea who might be waiting in the wings to take his place."

Andrews paused to let that sink in. "I'm not arguing, John. But do you have any idea how difficult it would be to pick one man out of Sudan? We don't even have a name, let alone a face. If Bashir doesn't give him up, who is capable of going in there to find him?"

"I would have thought that was obvious."

Andrews finally shifted in his seat to look at his subordinate. His gaze was steady and flat, completely unreadable. "I thought he was out."

"He *is* out. He was out the last couple of times we needed him, too, but that didn't stop him from coming back. If we're forced to get involved on a deeper level, I'd rather have him running point than anyone else. Besides, he's already over there."

"In Africa?"

"Right," Harper said. "He's been working with Blackwater for the last couple of months."

"Private security?" Andrews seemed surprised by this. "Is it one of our operations?"

The Departments of Defense and State regularly contracted out security work, including the safeguarding of foreign leaders and dignitaries overseas, to independent outfits through various governmental agencies, including the Bureau of Diplomatic Security—which technically fell under the purview of the DOS.

Harper shrugged. "I think it's direct between Blackwater and the government of South Africa, though we might have been consulted," he said. "Last I heard, he was running one of their mobile security units."

The director frowned, clearly uncomfortable with the prospect of bringing Ryan Kealey back into the fold. "You think you can talk him into it? The last time he did something for us, it nearly got him killed. Not to mention the other part."

Harper nodded briskly. "He'll get on board, one way or another." He sounded more confident than he probably should have, but he didn't want to give the director a chance to change his mind. What Harper hadn't said was that Andrews was right. Everything rested on what he had so tactfully described as the *other part*. The death of Naomi Kharmai, and its lingering effect on him. It was potentially the single greatest obstacle to drawing Kealey back into the fold, and Harper knew that when the time came, he would have to approach with the utmost care. To that end, he'd already arranged for a meeting in Baltimore with someone who could be of immense help.

Of course, the hope was that it wouldn't come down to getting Kealey involved, but somehow, Harper already knew that it would. The only question was how long the president would be able to stand up to Stralen, and what disastrous course of action might result from that uncomfortable union.

CHAPTER 4

JOHANNESBURG,
SOUTH AFRICA
JUNE

It was just after two in the afternoon as Alex Whysall stood in the sparkling white lobby of the courthouse, his back resting lightly against a towering marble pillar. The building was packed with reporters, photographers, and politically minded South Africans who had come to await the outcome of the trial currently in session, and the tension in the airy, spacious lobby was impossible to miss. The crowd had been building steadily since that morning, and now it felt as if the room was about to burst at the seams.

There were at least 100 people in the lobby alone, all of them clamoring to be heard over one another, and another 1,000 or so were standing outside the building. That was where the real threat was located, Whysall knew, and as he listened to the massive crowd chanting on the other side of the large, glass-paned doors, he unconsciously tightened his grip on his primary weapon, a Heckler & Koch MP5 fitted with a collapsible stock and a forward-mounted handgrip. His secondary weapon, a

9mm Beretta, was holstered on his right hip, but Whysall knew that if he had to use it, he would already be in serious trouble. Of course, the chances of things escalating to that point were slim to none, but he had to be ready for anything. It was all part of the job.

At twenty-six, Whysall was just one month out of his second three-year enlistment with the U.S. Marine Corps. During his time in the Corps, he had served as a staff sergeant with the 1st Force Reconnaissance Company based out of Camp Pendleton, California. As a Force Recon marine, Whysall had fought in Afghanistan during Operation Achilles, the NATO-led operation to clear the southern province of Helmand of Taliban fighters in 2007. He had been awarded the Bronze Star for his actions in that particular conflict, and he could still remember the day the battalion commander had conferred the medal. Most distinctly, he could remember the pride he had felt at doing his job well enough to earn that coveted decoration.

At the time he had not been able to conceive of anything he would rather be doing, and he had been eagerly anticipating his next enlistment. Then, while visiting his parents on leave, he had seen an advertisement for private security officers posted on the Internet. To put it simply, the numbers had stunned him. Blackwater Worldwide, once a little-known security firm with less than a hundred twenty-five thousand dollars in government contracts, had blossomed in the wake of the September 11, 2001, attacks on the World Trade Center. The company had expanded its operations across the board and was now offering six figures to former members of the U.S. military's elite units. As a long-standing member of Force Recon nearing the end of his enlistment, Whysall had been in a prime position to capitalize on the opportunity, and after much consideration, he'd decided that the money—nearly four times what he earned annually as an active-duty marine—was just too good to pass up. His second enlistment had ended a few months later, and once he'd received his discharge papers, he had immediately signed a one-year contract with Blackwater.

He had fully expected a posting to Iraq, and for a while, it had looked like that was where he was headed. Then, while he was attending the company's two-week training course outside the Great Dismal Swamp in Moyock, North Carolina, Blackwater had inked a lucrative deal with the South African government to provide protection for President Jacob Gedleyihlekisa Zuma and senior members of his party, the African National Congress. The company's executives immediately began shifting resources, and one week after his training had finished, Whysall had found himself on a plane to Johannesburg. Much to his surprise, he had been met at the airport by the head of the PSD, or protective security detail, to which he was assigned. His surprise at this unexpected courtesy, however, had turned to sheer disbelief when he realized who the man standing in front of him actually was.

Whysall suspected he knew as much as anyone else about Ryan Kealey, and that wasn't much. But it was enough. The former army officer had served in the 3rd Special Forces Group from 1995 to 2001, ending that assignment—his last in the U.S. Army—with the rank of major. Prior to that, he had served with the 10th SFG at Fort Carson, Colorado. It was said that he had been assigned to the elite 1st SFOD-Delta as well, though unsurprisingly, no one could verify that particular rumor. What was better known was the man's accomplishments over the past several years, during which time he had worked for the Central Intelligence Agency as an independent contractor.

Whysall was not easily impressed, but Ryan Kealey's résumé was beyond remarkable, and he had been gratified to learn that he would be working under the man in Johannesburg. During his time at the Blackwater facility in Moyock, Whysall had come to question the standard to which the incoming recruits were trained. Contrary to popular belief, not all of Blackwater's security people were former members of the SF community. In fact, some of them had no military experience whatsoever. Still others had highly questionable backgrounds. One man Whysall had trained with at the Moyock facility was Chilean, and there were whispers that he had served under the brutal regime of Augusto Pinochet during the late eighties.

Still, Whysall had been relieved to find that the PSD to which he was assigned in Johannesburg had none of those problems. Regardless of whether or not the stories about Kealey were true, there was no denying the fact that the man knew how to run a protective detail. This in itself was nearly enough to confirm for Whysall that Kealey had, in fact, been a Delta operator, as close-quarter protection wasn't part of the training program in any other branch of the military, save for the Marine Security Guard, which was assigned to U.S. embassies around the world, as well as the White House itself.

A loud roar from inside the courtroom jarred the former marine back to the present, and he felt a moment of shame for allowing his attention to wander. Straightening, he studied the doors leading into the main chamber and wondered what had just taken place inside. He checked his watch quickly and decided that it was too soon for the verdict to have been read. On the other hand, he doubted that the jury would be out for much longer, as the case was all but open and shut, which explained why he was there to begin with, along with seven other members of President Zuma's Blackwater security detail. ·

David Joubert, the man currently on trial, had been Zuma's close friend, business associate, and right-hand man when he was deputy president of South Africa under the previous administration, headed by Thabo Mbeki. Though they were fellow Xhosa tribesmen whose relationship went back to Zuma's childhood, Zuma had disassociated himself from Joubert shortly after the National Prosecuting Authority, South Africa's leading judicial body, had charged Zuma with two counts of corruption in 2005, adding fraud, racketeering, and money laundering a couple of years later—allegations that had clung to him even after he won the presidency four years later, ousting Mbeki from the post he'd held since Nelson Mandela left office.

In the eyes of many, including Whysall himself, Joubert was a sacrificial lamb. The intractable poverty and joblessness that beleaguered South Africa—and the entire continent—often led to the fortunes of African politicians turning on a dime. Before his parliamentary election Zuma had been a populist icon, the man who'd gained the backing of organized labor and vowed to bring new business and employment to the nation. But Whysall had been in enough of the world's poorer countries to know that hope and desperation blinded people to the stains on their chosen savior's robes.

The charges against Zuma stemmed from his association with Schabir Shaik, a Durban businessman who had been convicted of bribing senior officers in the South African Navy in order to win several lucrative contracts, including the construction of four Valour-class frigates valued in excess of one and a half billion rand, or a hundred fifty million euros, apiece. Additional charges linked Shaik—and, by extension, Zuma—to a French arms company. In that instance, the NPA claimed that Shaik had accepted bribes for military contracts on behalf of Zuma, who was alleged to have unwisely proceeded to launder the money through some of South Africa's largest banks. Ultimately, Schabir Shaik was sentenced to fifteen years in prison, and shortly thereafter, the National Prosecuting Authority had started to collect the evidence it would need to formally indict Jacob Zuma.

That had been four years earlier, and the problem lay in what had occurred since. Despite having been accused and barely acquitted of rape before his election, Zuma had found a solid base of support in South Africa's far left, which had grown disillusioned with Mbeki's habit of ignoring views that conflicted with his own, as well as his steadfast refusal to address the needs of the nation's vast lower-class community. Zuma's popularity was so great that the ANC had voted him in as its new party head in 2007, effectively putting an end to Thabo Mbeki's grasp on the presidency. The only problem had been the assortment of charges levied against Zuma, and they were dismissed on grounds of prosecutorial misconduct, finally clearing his path to power.

Whysall could not have said whether the dismissal had come on a legitimate, if convenient, technicality or quiet disclosures that Mbeki had been pressuring the NPA to disgrace and imprison his chief competitor. Both were rumored, but he was not inclined to plunge into the quagmire of African politics for the truth. He knew, and wanted to know, only as much as was necessary to do his job.

What he knew now was that the same constituency that boosted Zuma to the top had grown disillusioned less than a year into his first term of office. Winter in South Africa lasted from May through September, and the last had been marked with especially cruel, frigid weather. With millions homeless, and millions more living in unheated shacks, there had been walkouts by chemical, construction, and municipal workers demanding higher wages for themselves—and better housing for their families. As the strikes caused industry to grind to a halt, and unrest spread across the nation, Zuma had returned to his home province of KwaZulu-Natal to implore his most faithful supporters to remain patient with him.

It was no surprise when the corruption allegations resurfaced. Zuma's recurring problems represented new openings for his opposition. If he were again bogged down in legal proceedings, his career as president, one on which many others staked their own careers and reputations, would grind to an abrupt and final halt . . . and so would the government, at perhaps the worst of times. In the end it would be the South African people who suffered most from all the political and judicial machinations.

Again, Whysall did not know whether the latest accusations were legitimate. Many Zuma devotees were calling them "Mbeki's revenge," asserting he might have stirred the pot behind the scenes. The only sure thing was that Zuma held a secret trump card this time—an electronic and paper trail of evidence he'd supposedly uncovered indicating that it was his lifelong friend David Joubert, who had been appointed national police commissioner, that was responsible for the dealings he'd supposedly engaged in with Shaik.

Was his evidence real? Concocted? Had Zuma thrown

Joubert to the wolves to spare himself another trial? It was all too much of a tangle for Whysall, and he wouldn't likewise twist his brain into knots trying to figure it out. The simple truth was it wasn't his concern. Blackwater Worldwide was morally neutral, apolitical, and disinterested in anything but the protection of its client.

Bottom line, so was Whysall. For him the situation boiled down to this: Zuma's people had approached Blackwater just as the Joubert trial was getting under way. It had been discovered that several of the senior figures in the president's security detail were former members of the South African Police Service whose loyalty to Joubert ran deep. After discovering this alarming fact, Zuma had disbanded his detail in favor of an outside security contractor. Given its success protecting Paul Bremer in Iraq, Blackwater Worldwide had topped the list of possible candidates.

It still wasn't known if Joubert's supporters in the SAPS posed a credible threat, but for Blackwater it represented an inarguably profitable one. The outfit's senior executives had been more than happy to write up the contract, and on receipt of a substantial deposit they had immediately begun drawing up a security profile for the South African president. Now Zuma had an eight-man team at his disposal, as well as five armored vehicles and a Bell helicopter to provide aerial support. The convoy, Whysall knew, was currently waiting in the parking garage, the entrance to which had been sealed off by the local police, and the helicopter would be called in once the Joubert verdict was read.

What happened from that point forward was anyone's guess. For the most part, the huge crowd gathered outside cared nothing about what happened to Joubert. Many were die-hard Mbeki supporters; others disenchanted followers of Zuma. A sizable group of people asserted the whole trial was a distraction, a sham in which Joubert had willingly participated to turn attention away from Zuma's dishonesty.

For the Blackwater team it added up to a mess. In short order the courtroom doors would open, and they would have a potentially serious problem on their hands.

A familiar voice caught Whysall's attention now, and he quickly adjusted the secure Motorola receiver/transmitter nestled in his right ear. "This is Whysall. Go ahead."

"Whysall, Kealey. What's happening out there?"

Whysall took a quick look around, trying to gauge the mood of the crowd. Ryan Kealey, he knew, was inside the courtroom, sitting not more than a few feet from the South African president. Zuma had insisted on attending the last day of the trial, and despite his best efforts, Kealey had not been able to talk him out of it.

"The people out here are getting antsy," Whysall said. "And additional police units arrived in the square a few minutes ago. Six more vehicles and fifteen officers, for a total of fifteen and eighty—damned if I know whether they're friends or foes. Otherwise, there's nothing to report."

"Okay, just sit tight. The jury's coming out now. Make sure everyone is ready to move. Out."

"Copy that, out."

Whysall immediately relayed the information to the rest of the team, then returned his attention to the crowd milling around him. Approximately five minutes later he heard a rumble of activity on the other side of the courtroom doors. Whysall knew the sound could only mean Zuma had finished testifying in the main chamber.

Around him, beneath the building's gilded ceiling, dozens of reporters immediately began fighting for position, thrusting their microphones and cameras at arm's length over the rope line. Behind the assembled media, the crowd of onlookers and protesters pushed forward, so that the narrow aisle leading from the main chamber to the courthouse entrance seemed to grow narrower with each passing second.

Whysall studied the chaotic scene with a sense of rising dread. He didn't understand why the general public had been granted access. It made for a security nightmare despite the manned checkpoint and the magnetometer positioned inside the main entrance. As bad as it was inside the building, though, it was ten times worse outside. The Johannesburg police had set up blocks on either end of Von Brandis and Kerk, the two intersecting streets in front of the courthouse, but their focus had been limited to vehicular traffic. They had done virtually nothing to prevent the unruly mob from congregating in front of the building, and Whysall suspected that the police would not be inclined to wrestle with those people when the time came for them to leave, especially after what had just transpired inside the main chamber.

Jacob Zuma had just testified against the head of the SAPS. With some of Joubert's supporters having managed to find their way onto Zuma's security detail, it seemed possible—even likely—that many of the police officers guarding the building were privately supporting the crowd elements hostile to the Zulu president. That the police might not be eager to facilitate Zuma's

safe departure was something Whysall hadn't considered until this moment, avoiding it in his reluctance to
let his mind stray into the intricacies of South Africa's
affairs. But this was one instance when a client's standing with an internal arm of his own government might
well have a direct bearing on his safety.

Whysall knew what it could mean if he was right, and
he decided to pass his concerns up the ladder. Just as he
was about to speak, though, his earpiece crackled to
life.

"All lobby personnel, tighten up on the rope line.
We're on the way out."

Whysall immediately acknowledged the transmis-
sion, then listened as the rest of the team followed suit.
Thirty seconds later he was in position, and he watched
as the heavyset police officer standing in front of the
courtroom doors lifted a radio to his lips. The man
mumbled a few words, then stepped to one side of the
massive oak doors. The doors were pushed open from
the other side, and two plainclothes police officers
quickly locked them into place against the walls. Then
the crowd erupted as Zuma and his entourage swept
out of the main chamber and into the lobby.

CHAPTER 5

KHARTOUM, SUDAN

Walter Reynolds, the U.S. chief of mission in the Republic of Sudan, stood at the small, barred window of his corner office and sipped from a cup of steaming black coffee, his twelfth of the day. As he took in the sweeping view of downtown Khartoum—the chaotic jumble of dun-colored buildings, olive green trees, and domed mosques that formed the city center, all of it backed by the towering flats of Barlaman Avenue and divided by the twin routes of the Nile—he was suffused by a sense of burning resentment, the same bitter anger he felt each time he stopped to consider the prospect of another two years in the sweltering pit of North Africa.

Reynolds had assumed the post of chargé d'affaires just ten months earlier, shortly after leaving his previous post in Côte d'Ivoire, but he was already sick of the place. In fact, he had been ready to leave the day he arrived, and it wasn't just because of the heat.

In his thirty years with the Foreign Service, Reynolds

had come to understand just how vast the cultural gap between the United States and the rest of the world actually was. Nevertheless, he had always made an effort to appreciate the cultural practices of the countries to which he was assigned, even when he found them personally distasteful. He'd also learned that what counted as "acceptable" social behavior could vary greatly from country to country. He had done his best to take this in stride, and for the most part, he'd succeeded. After all, that was part of being a diplomat. Some level of feigned interest—or acceptance—was occasionally called for, and Reynolds could disguise his inner disgust with the best of them. During his time in Sudan, he'd found it necessary to do just that, and with far more frequency than usual.

At least, that was how it had been prior to the disastrous events of April 4. Since the barbaric attack on Camp Hadith, everything had changed, and Reynolds no longer felt the urge—or the need—to mask how he truly felt. Over the last two months diplomatic relations between the United States and Sudan had essentially ceased to exist, and up until the previous afternoon Reynolds had been expecting the inevitable call from the State Department that would bring him, his wife, and the rest of the embassy staff home. Privately, he'd been wondering why the evacuation was so long in coming. Now he was starting to suspect it might not happen at all.

Walter Reynolds was one of the few people who had known about Lily Durant's presence in West Darfur—as well as her closely guarded relationship to the president—right from the start. He had met her just once, on the day she had first arrived. That had been several months earlier. They had kept the meeting short for the sake of discretion, but despite the brevity of that encounter, he'd found her to be an exceptionally charming, if somewhat naïve young woman. The fact that she had volunteered for such thankless work was more than enough to earn his genuine admiration, as he had visited the camps of West Darfur, and he knew just how terrible the conditions actually were. Not just for the refugees, but for the aid workers themselves.

The knowledge that someone would actually choose to live in such squalor in order to help others had done much to restore his faith in humanity, which had been sorely lacking since he had arrived in Khartoum. The only thing that worried him was Durant's blatant lack of concern regarding her personal security. She had politely but firmly brushed off his warnings, despite what had happened to John Granville, a senior USAID official who had been killed in Khartoum some years back, along with his driver, a Sudanese national. Reynolds had painted a colorful picture with that story, trying to impress upon her the danger of working in such an unstable environment. But she would not be dissuaded, and he could not help but admire her tenacity even as he privately feared for her personal safety.

He deeply regretted that he had been right all along, and although he had tried, he couldn't seem to erase that terrible day from his memory. He could still remember every word of the frantic call he'd taken from Gregory Beckett, the doctor stationed at the camp in West Darfur. Beckett was the primary eyewitness to the entire event, as well as the first person to report what had happened. As he'd listened to the doctor describe what he'd seen, Reynolds had tried to tell himself that it wasn't true—that Beckett had either made a terrible mistake or was playing some kind of sick joke. But the lingering fear and shock in the younger man's voice had made it impossible for Reynolds to doubt what he was saying, and he didn't have to wait long to discover that his first instincts had been correct. The doctor might have been a coward who had fled at the first sign of danger, but he was telling the truth.

Beckett's call had come in at 6:00 a.m. local time, and by noon they had had all the proof they needed. Although his aides had strongly advised him not to, Reynolds had personally flown to West Darfur to identify Durant's body. He had not had a decent night's sleep since. Even with just a couple of months to reflect, he knew that the things he had seen in the charred ruins of Camp Hadith would haunt him for the rest of his life. If he had despised the central figures in the Sudanese government before he'd walked into that hellish scene, by the time his plane had touched back down in Khartoum, he'd hated them all with a passion . . . every single minister, general, and district governor who'd ever seen fit to support the monstrous regime of Omar al-Bashir.

And that was before he had seen the tape.

It had been released two days after the attack; presumably, it had taken that long for the copies to reach their final destinations, as none were later determined to have been hand-delivered. Al-Jazeera, the controversial Qatar-based Arab news network, was the first station to air it, followed soon thereafter by Syria Satellite, Tunisia National Television, and NBN in Lebanon. Less than an hour after Al-Jazeera ran the tape for the first time, it appeared on Somali TV. Seeking to one-up its competitors, the Mogadishu-based station elected to stream the recording over the Internet, giving the whole world access to the last horrific moments in Lily Durant's life.

Reynolds had tried to watch the tape, reasoning that it could not be as bad as what he had seen firsthand in the camp. He was wrong. The full-length recording was less than a minute long, but even with the volume turned down, he'd been able to sit through only the first fifteen seconds before the blind fear and utter despair in Durant's face had compelled him to turn it off. To make matters worse, her state of undress confirmed what everyone had feared right from the start: that her torture had gone far beyond a physical beating. The autopsy, which was carried out three days later at the National Naval Medical Center in Bethesda, Maryland, verified that Lily Durant had been raped repeatedly before she had died. Unsurprisingly, the cause of death was listed as the gunshot wound she sustained in the tape's closing seconds.

The public outcry that followed the tape's release had been predictably deafening, particularly in the United States, where David Brenneman was halfway through his second term in office. While his popularity with the voting public was lukewarm at best, the fact that his niece had been killed in such brutal, dramatic fashion had touched something deep within the American psyche, weary as it was from the Iraqi conflict overseas and economic turmoil at home, imparting a sense of moral outrage that united the country in a way that hadn't been seen since 9/11.

Or maybe the nation's outrage had less to do with morality than the need to vent amid the innumerable hardships people were going through. Maybe it was a collective purging of frustration in the wake of record home foreclosures, joblessness, and unending threats from abroad. One day North Korea was testing nuclear missiles in defiance of international condemnation, the next Iran was building them in its factories, and by the way, America, your stocks are worthless, Detroit has gone to hell, and your credit line's been cut.

Now, here in this place, the most heinous of acts had been committed against a U.S citizen on a humanitarian mission, a pretty young woman who could have been the girl next door but just happened to be the niece of the country's highest elected official. And the perpetrator was a foreign leader considered a pariah in the civilized world, a figure as hated and loathed as Osama. Knowing the man responsible had given the American people a clear target for their anger, and they had responded accordingly.

How did that old Rolling Stones song go? It had been a favorite in Reynolds's college days. *Rape, murder, it's just a shot away.*

Yes, he thought, *a shot away.* It was possible, he supposed, that a country in need of a bloodletting had found a convenient target for its wrath. That would certainly be the cynic's explanation, although he'd somehow managed to avoid it in spite of his backstage perspective on global politics, and intimate familiarity with the maneuverings that went on behind the scenes. . . . Call him a die-hard believer in man's higher nature.

Reynolds drank more of his coffee, realizing he should probably eat something to soak it up a bit, never mind that he hadn't mustered any kind of appetite today . . . a sure sign of his growing anxiousness. He already felt a hot, acidic gnawing in his stomach and knew it would turn into full-fledged indigestion by the time he was ready for bed. Sleeplessness, bad dreams, and stubbed toes during urgent midnight trips to the bathroom—there you had the touchstones of a career diplomat's dedication to his post.

He sighed. Whatever force, or combination of forces, had been driving the national consciousness back home, there seemed to be no doubt in anyone's mind that Omar al-Bashir was the guilty party. A poll conducted by *Newsweek* one week after the incident had shown that 84 percent of Americans believed the Sudanese dictator had ordered the attack. Of those, an astonishing 92 percent believed he had done so with the knowledge that the president's niece would be specifically marked. Al-Bashir, in turn, had vehemently denied any involvement, but that was only to be expected, and for the most part, his word carried no weight outside of Sudan.

Reynolds was a student of history, and he believed with every fiber of his being that in the weeks following Durant's death, David Brenneman had had more power at his fingertips than at any other time of his presidency. It was the kind of global support that gave its bearer a blank check, the ability to launch a devastating attack on the Sudanese government without regard for the consequences. And yet, shockingly, Brenneman had done virtually nothing to take advantage of the political climate. There had been no retaliatory strikes, no threats of retribution, no additional sanctions . . . nothing at all. Stranger still, there had been no explanation for the president's refusal to act. He had neglected to issue a statement, other than the usual condemnation of the Sudanese government's role in the ethnic cleansing of West Darfur, and in the weeks following the attack, he had said nothing at all about his relationship to Lily Durant, the sole foreigner to die in the raid.

Faced with this inexplicable silence, the hugely frustrated press corps had sought answers through alternative channels. But Lou Samberg, the White House press secretary, had been just as reticent to comment, as had the rest of the senior White House staff. In short, there was no explanation as to why the president was willing to let the Sudanese government get away with murdering his own niece. As the silence stretched on, it became more and more obvious that nothing was going to happen, and then the inevitable came about as a result. Public sympathy for Brenneman's personal loss began to erode, along with his approval ratings. Now, two months after that tragic incident, he was facing the darkest days of his presidency.

Reynolds tossed back what remained of the potent brew in his cup, turned away from the window, and took a seat at his desk, absently scanning the dusty surface, which was cluttered with books and stacks of unread files. He was conflicted inside. In the end a president's approval was a visceral thing for Americans, less about his specific policies than an estimation of character. To some extent, he couldn't blame them for abandoning Brenneman. After all, how could they be expected to support a man who wouldn't stand up for his own family? More to the point, if he wasn't willing to act on behalf of one person, how could he possibly be counted on when the lives of hundreds, thousands, or millions of Americans were at stake?

These were fair questions, and yet, Reynolds had met David Brenneman on several occasions, and he couldn't bring himself to concede that the press had it right. He couldn't accept the idea that Brenneman had sacrificed the memory of his niece, mainly because nothing in his past—including a record of commitment to fulfilling the promises he'd made as a candidate, and a willingness to buck the polls and his opposition in order to overcome Washington's inertial tendencies—suggested that he was the type to cave in without a fight, especially to a hardened thug like Omar al-Bashir. At the same time, the evidence was laid bare for all to see, and the senior diplomat had to admit that it didn't look good. Brenneman's inaction seemed to speak for itself, and even Walter Reynolds, one of the president's staunchest supporters, couldn't help but wonder if the pundits had been right all along. Maybe the man *had* lost his nerve.

As he sat there brooding at his desk, he checked his watch with a combination of annoyance and frustration. The person he was expecting was late, but Reynolds supposed that was his prerogative. After all, somebody with the consultant's political backing did not have to be prompt for anyone, especially a washed-up old diplomat with a terrible diet, an aversion to exercise, and the waistline to show for it. In recent months, Reynolds had taken to wearing oversize sport coats and loose-fitting pants to accommodate his bulk. The way he saw it, there was no point in being uncomfortable, as he and his counterpart in the foreign ministry were still giving each other the silent treatment. It was a battle of nerves that didn't seem likely to end anytime soon, and since he was holed up in his office all day, there was no reason not to take advantage of a less stringent dress code.

At least, that was the usual state of affairs. Today, in deference to the status of his mysterious visitor, he had made an effort to spruce up his appearance. He was wearing a crisp white dress shirt, a dark blue suit of worsted wool, and polished wing tips. A scarlet tie completed the picture. He was extremely uncomfortable—the tie was cutting off his air, and probably contributing to his reflux in some arcane medical way—but with three decades of government service in his portfolio, Reynolds knew when it was time to make a show of himself, and this was one of those rare occasions.

He had learned of the impending visit the previous day. When his secretary appeared in the door to announce that Scott Linton was on the line, Reynolds had smiled and heaved a sigh of relief. Even before he'd picked up the phone, he knew what it meant. Linton was a heavy hitter, the assistant secretary of state for consular affairs at the State Department, and his call could only mean one thing: that the U.S. Embassy to the Republic of the Sudan was about to be closed down, its staff pulled out of the country. With Linton's call, it had looked like the long wait was over. The president had finally decided to make a stand.

When he picked up the phone, though, it had not been Linton on the line. Instead, a young man had asked him to hold for Brynn Fitzgerald, the secretary of state. Reynolds, in a state of shock, had stuttered a few clumsy words in response to Fitzgerald's greeting, but before he could redeem himself, she had come straight to the point. A man whom she murkily described as— quote unquote—a consultant to the president would be arriving in Khartoum the following day, and she would appreciate it if Reynolds would extend him every courtesy during his stay in the country, which she characterized as open-ended . . . again, using her exact words.

Although Fitzgerald had relayed this request with unfailing courtesy, Reynolds was left with the distinct impression that the consultant's visit was not to be taken lightly. The veiled speech seemed only to confirm this notion, as did Fitzgerald's next instructions, which were delivered in a much firmer tone. Reynolds was to keep the consultant's visit a closely guarded secret. No one was to be told about it, and there was to be no record of his arrival or departure at the embassy. Reynolds, with no room or desire to argue, had agreed readily to these conditions, and Fitzgerald had promptly ended the call, leaving him with the better part of a day to muse over the strange conversation and what it might mean for him and his staff of seventy.

Although he had come up with plenty of possibili-

ties, Reynolds had not been able to hit on the true nature of the consultant's mission in Sudan. He could
think of nothing that would justify such secrecy, or a
call from someone as highly placed as Brynn Fitzgerald.
In fact, the whole thing was so unusual that he had
started to think he had dreamed it up.

But that clearly wasn't the case. His secretary was
standing in the door, and she was trying to get his attention.

"Yes, Joyce?" he asked, though he already knew.

"Your three o'clock is here, sir. He's on the way up."

Reynolds nodded and pulled at his tie. He still had
no idea why the consultant had traveled as far as he had,
or what he might possibly want, for that matter. But
there was no point in worrying about it now. He had
waited this long, after all, and he would have his answers soon enough.

"Good," he said. "When he arrives, send him right
in."

CHAPTER 6

BALTIMORE, MARYLAND

The redbrick town house that served as both home and office to Allison Dearborn, PsyD, EdD, was located in the Bolton Hill section of Baltimore, a short drive from the grand Victorian dome and towers of the Johns Hopkins Hospital, where she had completed her residency in the midnineties, after an earlier internship at Mayo, and now served as an affiliate clinical psychologist. For five years in between, she'd worked in Washington, D.C., as a screening, evaluation, and crisis-intervention counselor for the CIA . . . although once the Agency recognized her outstanding skills as a therapist, the latter area of specialization had come to occupy most of her time. Inside and outside the office.

When she left her position in 2008, Allison had insisted it was because she was a generalist by inclination and wanted to pursue various areas of academic study. It was a nice, pat reason she'd known would roll smoothly off her tongue and leave her superiors with few openings to urge that she reconsider her choice. Dreams and goals represented the intangible and, precisely for that reason, were hard to poke holes in. If she'd told the truth, namely, that her decision had been based on mental fatigue, there would have been a barrage of suggestions and incentives, which she'd have had to swat off one by one. *Take some downtime, ease your caseload, and how about we shift more of the obviously tough and complicated cases over to other therapists till you've reenergized your battery? Meanwhile, we can certainly slot you in for more frequent out-of-town conferences. Arrange for you to occasionally travel inside and outside the country. Rome, for example. Have you been to Rome? There's also Milan. Or our Paris branch. In springtime. Where enchanted music rises from the banks of the Seine and perfume fills every boulevard.*

Allison had always appreciated the respect she got from the Agency. She had likewise known it was much deserved. Her success rate was in the upper percentile—meaning she kept most of her patients productive or curbed their dropout rate. Her bosses therefore would have bent over backward to accommodate her if it meant she'd stay on; she was sure of it because they'd done it in the past. But at the time of her resignation she'd been disinclined to keep fouling off their pitches, however well-intentioned they might be.

And so Allison had claimed she needed a change based on personal objectives beyond and distinct from the job, and let it stand at that. She'd been careful to say nothing about the intensity in the eyes of her patients, and what it was like to feel them searing into her own, those looks speaking volumes about the fires burning inside them, communicating hidden rage, guilt, anxiety and, for some, nightmarish horrors beyond what they were able to share in words. Nor had she mentioned the nights she'd spent lying awake in the dark, agonizing over each one of those patients, worrying what might happen if she committed the smallest error in judgment or just had a momentary slip of attention. There were many individuals with aggression issues, deep-rooted guilt, even core identity conflicts, often compounded by drug or alcohol abuse. Some were trying to reacclimate themselves after returning from some foreign hell. Others had been on covert assignments and were trying to maintain some inner balance between their secret lives and honest, open relationships with families and friends.

Shortly before leaving the Agency, Allison had read an air force study that said over half the airmen on foreign deployment who committed suicide had attended regular counseling sessions. She'd had a strong hunch the numbers were similar, or greater, in the CIA. While she had been fortunate enough to have never lost a patient, Allison had spoken with other highly capable mental health professionals within the organization who weren't quite as lucky and beat themselves up regularly over the ones they had failed to save. And although she'd known better than to make her thoughts known to them, she always wondered, as they doubtless did, what key point in someone's unraveling had been missed. And why.

The questions had plagued her throughout her tenure at the Agency. Shrinks were as vulnerable to obsessive fears as anyone, and the one that had haunted Allison during her frequent sleepless nights was the possibility that her concentration might blink while someone was baring a dark, pained corner of his soul, just *blink* as some vital, wounded part of him briefly reared like a fanged undersea serpent from some hidden inner recess, and that she'd wake up the next day to read about him taking a Glock to his head and pulling the trigger, or overdosing on some prescription tranquilizer cocktail, or hanging himself while alone in a cheap roadside motel room. Or maybe taking the wife, kids, and brand-new puppy with him when he drove his car off a cliff.

As a therapist, Allison knew, your humanity was the tether that connected you to your patients; in fact, it could be a lifeline to some of them. But she recognized it was also a potential trip wire for the most volatile personalities. There was very little margin for error when interacting with them, and the danger, in her mind, was that the slightest lapse could have grave ramifications. Was it that you suddenly realized you'd forgotten to mail your loan payment in time to avoid late fees? Locked yourself out of the car? Neglected to open the pet door for the cat that morning? Or maybe to schedule a visit with the dermatologist to remove the suspicious little bump over your eyelid?

At the CIA Allison had frequently dealt with the institutional stigma against admitting to psychological problems. It had worn rather thin at times from the very beginning, but the real strains had sprung from the reality that she was very often playing for mortal stakes.

Now Allison, a tall, willowy blonde in her midthirties with her hair pulled back in a French twist, wearing small, round diamond earrings, a long-sleeved Ralph Lauren stretch polo under a matching gray sweater jacket, gray wool dress pants with flared bottoms, and peep-toe black suede dress heels, entered her second-story office with its window overlooking the poplar trees and cobblestone sidewalks along Murielle Lane.

Pausing to pour herself a strong black cup of Italian roast, she went swiftly across the room from the coffee maker, then sat down behind her large oak desk. The antique pendulum wall clock to her right—a made-in-Germany Hermle Black Forest she'd picked up at a yard sale near her niece's home in Oak Creek, Wisconsin, of all places—said it was a quarter to ten. Jonathan Harper was due for their hastily scheduled powwow in fifteen minutes. But if he held true to form, he would arrive in no more than ten, barring a calamitous traffic jam on the Capital Beltway.

She drank her coffee, settling in for the presumably brief wait. She hadn't thought about her CIA days for a while. But then it had been quite some time since she'd gotten a call from Harper, though he was still nominally under her care. Looking back on her eight years with the Agency, she considered it sad irony that its intelligence gatherers had assembled comprehensive reports on the major causes of death for every country and region in the world—not to mention almost every profession—but had failed to address its own problems in that regard. If you were interested in what took people's lives in Belarus, Algeria, or the Indian subcontinent, the information could be instantly plucked from its databases with a scroll and a click. Reach into the intercontinental grab bag for any of that data, and the Agency could—and typically did—generate reams of material on who was dying from childhood leukemia or old age, genetic conditions or environmental contaminants, pandemics, accidents, violent crime . . . and so on and so forth, including self-inflicted means. Incorporating these analyses into its overall intelligence tapestry, the CIA made recommendations on foreign strategy and policy to diplomats, and the loftiest of generals and heads of state . . . yet as an organization still had not quite figured out how to look inward. Or as one fellow academic, who wrote a white paper on the subject, had put it to Allison, the Agency was choking on evolutionary exhaust when it came to maintaining the mental health of its employees.

His snooty language aside, it was accurate that the CIA topped the list of government agencies whose human resources too often jumped aboard the Downbound Express into suicide and depression. And it had held that inglorious distinction for quite some time, followed closely by the Feebs, local police departments, all five armed services, and that old bad joke punch line, the rain-or-shine U.S. Postal Service . . . which, in absolute fairness, technically operated as a private enterprise and fell into a different pot from the others. Over the past decade, in fact, with field operatives increasingly deployed to countries like Iran, Afghanistan, and other war-on-terror hellholes, where poverty, disease, and the atrocities of armed thugs were so widespread as to be virtually atmospheric, the rates of depression and suicide had soared to unprecedented heights. According to the most recent studies, two-thirds as many agents had died by their own hand than had been officially killed in the performance of duty. *Officially*, because in her mind the line wasn't nearly that clear-cut. As Benjamin Disraeli was once supposed to have said, "There were lies, damned lies, and statistics."

Of course, it wasn't about numbers for Allison, not in the end, besides their underscoring what she already knew from her up close contact with men and women who had returned from the field or were engaged in clandestine ops. It was really pretty basic: stress and trauma were no less destructive than bullets.

The day Allison submitted her resignation, her department head, Edward Rockland, had made a strong, earnest appeal for her to stay on, offering to shift her to an analysis and research job within the Directorate of Intelligence, where she would have a chance for consultancies with senior government policymakers. When she'd declined the offer, he'd asked her to at least do him the favor of speaking with the deputy director of Management and Services, Office of Personnel, to see if there was anything else that might be done to convince her. Rockland was a legitimately decent guy who took good care of his people, and though she'd agreed to it out of respect for him, Allison was convinced he'd viewed that second meeting much as she had—as a requisite formality. Though she had heard him out with all due deference, his reconciled tone had made it evident that he had very little doubt her decision was a firm one.

Allison had brought that same polite yet unassailable demeanor to her sit-down with the DD-MS, although she went into it with an added measure of remove. Psychologically and emotionally, she was already well out the door, and all she could think about while quietly listening to his pitch was that old William Blake poem "The Tiger," with several lines in particular nearly jumping from her lips: *In what distant deeps or skies, burnt the fire of thine eyes? On what wings dare he aspire? What the hand dare seize the fire?*

The thing she'd recognized in herself upon deciding to leave the Agency was that she could no longer spend all her days trying to seize the fire in the eyes of its most damaged operatives. The heat was too strong; its overflow into her own daily life too consuming.

But there was a major catch. In the thirty-two years

since she'd come kicking, bottom down, into the American heartland via C-section, Allison had learned there was nearly always a catch somewhere. And for her it had been lurking inside her.

What was it she had been thinking about irony? As loath as she was to admit it, it was her constant yet maddening companion through life, a disobedient pooch she walked on a long leash while complaining it was always out of control. Because the inescapable paradox at her core, one she'd first done her best to disregard while formulating her exit strategy from the Central Intelligence Agency, and *then* closed off from her mind as she gave her spiel not once, but twice, was that she not only took gratification from helping people with dire psychological problems—and had chosen her vocation precisely for that reason—but was fascinated by the prospect of tackling cases others deemed tough or insoluble.

Although she now spent the bulk of her time doing research and lecturing at the university on Charles Street, Allison had found herself missing the rewards of people in need and had gradually begun taking a select number of Agency patients on referral.

Jonathan Harper had been the first of them, and the one that made her realize she could take on others on a limited basis without once again succumbing to the sort of nervous tension that had given her constant, tightly wound insomnia throughout her latter months with the Agency. And the whole thing had been pure serendipity.

It would have sufficiently floored her if someone of Harper's stature had sought her out on his own, but the wild, wild coincidence was that their connection had come through his wife, Julie, whom Allison had met during her time at Mayo in Rochester, Minnesota, long before she'd ever heard of Jonathan Harper or set foot in Langley. An attractive, slightly plump woman with a warm maternal disposition, Julie had been a head nurse at the clinic and had been considerably older than Allison when they'd gotten to know each other while treating a breast cancer patient who'd opted for in-house counseling. Always the type to take young people under her wing—particularly a green psych intern for whom buying groceries took a backseat to paying off student loans—Julie had invited her over to her place for dinner one evening after a late conference. Besides being pleasant, intelligent company, she had turned out to be quite the gourmet cook, making her company an irresistible draw for a young woman who considered preparing unburned toast a proud accomplishment even when she *could* afford the luxury of a trip to the supermarket.

At the time, Allison had known Julie's husband did sensitive work for the federal government and occasionally spent extended periods overseas on what she assumed were diplomatic missions. But neither she nor anyone else at Mayo ever had the slightest inkling that he was CIA . . . which was, of course, how he wanted things. Or to put it more correctly, how things had to be for the welfare of Harper and his family.

That carefully preserved secrecy about the nature of his work had never changed. Harper remained unknown to the vast majority of Americans. As the Agency's deputy director, he was the second most powerful person in the organizational hierarchy. Individuals in his position weren't supposed to be photographed in the newspapers or to appear with policy wonks on televised Sunday morning political shootouts. He was among the quiet ones. The ones who did the work of keeping the country safe and secure from behind the scenes. Anonymity was an essential part of his curriculum vitae.

Among the members of the intelligence community, however, Harper was a renowned figure, a man who not only had a close relationship with the president but had also been among those who'd once uncovered a plot to assassinate some of the world's most powerful leaders. That accomplishment alone would boldface most careers, but his exploits went back to the late eighties, when he had conducted some of the most incredibly daring missions of the Cold War behind the Iron Curtain—including one he had personally told Allison about, which involved his hanging from the skids of a Black Hawk chopper while snapping recon photos of ancient Thracian passes over the Balkans. And that itself had been part of an operation in which he'd smuggled a Communist defector and his family out of Sofia, Bulgaria, negotiating miles of rugged, wooded terrain to eventually rendezvous with a Sturgeon-class submarine in the Black Sea. . . .

Allison smiled a little. If she had heard that story from anyone but Harper, she might have smelled a very ripe fish.

To be sure, she'd learned nothing about his mysterious career from Julie during their time together at Mayo, or after moving on to her residency at Johns Hopkins, though they'd periodically stayed in touch with one another over the years. It was only after she'd been introduced to DCI Jonathan Harper sometime early in her tenure with the Agency that she'd registered the possible connection . . . and even then, her suspicions weren't fully confirmed until she attended a dinner symposium in Washington at which both Harpers were guests, arriving at the affair arm in arm.

Still, she would have never imagined the legendary Harper would wind up seeking her out for therapy. Never viewed him as being made of flesh and blood like anyone else. Until the unthinkable occurred about two years ago.

Allison's smile faded as she recalled the details of the shooting that nearly claimed his life. He'd been right on his doorstep after his morning run, doing some stretching exercises as Julie prepared breakfast inside. Right there on the doorstep of his General's Row home. Harper did not so much as glimpse his female assailant until the first shot left her gun, clattered around his rib cage, and punctured his right lung. The next two shots had caught him in the arm as he'd reflexively whirled around to face her, and it was lucky he *had* been turning in that split second, because otherwise those bullets would have struck him square in the chest and inflicted more serious damage than they did. As it was, the fourth .22-caliber slug to issue from her weapon barely missed his heart—and her intended fifth would have been the fatal shot.

What saved him was the chance proximity of a D.C. Metro police car over on Q Street. The officer inside the cruiser had heard the distinctive pops of gunfire, jolted to a halt, and pushed out his door just as the woman moved in to finish off the stricken Harper. He'd started pulling his gun, momentarily drawing her attention from her intended victim, but she had taken him out with one shot, killing him instantly. Meanwhile, Julie had heard the commotion, had come racing out onto the stoop, and had dragged her unconscious husband into the house.

Harper would later discover that he'd actually lost his vital signs for almost a full minute before the EMT wagon arrived. Were it not for Julie rapidly administering CPR and applying towels and pressure to staunch his hemorrhaging, he'd have died right there in his foyer, bleeding out on the carpet. He would later joke that marrying a nurse with a taste for expensive jewelry and clothes had finally yielded some practical dividends.

Besides Julie's resuscitative and emergency first aid skills, the commotion on the street would prove a major aid to his survival, the gathering crowd outside the house having forced the gunwoman to run for cover. Unfortunately, it also gave her a perfect chance to blend in amid the morning foot traffic. Despite roadblocks and cordons and airport alerts—and even with a massive deployment of law-enforcement personnel, which the Washington media would liken to the hunt for John Wilkes Booth in terms of its geographic scope and allocation of manpower—she'd managed to go to ground.

It was about a month after Harper was released from the hospital that Julie left Allison a voice mail telling her to expect a call from him in the "next couple of days." He'd been having bad dreams, night sweats, and sudden onsets of nervous tremors. He had feared for Julie's safety to an extreme degree, to the point where he grew nervous whenever she left the house, and even more ill at ease when she was home alone. For a while he insisted to Julie that those episodes would pass. But she'd known they wouldn't, not unless he got some professional help.

As it turned out, a couple of weeks, not days, would pass before Allison actually heard from him. Which came as no surprise. She'd dealt with CIA men for too long . . . their throwback macho ethos; the illogical shame born of associating trauma with weakness, vulnerability, and even cowardice; the assumption of guilt for everything negative they could not control. It was an embedded part of Agency culture that was difficult, and frequently impossible, to counteract.

Fortunately for Harper, his wife's stubborn insistence had done the trick. And to give him his fair share of credit as well, he had listened, admitted he had problems, and had the courage to do something about them.

Sighing over her coffee cup, Allison shook off her thoughts and glanced at the pendulum clock again. *Ten fifty-one.* It was starting to look as if Harper's compulsive earliness had gone by the wayside, after all. . . .

Her intercom buzzed, prompting a wry smile. She'd always been okay with the notion of a mostly random universe. But throw her a few token constants—nothing to tag her as *greedy*—and she could nestle into existence with a far greater degree of comfort.

She punched the speaker button. "Tell Mr. Harper to come right in, Martha," she said, rising from her chair before the receptionist could utter a word.

Harper entered a moment later. His graying hair impeccably trimmed, he looked fit and lean in a conservative gray Brooks Brothers suit, gray and red striped tie, white shirt, and buff cordovan wing tips.

"John, it's been a long time," she said, extending her hand.

He set down his briefcase and clasped her hand warmly in both of his. "Much too long," he said. "Julie sends her regards. She's been meaning to throw a get-together, invite some of our close friends for cocktails. But you know. . . ."

"We're all busy folks," Allison said, thinking they both knew her days of socializing with Julie were over, beyond their yearly exchanges of Christmas cards and occasional breezy hi-how-are-yous over the telephone. For all intents and purposes, their closeness had ended once Allison became her husband's therapist and was entrusted with confidences he could share with no one else, including, and sometimes especially, Julie herself. For Allison this had been expected; it came with the territory. The instant she'd agreed to assist with Harper's psychological healing, she had understood that her responsibilities as his doctor would not only override her longtime friendship with his wife but most likely also require its sacrifice.

"Pour you some coffee?" she asked.

Harper declined with a quick shake of his head. "Trying to cut down on the caffeine intake," he said. "My limit's six cups before noon."

She smiled. "That few?"

"Mondays, Wednesdays, and Fridays excepted," he said.

"And weekends?"

"Two cups at breakfast, maximum. Scotch and water the rest of the way."

Allison's smile grew a bit larger. "I suppose progress is progress," she said.

Harper was silent. After a moment she motioned him into the wingback leather chair in front of her desk, then went around to sit opposite him.

"So," she said, "how've you been?"

"Personally, fine," he said, hefting his briefcase onto his lap. "Professionally, troubled."

She regarded him closely. "I don't recall you ever having a clear-cut line of control there, John."

Harper gave a shrug. "You said it yourself," he said. "I've made progress."

Allison kept studying his features in the sunlight streaming through the window behind her. She could see small, radiating creases at the corners of his eyes and mouth, which hadn't been immediately apparent as he entered the room.

"When you called yesterday, you told me you needed to ask a favor," she said. "Which side of this new Harper line does it fall on?"

"The troubled part," he said. "As I think you might surmise."

"Does it have anything to do with Sudan?"

He gave her a sharp look. "Pretty astute of you."

"Not so much," she said, leaning forward. "I read the papers . . . follow the stories about Sudan. And right now that's monopolizing the headlines until you get to the gossip and sports pages." She paused. "It's evident that the president's been under pressure from nearly all sides to retaliate. I assume that whatever's coming at him publicly is being multiplied exponentially among his advisors. I also assume you're one of the people who have his ear."

"That's debatable," Harper said with a shrug. "I've taken the minority position, Allie."

"Can you tell me what that means without spilling state secrets?"

"Generally," Harper said, "it means I've urged patience. But after what happened to his niece, David Brenneman hasn't had much of it with Omar al-Bashir. Or with me."

"I get the sense your minority element isn't very large."

Harper smiled soberly. "He's six foot three and weighs about a hundred eighty pounds," he said. "And amiable."

"Will he admit to having a coffee jones?"

"I think you'd have to ask him in the capacity of his analyst," Harper said. "Given a choice right now, though, I'm very certain his preference would be to speak to you as a friend."

Allison sat looking thoughtful for a full thirty seconds. "I'm listening, John," she said then.

He took a long, deep breath. Allison noted that he had his hands on the hard-shell briefcase on his lap, his fingers spread out atop it, lightly pressing down on its black leather surface.

"You've heard of Ryan Kealey," he said.

"Of course," she said. "If memory serves, you recruited him, isn't that right?"

"Memory serves," Harper said.

Allison was nodding. "I was at Langley for nearly a decade," she said. "In all that time, I can think of only one operative who managed to become the lead story on the evening news. Although it's understandable how getting into a shoot-out on the streets of New York City can have that rather exceptional result."

Harper had to chuckle. "Kealey admittedly had a flair for the dramatic," he said.

"Past tense?"

"In terms of the Agency, yes," Harper said.

Allison raised an eyebrow. "I've been out of the loop, granted. But somehow I'm surprised to hear that."

"If you knew him, you wouldn't be," Harper said. "Kealey is . . . I suppose the word would be *unorthodox*. That's sometimes brought attention to him. But he's never gone looking for it. Or frankly even been keen on taking credit."

"Can you tell me why he pulled out of the game?"

"He's mostly been a reluctant player from the beginning, " Harper said. "And he's been through a lot of things. Carries a lot around with him."

"That isn't so unusual," Allison said. "The majority of my time at the Agency was spent trying to lift unnecessary burdens from people's shoulders. But I suppose that's true of any clinician."

Harper sat a moment, crossed his ankle over his knee. "A question, Allie . . . Why did *you* pull out?"

"Is it really important?"

"It might be for your understanding."

"Of Kealey?"

"And the reason I came here to talk to you this morning."

"Which is presumably tied to Kealey."

He gave a slow nod, waited, meeting her gaze with his own. After a while Allison shrugged.

"Every mind is a complicated piece of machinery," she said. "If there's one that isn't functioning to optimal performance, and you're going to muck around inside, you'd damn well better have steady hands. It's serious business, whether someone comes to you because he or she has intimacy issues, problems with self-worth, or is phobic about crowds, clowns, riding in a car, or chickens." She linked her fingers together more tightly on the desk. "But I didn't mean to switch metaphors, John. So getting back to yours . . . At the Agency every game is high risk. I just felt that I was wearing down. And that's when people make mistakes."

Harper watched her in silence for a moment, lightly drumming his fingers on the case. "Did you lose someone?"

"Bad guys get away. Patients die. Loss comes with the job when you're in the business of saving lives."

"That doesn't exactly answer my question."

Allison gave a fleeting smile. "I guess you'll have to settle, bub." She nodded her chin at the briefcase. "So what's in there that's got you tapping out finger rolls, and how's it related to the favor you've come to ask?"

Harper snapped his eyes down at his hands, frowning as if they'd been guilty of insubordination. Then he raised them back to her face.

"It goes back to what we were talking about when I walked in here. Sudan, President Brenneman, and your observation that retaliatory action may be imminent," he said. "I've already told you I believe it would be a mistake at this point. I can't tell you why I believe it, and I can't tell you what I think is necessary to forestall that course of action. . . ."

"But you're hoping to find a way do it."

He sat quietly again, his forehead seamed with concentration, the crow's-feet Allison had noticed around his eyes spreading and deepening. "I'm going out on a limb telling you this, Allie. But there are things that need to be looked into under certain people's radar. And I'm convinced Ryan Kealey is the only person capable of pulling off the job."

"Have you asked him if he's interested?"

"Not yet. And I can guarantee he won't be. But I'm going to try to persuade him. It means flying fifteen hours and eight thousand miles, and that's okay. When I reach him, though, I'm going to have only one crack at it."

Allison sat there thinking. She was no mathematical whiz. But basic addition wasn't a problem for her.

"You want me to profile him for you," she said, pointing her chin at the briefcase. "Based on . . . what information?"

"His psych workups and personal history. Files going back years before he was Agency. Everything about everything in Ryan Kealey's life." He lifted the case off his lap and placed it on the desk. "It's all in there for you to read and evaluate. And just to be harshly explicit, Allie, I'm requesting more than another psychological profile. What I want to know from you is how to push his buttons. Pull his strings. Manipulate him by any and all means possible. Whatever it takes to get him to come aboard."

She went bold straight in her chair, eyes widening, boring into him, her shoulders as stiff as wooden pickets.

"My God, John . . . this is *beyond* unprincipled. Do you realize how many ethical codes you're asking me to violate?"

Harper met her stare and didn't blink. "I'd be breaking a few myself," he said. "In fact, I've blown a few to smithereens just getting hold of his files. And probably more coming here to discuss them with you."

Silence.

"If I agree to do this," Allison said, "it would be done without conscience."

"No, Allie. It wouldn't. For a couple of reasons. The first is Kealey. It isn't as if we just lost him at the Agency. He's lost himself. I don't know how else to put it. But the course he's on right now isn't a good one. Or the kind that lasts long before there's a major train wreck."

The Downbound Express. Allison looked at Harper as if he'd prepared for their conversation by wiretapping her earlier thoughts.

"And your second reason?"

"If I'm right in what I'm doing—and successful—you might be helping to prevent a tremendous, unnecessary amount of destruction. Americans' lives are my primary concern. But we're talking about people in Africa and elsewhere. And about possible escalation on a level I don't even want to contemplate."

She was shaking her head with a mix of incredulity and denial. "John . . . I wish you could be more specific."

"I don't have to be," Harper said. "Look at the foreign governments with vested interests in Sudan. China. Russia. The old tried-and-true biggies. And then, of course, you have Bashir's Moslem brethren who are on the cusp of supporting him." He paused. "You used the word 'retaliate.' By definition that means hitting back. But contemplate for a minute what it would mean if the United States picked the wrong target for its vengeance."

The renewed silence between them surpassed the previous one in its length and weight. Allison could feel it pressing on her like the compounded gravity inside some inescapable black hole. She willed a breath into her lungs, trying to absorb everything Harper had told her, struggling to put it into some sort of order and context.

It seemed forever before she managed to exhale.

"I'm not a world rescuer—not in the sense you are," she said. "I take it one person at a time, you understand?"

Harper looked at her. "Yes," he said. "I understand."

She nodded, willing the immense weight that had borne on her to shift in his direction.

"Good," she said firmly. "Because if I'm going to make a pact with you, the devil, or both, I mean to be able to live with it. Maybe not easily, and certainly not without lasting regret. But what I'm requiring that you provide in return will allow me to tenuously hang on to my self-respect. And maybe salvage something else besides."

Harper's expression showed that he had grasped her meaning at once.

"Kealey," he said, articulating it with a single word. "You want Kealey."

"And your commitment that I will have a chance to help him, whenever he's through saving the world." Allison said with another nod. "God forgive me if it borders on psychological manipulation. But get him here to me, just get him here, and I'll prepare you for your meeting with him. And then find a way to live with this bargain."

Harper was very still for a time, before he leaned forward in his chair, reaching a hand out to her. When Allison took it, there was no double handclasp, and it wasn't nearly as warm as it had been. *No*, she thought, *not now. And maybe never again.*

She could tell Harper had felt the chill as he pulled his arm back across the desk, then rose from the chair.

"We'll talk soon?" he said.

"As soon as possible."

Harper nodded, turned, and walked toward the door, halting midway across the office. "One more question for you," he said with a glance over his shoulder. "If you don't mind."

Her gesture fell somewhere between a nod and a shrug.

"What's the clinical term for a fear of chickens?" he asked.

Allison looked at him, managing a faint smile. "Alektorophobia," she said.

Harper grunted. "I'll try to remember it," he said.

"To stump the guests when Julie and I finally get around to throwing that cocktail party."

Her hands on the briefcase he had left on her desk, Allie had nothing more to say as she watched him leave the room.

CHAPTER 7

JOHANNESBURG

As expected, the South African president moved directly toward the rope line, where the press pool was eagerly awaiting his statement. From where he was standing, Whysall could see Kealey walking a few steps behind Zuma. The man's dark gray eyes were in constant motion as he scanned the crowd for anything out of the ordinary, but otherwise, his face was completely unreadable. Seeing this, Whysall shook his head in grudging admiration. In his previous job he had come under fire on more than one occasion, and he had never been rattled, at least not in any meaningful way. Now his hands were sweating profusely, and every muscle in his body was painfully taut.

Kealey, on the other hand, appeared to be unnaturally calm, completely unshaken by the commotion surrounding him. Even his movements seemed to be fluid and relaxed, so much so that one would be hard pressed to notice the careful way he had positioned himself with respect to his principal. It wouldn't be readily apparent to most people, but Whysall noticed that Kealey was never more than five feet from Zuma. The weapon on his left hip holstered with the butt pointing forward to facilitate ready access with the right hand, he was in a perfect position to provide immediate cover without physically intruding on the African leader's space.

Whysall watched as Kealey stopped a few steps behind Zuma and drifted a little to the left so that he could scan the crowd while the president spoke. A hush fell over the crowd as Zuma accepted a few pages of paper from one of his aides, thanking the man with a gracious nod. Even his most ardent critics gradually stopped chanting their slogans, their jeers falling away as Zuma, seemingly oblivious to all of it, studied his handwritten notes. Then, when the room was completely silent, he slipped on a pair of reading glasses, lifted his stately head, and began to read.

"Ladies and gentlemen, members of the press. I am happy to report that today justice has been done in your High Court of Johannesburg. . . ."

Outside the courthouse, the crowd had swelled to nearly 1,500 students, union delegates, political activists, and unemployed workers. The statement that would exonerate Zuma at the expense of his old friend and confidant had been given under oath—and as the word spread, any semblance of cohesion between members of the throng evaporated in an eruption of violent confrontation. Fists were thrown, people trampled, and a car was set ablaze on the far side of the square. Screams of fear and pain mixed with chants both bitterly denouncing and extolling the Zuma government as the police tried in vain to hold back the crowd from the president and each other. Flowing outward over the pavement, it pushed angrily against the flimsy metal barricades that had been erected seven hours earlier on the intersecting streets in front of the building. At the same time, the police captain in charge placed a frantic call to Metro headquarters, seeking permission to use the array of nonlethal deterrents at his disposal.

In the confusion, no one noticed the young man who approached the police car parked alongside the curb on Kerk Street, 50 meters east of the courthouse. The teenager fumbled a key from his pocket, the same key that his brother-in-law—a sergeant with the South African Police Service and a longtime adherent of David Joubert—had given him the previous day. He reached into the backseat and found the plastic CNA shopping bag his brother-in-law had left for him. Pulling it out of the vehicle, he quickly checked the contents. Satisfied, he hit the automatic locks and closed the door behind him. He took a few seconds to check his position on the street and calm his nerves. Then he started moving toward the parking garage on the far side of the courthouse, the shopping bag dangling low in his right hand.

Ten minutes after he finished addressing the press in the lobby of the Johannesburg High Court, President Jacob Zuma and his small entourage passed through a steel doorway and into the concrete expanse of the fourth-floor parking deck. The deck had already been swept by Alex Whysall and four other men, and the motorcade was waiting, a total of five vehicles idling in the otherwise deserted parking garage. The entire deck had been cleared out the night before, and any cars that had been left behind had been towed that morn-

ing. It was the kind of precaution that wouldn't win
Zuma any new supporters at the courthouse, but Kealey
had insisted, and Zuma's chief of staff, a man named
Steve Oliphant, had reluctantly concurred.

Ryan Kealey followed his charge through the door
and started across the smooth concrete. The courthouse was attached to the parking garage, and in the
near distance he could hear the sounds of the riot taking place at the intersection of Von Brandis and Kerk.
With each step he took, the cacophony seemed to grow
louder, closer, and more threatening, and he could no
longer ignore the risk to the man he was charged with
protecting. Quickening his pace, he moved close to the
South African's left shoulder.

"Sir, may I speak to you for a moment?"

The South African president stopped in his tracks
and turned to face him. He looked mildly surprised by
the request, but he nodded once and walked a few steps
away from the waiting vehicles. Kealey followed and
quickly explained his concerns.

When he was done, Zuma nodded thoughtfully. He
looked carefully at his head of security and wondered,
not for the first time, what had brought him to this
place. It could have just been the money, of course, and
for most of the security contractors, he would have
guessed that to be the primary motivation. In Kealey's
case, however, he did not feel comfortable making that
assumption.

The American was of medium height, lean and tan,
with long, lank black hair that stopped just short of
being inappropriate for the job he was tasked with. As
usual, he was dressed casually in a faded black polo
shirt, pressed tan slacks, and a pair of rugged, expensive-
looking hiking boots. It was a uniform common to
every member of the security detail. Unlike his peers,

though, Kealey did not carry an automatic weapon. Instead, he was armed only with a 9mm handgun, which was holstered in a cross-draw position on his left hip. The man was as inconspicuous as he was effective— Zuma had learned as much over the last two months, much to his unspoken relief. He had expected a more visible presence at the start and had been vaguely disappointed, not to mention uneasy, when Blackwater had sent him Kealey and company.

As it turned out, the eight quiet professionals had managed not only to keep him safe but also to keep a remarkably low profile in the process. In fact, they were so unobtrusive that the South African media had yet to pick up on the fact that he had outsourced his personal security to an American firm. He didn't know how long that could last, but it was still a pleasant, if unexpected benefit to the whole situation.

At the same time the man standing before Zuma remained a mystery, and he continued to find that a little troubling. He didn't understand what could have prompted Ryan Kealey to sign on with Blackwater Worldwide. The man was a veritable legend in the U.S. intelligence community, and despite the CIA's best efforts, his government had been unable to completely conceal the full scope of his contribution to the nation's security. Zuma had wondered on more than one occasion what could have prompted the young American to walk away from all of that, though he had yet to come up with any likely scenarios. He suspected it had something to do with the haunted look that was never far from the young man's eyes, though he would never have presumed to ask. Simply put, it was none of his concern, and besides, it didn't really matter. The man's capabilities were all Zuma truly cared about, and they were undeniably intact.

The American was still awaiting an answer. Zuma sighed, shot a glance at his watch, and said, "What is your alternative, Mr. Kealey? Bearing in mind that I can't stand around all day waiting for the police to do their job."

"We have a helicopter providing sniper support for the run back to Pretoria. It holds only four, but we can squeeze in seven, and we'll send the rest of the men in the cars later, once the police manage to get things in hand."

"*If* they do, Mr. Kealey. I know you're aware of where I stand with many of them as a result of this trial."

Kealey grunted. "I've checked out the Metro captain in charge. He's no believer in Joubert, and I think we can trust him as much as anyone. He says they'll have the area secured in forty minutes or less."

"Is there room for my aide on the helicopter?"

Kealey glanced over at the chief of staff, who was already sliding into the backseat of the fourth armored vehicle, a white Toyota Land Cruiser. "He'll have to stay here, sir. I'm sorry, but I can't leave you with less than six security officers. Company policy."

Zuma appraised the younger man with a slight frown. Something about the way he said "company policy" made the South African leader think that Kealey couldn't care less about the company *or* its policies. Even the word *sir* was somehow impertinent coming from this man's lips. At the same time, he was standing there giving his honest, unbiased opinion, and that warranted some degree of respect and consideration. Zuma was a practical man, and he prized his personal welfare far above the formalities of his office.

He thought about it carefully. Usually, he didn't hesitate to follow the American's suggestions regarding his personal security. But on this occasion he desperately needed some time to confer with his chief of staff. He was due in Cape Town in two days' time, where he was scheduled to address the National Assembly regarding the budget he had submitted two months earlier. He needed every minute between now and then to pin down his position and clarify his arguments—and that, more than anything, made his decision for him.

"I'm sorry, but Mr. Oliphant and I have a great deal of work to do, and it cannot wait. I realize there is some level of threat, but I'm sure your people can handle it. Now, are we ready to go?"

Kealey hesitated, but the other man's words had made it clear that his decision was final. "Yes," he said. "We're ready to move."

He followed his principal to the armored SUV. Steve Oliphant was already seated in back, and Zuma took the seat next to him. The driver, a former commando in the Honduran army, closed the door behind the South African president as Kealey moved around the front of the vehicle to the passenger-side door. On the way he made eye contact with Alex Whysall and pointed toward the fifth vehicle, another Land Cruiser. Whysall nodded and started to move, as did the rest of the team. As the doors slammed shut on every vehicle, the sound reverberating off the cold cement walls of the parking garage, Kealey climbed into the fourth truck and shut the door, the driver following suit a few seconds later.

Ramón Flores looked over and raised an eyebrow. Kealey held up a finger, indicating he needed a minute. He turned on the radio and performed a quick communications check. Once he was satisfied that everything was in working order, he ordered the first vehicle to move. Flores followed a few seconds later, and the five vehicles began the short run down to street level.

* * *

It had taken the teenager ten long minutes to fight his way through the dense, riotous crowd, during which time he had nearly lost the shopping bag twice. Scrabbling hands had caught at the thin plastic on several occasions, and one man had made a halfhearted attempt to tear it out of the teenager's grasp, but the bodies around them had changed position at the last second. He had used the shift in momentum to pull away from his assailant, who was quickly swallowed by the surrounding sea of flailing limbs. Miraculously, the bag had stayed intact through the entire ordeal. Now, as he slipped unnoticed past one of the fallen barricades, the weight of its contents caused the plastic handles to cut into his hand, cutting off the circulation to his sweaty fingers. The pain was intense, but he did his best to set it aside, knowing that he could not afford the slightest distraction.

The entrance to the parking garage was less than ten meters away, and on the second level, through a narrow gap in the concrete decks, the teenager caught a glimpse of sunlight glinting off white paint. He couldn't hear the engines over the deafening roar of the aggressive mob, but he sensed that the vehicles moving rapidly through the garage were the ones he was waiting for. Returning his gaze to ground level, he kept moving forward, aware that the police officers behind him were still fighting and failing to keep the crowd back. They hadn't used the gas yet, but the teenager knew it was coming, just as he knew that the riot would eventually be contained. In his mind, the police were not to be blamed, despite the brute force they were using to put down the revolt. After all, his own brother-in-law was currently fighting to contain the violence, even though he privately supported the pro-Joubert factionalists. The two groups had no way of knowing that they wanted the same thing, but the teenager knew, and he was ready to act on behalf of them all.

The gate leading into the ground floor of the parking garage was already in the elevated position, as his brother-in-law had said it would be. The teenager could not detect any sign of a police presence in or around the concrete structure, yet he knew it was there. As he quickened his stride, he reached into the bag and found the plastic switch by feel. Summoning his courage, he flipped it over and started to run, his feet pounding over the sunlit cement. In his peripheral vision, he caught sight of a police officer in full riot gear shouting at him, telling him to stop. But he ignored the man and kept moving forward at a dead sprint, the heavy contents of the shopping bag bouncing painfully against his leg.

The first Toyota appeared without warning, the vehicle's glossy paint reflecting the white winter sunlight. The heavy truck swung a hard right onto Von Brandis, the street directly in front of the parking garage, and a second Land Cruiser followed less than five meters behind. The teenager kept sprinting forward, eyes fixed on the fast-moving motorcade. The rioting crowd was a dull, distant roar; the shouted commands of the police officer nothing but meaningless gibberish in his ears. All his attention was locked on the gleaming white vehicles in front of him.

The fourth Toyota had just made the turn when he flung the shopping bag forward with an underhand motion. He instantly turned to run as the plastic bag and its deadly contents slid over the pavement, coming to rest in the path of the oncoming vehicles. The police officer tackled him a split second later, slamming his head to the pavement, fracturing his skull in three places. The teenager was already dead when the bomb he had thrown went off, directly beneath the passenger-side wheel of the fifth and last vehicle in the Blackwater motorcade.

Aside from the driver, Alex Whysall was the sole passenger in the last Land Cruiser. As they passed under the raised gate of the parking garage, the driver, Stiles, was the first to see the young man running toward the truck. He shouted a warning as the African slung an object toward the vehicle. The young man immediately turned to run but didn't get more than a few steps before a police officer slammed him to the ground. Neither Stiles nor Whysall saw what happened from that point forward. Both men's eyes were glued to the white shopping bag that had just slid in front of their vehicle.

Reacting instinctively, Stiles swore and pulled the wheel hard to the right. He punched the gas, trying to clear the unknown object, but it was too late. A powerful explosion rocked the Toyota a split second later, lifting the front end a full two feet off the cement, tearing the front axle away from the frame. After what seemed like an eternity, the truck came crashing down with a resounding bang, slamming both men forward in their seats.

For a few seconds Whysall was too dazed to fully comprehend what had just happened. He was dimly aware of the frantic radio traffic coming over the dash-mounted unit, as well the roar of the angry crowd gathered in front of the courthouse, less than 30 meters west of their position. He couldn't see through the windshield, as the blast had turned the glass opaque, but through his side window, he had a clear view of the policemen standing between their incapacitated vehicle and the frenzied, swelling mob. Presented with a new target in the form of the smoking SUV and the security people trapped inside, a segment of the crowd had broken off from the larger mass and was now surging forward with renewed vigor.

Stiles was slumped over, his head resting against the partially fractured driver's side window. Reaching over, Whysall shook his shoulder and said a few words, trying to get a response, but the man didn't react. Whysall unbuckled his seat belt and shifted over to check Stiles's pulse, using his forearm to push down the air bag, which had deployed the instant the bomb went off. Stiles's pulse was steady and strong, and he realized that the driver had merely been knocked unconscious when his head had hit the reinforced glass.

Breathing a short sigh of relief, Whysall took a few seconds to appraise the situation and check himself for injuries. He didn't feel as if anything was wrong, apart from the whiplash he'd sustained when the front of the truck hit the pavement. But he knew full well that shock and adrenaline could temporarily mask the pain of almost any injury, no matter how serious. Still, a quick visual examination didn't reveal any obvious problems, and he couldn't just sit there and wait for help. The crowd was already on the move, and it didn't look as if the police could hold them back for much longer.

Why the hell aren't they using the tear gas? What the hell are they waiting for? The restraint being used by the South African Police Service and Johannesburg Metro PD didn't make sense to the former marine, especially after what had just transpired. The police officers knew exactly whose motorcade had just been attacked; that was the whole reason they were conducting crowd control to begin with. Looking over, he could see that the majority of the officers forming the wall were dressed in full riot gear: composite helmets, chest protectors, black rubber batons, and clear convex shields. They knew what they were up against, so why hadn't the captain authorized the use of nonlethal deterrents?

Whysall remembered his earlier concerns, thinking it appeared he'd been right all along. The police captain's loyalties seemed not to lie with the president, but with the official who had just been convicted. It would explain why the attack had been allowed to take place. Whysall wondered if someone had been given the wrong information—if they had been told that Zuma would be in the last vehicle—or if the man who had thrown the bomb had just made an error in timing.

Somehow, he doubted that it had been a real attempt on the president's life, as it was all but guaranteed to fail. But that didn't change the fact that he and Stiles were now dead in the water—stuck with a disabled vehicle, no clear route of escape, and a hostile crowd numbering in the thousands.

Reaching forward, Whysall grabbed the handset and pushed the transmit button, hoping that the radio still worked, praying the police could somehow restrain the mob, and silently doubting that they had even the slightest chance of surviving the next few minutes.

At that precise moment the four remaining vehicles in the president's convoy were racing east on Pritchard, approximately one kilometer east of the courthouse. Kealey had seen the explosion in the rearview mirror, but he'd ordered Flores to keep going. While he'd wanted nothing more than to stop and assist the men in the last vehicle, he had not been willing to risk so many lives—his principal's above all—without knowing the specific nature of the threat. He'd seen only a bright flash behind him, and it could have been anything, though the resulting shock wave had been severe enough to convince him that the vehicle carrying Whysall and Stiles had probably suffered a crippling blow.

He had been trying to raise the two men without success, which could mean only one of two things: either the radio had been knocked out during the attack, or the men in the last vehicle were too badly injured to respond. Kealey could only hope it wasn't the latter. Doing his best to ignore the commotion in the backseat, he placed a second call to the pilot of the Bell helicopter buzzing 500 feet over the incapacitated SUV. He had already ordered the pilot to maintain his position above the parking garage, where he would be able to keep watch on the developing situation.

"Air One, what's happening down there?"

"Copy, this is Air One. . . . I can't see any movement inside the vehicle, but it doesn't look like the officers on the ground can hold these people back for much longer." There was a brief crackle of static, followed by an unintelligible exchange. "Uh . . . Greenwald is asking for permission to engage, over."

"Negative," Kealey snapped. Bruce Greenwald was the shooter on board the helicopter, a graduate of the U.S. Army's famed Sniper School and a former marksman with the Los Angeles Police Department. He'd retired from the LAPD two years earlier with the rank of sergeant. He was a good man and a true professional, but Kealey could easily see things getting out of hand if he gave the sniper a green light. Besides, shooting into the crowd would only work to further enrage the protesters, placing the stranded Blackwater men at greater risk. "There's nothing to engage. Are those people even armed?"

A brief silence. Kealey could picture Greenwald scanning the crowd through his gun scope, searching for any sign of a lethal weapon and probably hoping to find one.

"Negative," came the reluctant response.

"Okay, Air One, tell him to hold his fire. Let me know if the crowd gets to the truck, over."

"Will do. Air One, out."

Kealey immediately tried to raise the stranded vehicle again, but there was still no response. They were now moving south through the business district, towering skyscrapers on either side of the busy street. The congestion had forced them to slow down, but Flores was skilled at finding holes in the traffic, and they were rapidly approaching the M2. As a blue sign flashed by, Kealey caught sight of the white lettering, realized they had missed their turn, and instantly turned to face the driver.

"What are you doing?" he demanded. "I told you to head for Marshalltown. You're going the wrong way."

The Gauteng Provincial Government Building was on Simmonds Street in Marshalltown and located less than two kilometers west of the Johannesburg High Court. After a quick check of the map in the glove compartment, Kealey had decided it was the best place to get Zuma and his aide secured before going back for Stiles and Whysall. Normally, he would have dropped the South African leader at the nearest police station, but some inner instinct warned him against that idea. According to the pilot of Air One, the SAPS units in front of the courthouse had yet to use nonlethal deterrents on the rioting crowd, which gave Kealey reason to think that at least some of the officers—and possibly even the captain in charge—were loyal to the man Zuma's testimony had essentially buried in the high court.

Flores was shaking his head. His mouth was set in a tight line, and beads of perspiration were running down his dark, weathered face as he skillfully navigated the busy midtown traffic. "We're not going back there."

"What the hell are you talking about?"

"You know the rules. If something goes down, we get the principal clear. That's what we're doing. Stiles and Whysall are on their own. There's no sense in risking four to save two."

"Fuck that," Kealey snapped. He knew the Honduran was referring to what he had learned at the training facility in Moyock. Blackwater policy was "to get off the X," or move out of the target area as fast as possible when a vehicle was hit in an ambush. In other words, it was every man for himself. But Kealey had no intention of adhering to that particular policy. "I don't know or care how they ran things in your army, Flores. There is no way I'm leaving those guys behind. Turn this truck around right now."

Flores swerved hard to avoid a red Opel that had braked to a sudden halt in front of them. He gunned the engine as they shot through an intersection, horns blaring behind them. The entrance ramp to the M2 was just a few hundred meters away, and from there, Kealey knew, it was a fast, straight run to Pretoria. There was just one more intersection between them and the highway, and once they hit the ramp, there was no turning back. The two men stranded outside the courthouse—the two men he was responsible for—would be as good as dead.

"No," Flores repeated. His heavily accented voice was

hard, and it seemed to leave no room for argument. "No way. We're getting out of here, and that's final. Who the hell do you think you are, anyway? I don't give a shit about the things you did with the CIA, Kealey. This isn't the Agency, and you don't have any real authority here. You can't make me—"

The words died in his throat, and he reflexively took his foot off the gas. The three lead vehicles jumped ahead immediately, as though the invisible chain that linked them had suddenly been cut. Kealey had drawn his Beretta 92FS and was now holding the weapon to Flores's left temple.

"Turn around," he said evenly. He was oblivious to the stunned silence in the backseat; his steady, uncompromising gaze was fixed entirely on the man sitting next to him. "We're going to Marshalltown, and then we're going back for our guys. Turn around right now, or I'll shoot you, kick you out of this fucking truck, and do it myself. Do you understand?"

Flores hesitated, his mouth working silently. His eyes were still fixed on the road ahead, but it was clear that he was thinking about just one thing: the gun currently pressed to his head. Both men were lost in their own private standoff, oblivious to the traffic around them, the delayed shouts of fear and confusion in the backseat, and the fact that the three lead vehicles had already hit the M2 and were essentially out of the picture.

Although Flores had taken his foot off the gas, they were still rolling forward. When they were halfway through the intersection, a blur to the left caused Flores to turn his head instinctively. Before Kealey could react, another vehicle plowed into theirs, crushing the truck's left front fender and knocking them out of their lane. The armored Land Cruiser lurched to the right and traveled another 20 feet before slamming into the rear end of a minibus. Kealey snapped forward in his seat, the belt tightening over his chest, forcing the air from his lungs. His right hand banged against the dashboard, and the Beretta slipped out of his grasp. Everything seemed to go black for an instant, a strange silence settling in the aftermath of the accident.

Shaking it off, Kealey groaned and reached under his seat, searching for the weapon he'd dropped at the moment of impact. Almost simultaneously a man shouted an order in Xhosa, one of the few local dialects Kealey recognized. Then gunfire erupted, rounds pounding into the armored exterior of the vehicle.

The instant the bullets hit, Kealey folded at the waist, twisting his body below the level of the windows. With a cold sense of fear, he realized that the crash had not been an accident at all. It was an ambush, and it had worked to perfection. The rear escort had been taken out with consummate skill, the helicopter was still back at the courthouse, along with Whysall's disabled Land Cruiser, and the other vehicles were already on the M2, moving fast for Pretoria.

They were alone, outnumbered, and completely exposed.

And no one was coming to back them up.

CHAPTER 8

KHARTOUM

"Before we begin," the consultant said as he sank into the comfortable armchair across from his host, "I'd like to thank you for seeing me on such short notice. I know things are pretty hectic around here, sir, and you must have a lot on your plate. I just want you to know that I appreciate your time. Not to mention your hospitality." He smiled agreeably and lifted his cup of coffee, which had just been provided by his host's secretary, Joyce, in the adjoining room, in a casual toast of sorts.

Walter Reynolds, who had spent most of the morning reading the *Washington Post* online and washing his gut with coffee, almost winced at the gratitude. Now more than ever he felt like a complete fraud in his neat two-piece suit, strangling tie, and polished wing tips. But shaking it off, he raised his cup to return the toast. It was an unusual gesture, he thought. In all his life he couldn't remember carrying out the ritual with anything other than alcohol, which was notoriously hard to procure in Sudan, God-fearing and genocidal republic that it was, much to his lasting annoyance.

Reynolds sighed as they both sipped at the hot liquid, his gaze never shifting from the man seated across from him.

The consultant, he had to admit, was not what he had been expecting. Reynolds wasn't sure why, exactly, but a few things stood out, including his age. For a man with such remarkable connections, he was young . . . no more than thirty-six or seven, and that was a conservative estimate. His dark hair, which could have been black or a very dark shade of brown, was lightly oiled and cut short to reveal a receding hairline, which, strangely enough, didn't seem to detract from his youthful appearance. His face was on the narrow side, but open and friendly, particularly around the eyes and mouth, and he wore steel-rimmed spectacles that pinched the bridge of his long nose, contributing to the overall air of subdued intelligence.

And that was what had thrown him, Reynolds realized. The consultant didn't seem to fit the mold. He wasn't loud, domineering, and demanding, like most people would be in his position, but quiet and unassuming. He did not have the fleshy, arrogant face of the stereotypical kingmaker, but that of an earnest scholar. He could have been a congressman on the rise, or a surgical resident in one of the country's better hospitals. In his youth he might have been the captain of the chess club or debate team at an Ivy League school, of which he was no doubt a graduate.

Reynolds idly wondered which one he had gone to. Had it been Harvard, the first choice for America's moneyed youth? Princeton, maybe? Yale? Perhaps he was wrong, Reynolds thought. Perhaps this youngster had come up the hard way. Perhaps he had gone to Brown.

Setting down his cup, the senior diplomat returned his attention to the document on his desk. It was a letter of introduction, delivered by diplomatic pouch several minutes earlier. The timing was extraordinary, and by no means a coincidence—it had arrived less than a minute before his guest had appeared in the anteroom. Reynolds lifted the top half of the single page and slowly scanned the twelve lines of concise text, even though he had already read the letter several times. A moment later he reached the signatures at the bottom. It was here that his eyes lingered. There were four signatures in all, and they represented some of the most powerful people in the U.S. government, among them the woman who'd called him the previous day.

Reynolds couldn't help but shake his head in admiration. It was a remarkable document in a number of ways, primarily for the powers it bestowed upon the young man sitting across from him. At first glance, they appeared to be nearly unlimited, though Reynolds reminded himself that the wording in the letter was hardly specific and could be interpreted any number of ways. In his thirty years with the Foreign Service, he had seen some incredibly vague terminology appear in official government documents, and this one was no exception. But still, to see all those signatures, and on one piece of paper . . .

He looked up and offered a smile, then flicked the fine linen paper with the tip of his finger. "Your credentials are very impressive, Mr. Landis. Beyond reproach, actually."

The young man couldn't help but smile at the name.

There was no harm in doing so. To the senior diplomat, it would look like he was merely returning the gesture. It had not been easy at first, and he had nearly slipped up a number of times, but he was now accustomed to hearing it.

James Landis. He had held that identity for exactly thirty days, and it was getting easier with each passing week. The chief of mission believed that he had arrived in-country that very day, mainly because that was what he was meant to believe. In reality, Landis had landed in the Republic of Sudan a month before, entering the country through Khartoum International Airport as Harold Traylor . . . yet another disposable name he'd jettisoned, along with his forged passport, after its purpose had been served.

Just getting into Sudan had been almost as dangerous as the things he'd been doing since. While he would have preferred to enter via a remote border crossing, preferably in the western territories edging up against Chad, most had been closed due to the escalating clashes over the oil fields and pumping stations in West Darfur. The few checkpoints that remained open were so volatile that for any Westerner to attempt a crossing—even a man of his unique and considerable talents—would have amounted to suicide. As a result, he'd been forced to take a direct flight into Khartoum, where alert officials and CCTV cameras were in far greater abundance. There had been some degree of risk in doing so, but he'd made it through customs unscathed, and forty minutes later he'd destroyed any evidence that Harold Traylor ever existed. That passport, along with a New York driver's license, a well-worn membership card to a video store in Albany, and several credit cards in the same name, had been burned in a back garden at the home of his sole contact in the capital.

Another stop along the road, another shed skin left behind.

Since those first precarious days, his network had expanded with astonishing speed, thanks largely to his contact's connections in Khartoum and the surrounding areas. The planning itself had involved weeks spent clustered around a table in the Harry S. Truman Building in Washington, D.C., home to the U.S. Department of State. In a soundproofed room on the ground floor, he and a rotating staff of ten had studied everything from the strength of the republic's dissident groups to the command structure of the Sudanese army. The lengthy strategy sessions had been hard to endure, even though he'd known just how important that information would eventually be to his own welfare. Now Landis was well into the operational part of his plan, but up until this point, he had only been setting the stage. Moving the pieces into place. The next stage was crucial. Fittingly, it would also be far more dangerous. The risks had been mulled over at length—not only by him, but by the men and women who had tasked him with his current assignment, the most challenging and important of his career. After much debate, they had been deemed acceptable.

One of those risks was the man seated across from him now. The problem, Landis knew, stemmed from an incident twenty-five years in the past. Walter Reynolds, then a junior economics officer stationed at the U.S. embassy in Asunción, Paraguay, had misplaced a stack of sealed bids submitted by various American contractors. The contractors, five in all, were competing for the right to build a four-lane vehicular bridge over the

Paraná River, a project valued in excess of ten million dollars. One week after the bids went missing, a Japanese company swept in out of nowhere and won the contract, outbidding the closest U.S. competitor by a mere twenty thousand dollars.

It was never proven that the missing paperwork had fallen into the wrong hands, but that didn't matter. The damage was already done, and someone had to take the blame. The incident had done much to derail Reynolds's career in the Foreign Service. It had also marked him as a man who could not be trusted with important information. The trick in this case, Landis knew, would lie in telling him exactly what he needed to know and not a word more. Eventually, Reynolds would be allowed to see the entire picture, but certainly not now, and maybe not until it was all said and done.

The chief of mission was droning on, saying something about the necessity of maintaining clear lines of communication between the various diplomatic outposts. It wasn't what Landis wanted to hear. Leaning forward in his seat, he cut the older man off with a genial smile and a wave of his hand.

"Sir, I understand exactly what you mean, but I'm afraid I don't have time to get into it now." It was partially true; he had several meetings lined up in the city, and they would take up the better part of the afternoon. For the most part, though, he just didn't want to be in the embassy any longer than necessary. "There is one thing I need to hear from you, and then I can brief you a little more thoroughly. If you're satisfied with that arrangement, we can proceed."

The man looked suspicious. Landis couldn't blame him; had the roles been reversed, he would have felt the same way.

"I suppose that depends," Reynolds said slowly, "on what you need to hear."

Landis pointed toward the document on the desk, which was facing away from him. "Sir, do you believe that this is a legitimate document? More specifically, are you comfortable with the terms stated in the letter, and are you willing to abide by them?"

The senior diplomat leaned back in his chair and smiled tightly. "Well, that all depends, doesn't it? I'm sure *you're* comfortable with the terms, Mr. Landis. This document seems to give you a good deal of authority. Essentially, it makes you my superior."

"That it does," Landis replied neutrally. He would have preferred to demur, but Reynolds was right, and it would be better if he understood the hierarchy right from the start. That way, they could avoid the argument later. "But again, are you willing to abide by the terms? Because if you are not, I need to know now so I can leave this building and make some calls."

The older man's smile faded away. "That sounds like a threat."

Landis knew Reynolds was thinking about the four names at the bottom of the introductory letter and what those people could do to his career.

"Not at all, sir," he replied calmly. "Far from it. I'm merely pointing out that by seeing this document, you already know a great deal, and that could endanger my work here. If you are not willing to cooperate, I'm going to have to leave the country and make alternate arrangements. Surely you can see the logic in that."

Reynolds mused over this for a moment. Then he nodded once, conceding the point. "If I agree to your terms," he said slowly, "will you tell me what this is about?"

"No, sir," Landis said. He strived to sound genuinely regretful, as though it wasn't his decision to make. "I can't and I won't. In time you'll know everything. I promise you. But for now, I just need to know that we're on the same page. And in case you were wondering, calling those people"—he pointed to the signatures at the bottom of the letter—"will get you nowhere. As the document states, I have full control on the ground for the duration of this operation. They will tell you exactly the same thing, only they'll probably be less polite about it."

The senior diplomat lifted his cup and took a long sip, thinking about it. The word *operation* said much in itself, he thought. It seemed to imply a prolonged, potentially dangerous task, and he realized that he had misjudged the man sitting across from him. Despite his rather ineffectual appearance, the consultant was clearly not the kind of man who worked from a desk. Regardless of what he was trying to accomplish in Sudan, Reynolds had no doubt that James Landis would be in it up to his neck . . . and assuming that was the case, it could mean only one thing for Reynolds and his staff of seventy.

He set down his cup and looked at the younger man. "We're not going home, are we?"

"No, Mr. Reynolds, I'm afraid you're not. The embassy will not be evacuated, and diplomatic ties will not be severed. But there *are* going to be some changes around here, and I assure you, they will be for the best. Now, can I count on your cooperation?"

Reynolds was still hesitant, but he was also boxed in, and—he had to admit it—more than a little curious. "Yes, you can."

"Good." Landis smiled. "Now, here is what I need from you."

* * *

Ten minutes later the consultant emerged from an elevator on the ground floor of the embassy. He crossed the scuffed floor of the crowded lobby, ignoring the cursory glance of a marine corporal standing post. As he headed for the main entrance, he did his best to skirt the restless crowd, his ears filled with the low, angry buzz of 80 people standing in line to get or apply for their visas. Unlike the people waiting in line, he was in a good mood, and it was getting better with each step he took toward the door. The meeting with the chief of mission had taken less than fifteen minutes, and it had accomplished a great deal. He had secured Reynolds's assistance—not only for the transfer of incoming funds, but also for the housing of personnel, should the need arise. The embassy was now a sanctuary of last resort—not only for him, but also for his assets, most of whom were Sudanese nationals—and the letter of introduction, which had made him uneasy to begin with, even though he'd understood the need for it, was now a pile of gray ash in the steel garbage can sitting next to Reynolds's desk.

Despite his warnings as to where it would lead, Landis had no doubt that the chief of mission had been on the phone to Washington the minute he'd left the room. What he'd said to the older man had been true. Regardless of who Reynolds called, he would be told nothing more than what he already knew. In fact, depending on who he called first, he would probably be told in no uncertain terms to back off and keep his mouth shut, which was fine with Landis. More than anything, the meetings back at the State Department had focused on the consequences of failure—on what would happen if it all went wrong.

It had been decided that the biggest threat to the entire operation was the possibility of a leak. As always, the damage it could do would depend entirely on where it was sprung. A leak on the local level, for instance—a botched recruitment, perhaps, or a note slipped from one of his assets to someone in Bashir's regime—would end up with Landis dead and his network rolled up; a leak in Washington might well lead to one of the biggest scandals since the Iran-Contra affair.

The national opposition to Bashir was as generally widespread as it was internally divided and fractious. There was the Justice and Equality Movement, or the JEM. And the United Resistance Front, led by Bahr Idriss Abu Garda, the JEM's deputy chief before his split with its founder Khalil Ibrahim—a man now seen by many former followers as no less an opportunist and demagogue than Bashir. Then, of course, you had the Sudan People's Liberation Army and its Abdel Wahid al-Nur and Minnawi factions . . . and others.

The man who called himself Landis thought it almost unimaginable that anyone in the United States government would be bold enough to try pulling these groups together, or even to decide a coalition was within the realm of possibility. But history had seen stranger bedfellows joined—if not quite united—for a common purpose.

Given the possible fallout—especially on the political side of things—Landis had never expected it to get this far. Somewhere along the line, he had expected someone to lose their nerve, and to some extent, he still expected it. Yet he did not intend to waste valuable time planning for that eventuality. If the powers that be decided to call a halt to the whole thing, he would not draw back easily for them. If it failed, the operation might still end up as a minor footnote in history. If it succeeded, it would be considered one of the most audacious ever conceived and seen to fruition.

Landis did not consider himself to be a vain man, but the prospect of being right there, on the knife edge of history, filled him with a kind of exhilaration he'd never known, and he wanted nothing more than to see it through to the end, regardless of how it played out.

He slowed as he approached the main entrance, then shifted course, heading for a discreet door set in the far wall of the lobby. Like all U.S. embassies and consulates, the building in Khartoum was secured by a detachment of U.S. Marines, all of whom had passed through a specialized training program at the Marine Corps Embassy Security Group, or MCESG, located in Quantico, Virginia. Post One, the security hub for the entire embassy, was located just inside the main entrance, where it served to deter an attack from the street. Inside the small, overheated room, Landis was met by the detachment commander. Reynolds had already called down for him, and the confused but compliant marine sergeant had the appropriate materials packed and waiting. Less than a minute later Landis was walking out the front door into the afternoon sunlight, an olive green rucksack slung over his right shoulder.

The car, a dusty black Ford Escort, was waiting on Ali Abdel Latif Street, engine idling. The vehicles lined up behind it were honking incessantly, turbaned men leaning out of their windows to scream insults in Arabic at the driver, who had parked with the rear end of the Escort jutting into the road, just as Landis had instructed.

He could see that the diversion had worked perfectly. As the confused scene played out, all eyes were fixed on the car in the road and not on the lean, dark-haired American descending the steps of the embassy. Hitting the street, Landis turned right and started weaving his way through the pushy pedestrian traffic, walking quickly toward the intersection at Nillien University where in two minutes' time he would be picked up by the man in the Escort.

Satisfied with what he had seen in the street, he had missed the one person who had not been distracted, a fellow American who'd been climbing the steps as he'd been descending. He did not see the man stop at the top of the steps, turn, and stare after him. The man was still staring after Landis as he turned the corner and disappeared from sight. Then, shaking his head, he walked forward and entered the building, a welcome blast of cool air hitting his face the second he opened the door.

Seth Holland was officially listed on the embassy's organization chart as a budget and resource manager with the Defense Institute of Security Assistance Management. In keeping with this exalted title, his office on the fourth floor was large and comfortably furnished, with French windows that opened up to the inner courtyard. It was the kind of office that, in the budget manager's absence, might be occupied by the CIA's chief of station in Khartoum. Fittingly, this was the position that Holland, a twenty-year Agency veteran, actually held.

Unlike the man in charge of the embassy, Holland's workload had increased sharply since the attack on Camp Hadith. But as he stepped into the elevator and jabbed the appropriate button, he wasn't thinking about reports of increased rebel activity in the Nuba Mountains, or the sharp, unexplained increase in anti-Bashir demonstrations, which had recently begun popping up all over the city. Instead, Seth Holland was thinking about the dark-haired man with the rucksack he had seen on the steps, and two thoughts in particular.

Who was that man, and where have I seen him before?

CHAPTER 9

JOHANNESBURG

Outside the parking garage on Von Brandis Street, the situation had gone from bad to worse. The police, unable or unwilling to hold back the mob any longer, had been overrun by hundreds of screaming men and women, a great many of whom had focused their rage on the crippled Toyota and the two men trapped inside. The truck was surrounded on all sides, and it was being rocked violently from side to side. The doors and windows were being kicked and beaten with bats, metal chair legs, and bare hands, but so far the heavily armored exterior had managed to withstand the furious assault.

In the front passenger seat, Alex Whysall was working frantically to repair the radio, even though he suspected the problem was not with the unit itself. The engine wouldn't start, which wasn't surprising in and of itself, given the force of the explosion beneath the vehicle. But it wasn't even *trying* to turn over, indicating that the battery was probably out of commission. Although the battery itself was surrounded by additional steel plating, it was possible that the explosion had severed the cables. This would explain why they couldn't communicate with the other vehicles in the motorcade, as the radio drew its power directly from the battery. Though Whysall had tried to reach the other vehicles using his portable radio, it didn't have the necessary range. In short, they were completely cut off from the rest of the team.

The only thing they still had working for them was the helicopter, which Whysall could see hovering southwest of their position and more or less directly over Kerk Street. He assumed it was reporting everything to Ryan Kealey, the head of the PSD, but Whysall had no way of signaling that they were okay. Stupidly, he had lent his cell phone to another man on the detail earlier in the day, and he'd forgotten to get it back. He only hoped that someone was on the way to get them out, and soon. It wouldn't be long before the mob found a way into the vehicle, and once that happened, they would not be able to defend themselves for long.

At the intersection just north of the M2, the second disabled Land Cruiser was coming under heavy fire. Kealey had managed to find his 9mm, but he was folded awkwardly to the side, his head crammed against the passenger-side door. Tilting it up and to the right, he screamed for the men in the backseat to keep down, then looked over at Ramón Flores. The Honduran was slumped over the steering wheel, his thick arms limp at his sides.

Kealey could hear rounds pounding into the rear windshield now, but the bullet-resistant glass seemed to be holding. He knew it was specced to stop anything up to a 7.62mm rifle round. Anything heavier than that would pass right through, and a sustained assault from weapons of a lesser caliber would eventually have the same effect. Either way, they couldn't just sit and wait for help to arrive; they had to move immediately.

The engine was still running. Kealey couldn't tell if the truck was drivable or not, but there was only one way to find out. Shifting his weight onto the console between the seats, he leaned into Flores, twisted his body to the right, and jammed his left foot onto the brake. Reaching back awkwardly, he shifted the vehicle into reverse without looking, then moved his foot onto the accelerator. The truck lurched back and careened off an unseen object before it started to pick up speed. Kealey could hear men shouting outside, and he was vaguely aware of people diving out of the way, but he ignored all of it, just as he ignored the two men lying prone in the backseat. Looking over the shoulder rest of the driver's seat, he swerved around two stationary vehicles, then swung the wheel hard to the left, whipping the truck back in the direction they had come from. The sudden maneuver brought the vehicle to a screeching halt.

In the rearview mirror, Kealey now had a clear view of two police Land Rovers, one of which had suffered obvious damage to the front end. The vehicles were white with blue stripes and lettering, and the light bars on both were flashing, though the sirens were off. They were parked about 30 meters away, and a quick count yielded six men. Four of them were already sprinting toward the damaged Blackwater SUV; two more were getting back into the Land Rovers, anticipating a possible chase. They were all wearing standard South African Police Service attire, and when Kealey saw the field dress uniforms, he endured a moment of doubt, even though he knew what he had to do. He shook it off, holstered his Beretta, and reached for the metal case tucked under his seat. Flipping the latches, he opened the lid to reveal the components of a Fabrique Nationale FNC Para.

Slumping low in the seat, he slapped the lower edge of the rearview mirror with the tips of his fingers, angling it so that he could see through the back windshield without exposing his upper body. Then, without taking his eyes off the approaching police officers, he put the assault rifle together by feel, sliding the bolt into the upper receiver before closing the upper and lower receivers into place with the front and rear pins. Locking the bolt to the rear, he slid one of the preloaded steel magazines into place, then let the bolt snap forward, chambering the first 5.56mm round.

A low groan to his right caught his attention, and Kealey snapped his head around, searching for the source. It took him a second to realize that Flores had regained consciousness, as the man was still slumped over the steering wheel. As Kealey stared at him, though, he groaned again and raised his head a few inches, a thin trickle of blood spilling out of his mouth and over his unshaven chin.

"Flores!" Kealey shouted.

The Honduran stirred but didn't respond.

"Flores, wake up! Come on, wake the fuck up! We've got to move! *Flores!*"

The driver wasn't responding. Movement in his peripheral vision caught Kealey's attention, and he turned his head to the right. Through the window behind the driver's seat, directly above the prone figure of Jacob Zuma, Kealey could see two of the SAPS officers who had ambushed them. The Africans had closed to within 20 feet of the Land Cruiser. Both men had their assault rifles up in a firing stance, and one was shouting something that Kealey couldn't decipher through the glass. The muzzles flashed, and the glass in the driver's side door turned opaque. The sound of the shots followed a split second later, and even inside the vehicle, they were loud enough to prompt another panicked cry from the president's chief of staff.

Kealey resumed shouting at Flores as the SAPS officers continued to fire on the vehicle, expending their 30-round magazines in a matter of seconds. Most of the rounds seemed to hit Flores's window, which was partially pushed in from the force of the incoming fire. Kealey could see that it wouldn't hold up for much longer, and he realized what their assailants were trying to do. By focusing their fire on that one part of the vehicle, they would be able to defeat the reinforced glass much faster than they would with sporadic fire to all the windows. It was a sound strategy, and it also offered the best chance of stopping the Toyota dead in its tracks, as the truck obviously wouldn't be going anywhere once the driver was killed.

They were quickly running out of options, and there was no time left to think it over. Operating purely on instinct, Kealey grabbed Flores's left shoulder and jerked him back in the seat. The Honduran's head bounced off the headrest, but he stayed upright, the muscles in his face working as he tried to return from the brink of consciousness. Leaning over him, Kealey put the muzzle of his FNC to the driver's side window and squeezed the trigger. A single round tore through the one-way resistant glass, penetrating the single flexible layer of Makroclear polycarbonate sheeting.

The muzzle blast was impossibly loud inside the Land Cruiser, and it worked where shouting had not. Flores came awake with a start, his eyes snapping open, his arms flying up in a purely defensive gesture. Before he could do anything else, Kealey jammed the muzzle of his rifle into the small hole he had shot through the glass, then twisted the barrel from side to side to work it through the tiny gap. When he had it all the way through, he leaned to the left, his shoulder pressed hard against the steering wheel, which was positioned on the right-hand side of the vehicle. He was unable to see his target's specific position due to the damage the window had sustained, but aiming in the police officers' general direction, he fired half a dozen rounds in rapid succession. By the time he squeezed the trigger for the last time, he was temporarily deafened by the force of the muzzle blast in the confined space.

He pulled back, jerking the barrel of the FNC free of the window. Flores was shouting at him, his face twisted in rage, pain, and confusion, but Kealey couldn't hear a word he was saying. Pointing through the front windshield, he shouted for the other man to drive. As if to emphasize his point, the driver's side window was suddenly hit with another burst of automatic fire, and Flores immediately slammed the truck into gear. It was more an instinctive reaction than a direct adherence to orders, but Kealey didn't care. All that mattered was that they were moving out of the kill zone.

The front windshield was one of the few windows still intact, giving Kealey a good view of the road ahead. As the ringing in his ears began to subside, he pointed to an upcoming side street and shouted for Flores to turn. Incredibly, the Honduran actually followed the order, spinning the wheel hard to the right.

As the vehicle swerved, Kealey twisted in his seat to look through the rear window on the driver's side. The top half of the window was clouded from the impact of incoming fire, but beneath that he could see the police officers running back to the Land Rovers, both of which had accelerated up to the officers' position. Kealey was disappointed to see that he hadn't managed to get lucky with one of his rounds. All four of the men outside the vehicles were still moving, though one appeared to be running with a lopsided gait, his free hand pressed to his left upper thigh, his dark face contorted in pain. As he watched them move, Kealey realized that they had fanned out to approach the Toyota. It was a smart tactical maneuver, as it made them less susceptible to incoming fire, but it also meant they had farther to go to get back to their own vehicles. Flores's fast departure had given them a short head start, but they didn't have more than twelve seconds lead time, and Kealey knew they would have to use it wisely.

They finished making the turn, and the view of the men abruptly gave way to a redbrick wall. The road they had turned onto was more like an alley than a side street. There was no sidewalk, and residential buildings rose up on either side, the walls crowding in on the narrow street. The asphalt was strewn with litter, discarded pallets of rotting wood, and other assorted debris, all of which served to impede their progress. There were pedestrians, as well, and as the Land Cruiser raced down the alley—Flores leaning on the horn the entire time—they pushed themselves flat against the walls to avoid the speeding SUV.

Flores was shouting questions, demanding some kind of explanation, but Kealey wasn't listening. His eyes were fixed on the road ahead. The point where the alley fed into the next street was partially blocked by the front end of an illegally parked car, and more vehicles were lined up on the far side of the street, parked bumper to bumper. He shot a glance at the rearview mirror, saw that it was still tilted down, and adjusted it quickly. The moment he did so, he saw the first of the two Land Rovers turning into the alley. The rear windows were down, and men were leaning bodily out the windows, trying to draw a bead on the lead vehicle. A few shots rang out. None of the rounds came close to striking the Land Cruiser, but even so, Kealey knew that they wouldn't stop coming. By attacking Jacob Zuma's motorcade, they had staked not only their careers but also their lives on the assassination attempt, and David Joubert was not in a position to protect them if they failed.

That last part was an assumption on Kealey's part, but there was no question that they were completely loyal to their former chief. Whoever had planned the ambush had clearly decided that the only way to secure Joubert's freedom was to kill Zuma, and given the prevailing attitude in the South African republic, Kealey decided it was a decent plan. With Zuma out of the way, his successor might be inclined to simply terminate the courtroom proceedings, or perhaps let them play out as a show of due process at work, and only then declare leniency once a verdict was reached.

A decent plan, yes. But it would succeed only if the policemen managed to get to his principal, and Kealey had no intention whatsoever of letting that happen.

Unfortunately, shaking them was easier said than done. The most obvious strategy would be to get to the government building in Marshalltown, but they would still be exposed as they moved from the truck to the building. The local police stations were also out, for obvious reasons. He knew there were probably better options, but the men chasing them undoubtedly knew the city better than he did, and he couldn't afford to prolong the chase. Looking through the windshield,

Kealey let his gaze linger on the illegally parked Peugeot at the end of the alley. With no time left to consider, he made his decision.

"Flores, hit that car. Hit it just forward of the wheel, then turn hard to the left. Stop once you're past the alley, but make sure these guys"—he gestured over his shoulder to the following vehicles—"don't have a visual on us. I'm getting out."

"*What?* You must be out of your—"

"Flores, just hit the fucking car," Kealey shouted. *"Do it!"*

The Honduran swore viciously, and when the Peugeot was less than twenty meters away, he jerked the wheel hard to the right, aiming for the sedan's front fender. The SUV's heavy front grille was dead center with the front wheel on the Peugeot's passenger side when they hit the stationary vehicle at forty miles per hour. Kealey flinched, closed his eyes, and braced himself at the moment of impact. He was thrown forward in his seat, but he traveled only eight inches before his body came to a sudden, jarring halt. The four-point seat belt snapped over his already bruised chest, driving the air from his lungs. The sound followed instantly; for some reason, the high-pitched explosion of glass seemed to drown out the earsplitting *crump* of the larger impact.

The Peugeot spun out of their path. The Toyota bounced to the left, then continued traveling forward. Kealey heard the men in the backseat shouting as they jumped the near curb. The vehicle's sheer weight brought it down hard on its damaged suspension, and the vulnerable undercarriage scraped along the asphalt, throwing up a shower of orange sparks. Flores swore as he lost control, the Land Cruiser slewing hard to the right. Flores turned into the skid without touching the brake, and Kealey opened his eyes in time to see another car directly in front of them, a woman's pale, frightened face behind the wheel.

They plowed into the vehicle with another violent explosion of metal and glass, driving it sideways over the cement and into the cars parked at the curb. People were scrambling for cover, covering their heads with their arms as the Land Cruiser shuddered to a halt, the engine all but giving out. The sudden quiet made the surrounding screams seem that much louder, but not for long. The 380-horsepower V-8 engine roared back to life as Flores jammed his foot onto the accelerator, simultaneously swinging the wheel hard to the left, turning it hand over hand. They lurched forward, the truck scraping against the woman's mangled sedan with a tremendous squeal that was somehow worse than the sounds thrown up by the earlier impact. They had barely traveled another five meters when Kealey, having managed to catch his breath once again, gripped Flores's shoulder and rasped, "Stop here."

This time the Honduran didn't bother to argue. He slammed on the brake, and the wheels locked up. They skidded to a halt a few seconds later. Kealey, having already removed his seat belt, immediately flung open the door. Clutching the FNC Para in his right hand, he stepped onto the glass-strewn pavement and shot a quick look back at the alley entrance. Over the screams, he could hear the steady whine of the approaching Land Rovers, but they had yet to hit the street. Better yet, the Peugeot they had hit at the mouth of the alley had spun into the street, effectively blocking the northbound traffic. He still had time.

Flinging a look over his shoulder, he said, "I'm leaving this door open. Drive forward another thirty feet and stop. Whatever you do, don't let that door close, and don't get out of the car. Their lives"—he jerked his thumb over his right shoulder, indicating the two African officials in the backseat—"depend on it. Understand?"

Flores nodded once, but Kealey didn't see the gesture of acknowledgment; he was already on the move. As the Honduran drove on, Kealey crossed the street to the side opposite the alley, ignoring the screams and the accusing fingers leveled in his direction. Stopping in the middle of the southbound lane, he brought the FNC to his shoulder and fired a long burst into the side of a black BMW parked next to the alley. The shots had the intended effect; everyone who had been pointing and shouting at him a second earlier started to scream and scatter, running for their lives. Ironically, the fact that he had fired his weapon had worked to draw their attention away from him. The pedestrians were now focused entirely on one thing, namely, their own survival.

Turning, he ran for the line of parked cars, all of which were pressed to the curb in the southbound lane. There was no room to run between them, so sprinting forward, he jumped and slid across the hood of a battered blue Mercedes sedan, using the chrome bumper as a springboard. The instant his feet touched the sidewalk on the other side of the car, he kept moving, jogging north at a fast, steady pace. Normally, he would have walked to avoid suspicion, but the only way to blend in here was to run, as the chaos on the street was near total. The rifle in his right hand was pressed against his outer thigh, the muzzle depressed. The weapon was as far out of sight as he could get it. Up ahead, he could see the Land Cruiser to his left. It was stopped in the northbound lane, a cloud of steam pouring out from the crumpled hood. Thanks to the expedient roadblock Flores had created by hitting the parked

Peugeot, there were no cars between the entrance to the alley and the Blackwater Land Cruiser.

Kealey didn't know if the SAPS vehicles had emerged from the alley behind him, but he couldn't risk turning to look. He wanted to peel off his long-sleeved polo, as he was wearing a different colored T-shirt underneath, and it might make him harder to spot if the police officers were smart enough to keep a roving eye on the scattering pedestrians. But removing the top layer of clothing would require taking his hands off his weapon, and he couldn't risk having someone try to wrest it away from him. The chances of that happening were small, and he would easily be able to retrieve it from anyone who might try to take it, but the fight—even though it would be very short and one-sided—would draw the wrong kind of attention, which was any at all.

A better alternative presented itself a few seconds later. In their haste to flee the scene, some of the pedestrians had dropped their shopping bags, purses, and other assorted items. Kealey, scanning the debris at his feet, caught sight of a crumpled blue baseball cap. Without breaking stride, he leaned down, scooped it up, and put it on, pulling the brim low over his eyes.

The squeal of tires to his rear announced the arrival of the SAPS Land Rovers. Kealey lowered his head and tilted his chin to the right as the vehicles sped past on the left, screeching to a halt just 15 feet behind the Blackwater SUV. They didn't seem to have noticed him, and he instantly quickened his pace, hoping to lessen the gap before they could act. He was 20 feet from the Land Rover bringing up the rear when the doors on both vehicles swung open, revealing the four police officers.

Once again, the drivers stayed in the trucks as the

rest of the men clambered out to the pavement. Without a moment's hesitation, they brought their weapons up and began unleashing a tremendous volume of fire on the rear windshield of the Toyota. Kealey, even though he was behind them, saw the exact moment they realized that the passenger-side door was hanging open. One man, presumably the leader, frantically waved a hand up and down in a chopping motion, the universal symbol for cease-fire. The automatic fire stopped a few seconds later, the sound echoing off the surrounding buildings, and the screams of panicked civilians once again dominated the chaotic scene.

Kealey was still running forward. His eyes were fixed on the men, all of whom were now looking to their left, searching for the man who had apparently fled the vehicle. As Kealey watched for a gap in the parked cars, a young woman ran toward him, screaming, clutching an infant child to her chest. Without really seeing her, he switched the rifle to his left hand and grabbed her arm with his right, swinging her around. Confused, the woman didn't even try to resist as he propelled her a few steps forward, then shoved her in through the open door of a sidewalk café. As he turned away, Kealey thought he saw a group of hands pull the woman into the safety of the building, but he couldn't be sure; he was already turning to reacquire his targets.

The four police officers were still searching the parked cars on the other side of the street. Clearly, they had decided that whoever had left the Blackwater vehicle had sought out the closest position of cover. It was the natural assumption to make, and Kealey had been counting on them to do just that. Now he approached unseen from the rear, but just as he was about to engage his first target, his earpiece came to life, jarring him out of the moment.

"Kealey, where the fuck are you?" It was Flores, and he was clearly panicked, the words coming out in an incomprehensible jumble of English and Spanish. "They're right on top of us, and they're armed to the fucking teeth. *¡Estoy saliendo de aquí! Do you hear me? Si no puedo manejar en otra parte, yo saldré de este camión y—*"

"Don't move," Kealey hissed. He was beside himself with rage, furious that the man had picked that crucial moment to distract him. "There's nowhere to drive to, Flores, because the truck is blocked in, and if you get out of that vehicle right now, you're a dead man. Do you understand me? They will kill you before your feet touch the ground, so *don't fucking move.*"

He didn't hear the Honduran's response, but he didn't need to; it was just another barrage of scared threats and angry demands. Still, it was a distraction, and he yanked the Motorola receiver/transmitter out of his right ear. Lifting the rifle to his shoulder, he dismissed the idea of moving closer, deciding it would be better to use the parked cars as cover. Besides, he didn't have time; the officers were already losing interest in the search, and one had stopped looking entirely. That particular officer was moving carefully toward the rear door on the driver's side of the Land Cruiser. His weapon was at the ready, his body crouched below the bottom edge of the windows. He was doing his best to approach the Toyota unseen, and it seemed to be working; Kealey didn't think that Flores had seen the man in his side mirror.

Kealey was just moving past a silver Ford Ikon, a delicatessen off to his right. Clearing the Ford's front windshield, he stopped, straightened, and found his first target. The FNC wasn't fitted with a telescopic sight, but at a distance of 20 feet, the iron sights were all he needed. The SAPS officer closest to the Land Cruiser

was just putting his hand on the door handle when
Kealey fired a three-round burst into the back of his
head. As the man started to fall, Kealey swung the barrel smoothly to the left, picking out a second target. At
the same time, he switched the FNC's fire selector to
single and squeezed the trigger.

Two rounds to the chest dropped the second police
officer, who had just finished turning toward Kealey's
position. The third officer almost had time to get his
weapon to his shoulder before Kealey's first round entered the base of his throat, puncturing his trachea. He
jerked the trigger of his R5 involuntarily, a dozen
rounds tearing a jagged line in the concrete as he stumbled away. His left hand whipped up to the tiny hole in
his throat, and as he backed into a Mercedes coupe,
Kealey's second round pierced his upper lip and blew
out the back of his skull, showering the roof of the car
with blood, fragments of bone, and brain tissue. The
man spiraled to the ground. On the way down, his limp
body tore the side mirror off the Mercedes. He landed
on top of it, twitched once, and stopped moving.

Kealey was already moving for cover. The fourth police officer in the open had managed to dive over the
trunk of a parked car and was now crouched behind
the vehicle, firing in Kealey's direction. It was panic
fire, though, and it was aimed too high. With his back
to the Ikon, Kealey could see the officer's rounds
punching into the front of the delicatessen, chipping
the brick façade above the plate-glass windows. The
angle, as well as the indiscriminate grouping of the
shots, told Kealey that the man was probably firing over
the hood of the car, which meant he had no idea where
his rounds were going.

Taking the chance, Kealey spun to the right and
stood, exposing his upper body. He snapped the FNC

up to his shoulder, but it was just as he'd suspected. The fourth officer wasn't visible, though his hands were. He was holding his R5 assault rifle over the hood of a red Fiesta, firing blindly across the street. Moving left, Kealey shifted his focus to the SAPS vehicles and saw that both drivers were still behind their respective wheels. Propping his elbows on the hood of an M-Class Mercedes, he sighted in on the driver of the lead SUV and prepared to fire.

Just as he acquired his target, the man flung open his door and started to climb out of the Land Rover. Since the steering wheel was on the right side, the officer was perfectly framed against his vehicle, and Kealey squeezed the trigger twice, both rounds striking the man in the center of his chest. A look of shock came over the driver's face. He reached out to grab for the door, but his legs were already giving way. The police officer dropped to his knees, then fell face-first to the cement, his handgun clattering a few feet from his body. He did not move again.

The second Land Rover was already reversing, the light bar flashing blue on top of the vehicle. Kealey ignored the vehicle, though he caught a glimpse of the driver's terrified face as the SUV hurtled past his position. Instead, he kept his sights fixed on the Ford Fiesta, which was parked 18 feet northwest of his position. The police officer crouched behind the vehicle had brought his weapon down, and Kealey could only assume he was reloading. Kealey had kept careful track of his own spent brass, and he knew that he had fired 23 of the 30 rounds in the FNC's magazine, including the long burst he had fired to scatter the pedestrians. That left him with more than enough ammunition to finish the work he had started, as long as he used it carefully.

He was still waiting for the police officer behind the

Fiesta to show himself when he spotted movement to his right. He turned to appraise the new threat and saw the driver's side door on the Land Cruiser swing open. He swore under his breath as Flores climbed out of the vehicle, a Glock 19 in his right hand. The Honduran turned right and began edging carefully along the side of the truck, the Glock extended at arm's length. His swarthy face was fixed in a strange expression, a combination of restrained fear and intense concentration.

Kealey watched the ex-Honduran soldier move with mounting rage and disbelief. He was tempted to shout out an order, to tell the man to get back into the vehicle, but some inner sense of self-preservation stopped him from doing so. He shot a glance at the Fiesta, but the police officer was still hidden from view. To Kealey's left, the second Land Rover was still reversing at a high rate of speed, and he turned in time to see the driver attempt a desperate, near impossible turn. He was clearly trying to swing the SUV back into the alley, but he cut it far too short, and there was a loud bang as the rear end of the vehicle smashed into the corner of the residential building, tearing away part of the redbrick wall. The truck died instantly, and even at a distance Kealey could see the police officer struggling in vain to restart the engine.

It was an incredibly easy shot, more akin to murder than a fair exchange of gunfire, but Kealey hadn't started this fight, and he wasn't about to hesitate now. Standing up, he moved to the back of the Mercedes SUV and leaned around the corner. Bending his knees slightly, he braced his right shoulder against the Mercedes and fired a three-round burst into the front windshield of the incapacitated Land Rover. He saw the driver jerk in his seat, then slump to the right. It was clear that his rounds had hit their target, but he fired another short burst, anyway, just to be sure. As the echo died away, he heard Flores calling his name. He did not respond, not wanting to give away his position, although he realized his last shots had probably done just that. Instead, he continued moving around the back of the M-Class Mercedes, the retractable stock of his FNC tucked in tight to his right shoulder.

One round left, he thought. *One round and a single target. So much for conserving ammunition.* Leaning around the rear passenger-side fender, he quickly appraised the situation. Flores had already moved into the open and was walking slowly forward, his gun up as he searched for targets. Kealey immediately adjusted his aim to the left, searching for the last surviving police officer, but the man was way ahead of him. He had already straightened behind the red Fiesta and was rapidly bringing his R5 up to a firing position, the muzzle level with Flores's chest. The Blackwater driver saw the threat and tried to swing his Glock to the right, his eyes opening wide, but he had already been caught out of position. Kealey, with a clear view of the whole scene, fired his last round as the SAPS officer pulled the trigger once. Kealey's bullet hit the man in the right side of the head, killing him instantly, but not before the officer's single round found its target. Flores jerked once with the impact, took a few stumbling steps forward, and dropped to the ground.

Kealey immediately left the cover of the Mercedes and started over to where the man had fallen. With a sense of relief, he decided that the Honduran had not suffered a serious wound, as he was already trying to sit up. His face was twisted in pain, and his left hand was pressed to his right shoulder. His unfired Glock was lying a few feet away.

Arriving on the run, Kealey crouched and pulled

Flores's hand away from the wound, ignoring the man's halfhearted attempts to push him away. The powerful 5.56mm round had pierced the right side of his chest, just above the first rib and below the outer edge of the clavicle. Judging by the absence of blood, the round had missed the major arteries in the region, as well as all the internal organs, none of which were situated in that immediate area. Moving around to check the man's back, Kealey found the exit wound, which was considerably larger than the hole in his chest. From the position alone, Kealey could tell that the round had driven through the center of Flores's right scapula before it left his body. It wasn't a fatal injury, but his earlier assumption had been wrong, as it *was* serious. The pain would be intense, and it would only get worse as the minutes passed. Flores had to get to a hospital immediately.

As the shock of the initial impact passed, the Honduran started to groan in pain. Kealey was already thinking about his next move. He looked around quickly, ignoring the distant wail of approaching sirens. Normally, the police backup would have arrived already, but the bulk of the city's force seemed to be focused on the courthouse at Von Brandis and Kerk, as well as the surrounding streets. Given the ongoing riot outside the Johannesburg High Court, it wasn't surprising that it had taken this long for backup to arrive on scene, and this realization led Kealey to another. If the SAPS officers who had ambushed them were originally assigned to stand post outside the courthouse, it would explain the ease with which they had obtained automatic weapons. And if they had drawn their R5s for the supposed purpose of crowd control, they had probably signed out some nonlethal deterrents as well—the same deterrents the policemen on Kerk Street should have been using the moment Whysall's vehicle was hit outside the parking garage.

He looked over at the first police Land Rover, which was still idling directly behind the Land Cruiser. The door nearest to him was hanging open, and the driver's corpse was lying facedown a few feet away. Rivulets of dark red blood were running out from under his chest, trickling down the gentle slope of the street. Looking the dead man over, Kealey took note of his outfit. It was standard SAPS winter attire: black tactical boots, gray field trousers, and a navy jacket over a gray short-sleeve shirt, the collar pulled outside of the jacket. A navy baseball cap bearing the SAPS gold star was lying next to the man's head, and his weapon—a standard-issue USP-9—was resting a few inches from his still right hand. There was nothing to suggest that he was anything other than a regular officer in the South African Police Service, except . . .

Except the handgun, Kealey realized. *The USP-9 isn't standard issue. So if these men aren't regular SAPS officers, who are they?*

The moment this question entered his mind, Kealey jogged over to take a closer look. Picking up the weapon, he saw that he had been right; it *was* a Heckler & Koch USP-9. The powerful 9mm handgun had been adopted by the SAPS Special Task Force a few years earlier, and that told him all he needed to know. The STF was an elite division within the South African Police Service. It was roughly equivalent to the SWAT team in a major U.S. city, such as New York or Los Angeles, only the STF was far more selective. In a police force numbering 130,000 officers across the country, less than 100 were active members of the venerable "Task Mag" units. For this reason alone, Kealey doubted that all six officers were assigned to the STF, but either way, the link would account for the heavy firepower the would-be assassins had brought to bear.

The police sirens were drawing closer. Turning his head to his right, Kealey saw flashing lights in the near distance. Over the sound of the two-tone sirens, he heard doors slamming shut and men shouting, and he realized the arriving officers had decided to proceed on foot, as the road to the north was blocked by abandoned cars. He assumed the occupants had fled when the shooting started, but unfortunately, the accidental roadblock—as convenient as it was—wouldn't do much to slow the new arrivals down. Even on foot, Kealey knew it wouldn't take them long to get to the Land Cruiser, which was parked no more than 200 meters from the officers' current location. Accounting for the cars blocking the way, he decided that he and the others had about fifty seconds to leave the scene. Checking his watch, he marked the time and started to move.

Jogging round to the back of the Land Rover, he popped the rear door and did a quick visual inventory. The cargo area was full of clothes, both civilian and police issue, as well as six boxes of ammunition, four spent magazines, a spare tire, and a fully loaded tactical vest bearing the SAPS departmental seal. Grabbing the vest, he squeezed each of the closed compartments, searching for the cylindrical shape of a CS riot control grenade. The fourth pouch felt right, and he ripped open the Velcro flap to check the contents. Two grenades were inside. He pulled the first one out to read the markings and saw that it was what he was looking for. Shoving one grenade into each of his pockets, he moved around the side of the vehicle and ran up to the rear door of the Land Cruiser. He tried the door and swore when he found it locked. Rather than try to convince the men inside to open it, he ran around the ruined front grille of the SUV to the passenger-side door, which was still hanging ajar. Hitting the automatic locks, he took two steps to his right and lifted the handle.

The South African president was still lying prone in the backseat, as was his aide, Steve Oliphant. Both men raised their heads cautiously when Kealey opened the door. They seemed stunned to find him standing there.

Fixing his gaze on the senior man, Kealey said, "Sir, we've got to move. It isn't safe here. . . . We have to change vehicles right now."

The man's mouth fell open, but nothing came out, and Kealey didn't have time to argue. Reaching in, he grabbed Jacob Zuma with two hands, then pulled him bodily out of the vehicle. The man seemed too stunned to react, but Oliphant immediately began shouting in protest. He reached out and tried to grab Kealey's arm, commanding him to release the older man. Ignoring him, Kealey gripped Zuma's arm and guided him gently but firmly back to the Land Rover. He had just pushed him into the backseat when the aide arrived on the run, his face a mask of indignant rage. Before he could say a word, Kealey gripped the lapels of his jacket, turned to the right, and shoved him up against the side of the SUV.

"What the hell do you think you're doing?" Oliphant sputtered. He tried to pull Kealey's hands away, but he didn't have the strength or leverage. "Get your hands off me! You have no right to—"

"Shut the fuck up! We have to get out of here. What don't you understand about that?"

The aide twisted his head to the right, toward the sound of the sirens. "We don't have to go anywhere," he protested angrily. "The police are coming. We should stay here and—"

"The police did *this!*" Kealey shouted, sweeping an

arm to his right to indicate the surrounding devastation. He tried to remember that the man had been doing his best to keep his head down for the past ten minutes, but it was hard to excuse this level of ignorance.

Oliphant fell silent and gradually stopped struggling as he took in the scene, his mouth agape.

"Don't you get it? It was the *police* who attacked us!" The African's mouth worked silently, but he had nothing to say, and Kealey took advantage of the dead air, knowing it wouldn't last for long. "Look, you were right about one thing," he conceded quickly. "More are coming, but we can't wait to see if they're on our side or not, so stop arguing and get in the vehicle. We're leaving. *Now.*"

Kealey released his grasp on the man's suit jacket, and this time Oliphant did as he was told. Without another word, he slid into the backseat next to his boss. Shutting the door after them, Kealey turned and sprinted the short distance back to Flores. The Honduran was still lying where he had fallen, blood streaming out from under his injured shoulder. At first, Kealey was afraid the man had lost consciousness. If he had, it would make his next task all but impossible. As he crossed the last few feet, though, he saw that Flores was still awake, if only just.

"Come on," Kealey urged, crouching next to him.

The man's eyes cracked open, but he didn't respond.

"*Come on.* We've got to get out of here." Kealey slid his right arm under Flores's left, then gripped the man's limp left hand with his, lifting him into a sitting position. "Ready?"

The Honduran nodded weakly. The slight movement caused sweat to drip from his face to his long-sleeved shirt, which was already soaked in blood and perspiration.

"Okay," Kealey said. "One, two . . ."

On *three,* he straightened his legs and heaved the man to his feet. It took all his strength; Flores had six inches and nearly 80 pounds on him. To complicate matters, the Honduran was already weak from shock incurred by blood loss. He made an effort to stumble forward without assistance, but even so, Kealey was forced to bear much of his weight for the short walk back to the Land Rover.

The rear cargo door was still in the elevated position. Turning to his left, Kealey did what he could to position the man's right thigh with the rear bumper, then pushed back and up, shoving the injured man into the cluttered cargo area. He would have preferred to put him in the front passenger seat, but it would be difficult to maneuver the large man into the tighter space, and time was no longer a luxury. As Kealey slammed the cargo door shut and moved around to the driver's side of the vehicle, he was confronted with this fact in the plainest possible terms. The closest police officer was clearly visible to the north, not more than 40 meters from where Kealey was standing, and two more were just a few steps behind. All three had their service weapons drawn. The lead officer was shouting a series of instructions in his direction, but Kealey couldn't hear what he was saying over the blast of the sirens, not that he particularly cared.

Realizing they would reach the Land Rover before he could reverse back to the alley, Kealey reached into his right pocket and withdrew one of the CS grenades. Stepping over the body of the Special Task Force officer he had killed a few minutes earlier, he moved behind the driver's side door. Crouching below the line of the window, he flipped off the grenade's thumb-clip safety, then pulled out the main cotter pin. Taking a single step back, he heaved the grenade over the door, aiming for a spot approximately 10 feet in front of the approaching police officers. Without waiting to see where it landed, he slid behind the wheel and closed the door.

Once inside the vehicle, he didn't waste any time. Oblivious to Flores's groans of pain in the back, he checked the glove compartment quickly, searching for a street map. As he rifled through the paperwork, he listened with one ear to the Tait digital radio mounted between the seats, which was already set to the appropriate channel. The responding officers were relaying information back and forth in a rapid, convoluted blend of English and Afrikaans. Straining to pick some information out of the frantic four-way exchange, he caught a few key words, but more importantly, he picked up on the anger and frustration in their voices. In his experience, the tension could mean only one thing—the second wave of SAPS officers was still searching for a clear route to the Blackwater Land Cruiser. And if that was the case, the alley behind the Land Rover was probably still empty, which gave them at least one clear route of escape.

Giving up on the glove compartment, Kealey moved on to the second most likely location. Reaching up, he flipped down the overhead visor, and a folded map fell into his lap, along with a few torn envelopes and a handful of business cards. Unfolding the map, he spread the thin paper over the steering wheel and slid his finger down to the M2, searching for their last known position. Finding it, he studied the surrounding streets, trying to determine which route they had taken.

It was hard to be certain, given the speed with which it had all taken place, but he was reasonably sure that the initial ambush had occurred at the intersection of Goud and Main Street. That was six blocks east of the Carlton Center, which marked the eastern edge of Marshalltown. If he was right, and they had traveled three blocks north before swinging into the alley, that placed them . . .

Kealey traced the route with his finger and landed on End Street, directly below the M2 overpass. That had to be where they were now, he decided, and a quick glance at the side mirror proved him right; behind them, he could see the sweeping arch of the double-decker highway. The concrete artery was held up by a long row of massive supporting pillars curving gently to the southwest, but while the road was imposing in scale and height, it was dwarfed by the surrounding buildings, most of which were residential in nature and at least ten stories tall.

Satisfied that he had their current location nailed down, Kealey went back to the map and started searching for the nearest medical facility. He found it quickly enough; the MBS Hospital was located in the urban sprawl of Doornfontein, ten blocks to the north in Region 8. He took a few seconds to memorize the route, his eyes occasionally flicking up to the windshield. Then he mentally checked off a number of possible detours he could use if they happened to run into a police roadblock. The hospital was his first and most important destination. If he could get there, he would feel comfortable leaving not only Flores but also Zuma and Oliphant in the care of the physicians on duty. He knew that Zuma's welfare was supposed to take precedence over everything, but he was not willing to abandon Whysall and Stiles to their fate outside the parking garage on Kerk Street. Not if there was something he could do to save their lives.

Looking back through the windshield, he saw that the grenade he had thrown forty seconds earlier had performed as expected, releasing a thick cloud of noxious gray-white smoke between their stolen Land Rover and the approaching police officers. He had been exposed to CS on several occasions, and he knew how unpleasant the effects could be. The officers unlucky enough to be in the vicinity would be suffering a number of symptoms. Their exposed skin would be burning; their noses would be clogged with mucus; their throats with bile and spit. There was a good chance they wouldn't be able to open their eyes, let alone find their way to the place where the Land Cruiser was parked, directly in front of Kealey's newly acquired vehicle.

The sight of the CS-laden smoke was reassuring, as was the fact that the responding officers had yet to find their way through it. He still had one grenade left, and if he could get to Whysall's disabled vehicle in the next few minutes, he might still have a chance at dispersing the crowd long enough to get the two Blackwater contractors out of the area. It was a long shot, but better than nothing at all, and as the head of the detail, he owed it to them to try.

Pushing the map onto the passenger seat, he threw the Land Rover into reverse and looked over his shoulder. With both eyes fixed on the rear windshield, he hit the gas and the SUV jumped backward, accelerating quickly. The Peugeot they had hit a few minutes earlier was still blocking the northbound traffic, giving him a clear run to the alley entrance. The only problem was the second police Land Rover, which was backed into the brick wall at a strange angle, the driver dead behind the wheel. The space between the front end of the SUV and the abandoned cars in the southbound lane was miniscule, no more than seven feet across, and Kealey knew there was no way they would make it through. Still, he was left with no other option. Keeping his eyes fixed on the short gap, he pressed the accelerator to the floor.

With his attention focused on the rear windshield, he not only heard but saw Oliphant cry out before he heard the shot. Jerking his head to the right, he saw the fresh hole in the windshield just as another round punched through the weakened glass, burrowing into the top half of the passenger seat. When he saw where the second bullet had hit, Kealey couldn't help but flash on the fact that he had nearly put Flores in that seat. He dismissed the thought just as quickly, and fighting every instinct he had, he turned away from the officers firing at the front of the vehicle. Instead, he focused on the rear windshield and the rapidly approaching gap.

A second before they reached the narrow space, Kealey realized he had badly misjudged the width. The gap was five feet across at most, and no matter how he hit it, they were going to collide with at least one of the stationary vehicles. Reacting instinctively, he cringed and reached over his chest with his left hand, his fingers grasping for the seat belt hanging loose at his right side. He had just managed to grip the material, his fist tightening around the expedient lifeline, when the impact came. The rear passenger side of the Land Rover hit the second truck, heaving them into the air. The rear wheels spun crazily as they sought for something solid to grab onto. Then the back end of the SUV came crashing down without warning, slamming Kealey back in his seat. They were still rolling backward when several more rounds passed through the windshield. The sound of incoming gunfire, more than anything else, shook Kealey out of his daze, and he reflexively hit the gas and turned the wheel to the left, swinging them out of the line of fire.

Now the second police vehicle was temporarily blocking the incoming fire, but it was also blocking their escape route. He backed hard into the vehicle, hitting it broadside, then pushed the accelerator to the floor, driving it sideways. Having created enough room to maneuver, he shifted the truck into drive, pressed down on the accelerator, and swerved to the right. Once they were back in the alley, he immediately slowed to a crawl and shot a glance over his shoulder, ignoring the people running ahead of the vehicle, away from the scene of the massacre.

"Is everyone okay?" he demanded. "Is anyone hit?"

Steve Oliphant shakily raised his head, then sat up. He was in a daze, too confused to immediately respond, but looking him over, Kealey didn't see anything to indicate that he had been injured.

Pointing at Jacob Zuma's prostrate form on the floor behind the front seats, Kealey said, "Check him. Make sure he's okay."

As Oliphant complied, Kealey called back to Flores, but there was no response, and he realized that the Honduran couldn't have come through the last collision uninjured, as he had been closest to the point of impact. He would have been thrown all over the place. If he had not already been unconscious when the crash occurred, he almost certainly was now, and that was the best-case scenario. The worst didn't bear thinking about.

Oliphant was saying something, and it took Kealey a second to decipher the words. When he did, his mounting despair was replaced by a surge of relief; Zuma had made it through unscathed. "Okay," he said. "We're getting out of here. Get low and stay there until I tell you otherwise."

Oliphant nodded and immediately slid to the floor, cramming his body into the narrow space between the seats. Apparently, he was done arguing. Zuma had raised his head to respond to his aide, but now he lowered it once again. Kealey could hear them moving around, though he didn't see them respond to his order as he hit the gas and fumbled for the Motorola receiver/transmitter he had pulled out of his ear a few minutes earlier. Pushing it back into place, he immediately heard the frantic speech of Jeff Venora, the pilot of the Blackwater helicopter. He cut in without hesitation, and the pilot came back a split second later, his voice laced with anger and barely contained panic.

"Kealey, goddamn it, where the fuck have you been? I've been trying to raise you for—"

"Just tell me what's happening," Kealey snapped. "Save the theatrics."

There was a brief pause, and Kealey could sense the other man biting back his instinctive reply. "The vehicle is still intact, but the situation is only getting worse. I don't know how much longer they can hold out, over."

"Any word from Whysall or Stiles?"

"Negative . . . Their radio must have been knocked out in the attack, over."

"Okay . . ." Kealey thought for a second as they hit the end of the alley. Swinging the wheel right, he ran through the route in his mind as the SAPS Land Rover shot north on Banket Street, the speedometer nosing up to sixty kilometers per hour. The hospital was now eight blocks away, and from there it was a five-minute run to the courthouse. "Just stay in position, Air One. I'm coming to get them out."

"You're what?" The disbelief in the pilot's voice was plain. "You must be crazy. They're surrounded on all sides. . . . You'll never even reach the vehicle, let alone get them out."

"I'm coming to get them," Kealey repeated. He didn't bother to acknowledge Venora's words, even though deep down, he knew the man was probably right. Regardless of the odds stacked against him, he had to try. "Just stay where you are. I'll be there as soon as I can."

CHAPTER 10

KHARTOUM

Seth Holland sat in his dimly lit office, staring at his computer screen in utter dejection. As he used the mouse to scroll slowly down the page, the faces of a unique, secret community blurred before his eyes. Dusk was falling outside his windows, a dark purple haze sinking over the city, but Holland could not take comfort in the end of the workday. He was beyond frustrated, and the late hour had nothing to do with it.

The answer he sought was just out of reach. He knew it, had known it for hours on end, for that matter, but now it was really starting to get to him. His patience—which was fleeting enough on the best of days—was long past the point of wearing thin.

The identity of the man with the rucksack had consumed him since that afternoon, when Holland had first spotted him on the front steps of the embassy. It had started as nothing more than vague curiosity, an itch that refused to go away. Hoping to rid himself of it,

Holland had gone directly from the lobby to his fourth-floor office, where he'd proceeded to place calls to several different departments on an internal line. He'd assumed that he would have his answer in a matter of minutes, as that was how this kind of thing usually played out. In this case, though, that assumption was wrong. He'd been shut down at every turn, and now, six hours later, what had started as simple curiosity had evolved into a very different sort of beast. And an implacable one at that.

Now he didn't just *want* an answer. Now he *needed* an answer.

When he first started looking into it, he had forced himself to do so with an open mind. After all, there was a chance that the whole thing was entirely innocent; that he had seen the man, or someone resembling him, in casual circumstances at some point in the past, and seeing him again had simply triggered that memory. It was a possibility that could not be discounted, but to Holland, it didn't feel right, and after twenty years in the Central Intelligence Agency, he had learned to trust his gut. Ever since that brief encounter in front of the building, every instinct he owned had been telling him that the recognition was rooted on a far more important level, a *professional* level, but since he couldn't be certain, he'd been forced to consider all the angles, even those that didn't seem likely.

That was how his search had begun: with all the angles. And with the basics. The vast majority of people who came to the embassy were there on routine business: registering births, replacing passports, seeking visas, or notarizing documents. For this reason, Holland's first move was to call the consular duty officer. It took him thirty seconds to explain what he wanted, and the fax came through a few minutes later. It was a list of every male who had appeared in the ground-floor office that day, along with any relevant personal information.

Holland was able to subtract five names right off the bat, simply because they had come in after the unknown subject had already left the building, and another nineteen because the men in question were either too old or young to fit the unsub's description. Another four could go because they were not Caucasian, leaving Holland with a grand total of sixty-three names. These he ran through the database at Langley, which he was able to access remotely via his desktop computer. Fifteen minutes after submitting the query, he received the reply. None of the names were flagged, at least in the Agency's records, which made it unlikely that he had encountered those people on the job. In other words, the list was useless, a dead end.

Undaunted by this temporary setback, Holland next placed a call to the public affairs officer, the man in charge of the Public Diplomacy Office. This was another long shot, since the man had only five full-time employees, but Holland wanted to be thorough. As expected, the answer came back in the negative. The PAO had not received any visitors that afternoon, and neither had any member of his staff. Subsequent calls to the Political/Economic Section and the Information Resources Center also failed to pan out. By this time Holland was starting to wonder if he had missed something, and he could no longer deny his rising consternation.

After two hours of trawling, he decided to take a break in the hope that a short rest would jar his memory. After asking his secretary to hold his calls, he kicked off his shoes, lay down on the couch in his office, closed his eyes, and let his mind drift back to the encounter. He allowed the images to unreel of their own accord, trying to focus on what he had seen. And exactly what *had* he seen? There was nothing to distinguish the man from a thousand others. A *million* others, maybe. A tall, lean, dark-haired man in his mid- to late thirties, wearing steel-framed spectacles, a navy sport coat, gray slacks, and carrying a rucksack of the army surplus variety. There was nothing unusual about that picture. . . .

Holland's eyes abruptly sprang open. *No, nothing wrong with the picture . . . except for that rucksack. Because that doesn't fit at all, does it?*

He tossed his legs over the side of the couch, then jumped up like a jack-in-the-box as the realization grabbed hold of him. That sack damned well *was* unusual. The more he thought about it, the greater his certainty. Why would a man dressed in business casual attire be lugging a military-style pack? It didn't jibe. Which led Holland to wonder . . . If he hadn't been carrying it all along, where would he get it?

The answer was obvious. The embassy was filled with marines, all of whom had ready access to that kind of equipment.

But why would one of them hand over his pack? And more importantly, what had been inside when he did?

With these questions blowing through his mind, Holland picked up his phone and called Post One on the ground floor. He asked for the detachment commander but was informed that he had just gone off duty. Holland left a message with the corporal in charge, asking the commander to get back to him ASAP. That had been two hours earlier, and he had not heard a word since.

Rubbing his eyes wearily, Holland stood and walked over to one of his windows. He stood there for a moment and studied the view. The sky was a rich, deep shade of magenta, the color fading quickly to coal black, and dusk had thrown long shadows over the inner walls of the courtyard. Below his window, he could make out a dark figure huddled against the rapidly encroaching cold. There was the flare of a match as the figure lit a cigarette. Then a second figure approached. Another flare, another cigarette. Coworkers, Holland assumed, sharing some watercooler gossip at the end of their shift. He envied them that camaraderie, the kind that could only exist between equals. Holland had no direct equal in the embassy, and since his work was not for public dissemination, there was no one he felt comfortable conversing with. It made for a very lonely posting. To make matters worse, he still had eight months to go in his current assignment.

It would have been much easier to bear if his wife had accompanied him, but she had flatly refused. Her decision to stay in Miami had stung him deeply, and he had unwisely lashed out at the time, calling her selfish and stubborn, as well as a few other things that did not bear repeating. Those accusations had let to a bitter argument that he deeply regretted. Like any job that involved long deployments and time apart, intelligence work was hard on families. The divorce rates in the ranks of the CIA were incredibly high, somewhere in the region of six to seven percent in the Operations Directorate alone, and Holland had no desire to add to those depressing statistics. Besides, he could see now that she had been right all along. North Africa—and Sudan in particular—was no place for Western women and children. What had happened to Lily Durant in Camp Hadith was proof enough of that.

Aside from Jake, their five-year-old son, Jen was the one good, stable thing in his life, and he had no intention of letting her slip away. He had made that promise to himself on the flight over, and he had not forgotten it. He only hoped that she knew how sorry he was. He'd apologized several times over the phone, and she had seemed accepting enough, but it was always hard to tell with her. Her birthday was coming up, though, and if she *was* harboring any lingering resentment, Holland figured the right gift would get rid of it once and for all. He'd seen a solid gold necklace on his last trip into the city center, and that had potential, assuming it was the genuine article. . . .

He stopped himself and nearly laughed aloud at his own naïveté. In the backstabbing, greed-driven *souqs* of Khartoum, that would be quite an assumption, and buying into it could only end one way: with one very happy shopkeeper and one very pissed-off wife.

The phone on his desk chirped, snapping him back to the present. Turning away from the window, he crossed the room in three quick strides and snatched it up. "Holland."

"Mr. Holland? This is Sergeant Sadowski. I was told you wanted to speak."

Holland closed his eyes and clenched a victorious fist in front of his chest. "Yes, Sergeant, that's right. Thanks for getting back to me so quickly, and I'm sorry to interrupt your downtime. . . . I know you don't get much of it."

"Not a problem, sir. What can I do for you?"

The CIA officer took note of the man's voice. It was calm, cool, and slightly curious, which presented him with a problem. Clearly, Sadowski had no idea who he really was, and judging by his clipped tone, he wasn't eager to do any favors for a mid-level budget manager.

Technically, the man's ignorance was good news. This was how it was supposed to be. The identity of the

CIA's station chief was a closely held secret in any embassy. Normally, it would have come as a relief to know that his cover had withstood intense scrutiny from within, but the secrecy wouldn't help him here. He needed answers, but he had almost no leverage with which to extract them. Holland instinctively knew that he might have to make a professional sacrifice to get them, and if that was the case, he might be getting back to Jen and Jake much sooner than he had anticipated.

And that, he silently acknowledged, would not be a bad thing at all.

"Sergeant Sadowski, I understand that you were on duty in Post One this afternoon. From zero six hundred to fourteen hundred hours. Is that correct?"

"Yes, sir, that's right."

Holland noted the wariness in the other man's voice. "Between, let's say, twelve hundred hours and the end of your shift, did you have any visitors? Anyone outside your chain of command?"

There was a tense pause, and the station chief knew he had pushed it too far. "Mr. Holland, I'm afraid I can't divulge that information. And frankly, I don't see how it concerns you."

"I'll tell you what, Sergeant—"

"Sir, I can't—"

"No, just listen," Holland said quickly. "According to your information, I am the budget manager for DISAM here in Khartoum. That is what you've been told, right?"

There was silence on the other end of the line, and Holland knew he had gotten it right. "Well, I'm telling you right now, that is not the reality. I do not work for that organization."

There was a brief, speculative pause. "So who *do* you work for, Mr. Holland?"

"I heard you were a smart man, Sergeant. I'll let you figure it out for yourself."

Another long silence ensued. Holland, listening to the sound of the other man breathing over the line, could almost sense the moment that Sadowski caught on. By his rough count, it took less than thirty seconds.

"I'm going to need some proof of what you're saying, sir, before I tell you anything. And that's assuming I even can."

"Look . . ." Holland didn't want to get into it over the phone. "Do you know where I'm located?"

"Yes," Sadowski replied. "Fourth floor, room four-oh-two."

Holland wasn't surprised to hear that the man already knew where his office was. At least once a month, the Marine Security Guards conducted a series of drills known as "Reacts"—which was short for Reaction. Each React started with a simulated emergency, such as a fire, a bomb threat, or a riot outside the embassy. From there, the MSG gathered in the designated React Room, a storage area for weapons, communications equipment, and other essential gear, where they received their orders directly from the detachment commander. As the man in charge of those drills, it was only natural that Sadowski would know the embassy's layout like the back of his hand.

"I'm up here now," Holland continued. "I wonder if you wouldn't mind stopping by for a few minutes. I promise you, it won't be a waste of your time."

There was a brief pause as the other man considered, and the station chief found himself holding his breath. Finally, Sadowski said, "I'll see you in five minutes."

Holland exhaled slowly in relief. "Thank you, Sergeant."

The line went dead, and Holland hung up the phone. As he stood there in the dark, he couldn't help but wonder if he had just made a serious error in judgment. Essentially, he had told the marine sergeant the truth: that he was the ranking CIA officer at the embassy. Not in so many words, of course, but the implication was clear, and a man with Sadowski's experience wasn't likely to miss the underlying message. Now he knew what only five other men at the embassy knew, including the four case officers who reported directly to Holland. It was the kind of information that hundreds, if not thousands, of Arab fundamentalists across the country would gladly kill for.

Holland shook off the lingering doubt. He had just committed an unforgivable sin in the eyes of his employers, but somehow, he knew that he'd done the right thing. He couldn't explain *how* he knew, but the identity of the man on the steps was worth the professional sacrifice. He was sure of it. And if it turned out that he was wrong, so be it. He'd made a calculated wager. Staff Sergeant Daniel Sadowski was a U.S. Marine who had served his country with distinction for years on end, not a gossiping secretary or some shifty, back-alley merchant in the city bazaar. Holland's true position at the embassy was as safe with him as it was with anyone else, including Holland's own subordinates.

Turning on his desktop lamp, he crossed to a large Gardall safe in the corner of the room. Crouching before it, he punched in a ten-digit code. The LED light to the right of the keypad turned green. He turned the handle and pulled open the heavy steel door. Inside there were two shelves. The bottom shelf held nothing but files, each of which was labeled with the appropriate security classification. The two objects he needed were on the top shelf. He had not touched either since he had arrived in Sudan eight months earlier. Grabbing them both, Holland closed the safe and locked it once more.

Just as he finished doing so, there was a knock on the door behind him. Getting back to his feet, he crossed the room, placing both objects on the edge of his desk along the way. He opened the door and recognized Sadowski on sight. The twenty-seven-year-old marine was a shade over six feet tall, with a wrestler's physique, flat green eyes, and hair clipped so short it was impossible to tell what color it was. He was wearing civilian clothes—khakis, a checked flannel shirt, and steel-toed boots—but it was what he held in his right hand that caught Holland's attention. It was a plastic shopping bag, weighed down in the middle. From the way he was holding it, it was impossible for Holland to determine the contents.

He extended a hand, and Sadowski switched the shopping bag to his left before they shook. Holland pretended not to notice. "Thank you for coming, Sergeant. Come on in."

Holland stepped back to give him room, and Sadowski crossed the threshold, looking around as he entered the room. For the most part, there wasn't much to see, which was exactly how Holland wanted it. The office was larger than most, but as spare as a janitor's. It contained nothing but a desk, a file cabinet, the safe, a few chairs, a couch, and a bookshelf lined with the standard foreign policy textbooks. There were a few motivational posters on the wall to round out the bland décor. It was everything one would expect from a mid-level public servant. The only things that didn't seem to fit were the items Holland had retrieved from his safe. Sadowski, a trained soldier, spotted them instantly. The first item elicited no reaction, but when he saw the gun, a Heckler & Koch USP Expert, a slight frown spread over his face.

After closing and locking his door, Holland crossed to his desk and picked up the gun. Sadowski tensed, but Holland merely held it out for him to take, butt first. The marine sergeant, after a second's hesitation, accepted the weapon, dropped the magazine, and checked the chamber reflexively.

"It's clear," Holland assured him.

As Sadowski reinserted the empty magazine, Holland picked up the second item on his desk, the credentials that marked him as an active field officer—GS-13, step 6—in the Central Intelligence Agency. He held out the plastic ID card. Sadowski stared at him for a moment, then set down the gun and accepted the proffered identification. His eyes flicked over it for a minute, as though he knew what to look for. Then he handed it back. Following Holland's lead, he took a seat in front of the desk and placed the plastic bag by his right foot.

"Well, I'm convinced," the detachment commander began. "You are who you say you are, Mr. Holland. I guess you can probably figure out what I'm wondering now."

The CIA officer nodded. "If I were you, I'd be wondering why I'm showing you this." He gestured toward the ID and the gun. "Why I'm bringing you into the loop."

"Exactly."

"Well, it's not for my health or yours, Sergeant. I'm telling you the truth because I need your help." He leaned forward and placed his forearms on his desk, fixing the young marine with a steady, serious gaze. "This afternoon I saw a man walk out the front door of this building with an olive green military rucksack. The way I see it, he must have gotten it from you or one of your men. I want to know what was inside that pack. And if you have a name, I want that, too."

Sadowski nodded slowly. "You don't want much," he said at length.

"I realize it's a lot to ask for. I also realize you are under no obligation to share this information with me. I'm requesting that you do so as a professional courtesy."

Holland let his eyes drift down to his Agency ID, which was sitting on the desk between them. His meaning was clear, but Sadowski didn't flinch.

"I'm not sure that's a good enough reason, Mr. Holland."

"Maybe not," Holland said. He smiled disarmingly. "But it's all I've got. Tell me, what time did you speak to Reynolds? Was it before or after this visitor showed up?"

It was a shot in the dark, but from the fractional movement that followed, the way Sadowski's eyes darted up to the left, Holland saw that he'd gotten it right. He felt a brief flash of satisfaction, but it couldn't last. What he had just learned—what Sadowski's body language had given away—was not what he wanted to hear, in a manner of speaking.

After striking out with the consular office and the PAO earlier in the day, Holland had started to suspect the worst, that the man with the green rucksack had met with just one person at the embassy—Walter Reynolds, the chargé d'affaires himself. Holland had been hesitant to fully consider that possibility, because if he was right, there was basically no chance he would ever get the answers he was looking for. He did not have a lot of respect for the chief of mission, whom he regarded as lazy and incompetent. But he was still the man in charge, and if he didn't want anyone to know who had stopped by his office, there would be no prying it out of him.

In other words, Sadowski was his last chance for answers, and he was starting to look uncomfortable. If he walked out, Holland would be left with nothing. With few options left, he decided to play his trump card. It was the one thing he knew would elicit a strong reaction from the man sitting across from him, if only because it seemed to elicit that kind of reaction from everyone.

"Sergeant, did you ever meet Lily Durant?"

Sadowski looked up, his face pinching into a frown of confusion. Clearly, he was trying to figure out where this was going. "No. I saw her once, when she first arrived, but I never spoke to her. At the time, I didn't even know who she was. I don't think anyone did. Why do you ask?"

"You know what happened to her, though."

"Of course." The staff sergeant's confusion was rapidly turning to anger. "What kind of question is that? Everyone knows what happened to her. Those fuckers raped and killed her in cold blood. Not only that, they had the nerve to record the whole damned thing, and we—"

He caught himself in time, but Holland knew exactly what he'd been about to say. "And we did nothing," he said quietly. "Right?"

Sadowski didn't respond, but the truth was written right there in his eyes. Holland genuinely sympathized with him. He had been trained to fight America's enemies the world over, but Lily Durant had been killed less than 1,000 miles from where he was standing, probably by the same government that was hosting them, and he had no choice but to stand there and take it. It would be hard for any man to endure such bitter cir cumstances, let alone a man with Daniel Sadowski's training and temperament. If the marine had left the building at that moment, weapon in his grip, and taken matters into his own hands, beginning with the presidential palace located a few miles to the north, Holland would not have been surprised.

"I understand how you feel, Sergeant. There are a lot of unhappy people out there. People who are less than pleased with how the president responded to this situation. Believe me, you're not the only one. Not by a mile."

Sadowski shook his head angrily. He seemed to have forgotten their earlier verbal sparring; his mind was now fixed on what had happened two months earlier, as well as everything that had occurred in the interim.

"It doesn't make sense," he said in a low voice. His face seemed to mirror the frustration everyone in the building was feeling. "Why didn't he authorize some kind of direct action? Hell, why are we still here? It was his *niece,* for Christ's sake. You think he would have . . ."

"Would have what?" Holland asked. He was genuinely interested. Everyone seemed to agree that David Brenneman should have acted in the wake of Durant's death, but few could agree on what should have been done. The ideas seemed to range from a strongly worded letter of protest to the complete destruction of the Sudanese capital. Holland had listened to these theories, and everything in between, but had heard few sensible suggestions. "In your opinion, what should he have done, Sergeant?"

Sadowski stared at him for a moment, eyes narrowed, as if trying to decide whether or not Holland was mocking him. Satisfied that he wasn't, the marine shrugged and grimaced, then ran a hand over his short, bristly hair.

"I don't know," he finally said. "I don't pretend to
have all the answers, Mr. Holland. But you want me to
be honest?"

Holland nodded. "Bluntly," he said.

"Putting it *bluntly,* sir, my guys think that we should
have evacuated our people, then launched a few cruise
missiles up the man's ass. It's kind of hard to disagree
with that plan of action, especially after what happened."

Holland nodded. He didn't have to ask for an expla-
nation. The "guys," he knew, were the marines under
Sadowski's command; the "man" was none other than
Omar al-Bashir, the president of Sudan.

"So you agree with them," he said. It was not a question.

Sadowski held his gaze for a minute. When he spoke,
his voice was low and tight, but completely controlled.
"Everyone knows that Bashir was behind what happened in West Darfur. He knew what he was starting
when he sent in the Janjaweed to destroy that camp,
and if he didn't know, too fucking bad." Sadowski nodded slowly. "We should have bombed him to hell and
back. Yeah, I do agree with that. Absolutely."

"But instead, we did nothing."

"That's right," Sadowski said. The scowl on his face
said more than he could have ever put into words.
"Nothing at all. It's complete bullshit."

Holland leaned back in his chair and studied the
other man plaintively. Having firmly established the
young marine's mind-set, he wasn't quite sure how to
approach the next topic. It was something he'd been
considering for the past couple of weeks, and while it
had started as nothing more than a stubborn idea, a
glimmer of insight inspired by events unfolding across
the country, he had not been able to shake it. Now, for

the first time, he was about to share his suspicions with somebody else, and he had no idea how they might be received.

"What if I were to tell you," he began slowly, "that I think we *are* doing something? Something no one knows about. Something no one is *meant* to know about."

A hint of curiosity broke through the young man's angry façade, and he looked at Holland with renewed interest. "Such as?"

Holland shook his head. "I can't give you any specifics, Sergeant, for the simple truth that I don't know. This is just an idea, and I can't prove a thing. But take a look around." He lifted his arms out to his sides, as though the answer could be found right there in the room. "Look at what's happened since April. Better yet, look at what *hasn't* happened. We've had . . . what? Four demonstrations outside the building over the past month?"

"Yes, that's right."

"Is that the normal state of things?"

"No," Sadowski conceded. He was starting to look interested. "The numbers are way down, as a matter of fact. Before the attack on Camp Hadith, we were getting an average of three a week, ranging from a few students with signs to a few hundred hard-liners with rocks, sticks, and plenty of American flags to burn. Lately, there's been almost nothing."

"Nothing for us," Holland corrected. "But last week there were three demonstrations in protest of Bashir's regime in Khartoum alone. Did you know that? Demonstrations *in protest* of his regime. Rallies were staged in Juba and Nyala as well. Of those that took place here in the city, two were staged at Nillien University, and one took place outside the al-Safa mosque in the Jarif district. They were put down by the local police, of course, and put down quickly, but each was attended by more people than the last, and another is scheduled for Tuesday, two days from now. Based on the evidence, I'd say the tide has turned in our favor, and the momentum is only building."

Sadowski looked intrigued, but also confused. "So what are you saying?" he asked. "Are you suggesting that we had something to do with those demonstrations? That we arranged for them somehow?"

"That depends on who you mean by 'we.' I can tell you unequivocally that the Agency is not involved with whatever is happening." Holland was breaking a number of serious rules by being so candid with the young marine, but he needed Sadowski's help, and he had already realized that he wouldn't get it for free. "At the very least, I would have been told up front if we had a part in it. Even if it was on the periphery."

The sergeant thought that through for a minute. "So you're wrong," he said. "If the kind of operation you're talking about *did* exist, the CIA would be the natural choice to run it. And since you claim to have no idea what's going on, these demonstrations must have happened of their own accord. Right?"

"That's possible," Holland conceded. "But when was the last time *anyone* in this city—let alone hundreds of people at a time—said anything negative about Omar al-Bashir in public? I don't see that happening without some kind of serious provocation."

"And you think we're responsible for that provocation."

"I think it's possible."

"But how could that happen without you knowing about it?" Sadowski demanded. He gestured toward Holland's credentials, which were still sitting on the desk between them. "You're the CIA station chief. Wouldn't you be the first person to be tipped off if something like that was going on?"

"Normally, yes," Holland said, barely managing not to wince at the younger man's statement of fact. It was strange and more than a little disconcerting to hear his title spoken aloud, and it served to remind him how big a risk he had taken by telling Sadowski the whole truth. "But I don't think we're in anything close to normal territory." He paused. No, not remotely close. In his view, they had entered a zone where everything became murky and ambiguous. "If Brenneman decided to go with an outside source for some reason, it might explain why we've been cut out of the loop."

Sadowski frowned and shook his head. "I don't see how that makes sense. Why would the president do that? Why put you in that position?"

"I don't know," Holland admitted. "But if it happened the way I think it did, it's the only possible explanation."

It took a few seconds, but then it clicked for the marine sergeant. "You think that the man who came to the embassy today is somehow tied up in this . . ." He stumbled for a second, searching for the right word to describe it. ". . . this *theory* of yours, don't you?"

Holland met the younger man's eyes. "I think it's a possibility, Sergeant, but again, I can't prove it. So in that regard, yes, it's nothing more than conjecture. That's why I need your help. That's why I need to see the disks you have in that bag at your feet. The security footage for the building from this afternoon."

Sadowski looked startled. "How did you . . . ?"

The CIA station chief waved it away. "What else could it be? I was starting to think that your visitor might have taken it with him."

"He did," Sadowski confirmed, sitting back in his seat. Now that the wall between them had melted, he seemed almost eager to talk. "Reynolds called down a few minutes beforehand and told me to give him the security disks and any backups, no questions asked."

"Is that all he took?"

"Yeah, that's it."

"Did Reynolds say who the man was? Did he give a name?"

"No. He just said that someone would be down for the disks. The guy showed up a few minutes later, and I handed them over. Then he said he wanted something to carry them in. He looked like he was in a hurry, and I didn't want any problems with Reynolds, so I just emptied my ruck, stuck the disks in, and sent him on his way."

"But you didn't give him the backups," Holland pointed out. "Why not?"

Sadowski shrugged. "It wasn't a normal request. More importantly, it was against protocol. I didn't like it, so I decided to cover my rear end, just in case. Believe me, when you join the Corps, CYA is one of the first things you learn about."

"And let me guess. The disks you have in that bag are just another set of copies."

The marine didn't take the bait. "Actually, these are the backup disks themselves. Your call caught me off guard, sir. . . . I didn't think to make any more."

"Right," Holland said dryly. "That's why it took you two hours to get back to me."

Sadowski opened his mouth to argue, but Holland held up a hand, cutting him off. "Relax, Sergeant. I'm not blaming you. I would have done the same thing in your position."

The marine nodded, clearly relieved to be off the

hook. He seemed to have forgotten that Holland had no actual authority over him. Reaching down, he grabbed the bag at his feet and placed it square on the desk. Holland pulled it toward him and withdrew the contents. There were four disks in all, each in a clear plastic jewel case.

"Why so many?" he asked. "How long was he here?"

"Not long. Maybe half an hour or so, but those recordings cover every camera we have, including those with a view of the street. I figured you would want everything."

Holland looked up. "You knew from the start that you were going to give them to me?"

"No," Sadowski admitted. "When I talked to you earlier, I was still on the fence." He didn't bother to say what had changed his mind. Instead, he nodded toward the small stack of recordable disks. "What are you going to do with them, sir?"

Holland had already thought this through. "First, you and I are going to go down to Post One. That's the only place in the building that has a multiplexer, and I don't want to have to flip from camera to camera, scene to scene. We'll watch these together. You know this place better than anyone, and you might be able to spot anything out of the ordinary. I want your input."

"And then?"

"That depends on whether or not I can identify him. Maybe seeing his face again will jog something loose. If I can pick him out, I'll pass the name up the line, along with a detailed report. If I can't . . . Well, we'll just have to see. Either way, I'm going to send these recordings to Langley. They'll run the video through the facial recognition software. Also, if the man's name is anywhere on file, they'll find it."

"But you're sure—"

"It's in there somewhere," Holland said, anticipating the question. As he stared at the small pile of disks, he knew they contained the information he had been seeking all day. It was strange to be that close and yet still not know. "*He's* in there somewhere. I've never been more certain of anything. And once we find out who he is, we'll have some answers."

CHAPTER 11

PRETORIA, SOUTH AFRICA

Jonathan Harper sat in the corner booth of the small bar and fought the temptation to stare at the door. He had ordered food, but he had no appetite. He had ordered a drink, but it remained untouched, as he did not want the alcohol to affect his judgment, to lower his guard. He had never been more conflicted.

Part of him—a very big part—wanted the man he was waiting for to make an appearance, as that was the whole reason he had traveled 8,000 miles to the South African capital. Another part of him wanted to get up and leave before he was forced to confront his old friend, a term he used—at least these days—with more than a little uncertainty. He'd been wrestling with this inner conflict for the past seventy-two hours at the very least. Much of that time had been spent debating the pros and cons of traveling to Pretoria, but even now, with the decision made, he still wasn't sure he was doing the right thing. His apprehension was only natural, he knew, but that didn't make it any easier to bear, and the moment of truth was fast approaching.

It had been almost a year since he had last seen Ryan Kealey, but he could remember their last meeting with crystal clarity, if only because of what it had led to. At Harper's request, they had met at a restaurant in downtown Washington. It was three months after an operation in Pakistan that had ended with the recovery of a senior U.S. official and the death of Amari Saifi, an Algerian terrorist who, with the help of a former Pakistani general, had struck at the heart of the U.S. government.

Brynn Fitzgerald, still acting secretary of state at the time, had been kidnapped after a bloody attack on her motorcade that left 18 people dead. One had been the head of her security detail. The other had been Lee Patterson, the U.S. ambassador to Pakistan and a college friend, who'd caught a bullet between her eyes.

It had taken Kealey and his team four days to track Fitzgerald down, and then they had moved in to extract her, assisted by a team of 24 Special Forces soldiers and some heavy support from the air.

The mission was successful, but Fitzgerald's rescue had not been without serious cost. Kealey was gravely wounded in the rescue attempt, and a fellow operative, Naomi Kharmai, died as an indirect result of the operation. She was killed—or presumably killed, as her body was never recovered—by Javier Machado, a retired CIA case officer with extraordinary connections throughout Europe and Southeast Asia. Machado had offered to help Kealey find Fitzgerald in exchange for a favor, but when the favor had proved too costly, Kealey had improvised, and Kharmai had paid the ultimate price.

Over the past couple of months Harper had realized

that was still accruing unwanted interest. For he'd become increasingly convinced it was Patterson's death that had sent Fitzgerald down the slippery slope of illogic into the place where fools like Stralen thrived.

At any rate, once the smoke cleared, an in-depth investigation—headed by the FBI and supported behind the scenes by the CIA—was launched into Kharmai's death, but not in time to bring any closure to the matter. The one person who might have been able to provide some meaningful answers, Machado, had already disappeared without a trace, abandoning his home in Spain, his wife, and his surviving daughter in the process. Kealey, after a lengthy convalescence, had disappeared in turn, and that was when the bodies began to pile up. An Arab fundamentalist in Paris, a money launderer in Antwerp, a smuggler in Karachi . . . It was the start of a series of killings that, over the course of the next several months, were to work their way across much of Machado's former territory. Presumably, the trail ended with Machado himself, although his body—like that of Naomi Kharmai—was never recovered.

This missing link did not affect the way Harper viewed the outcome. He knew Ryan Kealey better than anyone else, and there was no doubt in his mind that he had managed to track the Spaniard down. To the deputy director's way of thinking, the absence of a body only served as additional proof that Kealey had managed to locate—and eliminate—his primary target. Harper had never been more certain of anything.

He caught himself staring at the door again. Giving in to his jangling nerves, he lifted his scotch, drank half of it down, and thought back to the last time he had seen the younger man. It was three months after Naomi's death, a month before the killings began.

Toward the end of October a private ceremony was

held at the White House, the purpose of which was to posthumously award Naomi Kharmai the Presidential Medal of Freedom, the highest civil award in the country. Kealey refused to attend the ceremony, though he reluctantly agreed to meet Harper in the city later that day. When he finally arrived at the agreed upon restaurant, more than an hour late, Harper was shocked by his appearance. The bullet that nearly killed him had stripped at least thirty pounds from his already lean frame, leaving him looking more like the walking dead than one of the country's top counterterrorism agents. They ordered food, though Kealey left his meal untouched as Harper brought him up to speed on recent developments in the ongoing investigation.

Javier Machado was still missing, but one of his associates had turned up in Paris, a Hezbollah lieutenant by the name of Yassir Rabbani. As Harper described the circumstances, he waited for the inevitable volley of questions, but Kealey simply sat there listening. Later Harper would recall that the only time he had really reacted was at the mention of Rabbani's name, which he'd filed away with a slow, steady blink of his eyes. After another twenty minutes of awkward, one-sided conversation, they parted ways at the door.

And that was it. The last time Harper had seen him. Less than a month later Rabbani was dead, soon to be followed by the smuggler, the money launderer, and eventually, Machado himself. The dominoes falling one by one by one . . .

A gust of cold air brought Harper back to the present now. He looked up as the door was pulled open, but a young woman's indignant shriek of feigned offense, followed by a burst of drunken laughter, quickly dispelled his interest. He took another sip of his scotch and tried to relax. It was an impossible task; there was

too much to think about. Too much to anticipate.
Harper knew that the younger man wasn't happy with
the way Naomi had been pulled into the previous assignment, and as an extension, he felt sure that Kealey
blamed him, at least in part, for what had happened to
her. Or for what he thought had happened to her, anyway.

But not as much as he blamed himself. There could
be no doubt of that. It was precisely as Harper had told
Allison Dearborn. As long as Harper had known him,
Ryan Kealey had made a habit of taking too much on
his shoulders, including the welfare of the people he
worked with. In Naomi's case, the fact that they had
been far more than coworkers served only to compound the guilt Kealey had felt in the wake of her
death. At least, that had been Harper's impression during their final hour or two in Washington. Now, more
than a year later, Ryan Kealey was essentially a stranger
to him, and the deputy director had to rely on Allison's
profile to guide him, if not tell him what to expect
when the younger man finally showed up, assuming he
even did.

What was it Allison had said in her office?

*God forgive me if it borders on psychological manipulation.
But you get him here to me, just get him here, and I'll prepare
you for your meeting with him. And then find a way to live
with this bargain.*

Harper had made his promise, and thanks to Allison,
he had come prepared. Sitting next to him were several
folders filled with the evidence he'd acquired to support his case. Of far more importance were the two
small photographs in his jacket pocket. There was nothing especially unusual about either shot, other than the
status of their subjects, both of whom had played a pivotal role in recent events. But he was banking on the

fact that they would push all the right psychological buttons.

Another blast of cold air caused Harper to raise his head. This time it was the man he'd been waiting for. He watched with rising unease as Ryan Kealey entered the bar, his eyes moving over the scattered occupants, drifting from left to right. Finally, his gaze settled on Harper. When their eyes locked, the deputy director saw the one thing he had not been expecting—nothing at all. No expression of any kind. Kealey did not look surprised in the least to see him, but he didn't seem pleased, either. His face was completely blank.

At least, that was how it would appear to most people. After an initial moment of surprise, Jonathan Harper realized he'd simply needed a moment to reorient himself to Kealey's ways and measure him within his distinct frame of reference. He had known him for nearly eleven years, and he could see through the neutral façade. Even from across the room, he could sense the bitter anger that resided beneath his calm exterior. It had been there the last time they had seen each other, but it had been there before that, too. Naomi Kharmai wasn't the first person Kealey had lost to his line of work. There had been Katie Donovan before her. And even before that, the little girl in Bosnia.

Kealey was still staring in his direction, clearly debating his next move. In that frozen moment Harper felt sure that he would simply turn and walk right out the door. Instead, he started across the room, and Harper breathed a quiet sigh of relief. Despite the assurances he'd given Director Andrews two months earlier, he had known it would not be easy to draw Kealey back into the fold. For this reason, he'd hoped that it wouldn't be necessary, but recent events—not only in Sudan, but in Washington, D.C.—had forced his hand. Now that it *was* necessary, at least in his judgment, he knew that he couldn't afford to fail, and everything would hinge on how he handled the next few minutes.

He watched as the younger man approached. Instead of sliding into the opposite seat, though, Kealey stopped a few feet away and fixed him with a calm, steady gaze.

"What are you doing here?"

Harper did not immediately respond, even though he knew he was pushing his luck by ignoring the question. Instead, he took a moment to look the other man over. Kealey had replaced most of the weight he'd lost the previous year, but while his upper body was reasonably filled out, his face was still gaunt, suggesting that he'd packed on the pounds in a hurry. The lingering effects of the bullet he'd taken in Pakistan showed in the hard lines that creased his deeply tanned skin, as well as the dark shadows beneath his deep-set eyes. He had not shaven in several weeks, judging from the thick, uneven growth on the lower half of his face, and his lank black hair looked as if it hadn't been trimmed in months.

The man's appearance did not inspire a great deal of confidence. It never had, for that matter, but Kealey seemed to have reached a new low in that department. Harper couldn't help but feel that if he were to take away the black leather jacket, dark jeans, and Columbia hiking boots, Ryan Kealey, in his current state, would look more like a transient than the highly trained counterterrorist operative he actually was. Before flying into Pretoria, Harper's primary concern had been whether or not he could talk the younger man into coming back. Now, faced with this less than encouraging picture, he was starting to wonder if he should even try.

Harper shook it off, reminding himself of what

Kealey had done the previous week. On the flight over, he had read a detailed account of the attack on Jacob Zuma's motorcade in Johannesburg. The details of that report, if nothing else, assured him that Kealey had not lost a step in the last year, despite the lasting effects of his wounds. More than that, Harper reminded himself that the man standing before him had never failed to achieve his given objective, and perfect track records were hard to come by in their line of work. That the current situation had nothing to do with Kealey's specialty didn't concern the deputy director in the least. Kealey's skills were not only unique but highly transferable, and Harper had no doubt that he would able to bring them to bear in the forthcoming weeks, assuming he accepted the task at hand.

Still ignoring the pointed question, Harper appraised the younger man carefully, his face giving nothing away. "How have you been, Ryan? It's been a long time."

"Not long enough," Kealey replied. His flat tone seemed to indicate that Harper's visit was nothing more than a mild inconvenience, easily remedied. "Why are you here, John? What do you want?"

Harper sighed wearily and gestured at the opposite seat. "Sit down for a minute, will you? I flew eight thousand miles to see you, Ryan. . . . It's the least you can do."

Kealey stared at him a long while, impassive, then slid into the booth on the opposite side. Harper was momentarily surprised by the man's ready compliance, but he quickly realized that the gesture meant nothing at all. Although it was warm inside the bar, Kealey hadn't removed his jacket, and he hadn't ordered a drink. There was nothing keeping him there but the history between them, and Harper knew that would take him only so far. He would have to get to the point quickly, or risk losing the man once and for all.

"You don't seem surprised to see me," he said.

"When my bodyguards disappeared this afternoon, I decided it could only be one of two things," Kealey replied. "Either someone in the SAPS got the security pulled so they could get to me, or you were in town. I was hoping for the former."

Harper ignored the unsubtle jab. The "bodyguards" Kealey was referring to had been supplied through a directive issued by President Jacob Zuma himself. The orders had been handed down less than twenty-four hours after the failed assassination in Johannesburg. Since officers in the South African Police Service had been behind the attempt on Zuma's life, the entire organization had been deemed compromised. With few options remaining, Kealey's protective detail had been culled from the ranks of the South African Army. His personal security team consisted of four enlisted soldiers and one officer, an infantry captain, all of whom had been pulled from their regular duties at Special Forces headquarters in Pretoria.

Despite the lengths to which Zuma had gone to protect Kealey in the wake of the incident, the American's future in South Africa was far from assured. Harper had learned as much through a brief conversation with Zuma himself, which had been conducted by telephone earlier in the day. While the South African leader credited Kealey with saving his life, the fact remained that he had killed six police officers on a crowded street in broad daylight. That kind of bloodshed could not be covered up, and South Africa was a far cry from Iraq, where a similar incident might have been met with a slap on the wrist and a plane ticket home.

Kealey was now officially under house arrest at the Pretoria Hof Hotel, though the term *arrest* could only be used loosely in his situation, if at all. Instead of being confined to his room, he'd been given the freedom to move about as he pleased, which explained how Harper had come to learn about the bar. According to the Special Forces captain in charge of the detail, Kealey had visited the Elephant & Castle on the Selikaats Causeway five out of the last eight nights. For this reason, as well as the bar's relatively secluded location, Harper had selected it as the place he would first make contact. His intention in showing up unannounced had been to grab the upper hand from the outset, but apparently, Kealey had been ahead of the game the whole time.

Harper wasn't bothered by the fact that Kealey had seen him coming; in fact, he was reassured by the younger man's instincts, which were clearly as sharp as ever. Those instincts—as well as his ability to act on them—were a large part of the reason Harper had sought him out in the first place.

The deputy director tapped a folder sitting to the left of his untouched meal. It was stacked on top of two smaller folders, but Harper wasn't ready to get to those just yet. "Do you know what this is?"

Kealey didn't bother to glance at the bulky manila folder. "I can guess."

"It's the official incident report compiled by the South African government following the attack on Zuma's motorcade. Have you read it?"

"No."

"But you wrote part of—"

"I haven't read it."

Harper let the interruption slide, mainly because he didn't have any other choice. Moving his plate out of the way, he pulled the folder in front of his body but didn't bother to open it up. "I don't get it, Ryan." He rested his hands on top of the folder and stared across the table. "I've read this thing from cover to cover, and I have to say, it doesn't make a whole lot of sense. You pulled a gun on this guy Flores when he refused to follow your orders, and you threatened to shoot him if he didn't turn around and drive you back to Marshalltown. Then, less than ten minutes later, you risked your life, not to mention the lives of your principal and his aide, to get him out of there safely. Can you explain that?"

Kealey returned his steady gaze. "I don't need to explain it, John. Not to you. Besides, you already know the answer. I never liked Flores, but he was part of my team. I was responsible for him. It's that simple."

"So you weren't willing to leave him behind, but you *were* willing to shoot him if he didn't follow instructions. Is that right?"

The younger man shrugged. "I wouldn't actually have done it. I just needed to get my point across."

Harper didn't believe that for a second, but he wasn't about to waste time arguing. Instead, he opened the folder and flipped idly through the pages. "There's a lot of uncomplimentary stuff in here," he said. "Flores is just the tip of the iceberg. For instance, a man called Steve Oliphant signed a sworn statement the day after the incident in which he accused you of physically assaulting Jacob Zuma."

Harper looked up to see if Kealey grasped the full gravity of that statement. Judging by his indifferent expression, either he didn't understand the serious nature of the charges leveled against him or he just didn't care. Harper knew that he was dealing with the latter scenario. Kealey understood perfectly well what he had done, and he clearly wasn't about to apologize for it. "He accused you of assaulting the *South African presi-*

dent," Harper repeated. "I assume you can see the problem that causes."

"If it does create a problem, it's mine, not yours," Kealey pointed out. "Besides, why does it matter? Who cares what this guy is accusing me of?"

"It matters because the aide says that you—"

"I saved that man's life, John. Zuma himself says as much on page eighty-four of that so-called report, so the aide can bitch and moan as loud as he wants. I thought you said you read the whole thing."

"I thought *you* said you didn't read it at all."

Kealey didn't respond. Harper closed the folder and pushed it out of the way.

"It also says that after the firefight in downtown Johannesburg, you returned to Kerk Street in time to pull two of your teammates, Alex Whysall and Russell Stiles, from their vehicle, which was knocked out of commission by an IED in front of the courthouse. Both men credit you with saving their lives."

Kealey shrugged. "Whysall and Stiles were marines before they signed up with Blackwater. They would have done the same for me. That's what Flores didn't understand, and that's why he'll have a hard time finding anyone else willing to work with him."

"He'll have an easier time than you," Harper pointed out. "The South Africans weren't the only ones to compile a full report. At the prompting of the State Department, Blackwater carried out its own investigation. The team as a whole was cleared of any serious wrongdoing, but you weren't so lucky. The head office basically laid the blame for the entire incident at your feet. They accused you, among other things, of exposing your principal to unnecessary risk by ordering your driver to stop in a hostile area."

"This isn't news to me. I was there, and I know what happened. What are you getting at?"

"I'm wondering why you didn't stand your ground. Why you let them pin it all on you."

"Why would I fight it?" Kealey asked. "I took that job only as a favor to Paul Owen in the first place. Given Zuma's high profile and the nature of the threat, he asked me to run the detail, and I accepted with several conditions. The first was that I didn't have to sign a contract with Blackwater. The second was that I had complete control over the way I ran my PSD. Since he was willing to meet both conditions, I took the job. Believe me, I didn't want it that much to begin with. Getting kicked off the team is no big loss to me."

Harper took a second to break that statement down. Paul Owen had been Ryan Kealey's commanding officer during the younger man's time with the 3rd Special Forces Group. Later the two men had served together in the 1st SFOD-D, otherwise known as Delta Force. While they were stationed at Bragg, Owen was promoted to the rank of lieutenant colonel and Kealey to major, the rank he retired with in 2001. Over the last few years Owen had been "sheep-dipped," or "borrowed," by the CIA to take part in covert operations abroad on several occasions. Most recently, he'd been involved with the recovery of the secretary of state in Pakistan. He and Kealey had worked on that assignment together, butting heads more than once in the process.

Harper had been as surprised as anyone when word trickled down eight months earlier that Owen, after twenty-two years in the army, had decided to retire as a lieutenant-colonel, even though he was scheduled to receive a long-overdue promotion to O-6. The reason for his abrupt departure became readily apparent when he signed up with Blackwater Worldwide less than a month after separating from the armed forces. Unlike most of the former SF operators who signed up with the company, though, Owen did not find himself back on the front lines. Instead, he took a high-level executive post at Blackwater North, the recently established training facility in Mount Carroll, Illinois, where he currently served as program director. Essentially, he was now in charge of the entire facility.

It didn't surprise Harper that one of Owen's first acts with the company had been to actively recruit Ryan Kealey for Zuma's detail in Africa. It would have seemed like a smart move right from the start, and had he been in Owen's position, Harper might well have done the same thing. Having a man with Kealey's reputation on the payroll would only boost Blackwater's already sterling reputation as the leading security firm in the world. Nor did it surprise him that Kealey had elected to fall on his sword rather than allow Owen to take the blame for what happened in Johannesburg. Harper was sure that Owen had tried to talk him out of it, but the retired colonel had more to lose than Kealey did, and Kealey would have been the first to remind him of that fact. Harper couldn't help but wonder what Paul Owen regretted more—being forced to dump the blame on Kealey's head or recruiting the man in the first place. It was a question worth considering, he knew, as there was a good chance he'd be asking himself the very same thing in the near future.

"So what are your plans now?" Harper asked carefully. "Assuming, of course, that the National Prosecuting Authority decides to overlook your role in the death of six uniformed SAPS officers, where will you go from here?"

Kealey leaned back in his seat. "That sounds more like a warning than a question."

Harper shrugged. "Zuma is under a lot of pressure to hold someone accountable, Ryan. Remember, the South African people didn't see the attack on the motorcade. All they saw was the aftermath, and they're not exactly happy with the way it turned out. You'd be surprised at how many people were behind those six cops you killed. Now those people are screaming for blood. There's no guarantee that Zuma won't buckle under the weight of public opinion, if only to stave off the inevitable for a few more months, and if he does, there's a good chance you'll end up facing the sharp end of the stick. You can see why that would be a problem for us. The idea of you taking the stand in the Pretoria High Court does not make the director comfortable."

"It won't get that far."

"What if you're wrong?" Harper persisted. "Because I have to tell you, if it *does* get that far, the Agency will have no choice but to disavow. Do you understand that? If and when the NPA decides to file charges, you'll be on your own. I won't be in a position to help you."

"So you'd prefer to help me now. Is that it?"

Harper had been doing his best to ignore the younger man's combative attitude, but he could no longer contain his rising frustration. "Ryan, why are you making this so difficult? I *am* trying to help you, for Christ's sake. I'm offering you a way out, and if you had any sense at all, you'd listen to what I'm telling—"

"I don't need your help, John, and I didn't ask you to come here. Besides, I know how this works. I can see through your bullshit. Maybe I couldn't before, but I can now. You wouldn't be offering to bail me out unless you wanted something in return, so why don't you do us both a favor and get to the point?"

Harper exhaled sharply. *Okay, Allison, here we go. God forgive us both,* he thought, then reached into his jacket pocket and withdrew the first photograph. He looked to make sure it was the right one, then placed it faceup on the table and pushed it across with two fingers. Kealey looked down at it but did not react.

"You recognize her?"

"Yes," Kealey said. He was still looking at the photograph, which featured a dark-haired woman in her midtwenties. The aid worker was surrounded by a cluster of dark-skinned children, most of whom were badly undernourished but smiling broadly regardless, just like their benefactor. To anyone who didn't know how the story ended, it probably would have seemed like a heartwarming image. "Lily Durant."

"I'm guessing you know what happened to her."

"I know." Kealey studied the photo, his eyes narrowing, his jaw tensing slightly. It was a nearly imperceptible change in his expression, but Harper, a self-taught expert in kinesics, or nonverbal communication, caught it at once. The younger man looked up and pushed the photograph back across the table. "Is that what this is about? Did Brenneman send you?"

Harper looked at him. "I'd be out of a job if he had any inkling I was here."

For the first time Kealey was left without a ready response. "So why *are* you here?"

Harper slumped back in his seat and let out another slow breath. "You were right," he finally admitted. "About what you said before. I need your help. But that isn't the only reason I came. Give me five minutes to explain, okay? You won't regret it."

Kealey shook his head and looked away, staring absently at a couple sitting a few tables away. Then he returned his attention to Harper, a wan smile on his face.

"I always regret it, John. Every time you come looking for me. I don't see why it should be any different this time."

"You're going to want to hear what I have to say. I know you don't trust me. But trust me on that one point. Five minutes and you'll know everything."

Kealey shook his head again, but he didn't make a move to leave. Harper knew better than to break the awkward silence, though he was sorely tempted to do just that. As he waited for the younger man's response, he thought back to what he had seen a moment earlier. The way Kealey's face had changed with the mention of the president's niece confirmed what Harper had known all along—and what Allison Dearborn had reinforced in his mind. His best chance at getting Kealey back lay with Lily Durant. Or very specifically, with what had happened to her.

Allison had given him what she'd called her "psycho-babble one-oh-one" on the different analytical terms for what drove men in his line of work—a rescue personality, instinctive-cooperative behavior, the Jungian hero model. There had been those, and others he couldn't remember. But when you cut through the obtuse scholarly language, she'd explained, it came down to them being core idealists.

It isn't so unusual. There's a reason the Superman character has been popular with boys for almost a century. He embodies their desire to be identified as strong and helpful. And some of them actually grow up to be that way.

That was Allison, Harper thought. He respected her ability to keep things simple. Perhaps more importantly, he *liked* her because of it. And thank heaven he'd walked into her office, and not some other shrink's, after he was shot. Though he wouldn't have admitted it to anyone, not even his wife, Harper knew he would have never followed through on their first counseling session if she'd flaunted her doctorates and rained jargon on his head.

Harper well understood that Ryan Kealey was not the type to let the rape and murder of an innocent woman go unpunished. He believed he was supposed to be saving lives and righting wrongs. But whether you were a cop, a fireman, a law enforcement agent, or a surgeon, you had to maintain an emotional firewall, a hard line of defense against the stress and disappointment that accompanied those inevitable losses.

How had Allison put it? *Bad guys get away. Patients die. Loss comes with the job when you're in the business of saving lives.*

The problems often came when someone like Kealey assumed personal responsibility for events that were beyond his ability to control. When the expectations he placed on himself collided with reality, and he started measuring himself against failure and loss rather than success. Then *every* failure became a blow to his sense of worth, and as they compiled, they led to a massive guilt complex.

The upshot was frustration, bitterness, rage, and sometimes a blurring or complete disintegration of behavioral boundaries.

Harper supposed he should have understood what he had in Ryan Kealey when he'd first read his biographical data. Years before they'd met, before Callie Palmer and Naomi Kharmai, when Kealey was with the 1st SFOD-Delta, the death of an innocent young girl in Sarajevo had led him to actions that went far beyond—no, Harper had to be honest with himself—that *shattered* any acceptable standards of conduct. The punishment he'd visited upon the perpetrators, a group of Serbs in the local militia, had nearly landed him in a military prison for the rest of his life. Instead, he'd been quietly shifted out of that theater of operations.

Harper knew a little of how it felt wanting to be Superman, and admitted it was a large part of his connection to Kealey. But he'd always had a healthy pragmatic streak to keep his ideals in check. Kealey, on the other hand, had his sense of justice, his moral code, and no tempering characteristics. It was at the core of what made him special . . . and what made him a dangerous risk.

And, Harper thought with a lack of regret he found almost stunning, *what may just allow me to push his buttons.* Regardless of the anger Kealey was feeling toward Harper and the Agency as a whole, he would want a hand in tracking down the people responsible for Lily Durant's death. Or so Harper hoped and prayed. He was banking everything on it.

Kealey had been gazing across the room for what seemed a very long time before he turned back to look at him. As if on cue, he said, "Is this about Durant?"

"Yes," Harper replied. He felt a sense of quiet satisfaction that he'd gotten it right. He really and truly was one calculating son of a bitch. "In a way."

"Don't jerk me around, John. Is it about finding the man who killed her or not?"

"Yes, but there's more to it than that. Much more. Will you hear me out?"

Kealey shook his head again, but it wasn't a refusal. Harper waited patiently. Finally, Kealey turned his attention away from the couple to look the older man right in the eyes.

"I'll listen, but that's all. I'll listen for her."

And not for you, was the unspoken sentiment.

Harper ignored it. He felt a surge of relief, though he managed to keep it from showing on his face. He still didn't have what he'd come for, but at least he knew that he hadn't flown 8,000 miles for nothing. He now had the chance to get Kealey back on board, and for the moment, that would have to suffice.

CHAPTER 12

PRETORIA

"So how much do you already know?" Harper asked, taking a second to glance at his watch.

It was now past eight in the evening, but the bar was still remarkably quiet. Aside from the couple at a nearby table and a few men hunched over their beers on the far side of the room, the place was empty. If it hadn't been for Springsteen's "Born to Run" coming over the speakers at a moderate volume, the room would have been just as quiet as it was deserted. Harper was grateful for the solitude and the music, which served to cover their conversation, though he found himself wondering what had drawn the younger man to the bar in the first place. There didn't seem to be much to recommend it . . . but then it occurred to Harper that right there might have been the basis of its appeal for Kealey. A place like this was indistinguishable from countless other places like it, and that very possibly suited his desires—to simply be somewhere, unnoticed, out of sight.

Harper suppressed a frown. Or maybe he was over-thinking and Kealey just liked the goddamned beer on tap.

Kealey, meanwhile, had shrugged in response to his question. "What I know is basically just what the networks reported. The Janjaweed raided the camp and Durant was killed, along with forty or so refugees. A doctor called it in, some guy from UNICEF, and the embassy sent some people out to identify her body. The ambassador flew out there himself, if I remember correctly. Al-Bashir denied involvement and promised to find the people responsible, but nothing came of it. No surprise there."

Harper nodded again, sat back in his seat, and lifted his scotch. He'd just walked up to the bar for a second round, but even though he'd offered to pick up the tab, Kealey had refused a drink. Harper knew that the younger man's newfound abstinence didn't mean a thing and was probably based entirely on his presence. Earlier in the day he'd asked the SF captain in charge of Kealey's security about the American's drinking habits. The question was spurred by the captain's revelation that Kealey had visited the Elephant & Castle on five of the last eight nights. It had immediately set off Harper's internal alarm.

Unfortunately, the South African's answer had done nothing to alleviate his concerns. Kealey had run up quite a tab on the nights in question, and even though he seemed to handle it well, at least according to the captain, Harper was less worried about the drinking than he was about what was causing it, and wouldn't have needed Allison's input to know it was a manifestation of Kealey's overbearing guilt. He had not been able to forgive himself for the choice he'd made in Pakistan the previous year, the one that indirectly led to

Naomi's death. And he'd been punishing himself ever since. The heavy drinking was only a signpost, a symptom of much deeper issues.

Harper couldn't help but wonder how this internal conflict would affect his ability to carry out the task at hand, assuming he was willing to take it on to begin with. But it was just a passing thought. In for a dollar, in for a pound. Of flesh.

The deputy director let none of this show on his face. Setting down his glass, he said, "So you think Bashir ordered the attack. You think he wanted her dead."

"Actually, no. I don't think that at all."

Harper supposed he shouldn't have been surprised. He'd come to send Kealey into the fire. But he'd also missed him—and the chance to test his thoughts against Kealey's razor-sharp perceptiveness. "Why not?"

"It doesn't make sense, for one thing," Kealey said. "He would know it could only give the ICC and the United States a common agenda . . . and a sound justification to act on it. Russia would kick and scream at anyone taking any unilateral action against Bashir. So would the Chinese. But with the World Court already declaring him a criminal, and American blood on his hands, that's about all they could do."

Harper willed his face to remain neutral. "Arrogance and power have led smarter men than Bashir to overextend their reach before."

"Except Bashir's got something more valuable to a dictator than brains, and that's a well-developed survival instinct," Kealey said. "For him to do anything this drastic, he would need to have something to gain. And there's nothing. In that respect, he's like any other dictator. He's interested in two things—one of them being power, which you already mentioned. And he's got all he's ever likely to have."

"Which leaves money," Harper said.

"Right," Kealey said. "But killing Durant does nothing to boost his bank account. There's no upside to ordering her death, so why would he do it?"

"Pride? Anger? Separately or in combination, take your pick," Harper suggested. He was, of course, still playing devil's advocate here. But he wanted to see how far the other man had thought it through—and was admittedly enjoying it. "The sanctions Brenneman approved back in February are nothing to sneeze at, Ryan. The Sudanese defense minister had his personal accounts in the U.S. frozen and eventually seized. We're talking about several million dollars, and the minister is a first cousin to Omar al-Bashir, not to mention one of his closest advisors. You don't think that would be enough to provoke some kind of retaliation?"

Kealey shook his head. "His only concern for his family is that they stick close to protect him. And if he really wanted to, he could throw him that much money as a bone. It's chump change compared to what he stands to lose . . . enough to prompt a lot of talk, but that's it." Kealey shrugged. "Anything Bashir does to us is going to come back to him tenfold. He knows that. More to the point, he's seen it happen in Iraq. After he pulled out of Kuwait back in ninety-one, Saddam did nothing but talk and wave his sword in the air, and that in itself was enough to bring him down. Bashir knows what he's up against. And I don't think he's behind the attack."

Harper managed to look skeptical. "You realize that opinion puts you in the minority."

"Yeah, I know. But it's what I think," Kealey said. "Tell you something else. If he'd known what was coming ahead of time, my guess is he would have done everything in his ability to stop it."

"If that's so . . . if he didn't give the order . . . wouldn't you say it's a little surprising he hasn't come up with whoever *is* responsible?"

Kealey shook his head. "Sudan is neighbored by something like eight or nine countries," he explained. "Two or three share a border directly with West Darfur. The militiamen could've slipped into Chad or Libya long before the fires burned themselves out at the camp. Or they could have headed into the mountains. Either way, they wouldn't be easy to find, even with aerial coverage."

"But it's open terrain. There's hardly any vegetation. If they had planes—"

"We're using Blackbirds and Predator drones in Pakistan," Kealey pointed out. "The most technologically sophisticated spy planes on the planet . . . and we still can't find Osama bin Laden and his top cronies. I've never been that far north in Africa, but as far as I know, it's the same kind of landscape. Plenty of caves and small villages to lose yourself in."

Harper nodded. Yes, indeed, he'd missed the hell out of this. The thoughts were jumping back and forth between him and Kealey like those brightly colored bouncy balls kids got from gum machines. "And what do you think about what came after? About our response?"

"*Lack* of a response, you mean." Kealey shrugged. "What can I tell you? If I'm right—if Bashir wasn't directly responsible—it's probably a good thing that we didn't hit them. God knows the man doesn't deserve to live, but you can't kill him for something he didn't do. I'd need a lot more than ten fingers to list the problems it would create for us in the region. Just look at what's happening in Kenya." Another quick shrug. "On the other hand, someone ordered the attack, and someone pulled the trigger. Those are the people you have to find."

And kill, Harper thought but didn't say . . . although Kealey's expression told him he knew that was a critical part of it. *Thing is, Kealey, the word is "we." We need to find them. I still need you to realize that. Because as much as we're alike, the very thing that separates us is the thing that makes you the perfect man for this job.*

Not for the first time, Harper found himself wondering about Kealey's quick and utter readiness to take another person's life. It was a question that had always bothered him. Did he feel anything at all for the six police officers he'd killed the previous week? Did his recent spate of heavy drinking stem in part from those deaths, or was it rooted entirely in what had come before? Somehow, Harper doubted that he had lost even a minute of sleep over the dead SAPS officers, which left only the not-so-distant past. In that respect, the drinking could almost be seen as a good thing. At the very least, it meant that the man had managed to retain some semblance of human empathy despite the things he had seen and done over the last twelve years.

The waitress, a slim, attractive blonde in her mid-twenties, approached to collect Harper's plate. She lingered long enough to shoot a meaningful smile in Kealey's direction, but he didn't seem to notice.

A few years earlier Harper would have waited until she walked off. Then he would have made some kind of comment about that long look, and Kealey would have said something back, and they would have shared a laugh. But those days were clearly gone. With this realization, Harper felt a twinge he attributed to some bittersweet mixture of nostalgia and regret swirling around inside him. He could see how far he and the Agency had fallen in Kealey's eyes, and he could see how willing he was to use Kealey at all costs, and both troubled him deeply—especially when he stopped to consider how much the younger man had given his country.

He waited until the disappointed waitress had wandered off, then said, "You were here when the attack took place, weren't you?"

"Yes. But you already knew that."

"What was the mood like?" Harper asked, noting the tension in the other man's voice.

"The mood?"

"Here on the ground. How did people react when they heard she was dead?"

Kealey shook his head slightly, a look of anger and confusion coming over his face. "I don't know, John. What does that have to do with anything?"

Harper, seeing he had pushed it too far, tried to backtrack. "I'm only asking because—"

"I don't care why you're asking," Kealey snapped, raising his voice a couple of notches. A few tables over, the couple stopped talking and turned to look at them. "You said you wanted five minutes, and I gave it to you against my better judgment. I've answered all the fucking questions I'm going to, okay? You said you wanted to explain why you're here, so start explaining. Either that or go home and leave me in peace."

He made a move to slide out of the booth, and Harper immediately raised a hand in a gesture of contrition. "You're right," he said quickly, his voice little more than a murmur. "You're absolutely right." Kealey stopped before he could get to his feet and turned to look at him. "I'm not trying to waste your time, Ryan. I just wanted to get a feel for how it all played out on your end. I'm sorry. . . . It won't happen again."

For a few seconds Kealey didn't respond or react in any way. Then, to Harper's relief, he eased himself back into the booth. The couple was still looking at them, shooting little concerned glances in their direction, and for a second Harper thought they might have to move. But then the couple put their heads together in whispered conversation, reached a decision, and stood to leave. Harper waited until they were completely out of earshot. Then, realizing he could no longer delay the inevitable, he launched into the story.

He began by describing the meeting that took place at Camp David the night Lily Durant was killed. He recounted as much of the actual conversation as he could remember, emphasizing Stralen's hawkish rhetoric and the president's grief-stricken state. From there he went on to describe the next two meetings he'd had with the president.

The first occurred the day after that midnight assembly at Aspen Lodge. Harper had requested an audience through Stan Chavis, the White House chief of staff, and was received by Brenneman in the Oval Office. By that time Walter Reynolds had identified Durant's remains in the charred wreckage of Camp Hadith, and her body was already en route to Andrews Air Force Base. It was the worst possible time to try and talk the president down, but it had to be done. Once again, he implored Brenneman not to make a rash decision with respect to a retaliatory strike but was rebuffed for a second time. If anything, the president was even more distracted and desolate than he'd been the night before.

·The second and last meeting took place two weeks later. By this time the CIA had been effectively cut out of the decision-making process, at least with respect to Sudan, and Harper had been trying in vain to get another audience with Brenneman when the summons finally arrived. He and Robert Andrews had walked into the Cabinet Room two hours later to find the president waiting, along with Jeremy Thayer, the national security advisor, Brynn Fitzgerald, the secretary of state, and General Stralen and a couple his aides from the Defense Intelligence agency. The discussion that followed was both highly unusual and very uncomfortable, at least for the two senior CIA officials. It began with Thayer recounting the incident at Camp Hadith down to the last detail, including the brutal rape and murder of Lily Durant. To Harper's surprise, the president absorbed Thayer's carefully chosen words with remarkable poise. When Thayer was done, Fitzgerald laid out the evidence linking Omar al-Bashir to the Janjaweed raid on the camp.

As it turned out, the case was entirely circumstantial—and that wasn't good from the standpoint of validating an open U.S. response. Other than the thoroughly documented links between the Janjaweed and the Government of Sudan (GOS) forces, the State Department had been unable to turn up ironclad evidence that Bashir had directly ordered the attack. Since Bashir had refused to allow an FBI team into the country, the Bureau had not been a factor in the investigation, which had seriously hampered their progress.

By the time Fitzgerald was done, Harper could no longer contain his disbelief, which had been rising steadily during her speech. The fact that the Agency had been cut out of the loop had done nothing to stop him from compiling evidence on his own, and he was willing to suffer the consequences for launching an unauthorized investigation if it enabled him to bring this farce to a halt. But as soon as he started to make his case, the president cut him off at the knees. To the shock of both CIA officials, Brenneman calmly but firmly ordered them to shut down the investigation, an order that essentially absolved the Sudanese dictator of any blame, regardless of whether or not he was actually responsible. When Harper tried to point this out to the president, Brenneman brought the meeting to an abrupt halt and dismissed everyone present, save for one man. . . .

"Let me guess," Kealey said. "Your friend Joel Stralen."

Harper formed a gun with his thumb and forefinger and fired at him. "Good guess," he said, then finished recounting the particulars of that second meeting. He sat quietly looking down at his drink for a while, then emptied his glass.

"So," Kealey said, "what do you make of it?"

"I think Stralen talked the president into making a bad decision," Harper said. "A decision based on emotion rather than facts."

"And Fitzgerald and Thayer?"

Harper looked at him. "You tell me," he said. "Just so I know my antennae haven't been picking up scrambled signals."

"Based on what I'm hearing from you, I'd guess Fitzgerald and Thayer are somehow involved. Maybe not in a direct way, but certainly on the periphery. I think that whole meeting was scripted in advance, set up as a way to shut you down."

"'You' meaning . . ."

"The Agency," Kealey said, sounding impatient. "I thought I was pretty clear on that, John."

Harper realized at once what Kealey was doing—trying to emphasize the fact that he was no longer tied to the CIA. He was putting himself on the outside, distancing himself from the current situation. It wasn't a good sign, but Harper brushed it aside. He wasn't about to quit just yet.

"It sounds to me like you caught Brenneman off guard when you said you'd initiated your own investigation," Kealey went on. "Is that right?"

"Without a doubt. To be honest, we hadn't managed to come up with anything resembling hard proof, either . . . which is kind of ironic if you think about it. If he'd even bothered to hear me out, he would have been able to shut us down for the right reasons. But the way he did it leads me to think the whole thing was a scam, set up to provide the illusion of closure."

Kealey didn't respond right away. In the sudden quiet Harper could hear the elevated voices of the two men at the bar. They seemed to be arguing about something, though he couldn't tell what. Then the younger man's voice brought him back to the matter at hand.

"So let me try to sum this up," Kealey said. "You think the president is up to something in Sudan. And you think he cut you and the rest of the Agency out of the loop."

"Yes. At least, that's my best guess for the moment. And it appears you'd agree with it."

"I probably would," Kealey said. "From what I'm hearing, anyway."

"Have you ever known me to relay inaccurate information?"

"No." Kealey's eyes landed on his. "But convincing me won't solve your problem. And it doesn't sound to me like you have much in the way of proof."

Your problem. Again Kealey was intentionally—and unsubtly—distancing himself.

"I've got more than you think," Harper said. He extracted a few sheets of paper from a second folder and slid them across the table.

Kealey reluctantly turned them around and looked them over. And while Harper wasn't sure how much he knew about the intricacies of international banking, he would surely know enough to realize that he was looking at the record of a wire transfer initiated one month earlier, on April 30. Sixteen days after Durant had died in West Darfur. Harper waited as he quickly scanned the lines. According to the paperwork, a total of five million dollars had been wired from the Royal Bank of Canada in Nassau to the Paris branch of Bank Saderat Iran, or BSI. Other than the timing and the size of the transfer, nothing about it seemed unusual.

Before he could say as much, Harper jumped in to explain. "All you see there is the SWIFT codes, which is why it probably doesn't make a whole lot of sense to you. But I checked them out. The money originated with the Cowan Group, an incorporated company registered in Maryland. The full amount landed in an account belonging to Saud Bahwan Holdings, a shell company supposedly based in Ankara. Everything I've managed to dig up, though, indicates that SB Holdings is actually run out of Paris."

Kealey slid the documents back across the table. "Okay, but what does that have to do with—"

"I'm getting to that," Harper said. "Four hours after the initial transfer, a man with the proper ID and account number showed up at the Paris branch of BSI. This man, David Khadir, met with a senior manager and started wiring the money out of France. It took about two hours to send the full five million to fifty separate accounts in a half dozen countries, including Switzerland and Luxembourg. I'm sure you know what that means."

Kealey did. "He was smurfing the funds."

"Right."

Kealey took a second to think that over. Smurfing was one of the most reliable ways to hide both the source and final destination of illicit funds being transferred through the world's financial institutions. He'd learned about the process two years earlier, Harper knew, when they had worked with the Financial Action Task Force to trace the electronic funds of an Iraqi terrorist. In fact, Harper had been put on to Khadir and the wire transfer he received one month earlier after going back to the FATF to get the information, as the task force was one of the few official entities that could cut through the red tape so quickly.

He explained this to Kealey. "I brought it to their attention . . . and as it turned out, they already had their eye on Khadir," he said. "The story doesn't relate to us, so I won't get into it. Suffice it to say that the FATF doesn't know everything, including Khadir's real name. He's actually Simon Nusairi, a Sudanese national who'd been living in Marseille till very recently. I've got a reasonably extensive dossier on him courtesy of a friend in Interpol."

Kealey looked at him. "The Agency dealing with Interpol? You must be kidding."

"Who said anything about the Agency?" Harper smiled. "I said it was a friend . . . but we'll get around to that later." He started to push across another manila folder, but Kealey blocked it with his hand.

"Why don't you just tell me why you were looking into this in the first place?" he said. "How does it relate to Lily Durant?"

Harper sighed and pulled his drink in front of him but didn't bother to lift the glass. He realized to his disappointment that it was empty. "After that last meeting at the White House, I started to dig a little bit deeper," he said, gesturing for the pretty waitress. "The fact that Stralen was involved put me onto the Cowan Group, which is actually a front for a secret fund administered by the Department of Defense. It comes out of their operations and maintenance budget. There are six of these funds, one for each regional Unified Combat Command. Essentially, the DOD set them up to finance CINC discretionary projects." He didn't have to explain the term; they both knew it referred to the combatant commander in chiefs of the regional commands. "Usually that means training and joint exercises, but the money can be used however the commander sees fit. There's virtually no oversight. Each regional commander has access to one of these accounts, and as it happens, the Cowan Group is administered by U.S. Africa Command, the newest UCC."

"What kind of money are we talking about?"

"A fraction of the DOD's annual budget, but it's enough to suit their purposes," Harper said. "After the wire transfer to SB Holdings in Paris, the balance in the Cowan account was just under fifteen million dollars. I imagine the other commanders have access to similar figures."

"How do you know this?"

"About the Cowan Group, you mean?" Harper smiled. "Before I was promoted out of Operations, the OMB accidentally sent me a copy of the report." The OMB was a reference to the White House Office of Management and Budget, one of the least effective entities in the U.S. government. "This was when they were first setting up AFRICOM, so with all the paperwork fly-ing around, it's not surprising they slipped up. I filed the information away and destroyed the report. They caught the mistake eventually, but they had no proof I ever received it, so the whole thing was swept under the rug. They never bothered to open a new account."

"They may have let it slide the first time around, but they'll know something's up if you sent this as an offi-cial request through the FATF."

"It wasn't official," Harper said. "I've made a few friends on the task force, mostly because I gave them credit where credit was due. Thanks to my testimony in front of the Senate Intelligence Committee last year, they saw a big boost in their funding. They checked this out as a favor to me. There won't be a paper trail."

"So how does Nusairi figure in?" Kealey asked. "How did you find him to begin with?"

"Once I found out that David Khadir authorized the dispersal of the incoming funds in person, I convinced the bank president in Paris to give us the security tapes from the end of April."

"With a little help from your Interpol friend?"

"And gratefully so," Harper said with a nod. "I flew over and picked them up personally, though. The bank president was kind enough to point Khadir out, and we ran the tape through our face-recognition software. The search came up empty, but MI Five got a hit and sent us what they had."

"The Security Service, Interpol . . . sounds like you've been having quite the house party for spooks," Kealey said. "How do the Brits know Nusairi?"

"He was arrested in London a few years back for as-saulting a police officer during a protest outside the Su-danese embassy. Put the bobby in the hospital. They gave him a light sentence . . . eighteen months . . . but he didn't even do that much time. If I remember correctly, he was out in under a year."

"Uh-huh." Kealey's mind was plainly working. "He must have some major family connections."

Harper nodded. "His uncle was Khalil Osman—the businessman behind the Kenana sugar plantation. His father, a partner in the Kenana development, headed the Sudanese consulate in London for almost two decades."

Kealey grunted. "Did he graduate from Oxford or Cambridge?"

"Oxford."

"Law degree?"

"Social anthropology," Harper said with a small grin. "For all his wealth and privilege, Nusairi was a vocal critic of Bashir who developed a groundswell of support among the poor people of Sudan. They tolerated him to a point, but when he went from advocating civil disobedience to inciting riots, his family intervened to keep him from being imprisoned or worse. And even then they eventually had to disown him to save face."

"Which I'm sure only enhanced his popularity."

"Exactly . . . He became a kind of folk hero," Harper said. "The man who renounced all the advantages of birth to champion common causes. Give him credit—he had the courage of his convictions."

"And a violent streak."

"That too," Harper said. "The Bashir regime deported him, of course, and from there he dropped off the grid. This is the first we've heard of him in a half decade."

"What does Nusairi think of Omar al-Bashir?" Kealey wondered aloud.

"Well, the protest he was arrested at was a demon-stration against Bashir's regime, if that's any indication. Specifically, they were protesting the ethnic cleansing in Darfur. That was about the time it really started to get into the news and everything. The genocide, I mean."

"So five million dollars is wired from a secret DOD account to a Sudanese expatriate living in Marseille. Why? And where did it go from there?"

"Well, I'm sure Joel Stralen could give us the answers to those questions," Harper said dryly, a trace of anger touching his voice. "But I doubt he will. Neither will the AFRICOM commander, though I'd be surprised if he knew anything more than we do."

"So you want to ask Nusairi in Marseille," Kealey said, coming directly to the point.

Harper looked at him. "Our most recent line on his whereabouts is that he's in Africa now," he said. "And I want you to talk to him."

Kealey grimaced and started shaking his head. "I don't—"

"Hold on," Harper said, cutting him off before he could refuse. "There are a few other things you should know before you make your decision." Reaching into his pocket, he withdrew the second photograph, glanced at it, and set it down on the table. Pushing it over, he said, "Do you know who that is?"

Kealey managed to avoid the photograph for a few seconds. But Harper could tell that he'd already heard too much. He could read the physical cues—a slight raising of his right eyebrow, the way he leaned forward in his chair.

Finally, Kealey looked down. The man in the picture had dark hair and narrow, friendly features, and wore steel-rimmed spectacles of the kind that looked as if

they might have been issued during World War II.
Though Harper knew it would have been more than
ten years since Kealey had last seen the face, it was apparent he nevertheless recognized him at once.

His eyes opened wide, and his head jerked up. Staring at Harper, he said, "Where did you get this?"

"Khartoum. The image was captured by a security
camera outside the embassy ten days ago. I take it you
know him."

Kealey nodded absently and looked back at the
photograph. "I can remember teasing him about those
glasses. . . . It was one of our lighter moments in Sarajevo."

"I'm sure they must have been few and far between."

Kealey glanced up at Harper without comment, returned his attention to the snapshot. "He hasn't
changed much in fourteen years," he said. "At least not
noticeably. There are no gray hairs, no new wrinkles,
not even a couple of extra pounds." He sat lost in
thought for a moment, then shook his head and looked
up. "What's Cullen White doing in Khartoum?"

"We don't know yet," Harper said. "But we have some
ideas, thanks to our man in Khartoum. His name's Seth
Holland. . . ."

Harper explained how Holland had talked the detachment commander into turning over the MSG's security footage, despite the ambassador's orders to the
contrary. He explained how Holland and White had
worked together briefly back in '95. The event that
brought them together was the interrogation of a Serb
general captured in Srebrenica in the closing months
of the Bosnian War. Given the fourteen-year gap and
White's minor role in the interrogation, it wasn't surprising that Holland hadn't been able to put a name to

the face. But that didn't matter, as White was quickly
identified when the recordings were sent via an encrypted link to Langley. A twenty-year veteran of the
Operations Directorate picked him out just by looking
at a still image from the embassy's cameras, and the
Agency's biometric identifiers proved the officer right.
The only thing they hadn't been able to figure out was
why White had met with Walter Reynolds in the first
place.

"Why can't you just ask him?" Kealey asked when
Harper was done explaining it. "Call Reynolds up and
ask him. See what he says. He's a diplomat. . . . The
worst thing he'll do is tell you to go fuck yourself. Even
if that happens, you'll be no worse off then you are
right now."

"We can't ask him for the same reason we can't go
to Fitzgerald," Harper pointed out. "Anything I say to
them is bound to find its way to the president, and he
clearly doesn't want us involved in this. We have to
tread carefully if we're going to get any answer. . . . I
can't risk having him shut me down completely."

Kealey thought about that for a second. "Do you
think White is still in Sudan?"

"I don't know." Harper could see where Kealey was
going with this. "It's anyone's guess. Holland has only
four case officers under his command, and he hasn't
been there long enough to cultivate any real assets. So
he's limited in what he can do. He's had a few locals
watching the embassy since we identified White, but he
has yet to make a reappearance. However, another man
has showed up on several occasions, and thanks again to
our friends at MI Five, we've managed to put a name to
the face."

The deputy director opened the last folder and withdrew a grainy 8 x 10, explaining its significance as

Kealey examined the photograph. "His name is Ishmael Mirghani. He's forty-six years old, a Sudanese national and a graduate of Assiut University in Egypt, where he received a degree in electrical engineering. That was over a decade ago. We don't have any record on him prior to that year, but we have plenty since."

"A late bloomer," Kealey observed.

"Maybe, but he bloomed nonetheless," Harper said. He paused as their waitress left a fresh drink in front of him, smiled at her, and reached for it. "How much do you know about the predominant rebel groups in Sudan?"

"Not much."

"That's what I thought," Harper said and brought his glass to his lips. He was disappointed, but he wasn't surprised. Kealey had operated in Africa only once before and never in Sudan. He had no reason to know about the country's politics. "For the time being all you need to know is that the two most prominent ones are the Sudanese Liberation Army and the Justice and Equality Movement, otherwise known as the JEM. Both have been thorns in Bashir's side—enough so that Bashir was forced to cut a deal with them. He later reneged on the agreement, but they're still a factor. Especially now. We've seen a lot of increased rebel activity since the attack on Camp Hadith, particularly in the south, and there has been a series of mass demonstrations against Bashir's regime in the larger cities, including Khartoum. Holland has been sending me detailed reports on all of it, and frankly, I'm just as concerned as he is."

Kealey made a winding gesture. "And Mirghani fits in exactly how . . . ?"

"He was a senior figure in the SLA until recently. A field commander at the very least."

"He isn't with the group any longer?"

Harper shook his head. "We believe he may have left and founded his own offshoot," he said. "The Darfur People's Army."

"Original." Kealey chuckled a little.

"What can I tell you?" Harper said. "Anyway, so far Mirghani's managed to stay off the regime's radar. And ours, for the most part. We don't know why he left the SLA. Nor do we know whether he's still connected to the group, or gone completely off on his own toot, or formed affiliations with other rebel factions . . . the JEM being a possibility. Either way, it makes me think something's brewing in the hinterlands."

Kealey nodded thoughtfully and said nothing.

A long moment passed. Sipping his drink, Harper rode out the silence. The escalating situation in Sudan—particularly in Darfur—had been all over the news for the past several weeks, and he supposed he'd understated just how serious it was. To put it bluntly, the country was on the verge of a full-blown revolution.

"So what was Mirghani doing at the embassy?"

"We don't know. All we know for sure is that he met with Reynolds on three separate occasions, and each time he left with the MSG's security footage. According to Holland, Reynolds ordered the detachment commander to turn over the disks, just like he did with White. We have no idea what they've been talking about, but we're ninety percent sure Mirghani is working with White. Or for him, maybe."

"I assume you've tried following him."

Harper nodded. "We've tried, sure. But the man knows what to look for. He's different from most of the rebels in that respect. Whoever trained him did a damn good job. . . . We haven't been able to track him. He shakes the surveillance every time." A shrug. "I suppose it doesn't help that we're using locals and not trained officers. The problem is that Mirghani would spot our men in a matter of minutes, and we can't risk losing him altogether."

"Fair enough. But how is Mirghani tied in with White?"

"We don't know that, either," Harper admitted. "What we do know is that Mirghani can be directly linked to Simon Nusairi. They're cousins. First cousins, related by blood. I guess family makes the world go round."

"And here I thought it was money."

Harper shrugged. "In this case the two are inseparable."

Kealey showed the faintest grin. Watching him, Harper almost could have imagined this was another time and place. Say, five years ago at the Dubliner Pub in D.C. Kealey had liked the amber draught ale and hot corned beef sandwiches. He'd usually gone for Guinness and the shepherd's pie.

Harper reached for his whiskey and drank in silence.

"Okay," Kealey said after a while. His thin smile was gone. "So what do we have here? One month ago five million dollars disappears from a secret DOD slush fund. Soon thereafter it lands with Nusairi, a Sudanese national living in France. Nusairi is wholly opposed to Bashir's regime, just like his cousin, who is almost certainly working with Cullen White, a disgraced former CIA officer. It seems pretty clear that the money was meant for White to disperse all along."

Harper nodded. "That would be my guess as well," he said.

"But what's he using it for?"

"That's another question we can't answer right now," Harper said. "But the recent upheaval can't be a coincidence. The demonstrations, the increased rebel activity in the south . . . I just don't buy the timing. Nor do I believe a word of that meeting I had to sit through in

April. Stralen is up to something, and he's managed to pull the president into it. Fitzgerald and Thayer are involved, too, and they're doing their best to shut the Agency out. I want to know what's happening, Ryan. So does the director, and that's why I'm here. We want you to talk to Nusairi. We need you to figure out what's going on in Sudan."

"Now there's a surprise." Kealey pushed the photograph of Mirghani back across the table. "And what exactly do you want from me? Am I supposed to talk to Nusairi, or would you like me to the find the man who killed Lily Durant? Because last time I checked, we don't have any idea who did it, and Bashir certainly isn't about to hand him over, assuming he even knows who's responsible."

"We're hoping Nusairi might be able to shed some light on that."

Kealey shook his head in disbelief. "That's a stretch, John. I can't believe you don't realize it. There's nothing to indicate that Nusairi is linked to the men who raided the camp. If your theory is right, and Nusairi is opposed to Bashir's regime, we're looking at the exact opposite scenario. If he knew who did it, he would have already made it public."

Harper straightened in his seat. "Maybe you're right, Ryan," he said. "But I haven't told you it's going to be easy. Nusairi is our starting point, and we have no choice but to see where he takes us. Right now he's all we have."

"He's all *you* have," Kealey corrected. His eyes locked with Harper's. "I'm sorry. But I want no part of this."

He started to slide out of the booth, and Harper knew it was time to bring out his hole card. *Okay, Allison, here we go into the proverbial breach. For the sake of every-*

*one involved, I hope it's worth bulldozing through all those
lines of ethicality you talked about.*

"How do you put relative value on good people's
lives, Ryan?" he said. "I'm just wondering."

Kealey paused, staring at him. "What are you talking
about?"

Harper put his hands out in front of him, palms up
in the air, as if they were two sides of a scale. "Here's Lily
Durant," he said, motioning with his right hand. "And
here's Naomi Kharmai." He moved his left hand. "I'm
just trying to understand the way you measure one
against the other . . . and then decide the president's
niece had less intrinsic worth. Or was what you did for
Naomi more about purging your own conscience?"

Kealey had frozen across the table, his eyes still boring into Harper. They were suddenly hard as stone.
"You miserable son of a bitch."

Harper remained very erect. He turned his hands
over, set them down flat on the tabletop. "We've been
working with the Feebs to find Javier Machado and
other members of his network. It would help us get to
the bottom of some lingering questions about Brynn
Fitzgerald's abduction. And Naomi's death. But they're
gone, poof, like ghosts after the midnight bells have
rung. No one knows what happened to them . . . which
you might agree is probably for the best overall."

"Is this a threat, John? Because you don't scare me."

"In all the years we've known each other, I've never
for a second believed anything scares you, Ryan." He
didn't blink. "Except maybe failing at what it is you do
best."

"What kind of ambiguous horseshit is that?"

Harper shrugged. "I was actually trying to be tact-
ful—serves me right for overrating my people skills," he

said. "But to answer your first question . . . I consider you a friend, and there's no threat, implicit or explicit, in anything I've said. But I am making an appeal."

"To what? Some kind of guilt complex you've decided I'm carrying in my brain?"

Yes, Harper thought.

"No," he said. "Your sense of justice."

Kealey's lips peeled back in a humorless grin. It was almost a rictus. "Now there's a platform for your high and righteous sermon. *Justice.* For Lily Durant, I assume. But how does she figure into this? I mean really figure in. Because as far as I can tell, it's got nothing to do with finding the people who killed her and everything to do with settling some kind of interagency feud."

"You're dead wrong," Harper said with an adamant shake of his head. "In fact, we—that is, the director and I—agree that finding the man who pulled the trigger in West Darfur might be the only thing that can bring this all to a halt. Everything Stralen has done so far has been because of what happened to Durant."

"Except it doesn't seem Stralen has done anything without the president's approval."

"Come on, Ryan. You're acting like you haven't heard a word out of my mouth. If Lily Durant hadn't been the president's niece, or if they hadn't been as close as they were, maybe Stralen wouldn't have been able to talk him into it . . . whatever the hell 'it' may be. But she *was* his niece, and they *were* close, and he's been making political decisions based on misplaced emotion."

Kealey shook his head. "I've got news for you, John. Lily Durant can't be brought back to life. No matter what the hell we do."

We. Harper filled his lungs with air, exhaled slowly through his mouth. There you had it—the word he'd wanted to hear. Allison had more than earned her chit.

"No," he said. "She can't. But if you can find the man who killed her, we can take the emotional element out of it. Perhaps then he'll be more likely to listen to reason."

Kealey gave him a long look, settling back into the booth. "And justice will have been served. Is that right?"

Harper's smile was tinged with sadness.

"As much as it can be," he said.

CHAPTER 13

NORTH DARFUR

The Beechcraft A36 Bonanza wasn't much of a plane, even by North Africa's lax aeronautical standards. Certainly, it would never have passed an FAA inspection. The exterior was painted eggshell white with a brown stripe running the length of the fuselage, a dated color scheme betraying the aircraft's twenty-nine years of service. Fresh paint on the port wing hinted at recent damage to the wing's leading edge, a defect that would have grounded any pilot with an ounce of concern for the lives of his passengers. But for all its faults, the single-prop plane was ideal for the ninety-minute flight from Khartoum to Nyala Airport. They were now less than twenty minutes out, having departed the Sudanese capital just after eight that evening, and both passengers were eager to get on the ground, though only one showed any sign of his inner turmoil. Ismael Mirghani was sweating profusely, despite the frigid air inside the cabin, and his hands were in constant motion, searching for some way to fill the time.

The second passenger was oblivious to Mirghani's fidgeting. His interest was fixed on the reading material he'd picked up at Khartoum International. *Al-Rayaam* was by far the largest and oldest newspaper in Sudan. It could trace its roots back to the 1940s, but as he read through the headlines, Cullen White was disappointed to see that its reputation for honest, straightforward reporting was completely undeserved. As far as he could tell, *Al-Rayaam* was nothing but another mouthpiece for the Sudanese president. The paper neglected to mention the demonstrations that had taken place the day before in Zalingei, Tulus, and Al-Fashir. Even the massive protest in Khartoum—a demonstration that had cost White more than three hundred thousand dollars in bribes and "donations" to organize—had been largely ignored.

That in particular bothered him more than he cared to admit.

The article he was looking for was buried in the back of the political section, a bad sign right from the start. Anything that showed Bashir in a positive light would have appeared on the front page, but the fact that they'd printed the story at all meant they had skewed the facts to their liking. When White finally managed to find the passage, he read through it quickly:

> *Approximately three hundred students gathered in Martyrs Square outside the presidential palace Tuesday to protest the ongoing violence in West Darfur, despite clear indications that the army has been working hand in hand with local leaders to ease the SLA's stranglehold on the region. According to Deputy Police Commander Mohammed Najib al-Tayeb, the incident outside the palace could have been easily avoided.*
>
> *"These young men were clearly misguided," al-Tayeb*

said in a written statement to the press. "For this reason alone, it is difficult to hold them accountable. In many ways they are victims themselves. Victims of Zionist propaganda and colonial lies, and I sincerely hope that they use this opportunity to examine their choices. If they hope one day to have a country of their own, they must learn to stand as one, united against the imperialists."

The deputy commander was pleased to announce that the dispersal of the crowd resulted in no serious injuries, though he noted that additional police units had been dispatched around the square to prevent another such incident.

White lowered the paper and shook his head in disgust. He had watched the demonstration gather outside the palace from the safety of a nearby rooftop and had seen what had actually transpired. Needless to say, it was nothing like what the paper reported. More than 4,000 people had been in attendance that day, and they had not run at the first sign of trouble, holding their ground against the rapid response of the state police and the brutal tactics they'd employed to put down the revolt. By the time the crowd eventually broke up, White had lost track of how many ambulances had come and gone. And though he didn't have access to any hard numbers, he guessed that at least 100 protesters had been taken into custody before the square was finally cleared of people. The brutal efficiency of the state police made him grateful he had not tried to recruit their deputy commander, an act that would have surely resulted in his immediate arrest.

It was disheartening to see that his work was being so thoroughly dismissed by Sudan's major news agencies, but with just five weeks in-country, he was already mak-

ing some serious inroads, and he knew it was just a matter of time before the truth came out. To a certain extent, the regime could control what was printed, but
many of Sudan's most popular publications had flour-
ished regardless, including the *Tribune* and the *Mirror*,
two of the more successful independents. It was no coincidence that the former was based in Paris and the
latter in Kenya. For Sudanese nationals, freedom of the
press was something that could be found only online or
outside the country, but it *could* be found. Sudan was
not immune to external influence.

White couldn't help but smile at the thought; he was
proving as much with each passing day.

It had been ten days since he'd visited Walter
Reynolds at the embassy in Khartoum, and he'd accomplished a great deal in the interim. He'd met quietly
with public figures in and around Khartoum and the
capital cities of the three federal states in Darfur: Al-
Fashir, Al-Geneina, and Nyala, his current destination.
Prior to the meeting with the ambassador, he'd spent
several days in Juba, the regional capital of Southern
Sudan, where he'd worked with the local SLA commander to stage a large demonstration in Buluk Square.
That event had cost the U.S. taxpayers a hundred thousand dollars, but it had been a major success. A huge
mass of people had shown up to protest the government's nationwide expulsion of aid workers from the
International Red Cross, the World Health Organization, and UNICEF, the United Nations Children's Fund.
Most of those workers had been based in the south,
where they had been in the midst of a campaign to
eradicate the polio virus, which had popped up six
months earlier, after seven years in remission. More
than 400 children had been infected in Juba alone, and

with the aid workers out of the picture, it seemed likely the virus would continue to spread. The epidemic had almost been enough to incite a revolt on its own, and with the support of the SLA, which carried a great deal of sway in the area, White had convinced the locals to stand together for much less than he'd initially anticipated. Most of the funds he'd dispersed in Juba had gone to families affected by the polio outbreak, and that was money he didn't mind spending.

He put the paper aside and stared out the window, letting his mind drift. Technically, there was nothing surprising about the way things had progressed. He was, after all, adhering to the timeline they'd developed during those endless meetings at State, but he'd never really expected things to go according to plan. Even before his plane touched down in Khartoum, he'd come to terms with the fact that something would happen to throw him off track. Something to delay his forward progress. But much to his surprise it had never happened, and now he was about to finalize the arrangements they had made back in April. The importance of the meeting he was about to attend could not be overstated. As it stood, the work he'd accomplished over the past five weeks could all be undone with a single call, but that was about to change. The window for retreat was rapidly closing, and in less than two hours there would be no turning back.

White smiled to himself as he gazed into the pitch-black night. Everything was coming together as planned, and he had accomplished most of it all by himself, circumventing Bashir's regime at every turn. As Harold Traylor, he had entered Sudan on a false passport without incident, a remarkable feat given the countrywide security clampdown that was put into effect after the massacre at Camp Hadith. As James Landis, he had bought politicians, recruited senior rebel leaders with the SLA and the JEM, and engineered mass demonstrations in five major cities in the largest country in North Africa. As Cullen White . . .

The smile faded, and he saw his reflection change in the port-side window. As Cullen White, he had made mistakes. That was the cold, hard truth, and though he had tried to run from his past, he had never been able to leave it behind. Over the years he had tried to console himself with the fact that he had been young, that there was no way he could have seen what was coming. But he had never really been able to convince himself. Nor had he been able to convince his immediate supervisors. As far as they were concerned, his age was no excuse for what he had done, or rather, for what he had failed to prevent, and they had reacted accordingly. He'd been with the Operations Directorate for less than a year when Jonathan Harper, the DDO at the time, had brought him back to Langley to ask for his resignation in person. That was in '96, a few months after the incident that marked the end of his career with the Central Intelligence Agency.

The ensuing years had seen him drift from one meaningless government job to the next. After his embarrassing departure from the DO, he was shuttled over to State, where he worked as a passport specialist at the Washington Passport Agency, a consular officer in Gabon, and a cultural attaché in Dubai. Those were just a few of the figurehead titles they had seen fit to saddle him with. Middle-management roles in thankless posts, the career path to nowhere—to becoming another Reynolds. White knew they would have loved to cut him loose completely, but it was a risk they couldn't afford to take.

He never asked why they had kept him close, mainly because he didn't need to. Despite his short-lived association with the Agency, he had seen and heard a great deal—much more than he should have, given his age and rank. It would be just as dangerous for them as it would be for him if the truth came out. But they had learned from their earlier mistakes. He was never again placed in a position of authority or given any real responsibility. Nor was there any chance of his security clearance being reinstated, and while his promotions arrived on schedule, his workload did not reflect his seniority. Nor did his staff. In his thirteen years with the State Department, he had never had more than three people working under him. At least to his way of thinking, that spoke volumes about the contempt his superiors felt for him.

At first, he had tried to make the best of it. He had sought in vain for some way to redeem himself, but nothing he did seemed to make a difference. As the years rolled past, his bitterness had gradually seeped to the surface. Much of his rage was focused on the people who'd sold him down the river, his former employers at Langley—and for good reason. After all, there was no question that they were the ones at fault.

He'd been twenty-three at the time, just six months out of the Career Training Program at Camp Peary. *Twenty-three years old.* Even now White had to shake his head at the sheer stupidity of it. There was no way he should have been given the responsibility they'd thrust upon him. But they'd done it regardless, and in retrospect, it was easy to see what a bad decision that had been. Even he could admit as much, though it pained him to do so. . . .

Catching himself, he grimaced and shifted his eyes

away from the window. He did not want to dwell on the past. It had no bearing on what he was doing now, and besides, he was not the same man he had been back then. He had been immature and ill equipped for the work he was tasked with, but those days were over. Ironically, his work with the State Department—which was meant to be more of a punishment than anything else—had provided him with many of the skills he'd lacked as a young operations officer with the CIA.

The three years he'd spent in Jordan had given him rudimentary Arabic, which he later improved on, and an endless stream of embassy functions in half a dozen countries throughout Africa and the Middle East had taught him about the dark side of diplomacy. He'd learned how to spot the intelligence officers posing as minor functionaries, and an interview with a stunning female reporter from *Khoa Ditore*—a supposedly independent newspaper in Kosovo—had shown him just how far the host government was sometimes willing to go to recruit a source, even someone as lowly placed as himself. He could still picture the reporter's silky black hair, bloodred lips and full, perfectly formed breasts. He remembered the way she had leaned forward to give him a glimpse of her cleavage, the smell of her perfume as she whispered her proposition an inch from his ear.

White had possessed photographic recall since he was a child, and even now, eight years later, the memory was still enough to bring about a physical reaction. And that was the memory alone; confronted with the real thing, he had not been able to resist the temptation. He had told her what she wanted to know, and she had rewarded him with the best sex of his life, right there on the ratty couch in his small corner office.

The memory brought a smile to his face. White still wondered how she might have reacted when she learned that he'd made it all up, but he didn't feel the slightest bit of guilt. She had tried to manipulate him, and he had simply reversed the process. That was the name of the game. It was also the most important thing he'd learned during his time overseas—namely, how to manipulate people. He'd learned how to determine what they wanted, which told him in turn how to get what *he* wanted. The trick, he'd discovered, was simply listening. Listening to their problems, hopes, fears, and desires. It was amazing what people would say when given the chance, even at an embassy function, where they were surrounded by their countrymen and more than a few of their own intelligence officers, many of whom would gladly kill the loose-lipped official for speaking out of turn.

Cullen White had quickly seen the value of his ability to draw people in and secure their trust, even if he didn't understand where it came from, and he'd done his best to use it to his advantage. At first, he had passed everything on to the CIA, mainly because he didn't see any alternative. That was back when he still believed in the possibility of redemption. Later, when he realized they would never take him back, he still took notes and retained what he knew, but he no longer shared his insider knowledge . . . at least not until his posting to Liberia.

That was when he had first met Joel Stralen, the man who had vowed to help resurrect White's moribund career. He was one of the few men with the power not only to make that kind of promise but to actually follow through on it. And in the years that followed, he proved true to his word.

Although it had been a decade since their first encounter, White could remember that meeting in its entirety. At the time, Stralen was a brigadier general in the DIA and the commander of the Directorate for Human Intelligence. As such, he was the primary liaison between the DIA and the CIA, as well as the head of the Defense Attaché System, the DOD program that provides military and civilian attachés to hundreds of offices around the world. White had been getting ready to leave for the day when he turned to find the general standing in the doorway to his tiny office. Stralen quietly asked him for a few minutes of his time, and White, assuming he'd done something wrong, reluctantly agreed. Five minutes later, over stale coffee in the ground-floor cafeteria, he learned the real reason for Stralen's visit.

It was the fall of 2000, and the UN Security Council was a body divided. Three of the permanent members—the Americans, the French, and the British—were in favor of imposing limited sanctions on the Republic of Liberia, while the other two—the Chinese and the Russians—were opposed. A similar measure had already been passed with respect to Sierra Leone. Security Council Resolution 1806 had placed an eighteen-month restriction on the export of so-called "blood diamonds" from the West African nation, the site of a decade-long civil war between the sitting government and the Revolutionary United Front. The RUF was a powerful dissident group funded primarily through the sale of black-market diamonds in Western Europe. Those sales were worth an incalculable fortune each year, proceeds that were naturally used to purchase small arms for the estimated 25,000 members of the RUF.

The Security Council had seen evidence linking Liberian president Charles Taylor to key members of the RUF, and it was believed that Taylor was taking a cut of the profits in exchange for funneling the diamonds safely through Liberia to the waiting markets in London, Antwerp, and Prague. Before the Security Council was willing to move, though, it wanted hard evidence in the form of an eyewitness. Preferably someone in the Liberian government, a politician of note who could conclusively tie Taylor to the RUF. Stralen believed that the man they were looking for was the Liberian finance minister, Thomas R. Craven. In his opinion, Craven was the weakest link in the chain, and he wanted White to offer the minister immunity, asylum in the United States, and one million dollars in exchange for his testimony before the Security Council.

White had not felt the need to point out the gross illegality of Stralen's proposal, as it was plain enough to both of them. If the terms of the offer ever came to light, the U.S. government would soon find itself embroiled in a scandal of unprecedented scale. The dangers involved were very real and hard to ignore. At the same time, purchasing testimony from a foreign diplomat was not something easily done, and despite his misgivings, White was secretly flattered that the general had seen fit to entrust him with such a delicate task. More importantly, he sensed that Stralen was sizing him up for something more, and that was enough to seal his decision. He agreed to help, and one week later he attended a function at the presidential palace in Monrovia. Thomas Craven was also in attendance, and White, having already met and talked to the man on several prior occasions, managed to corner him long enough to relay the offer.

Incredibly, Craven had agreed on the spot. Later White learned that the minister had been on the verge of dismissal, anyway, and was only too happy to have the opportunity to turn the tables on Charles Taylor.

As it turned out, he never got the chance. The UN decided to move forward without Craven's testimony, and Stralen's offer was quietly rescinded. It was easily done; there was nothing on paper, and Craven could hardly go public, as that would have exposed his own treachery to Taylor, who was still in power. But the fact that White had succeeded in his task was not in dispute, and Joel Stralen—never one to forget a favor—showed his appreciation by offering him a unique, secret position in the DIA.

A week after the UN announced its decision to proceed with the sanctions in Liberia, they discussed the terms over lunch in a Monrovia hotel, with two of the general's men standing guard outside the door. Stralen envisioned him as a troubleshooter of sorts, as opposed to a full-time civilian employee, and White felt the same way. The offer came with just one caveat. Owing to his previous position with the CIA, which even then Stralen regarded as a rival agency, White would not be permitted to publicly acknowledge his new role with the Department of Defense.

White was not dissuaded by this minor catch and quickly agreed to the general's proposal. In the years that followed, he performed a number of tasks for Stralen while maintaining his pedestrian status with the State Department. The difference between his dual roles could hardly be greater. As a low-level staffer at State, he had spent years shuffling paper, filing reports, and placating angry Americans stuck in foreign locales. As a contract operative with the Defense Intelligence Agency, he had recruited agents, purchased classified material from foreign diplomats, and paid off assets on a sliding scale of importance, ranging from a custodian in the Jordanian parliament to a brigadier general in the Iranian army. Over the course of ten quiet years with the DIA, he had risked life and limb on any number of occasions . . . but never to this latest degree. He supposed everything that had come before was a precursor at best, a practice run for the main event.

White smiled as he considered the irony. In a way, he had proven his supervisors at the Bureau of Consular Affairs correct. They had told him he would never rise above the level of GS-12, and as it turned out, they had been right all along. He would never reach the top of the General Schedule, the government's internal pay scale. At least not at the State Department. He didn't care in the least. His work there was a thing of the past—all that mattered now was the task at hand. What he was doing in Sudan was easily his most dangerous and ambitious operation to date, and it could end only in one of two ways: with complete success and a triumphant return to the States, or with utter failure and a prolonged, agonizing death at the hands of Bashir's secret police. Given the stakes, he could not afford the slightest distraction.

White was reassured by the fact that he wasn't alone. He was supported not only by Stralen but also by Secretary Fitzgerald, Jeremy Thayer, and—if Stralen was to be believed—the president himself. His support on the ground was even stronger, and to White's way of thinking, far more important. Ishmael Mirghani, the man sitting across from him, was his most trusted lieutenant. He also happened to be the first person White had met in-country—it was Mirghani's back garden in which he had burned Harold Traylor's passport less than an hour after landing in Khartoum.

But for all his skills, Mirghani was just one man. Standing behind him was the network White had helped establish over the past five weeks. These were the people he relied on the most, as they quite literally held his life in their hands. His survival depended on their silence, as well as their loyalty. He believed he could count on both. The network reached from Al-Geneina in the west to Sannar in the east, from Ad Dāmir in the north to Juba in the south. It consisted of seasoned fighters with the SLA and the JEM, men who would endure days of torture before breaking their word. Men who would die for the opportunity to bring down the Black Crow, the name they had given Omar al-Bashir in the secret training camps of the Nuba Mountains and the Jebel Marra, the volcanic peaks of central Darfur. It was an opportunity White fully intended to give them, and perhaps sooner than they might have imagined.

Perhaps most importantly, he was supported by the gifts he had brought to this impoverished region. White had seen the poverty with his own eyes, but he still found it hard to believe. In Sudan the average person earned less than twenty-three hundred dollars a year, though most survived on a fraction of that. The contents of the black duffel bag tucked between his feet could have fed 11,000 refugees for three months, were he to use it that way. But that would be a short-term solution at best, and it wasn't part of the plan. The money wasn't destined for the IDP camps of North Darfur, or for the SLA fighters scattered throughout the region. At least not directly. Instead, it was meant for one man, and one man alone.

During the endless round of meetings and briefings at State, they had referred to him as "the Exile." Although the title seemed dramatic, that wasn't the intention. Each of the six candidates had been assigned a code name, all of which were drawn from their respective personal histories. Those histories, in turn, had been compressed into a series of dossiers. The dossiers consisted of each man's political and religious affiliation, criminal record, sexual orientation, and financial status, as well as a dozen other parameters by which they were secretly judged. Considering the stakes, it was a lot to take into account, and the heated debate had gone on for weeks.

Admittedly, the Exile had not been their first choice. A few of the other candidates had less controversial backgrounds, more palatable politics, and fewer skeletons in the closet, which automatically pushed them to the top of the list. But in the end, the Exile was determined to be the person with the necessary connections—the man with the grassroots support that would be needed to uproot the current regime. For these reasons, he had made the final cut.

White shot a glance at his watch as the engines reduced power, the pilot preparing for the final descent into Nyala Airport. The question had been bandied about by a dozen analysts from three different agencies, but its answer had come down to a lone, gutsy decision. It always did.

Joel Stralen had placed his wager on the Exile. In a very short time White would find out if the general's bet had paid off.

Wearing beige linen trousers, a pale blue shirt, and a traditional kufi over his tightly curled black hair, Hassan al-Saduq was relaxing in the courtyard of his residence in Quaila when the cell phone trilled on the table beside his rattan chair.

"Yes?" he answered.

"Hassan. *Kayf hallak,*" said the caller. He quickly shifted from the Arabic greeting to English. "I thought I would let you know we've landed."

"And the car I sent?"

"It met us at once. We're already on the road out."

"Good, good," Saduq said. "Edgard is my best driver. He knows more shortcuts from the city than my wives know ways to charm expensive gifts from me."

Mirghani ignored his minor jest.

Saduq thought he'd detected a slight nervous edge in his voice. "How was your flight, my cousin?" he asked.

"*Ilhamdu lilla 'asalaama . . .* I survived," Mirghani said. "To tell you I'm in one piece would be to ignore the rattling inside me."

Saduq chuckled. "And your fellow passenger?"

Mirghani hesitated at the other end. Then his voice lowered a notch. "I suspect nothing rattles him, inside or out," he said in a heavy tone, back to speaking Arabic.

Saduq thought for a moment. Mirghani and their visitor would not take long to reach him from the dusty airport 100 kilometers to the south, and he saw no cause to be anything but relaxed when dealing with the foreigner. Like himself, Cullen White was a facilitator, which gave them much in common. The difference was that White would believe the men they represented each had at least as much to gain as to lose—that, if anything, the Americans held some greater leverage.

Saduq, however, understood better. He knew the

true endgame, after all. If White even caught a hint of what he had been helping to set in motion—a mere *hint*—he would call their bargain off and go racing back to his Washington puppet master in a heartbeat.

"Does something beyond the crudeness of your transport trouble you?" Saduq said.

"Why do you ask?"

"I know you well enough to hear it in your voice." Saduq shrugged to himself. "If you can't discuss it now, though, we'll talk when no outsiders are present to overhear us . . . recognizing Mr. White's linguistic fluencies."

There was another brief pause before Mirghani replied, "It's all right. I'm simply a bit anxious."

Saduq believed he understood. Ishmael had no shortage of courage; his problem, rather, was a lack of audacity and vision. It had been like that since they were children—Ishmael willing to be bloodied in fights, but always in reaction. It had left Saduq the clever student to engineer the bully's fall, as it now left Saduq the trader to give the fighter encouragement. "We've gone far along a precarious course. And now the goal is in sight."

"Yes."

"Again, cousin, we can speak of things later. In the meantime my advice is to keep your eyes on the short step. Look too far beyond and you'll stumble. It's a lack of attention to the small things that trips us up." Saduq reached for his glass of mixed fruit juice, gulped what was left in it, and produced an audible sigh of pleasure. "I'll expect you within the hour. Tell our guest I extend my welcome and goodwill."

Saduq ended the call and gazed out at the field behind his house, the curved stucco walls of its U-shaped court shading him on two sides from the sun, his loafers off so his bare feet rested on the warm granite tiles underneath them. He had built the home near the waterfall above the village, close enough to the Jebel Marra for its rugged volcanic slopes to be easily seen from his bedroom window. Farther back across the dry grass, beyond a meandering stand of flat-crowned acacias, he could see the favorite among his horses ambling tranquilly in its expansive corral.

He had named the white barb Jaleid, after the Arabic word for *snow*. With its powerful brow, flowing mane, long, straight back, and proud posture, the creature was of rare pedigree, bought from Bamiléké horsemen whose stock had a lineage traceable to the nineteenth century. One of the oldest known African breeds, it was loyal, intelligent, and a swift, supple runner for its size, famed for its ability to negotiate the ravines and slopes of its native environment. The ancient horse people of the northern steppes had rendered the steeds in the cave paintings of Hoggar and Tassili. Hannibal's troops had mounted them in battle against the Romans. Brought to Europe along with other African plunder after the sack of Carthage, they would become warhorses in Julius Caesar's cavalry a millennium later. Centuries after Rome itself fell to conquest, the Berbers, from whom the breed inherited its name, had stormed into the Iberian peninsula atop their backs. In the First World War German occupation forces would saddle them to patrol Macedonia's rugged terrain, while decades later Rommel boasted that his soldiers were prepared to ride them through the streets of a vanquished Moscow in a symbolic show of power and triumph.

It was, Saduq mused, one of the few instances in history when the hooves of the ancient warhorse had threatened, and then failed, to drive their pounding thunder into the minds and hearts of an enemy.

Whether or not Rommel had taken a lesson from that unkept promise, it was eminently apparent to Saduq. However confident one was of one's plans, it was a mistake to declare them in advance. Victory held its own moment for the warrior. Trumpeting its glorious noise before the strike was an error born of pride and arrogance.

Now Saduq reclined in his chair. In a few hours it would become uncomfortably hot and he would have the stallion returned to its stable. For the present, though, both would enjoy soaking in the late morning warmth.

He closed his eyes, relaxed. When his maidservant came out to stir him with the gentlest of touches, he was surprised to realize he must have fallen into a light sleep.

"Yes, Ange?"

"Sayyid, Mirghani has arrived. With another."

Saduq yawned, checked his wristwatch, sat up. Incredibly, he had dozed for almost an hour.

"Give me a minute and then show them out here," he said. "We'll need cold drinks. And something for them to eat."

Ange bowed her head and turned toward the house. Saduq watched her retreat, then meshed his fingers, stretched his sinewy arms out in front of him, and slipped his feet back into his shoes.

A moment later he rose to meet his company.

"Mr. White . . . Ishmael. Please make yourselves comfortable," Saduq said and gestured them toward chairs facing the one from which he'd stood. "We'll have some refreshments in just a bit."

White shook Saduq's hand, looking around the courtyard. The split-level home through which he had passed was relatively simple in design, but spacious and well appointed. The art on the walls was expensive, and its furnishings and fixtures modern, as were the appliances he'd glimpsed while following the young female servant who had met them at the door. Even in the States, it would have been considered upscale; here in Darfur it was lavish beyond most people's dreams.

Skirting the village along the ungraded dirt road that brought him from the airport, White had seen plenty of its more typical dwellings—family compounds made up of crude, rounded huts with conical thatch roofs and mud foundations grouped together within irregular wooden fences. Each hut held anywhere from eight to ten family members, with some having zarebas, or animal pens, outside for their shared livestock—a few cows, goats, and pigs, a smattering of chickens, some bowed pack mules, and the lean, mangy dogs meant to guard them against poachers. Other flat-roofed earthen structures within the compound were used primarily for the storage of millet, onions, and dried tomatoes, or contained basic farming tools, or held firewood, used to provide heat and fuel the cooking pits for the extended family's common meals. There was, of course, no electricity, with the only available water carried in buckets from the *haftir*, earthen reservoir tanks built near the beds of the wadis before the winter dry season approached and the streams ceased to flow for long months on end.

Once, when he had known a great deal less about life,

White might have been compelled to reflect on the juxtaposition of those impoverished living clusters and Hassan al-Saduq's very ample surroundings. Might have spent a few silent minutes comparing the thoroughbred horses in their corrals out back of the courtyard—especially the majestic white specimen in the nearest enclosure—to the bowed, underfed mules he had first seen outside the villagers' huts, and then again on the road, bearing whatever extra eggs, milk, and cheese they produced down to the market for sale or barter. He might have pondered, too, how Saduq managed to exhibit his personal extravagance without engendering hostility among those who owned next to nothing. While it would have been easy to appreciate why they would fear him, their protective allegiance might have been a source of curiosity.

Now Cullen White took it all in matter-of-factly, recognizing the symbiosis that existed between the powerful and the deprived in the world's most godforsaken corners. It was like the relationship between the shark and the pilot fish. Men like Saduq kept dangerous predators at a distance with their own ferociousness, while allowing their weaker followers to stay close and protected, and feeding them enough to appease their hunger. In return, they would always stay close, attaching themselves to his sides when it benefited him. But he would see they never slept with their bellies full or were left without their critical dependency.

He sat, dropping his pack between his legs as he waited for the other two men to lower themselves into their chairs.

"So," Saduq said. "How are things in Khartoum?"

"Tense," White said. He recalled to his frustration reading the newspaper stories on the plane. "I would think you'd have good sources of information about what goes on there."

Saduq grinned. "One can never have too many," he said. "I take it this unrest is because of the economic sanctions?"

"There seems to be a lot going on." White was looking at him. "From what I can tell, it isn't easy to find somebody in the city who isn't upset about something or other."

Saduq grunted. "A pity. Like Ishmael, I was born in the capital. And spent my childhood there."

"You sound homesick."

"It is always difficult when we must remain separated from our roots, Mr. White."

White merely shrugged. That had never been among his problems.

The maid returned with a tray of cold juice, fruit and cheese hors d'oeuvres, set it on the table, and left. White reached for his juice and drank, appreciating its tangy sweetness. He realized he'd worked up quite a thirst during the trip.

"We should get right down to business," he said. "Are you all set for the purchase?"

Saduq nodded. "I will be flying out tomorrow," he said. "By the following night it should be complete."

"A deal is done when it's done," White said, shaking his head. "For me that won't be until the shipment is in-country. In the meantime a thousand different things could go wrong, and any one of them could spell serious trouble."

"I understand your concern," said Saduq. "But this transaction is not the first of its sort that I've brokered. Nor do I expect it will be the last. And my participation aside, it isn't altogether without precedent."

White met his gaze. He was remembering the RUF affair. And Iran-Contra, the ballsiness of which Stralen had always applauded, although he insisted the idea of negotiating with supposed Iranian moderates had been a foolish pipe dream. His objection to the former deal, and not the other, was all a matter of context—one fell within his system of moral and political values, and the other didn't, and for Stralen that made things very simple. But his respect for the general aside, White hadn't bought the comparisons. The ramifications simply weren't proportional, not as matters stood, let alone at the scale they were quickly approaching.

"Precedent or otherwise, I need to know there won't be any last-minute surprises," he said after a long moment.

"If my personal guarantee is not sufficient, then I would hope my cousin's would be, Mr. White."

Mirghani hefted his vast bulk forward, took a wedge of cheese from the platter, and placed it on a slice of bread. "You should have no concerns," he said, pushing the food into his mouth. "The merchants are reliable men."

"They're pirates," said White.

"Yes." Mirghani chewed, swallowed. "But it's in their interest to deliver. They don't want a reputation for reneging on bargains. While I have no doubt they'll spend their skim in the bars and whorehouses of Eyl, it is worth remembering that President Ahmed's Majeerteen clan controls Puntland, where they make their base. And that his transitional Somali government is in need of financial support."

White turned his sweating glass in his hands. "May the circle be unbroken," he said in an undertone.

"What was that?" Mirghani asked.

"American gospel."

Saduq's grin had reappeared, accompanied by a look of secret amusement. "Speaking of America, Mr. White, I believe your Revolutionary army had no qualms about buying thousands of weapons, and millions of pounds of gunpowder, from pirates. Without those supplies they could never have sustained their war against the British."

White regarded him in silence, almost smiling himself now. He wondered what his former bosses in the Agency would have thought if they'd heard him elevated into the company of George Washington.

Finishing his drink, he lifted the rucksack from the ground and set it on the table. "Here you are," he said finally. "With my thanks for the history lesson."

Saduq took hold of the rucksack's strap, pulled it across to his side. And that was that, White mused. There was no going back. For him, for Stralen, for anyone. And in an unexpected way, the finality of it took a weight off his shoulders.

He reached for a piece of fruit and reclined in his chair, admiring the barb in its corral across the field.

"A magnificent creature, is it not?" Saduq asked.

White looked at him, nodding. The broker didn't miss much, a valuable trait in his line of work.

"The horse was bred by the Bamiléké . . . an offshoot of the Bantu tribe that migrated into Cameroon hundreds of years ago," Saduq said. "Driven from their home near the Niger basin by internal conflict, they overran the Pygmies in their new land. Exiles themselves, these tribesmen became conquerors by necessity." A pause. "African history is different from yours, Mr. White. It is an ancient tapestry spun with many recurrent themes. Nothing here is new to us, and all that comes has been seen before."

White continued to regard him. "Should I take that as another historical reminder?"

Saduq shrugged. "I would prefer you consider it a bit of perspective . . . volunteered without added cost."

White considered that for a long moment, nodded. He again felt vaguely as if Saduq was toying with him.

"I'll try not to forget it," he said.

CHAPTER 14

YAOUNDÉ, CAMEROON

Bumping up against the hotels and high-rise apartments between Avenue Monseigneur Vogt and the railroad tracks, running nearly to the wide front steps of the Cathedrale Notre Dame des Victoires, with its pitched gable roof, lofty white crucifix, and swirl of Christian hymns and animist chants spilling on the streets at Mass time, the Marché du Mfoundi was the busiest open-air market in Yaoundé, the capital city of Cameroon.

Displayed under faded, slightly tattered pastel sun umbrellas were meat, fish, vegetables, religious totems, folk medicines, sculpted wooden figures, handcrafted rugs, garments, and baskets, and merchandise of countless other varieties. French and English could be heard mingling with Beti dialects as buyers and sellers haggled over prices at the crowded vendor stalls. Motorcycle taxis and yellow cabs weaved through traffic, cutting off cars, vans, and trucks of assorted vintage, startling pedestrians as they veered past. In the near distance, nestling Yaoundé's spaghetti tangle of streets and avenues on all sides, the Central African hills rose with their shags of green forest, tumbledown shanties, and rugged dirt roads, over which many of the vendors made their way down to the city's market-places each dawn, carrying their goods in mule carts or flatbed trucks, hoping to return with lighter loads and something of a profit before nightfall brought its threat of predatory thieves and bandits.

A short walk from the market, Ryan Kealey emerged from his hotel into the warm noonday sunshine, feeling just a little the worse for wear after his trip, which had been long but fairly comfortable. The flight out of Johannesburg on Kenya Airways had been followed by an extended layover at JKIA, west of Nairobi, where his connection, a sleek Boeing 737, had arrived after an hour's delay for the final sprint to Yaoundé's Nsimalen International. Informed he'd missed his hotel's cour-tesy shuttle, Kealey had hailed a taxi for the thirty-minute drive to the Hilton on Boulevard du 20 Mai. As Harper had promised, a prepaid reservation had been made for him there.

He'd left South Africa at eleven o'clock the night be-fore and spent nine hours in travel, reaching his hotel room at about six in the morning due to the difference in time zones. Gaining the two extra hours hadn't hurt—it had given him a chance to rest up before he met his contact. Though he'd been convinced he was too wired and out of synch to sleep, he'd set his cell phone alarm for ten thirty just in case and actually dozed off on a chair while skimming through a compli-mentary copy of the *Tribune,* the country's bilingual French-English newspaper.

When the alarm went off, Kealey showered, changed his clothes, called room service for some coffee, and headed out toward the market feeling decently refreshed. The temperature even in the full sun was probably in the seventies—about what it would have been in Johannesburg, where the winter climate was similarly moderate.

Now he crossed the boulevard on Rue Goker, passing a statue of John Kennedy on the avenue named after the assassinated U.S. president. Among the people here he was a heroic figure, his status rising almost to the same level of myth as in the States—and the reason, for Kealey, was no mystery. A lifetime ago, when he'd lectured in international relations at the University of Maine, he'd reminded students that the Peace Corps, which most of them believed had sprung from charitable ideals, had actually been brainstormed as a proactive—and cannily pragmatic—foreign policy initiative for staving off Soviet influence in the third world. In Cameroon, then a young republic after gaining independence from French colonialism, Communist maquisards had been entrenched in the bush, launching repeated terrorist strikes at its pro-Western government. It had been an early test of Kennedy's Cold War plan to offer the carrot before the stick in strengthening American interests. And in this country, at least, it had proven an effective tool.

Kealey went several more blocks on the avenue, then turned right toward the marketplace. It was full of activity, people milling about everywhere, some dressed in Western clothes, others in flowing, big-pocketed cotton shirts and pants with embroidery and colorful patterns spun into their fabric.

His dark eyes scanned the street through the jumble

of shoppers crowding the stands—tourists, locals, men and women of every age. Mothers in traditional *kabbas,* many with three or four children while barely out of adolescence themselves, held babies in carriers against their breasts and urged dawdling toddlers along with quick tugs on their wrists.

Up ahead at the curbside, Kealey noticed black coils of cooking smoke wafting from a food stall occupied by two women in traditional robes. Their skin the color of burnt caramel, Kealey guessed them to be mother and daughter, with the younger of the pair stirring the contents of a large saucepan on a barrel-shaped, coal-fired oven. He could smell roasting peanuts and a sweet, not quite identifiable overlaying scent in the thick smoke.

After a moment he checked his chronograph wristwatch. It was 12:20. Still a little early.

There was a gray-bearded man to his left standing over an assortment of knives spread out on a threadbare woven carpet, and Kealey decided to kill a few minutes by having a look. The vendor had a large choice for sale—machetes, bowies, hunting knives, a whole array of combat blades.

Kealey picked up a Spanish-made Muela Scorpion with a rubber grip and seven-inch black chrome finish blade, then simultaneously tested its balance and examined it to make sure it wasn't a knockoff.

"How much?" he asked.

"Eighty euros," the man said.

Kealey leaned over to put it down.

"Sixty, no lower." The vendor lifted its sheath from the carpet to display it. "Come with this!"

Satisfied, Kealey got out his wallet, paid for the knife, and slipped it into his carryall.

A moment later he wound his way toward the food

stall, paused a short distance from it, and stood quietly observing the female vendors. There was something at once sad and impressive about them. It was hard for him to separate the feelings or even know where they came from. He did not examine them any more than he had any others inside him, not for a very long time. He was keeping things simple. Blackwater was done. There was nothing more for him in South Africa. And he had agreed to do a job for Harper. He did not want to look further back than that. Or beyond it.

Kealey checked his watch again, grunted with mild impatience. Half past noon, not early anymore. At the food stall, the elder stood in front of the oven, repeatedly sliding baking sheets out of its front door and shaking their contents into plain white cardboard food containers. He watched quietly as she arranged the containers on a wooden table beside her or held them out to passing customers.

"Are you on line for the honey peanuts?" someone said from behind him. Speaking in a soft, French-inflected female voice.

Kealey turned. The woman facing him was tall and slim, with slightly up-slanted eyes and long, glossy black hair gathered into a ponytail. She had on a light cream-colored, midlength skirt, a yellow sleeveless halter, and open-toed sandals.

"I prefer an African fool," he said and took her hand. "Ryan Kealey."

"Abigail Jean Liu," she said. "Though Abby would be fine."

Kealey nodded, looking at her in silence.

"As far as your mango custard . . . I am afraid you're looking in the wrong place for a chilled treat," she said.

Kealey kept his eyes on hers. "Anywhere else you'd recommend?"

She tilted her head sideways over her bare, tanned shoulder. "There's a delightful café over on Avenue de l'Indépendance, where it is served with a touch of lime. . . . I was just going in that direction, if you'd like me to point it out."

Kealey gave another small nod. "I'd appreciate it. If you don't mind."

He identified her smile as altogether professional. "Not at all," she said. "In fact, I might just stop in and have a bit myself."

"You don't seem too thrilled with the custard," Abby said.

Kealey sat with his dessert untouched, his folded napkin on the table beside the parfait cup. "I've never liked mangoes," he said. "Or cloak-and-dagger routines."

Abby spooned some of her own serving into her mouth. "I'm sorry in both instances," she said. "One is a delight to me. The other, unfortunately, a necessity."

Kealey was silent, thinking. The café, Exotique, was run by an expat Frenchman named Gaston who'd seemed to know her well, engaging her in several minutes of familiar small talk before showing them to a small outdoor table set apart from the rest in the small rear garden.

"I don't know how Interpol operates," he said quietly. "But an arranged public meeting and code phrase are rigmaroles I'd rather have skipped."

"And your preferred alternative?"

"You knock on my door at the hotel. We make our introductions. And then we talk," Kealey said. "It lessens the high intrigue but gets right to the point."

Abby Liu delicately ate her custard. She was looking at Kealey, but there was something in her gaze . . . a keen peripheral awareness, which didn't escape him. "This is Cameroon, not South Africa," she said. "The clerk at your hotel's registration desk, the bellhop, or housekeeper could well be a relative of one of the pirates that raid the coastline. Or a member of the gendarmerie that's in bed with them."

He was thoughtful a moment. "Beware of prying eyes, that it?"

Abby nodded. "And ears," she said, barely moving her lips, speaking in a voice as hushed as Kealey's. "As an American, you're an instant red flag. Putting aside the affiliation you mentioned, I am a French citizen of Chinese descent. If nothing else, that makes me easy to spot and track. An odd-looking vegetable in the patch, if you will. Our meeting cannot help but draw notice."

"And you think a crowded market is less conspicuous than, say, your office?"

Her lips tightened at the corners. "Mr. Kealey, I hardly appreciate you making light of my understanding and experience."

"I'm not . . . and feel free to drop the 'mister.'" He paused, motioned vaguely to indicate their surroundings. "This place—"

"Gaston can be trusted." She'd cut him off. "I prefer we leave it at that for now."

Kealey nodded, his hunch confirmed. The café was an Interpol safe harbor.

"Another point worth bearing in mind," she said. "I use the term *pirates* as a convenient reference. But it is a misnomer. Or at the very least an oversimplification. While some groups in this region are wholly mercenary in their motives, others are political extremists or religious militants. Their connections aren't easily sorted out."

Kealey gave her words a minute to sink in. "Anything else before we get down to business?"

"You should pretend to enjoy your African fool or risk looking conspicuous."

"And if I don't?"

Her eyes suddenly gleamed with humor. "The legal penalty is life imprisonment," she said. "Also, I might be tempted to eat it rather than let a serving go to waste . . . and I try to limit my calories."

Kealey made no comment. Lithe, trim, athletic, Abby Liu had the look of yoga with light weights, and possibly martial arts—he would bet t'ai chi ch'uan. It was hard to imagine the extra calories would be a problem for her.

"All right," he said, "what do I need to know up top?"

She leaned forward. "Six weeks ago a ship loaded with military equipment was seized by pirates in the Gulf of Aden. It was a Ukrainian-flagged vessel, but much of its cargo came aboard in Iran."

He raised an eyebrow. "What about its destination?"

"The endpoint of record was Egypt."

Of record. Kealey did not miss the implication. "The last time something like this happened—must be three, four years ago—the Russians went into an uproar and sent battle frigates from the Black Sea after the pirates."

"Yes."

"That shipment was legal . . . arranged by an officially recognized arms merchant and bound for Kenya."

"Yes."

"But the cargo you're telling me about sounds like an altogether different story."

Abby nodded. "It was going down into Sudan."

Kealey was silent a moment, thinking. "A Russian-Iranian arms deal with the Sudanese . . . in flagrant violation of international sanctions."

"And with the cooperation of certain Egyptian officials."

He grunted. "I guess it's obvious why none of the parties involved would want to make a stink."

She shrugged her shoulders. "Obvious, yes. But it is also an open secret that Bashir's government has its supporters. And that the arms blockade imposed by the United Nations has been porous. As far as Egypt, there are deep ethnic and historical ties." A pause while she spooned more custard into her mouth. "Of far greater significance is the composition of the shipment, and where it may wind up."

Kealey looked at her. "Let's hear it," he said.

"We believe there are as many as thirty-three Zolfaqar main battle tanks. A dozen ANSAT/Sharaf helicopters. An indefinite number and variety of armaments."

Kealey dipped his spoon into his custard and idly held it there by the handle. Back in his Agency days, he'd read intelligence reports asserting the Zolfaqars and choppers were reverse engineered from American technology. In the case of the tanks, he'd heard rumors that Iranian forces had captured an M1 Abrams that had crossed the border with Iraq sometime during the 2003 invasion, using its chassis as the basic design for their own MBTs. The choppers were supposedly advanced, muscled-up versions of the Cobra attack birds that had been gifted to the shah before the Islamic takeover.

He fidgeted with the spoon, half twirling it between his thumb and forefinger. *May wind up.* Given Harper's reason for urging him off on his junket across the African continent, he had a general hunch who the prospective buyer might be.

Kealey took a careful glance around. Either business was slow at this hour or Gaston was discouraging customers from the garden. A glance through the glass patio doors leading to the café's interior told him it was probably the latter—there were plenty of people at the inside tables. But the only others in the garden besides Abby and himself were a middle-aged white couple in matching white shorts who had the unmistakable look of tourists, and a dark-skinned teenaged girl sipping coffee while watching videos on a notebook computer. He was certain none of them were eavesdropping. Or even within earshot if he kept his voice down.

"How did you find out about the pirate grab?" he said after a while.

"With a grab of our own," Abby said. "Pirates choose their targets by different means. Years ago they were mainly opportunistic. But they have since extended their tentacles into customs offices around the world."

Kealey considered that. "If they get a shipping officer on the take, he can tell them where a ship's going. Give them the route it's taking to its destination. Even tip them to what's on a manifest."

"And if he is in the right position, items *not* on the manifest," she said. "Since the nominal buyer was Egypt, the tanks and helicopters were technically legal cargo. We don't know whether any banned armaments may have been aboard, but it is certainly possible."

"So you've got an inside man working all ends against the middle—someone you nailed and cut a bargain with." Kealey was nodding. "He gets paid to set up illegal trades by one party, passes that information to the pirates, then sings to your people about it."

"And in exchange we let him stay out of prison."

Kealey sat there a minute, recalling Harper's rundown on Simon Nusairi and his alter ego David Khadir.

"The pirates... Are they connected to our man from Paris, Marseille, and recent parts unknown?" he said.

Abby gave him a look. "I couldn't tell you with certainty whether there's a direct line of communication between them, " she replied. "What we know is that our man, as you say, has linkages to many individuals and organizations whose reputations are the definition of nonexemplary. One is Ishmael Mirghani—"

"The war chief who cut loose from the SLA and the JEM?"

"Then started the Darfur People's Army, yes," she said. "I see you've been well briefed."

"Well enough to get me on a red-eye to Cameroon," Kealey said. "Now I'd just like to know what I'm doing here."

"I'll come to that in a moment." Abby nodded her head at his parfait cup. "First, I thought we agreed you would have some dessert."

He stared across the table. "You're serious."

"And you are noticeably not eating it," she said. "Have a taste, please."

Kealey frowned, slowly scooped out a mouthful, and ate. Abby sat watching him, that amused sparkle in her eyes again.

"How is it?" she asked.

He shrugged. "Like I'd expect mango custard to be."

Abby chuckled, and Kealey suddenly felt an alien smile touch his lips. It took him by surprise.

"Is the name Hassan al-Saduq at all familiar to you?" she asked.

He shook his head in the negative.

"Saduq has been a middleman for a great many arms deals over the past two decades, primarily between the Russian Federation and various nations in Africa and Central Asia. He has a long-standing relationship with the Federal Security Service."

"KGB lite."

"A fair characterization," she said. "I suppose you could make a similar comparison between Saduq and Adnan Khashoggi. Although not one to hobnob with Western aristocrats and celebrities, Saduq has accumulated substantial wealth and invested millions in Russia's Sudanese oil exploration."

"Are you telling me he's the one who did the deal that the pirates mucked up?"

"We can't prove it but believe that to be true," Abby said. "What we do know is that Saduq is about to meet the pirates to negotiate the shipment's resale."

Kealey locked eyes with her. "To Mirghani?"

"Yes."

And through him to Nusairi, Kealey thought. He stared at Abby some more, blew a long stream of air out his mouth. "Saduq . . . He set up his own customers to be hijacked."

"Again, it is what we believe."

"And when is the meet set to happen?"

"Tomorrow night."

"Here in the capital?"

She shook her head. "In Limbe, if our intelligence is correct."

Kealey drew an imaginary map. The coastal city was about 90 klicks—or 50 miles and change—to the southwest.

"This intel," he said. "How about sharing how you got it with me?"

Abby started to reply, glanced over to her right, closed her mouth. A tall, heavyset man with skin the color of roasted almonds, Gaston was approaching their table from the doors to the indoor café.

"Abby, *mon amie*, please excuse the interruption," he said, flashing Kealey a courteous smile. He tilted his head back toward the glass doors. "It is likely a coincidence—they occasionally stop here as they make their neighborhood rounds—but two uniformed agents of the city council have stopped in and requested an outdoor table of my barista."

She nodded her appreciation. "*Merci,*" she said. "We will be on our way in a moment."

Kealey glanced through the doors as Gaston withdrew, saw the uniformed men standing at the counter.

"They different from the gendarmes?" he asked.

"Council agents are civil functionaries. . . . You might consider them the equivalent of housing inspectors. In Yaoundé they mainly chase off unlicensed street vendors. Their latest big campaign was to clear the streets of call-box owners—people who run phone lines from indoor connections to the street and charge a small sum to customers who need to make emergency calls. Many in the city cannot afford mobile phones and depend on them."

"And how're they a problem?"

"They aren't . . . but they make easy marks for shakedowns." Abby shrugged. "Officials here line their pockets any way they can, which is why I trust none of them."

"What if it's one who's got his hand out to you?"

"I just assume he'll be holding his other hand out to somebody else."

Kealey grinned but said nothing.

"I will tell you more when we have time," she said. "Right now we'd best make our plans."

"When do we leave for Limbe?"

"Tonight," she said. "The drive is only a bit over an hour."

"The two of us going alone?"

She shook her head. "I have some associates who *can* be trusted. A couple with RB Yaoundé—the regional Interpol bureau. And another few that are dependable."

He nodded, waiting for the rest.

"We'll pick you up at nine o'clock," she said. "Walk two blocks from your hotel, turn the corner, wait halfway down the street. You'll be between the Avenue Foch and Rue de Narvik."

Kealey looked at her. "More cloak and dagger?"

Abby Liu shrugged, collected her purse from where she had hung it over her chair.

"Don't push me, Kealey," she said, her eyes flashing again. "It's enough I haven't insisted you eat more of your African fool."

Closed up for the night, the cluster of variety shops had gaudy window signs that advertised everything from used DVDs and children's clothing to cigarettes, aphrodisiacs, and condoms. Kealey was standing outside them in the night when the vehicle pulled up against the sidewalk—a gray BMW SUV X5.

Its darkly tinted passenger-side window rolled part-way down, Abby Liu looking out at him. Then the rear door swung open.

"Better get in," she said.

Kealey leaned forward to glance inside, saw two men in the rear, behind Abby and the driver, then rapped the door with his knuckle as he slid into the backseat with them. As he'd expected, it had the solid thump of 3/16-inch armor plate.

The car swung from the curb, glided off along the lightless street.

"Etienne Brun, Léonard Martin . . . Ryan Kealey," Abby said, shifting around to face him over her back-rest.

Kealey looked across the backseat at his fellow passengers. Sitting farthest from him, against the opposite door, the one named Brun had extended his arm as Abby made their introductions. He was a wiry, light-skinned black man with a shaved head.

Kealey gripped his hand, looked at the man between them, shook his as well. Martin was white and broad-shouldered, his longish blond hair combed straight back from a high forehead.

Kealey settled back, met the driver's gaze in the rearview mirror.

"Dirk Steiner," the man said in German-inflected English. The soft bluish glow of a dashboard GPS unit revealed his sharply angular features. "I have heard much to recommend you, Mr. Kealey."

Kealey grunted. "I hope it outweighs whatever else you've heard about me."

The man laughed a little but said nothing, his eyes on the winding road ahead of him.

"Etienne and Leo are both Interpol colleagues—

we've been working together for a while," Abby said. "They're specialized officers for maritime crime. Dirk's our liaison with the EU's antipiracy task force."

Kealey thought for a while, then shrugged.

"I suppose it leaves me the odd man out," he said. "Since I don't know a single goddamned thing about pirates, boats, or water."

A faint smile crinkled Abby's features. "Somehow I doubt you're being altogether truthful," she said. "Be that as it may, I've been advised that you do have other knowledge and abilities that ought to be valuable to us."

"Namely?" Kealey asked.

She turned around in her seat and then reached under the glove box. When her hand reappeared a moment later, it was holding something low between the two front seats.

Identifying it at once, Kealey reached forward and took the weapon from her grip. It was a Brügger & Thomet MP9 tactical machine pistol with a high-capacity magazine and sound suppressor attached to its bore.

Abby returned to watching him over her backrest as he examined the carbine on his lap. "Does your skill set include using that particular item?" she asked.

He looked at her in the dimness of the SUV's interior, their eyes meeting, then holding steadily. "What exactly are we getting into here?"

"I told you about Hassan al-Saduq's meet tonight, yes?"

He nodded.

"Well, Saduq owns a pleasure boat . . . a small yacht," she said. "We have learned it is currently anchored in a Limbe marina."

Kealey's eyes remained locked on hers. "Is that where you intend to take him?"

"There or in the bay, however circumstances dictate," she said. "Ultimately, it will be your call."

"Why the hell is that?"

Abby did not so much as hesitate for an instant.

"It should be apparent, Kealey," she said. "We're counting on you to lead us."

CHAPTER 15

LIMBE, CAMEROON

"Nicolas, you will please excuse my tardiness?" said Hassan al-Saduq. He sat at the table. "I trust your wait has been agreeable."

Chewing his *tomate cravettes*, Nicolas Barre looked across the hotel dining room, where a sultry blond singer in a black strapless gown was accompanying her own smooth French vocals on the keys. "My men have had enough to occupy them," he said. "Hopefully not too much for their own good."

Saduq grinned. "I'm told boredom is a killer."

"Perhaps," Barre said. His eyes were on the blonde. "But I've no fear of losing any of them to it here at this fine establishment."

Saduq sat at the table, his smile growing broader. Even through the melancholy piano music, his attentive ear could detect the clatter of roulette wheels in the casino across the lobby of the Hotel Bonny Bight.

Barre had reached for his wineglass and washed a mouthful of shrimp down with a gulp. "I suppose the diversions will keep my dogs from raising too much hell, since I won't be back to rustle them together," he said. "It would be best for the city of Limbe—most especially its innocent young women, I think—if I brought them along with me."

Saduq laughed. "I have five wives, and not one would have even flirted with innocence if I'd caught her out of the womb," he replied, deliberately avoiding the issue. He had not gotten as far as he had in life without being cautious, and their transaction was simply too sensitive to be conducted within range of very many eyes and ears. At his insistence, Barre would come onto the yacht alone. Barre, however, had accepted that condition only after putting forth one of his own, stipulating that he rendezvous with a motor launch approximately three kilometers offshore once their deal was cemented. His reasoning was evident enough. The meeting with the launch was insurance—if he did not show up, the sea rogues aboard would be instantly put on alert for a betrayal. And would be prepared to react in an unpretty manner.

Studying the pirate, Saduq could hardly fault him for seeking to equalize the terms of their handoff. He, too, had survived as long as he had thus far only by making wariness his close friend and ally.

Barre ate under his momentary scrutiny, digging into his meal with enthusiasm. He was a whipcord lean Somali with a deep mahogany complexion, a diamond stud in his right ear, and a black scorpion tattoo peeking over his shirt collar. "Will you be joining me, Hassan?" he said, glancing up from his dish. "The shrimp is exceptional."

"I prefer to dine once we've concluded our business," Saduq said. "But don't rush. I would hate to see good food wasted."

Barre took another bite of the tender shrimp, then drank more of his wine as the lounge performer continued singing, her voice sultry and wistful, the notes gliding from her baby grand piano in minor arpeggios: *"Les feuilles mortes se ramassent à la pelle. Tu vois, je n'ai pas oublié. Les feuilles mortes se ramassent à la pelle. Les souvenirs et les regrets. . . ."*

"She is a strikingly beautiful woman," Barre said. His eyes had held on her. "Do you understand French?"

Saduq gave a small shake of his head. "Barely enough to exchange pleasantries."

"She sings of a lost lover, the passage of seasons, and lingering regret," Barre said. "Such an emotional delivery . . . I wonder if she carries some personal sorrow."

Saduq chuckled. "Would you try to make her forget it?"

"Do not laugh," Barre said with a shrug. "I may return here some other night and introduce myself to her."

Saduq looked at him. "Tender soul that you are, Nicolas, I have no doubt you'd be ready with a healing touch," he said. "But I have found the best way to avoid sadness and regret is keeping my mind on one thing at a time . . . and for *this* night it is the business at hand."

A 52-foot Ferretti with an open flybridge, broad sky lounge, and streamlined hull, the motor yacht rocked gently in the berthing area with other quayside luxury vessels, her interior and running lights on.

"There's Saduq's boat," Abby said, pointing out the right side of the windshield. "The *Yemaja.*"

Kealey studied it from the SUV's backseat as they approached. The name on its hull was easy to spot in the streetlights along Avenue de la Marina. A couple of dark-suited men stood near the foot of the dock, no less visible to him.

He shifted his gaze to the glass-fronted, balconied, four-story building up the harbor, its entry spilling more brightness into the night. "Is that the hotel?"

Abby nodded. "We believe our friend Hassan has a silent stake in its ownership—he isn't hesitant to diversify his portfolio," she said. "Still, we've managed to slip a casual employee onto its staff."

Kealey grunted. A short while ago Abby's cell phone had trilled, and when she disconnected after a brief exchange with the caller, she'd reported that Saduq had arrived at the hotel to join another man in its restaurant.

"This plant of yours . . . he's sure Saduq is alone?"

"*She* is, yes," Abby said. "Or entered alone, at any rate. Danielle plays a fine piano in the dining room, has a lovely voice, and is quite observant. Unfortunately she cannot see through walls."

Kealey thought in silence. He was willing to bet the arms broker had bodyguards with him somewhere—besides the two at the dock. And then there was the posse Abby had said accompanied Saduq's contact. According to her information, he'd brought at least four men into the place with him, though they had vanished into the casino once he was seated at his table.

"Take it slow going past the boat," Kealey told Steiner, leaning forward. "Or as slow as you can without being conspicuous."

Steiner nodded behind the steering wheel and moments later was driving by the yacht. Kealey hastily counted three men moving about the deck and guessed they represented close to the *Yemaja*'s entire staff. A boat that small, Kealey figured Saduq could take it out into the bay himself if he had a pilot's license. But if he was going to hold an important meet aboard her, there would be a man at the helm, maybe a hand or two to assist him. You could probably add a galley steward to the crew list, since Saduq would be the type to like sailing in style. That would be about it.

"What's next?" Abby asked from in front.

Kealey had been grappling with the same question. His eyes intent, he noticed a dimly lit outdoor parking lot at the end of the dock, a row of tall royal palms forming the boundary line between its far side and the hotel grounds.

"Any idea who belongs to those vehicles?" he said, nodding toward the small number in the lot.

"It is general marina parking," Brun said across the backseat. "Also for the hotel's staff."

"What about its guests?" Kealey asked.

"The Bonny Bight has valets. An underground garage," Brun said.

Kealey was noting that quite a few of the outdoor lot's available spaces were well back in the shadows. It gave him, if not exactly an idea, then the bare seed of one. "Okay, let's pass the hotel so I can have a look at it," he said. *And a chance to think.* "Then we'll hurry up and make some plans."

Steiner nodded again and cruised by the front of the hotel. Outside were landscaped shrub islands and a circular drive that wound around to a separate drive adjacent to the resort—one Kealey assumed led to the underground garage. Cleverly recessed floodlights illuminated the elongated dome awning over the glass entrance doors, and a white-gloved doorman and valet stood talking behind them in the vestibule.

Steiner had continued on for only a short distance before the multilane Avenue de la Marina tapered off into an undivided blacktop, its streetlamps falling away, a mix of wild saw palmettos, figs, and mangroves shagging the roadsides. Peering through the brush to his left, Kealey made out a black curve of beach in the throw of the SUV's headlights. They'd gone far enough.

"We'd better double back now," he said. "Pull into that open-air lot. Find a space that's dark."

Abby glanced around at him. "Are you going to share what you intend to do afterward, or will we have to guess?"

Kealey gave her a cool look. "You asked me to lead the way on this ride," he said. "I don't remember hearing you lay down terms."

"I didn't," she said. "But I wasn't expecting to follow you blindly—"

"Nobody said you would." Kealey's tone was as controlled as his expression. "I need to figure some things out in a hurry. I also need a pair of binoculars if we've got them. I'll tell you what I'm thinking when we reach the lot."

As Abby reached into a dash compartment for the binocs, Steiner swung the SUV around in reverse, his cargo hatch pushing into the brush at the verge of the road. Then he was driving back toward the harbor.

The glasses to his eyes, Kealey looked out at the *Yemaja* through the SUV's tinted windows. Three crewmen had stepped onto the deck. One was lowering the yacht's sea stairs; another stood over the anchor winch toward the stern. The third, its pilot, was up on the flying bridge. They were preparing to set sail . . . and it appeared they'd be ready as soon as she was boarded.

Passing the hotel now, Steiner turned into the parking lot and rolled into one of its open spaces near the entrance, his front end facing the yacht on Kealey's instructions. Then he cut his engine and lights.

"We're going to hijack her," Kealey said after a moment, his binoculars lowered.

Four pairs of eyes stared at him in utter surprise.

"What?" Abby said. She looked as if she hadn't comprehended him.

"There are too many moving pieces," Kealey said. "We have to simplify our part of things."

They all continued to sit with their attention fixed on Kealey.

"I still don't know what you mean," Abby said.

"Then think about it," Kealey said. "We can't just grab Saduq on the dock and risk his friend bolting off on us. If we're going to be sure exactly what's going on here, we need both of them."

"No, Kealey. You're wrong," said Abby. "Saduq is our link to Ismail Mirghani. And Mirghani to whoever might have—"

"You told me yourself you can't prove anything when it comes to Saduq and the Russian arms deal," Kealey replied. "What exactly is it you figure to do? Wave your Interpol badge in his face and politely ask him to fess up?"

"We can do more than that," Martin said beside him.

"I'll ask it again. *What?* You can't arrest him without a warrant."

"But we can bring him in for questioning," Abby said.

Kealey's grin was scathingly harsh. "I hope that was a joke. You don't really believe he'll talk without serious motivation."

"Such as?" Abby asked.

"Leave that to me."

"Kealey, we can't just break the law and abduct those men," Abby insisted. "*They're* the bloody thieves and bandits—"

"And this is our chance to get them rolling in the mud together," Kealey said. "There's nowhere on the boat they can run that can take them too far."

She was shaking her head. "Say we go along with your idea. There are only five of us. We don't know how many guards Saduq has back at the hotel. The same applies for the man he's come here to meet."

"That's what I meant by moving parts," Kealey said. "We take the yacht, it cuts some of those parts out of the equation. My guess is those two won't have much company. It's obvious they want to put distance between themselves and any possible surveillance. But their business is happening where it is to keep eyewitnesses to a minimum—and I'm betting that includes their own men."

Abby regarded him for a long moment. "Kealey, this is absolute madness."

"Maybe so. But call it what you want. I'm here to get the job done." Kealey shifted in his seat to look out the rear windshield, snapped his head back around toward Abby. "It's push time, Abby. You asked me to lead you— I didn't offer. So do we move or head back to Yaoundé for more of your custard?"

Abby was silent. She'd also glanced out the rear and seen the men leaving the hotel. After a moment she inhaled, formed a spout with her lips, expelled a stream of air. "All right. Tell us what you have in mind," she said finally.

Leaving the Hotel Bonny Bight together, Saduq and his companion turned right, strode by the parking lot, and then walked along the edge of the quay on the Avenue de la Marina. They would have to pass six or seven other craft before they reached the *Yemaja*.

In the BMW's backseat, Kealey adjusted the MP9 carbine's concealed black carry pouch on his waist and then zipped the front of his jacket shut over its spare magazine rig.

"Ready?" he asked Abby.

She looked around from making her own preparations, nodded.

"Okay," Kealey said. "The rest of you sit tight. And stay alert."

He grabbed his door handle and exited the SUV, then moved to the front passenger door and opened it. Abby slipped her arm through his as she got out.

"You're too tense," he said in a hushed voice.

She shot him a look. "What do you expect?"

"For you to pay attention," Kealey said. "Now loosen up so those guards don't make us on sight." He waited a second, felt her body relax against him. *Better.* "Come on, let's walk."

They left the parking lot and then turned up the street, strolling toward the yacht about 10 yards behind Saduq and the pirate. The press of her hip and shoulder made Kealey think of Naomi Kharmai—he would have guessed they were about the same height and weight, Abby perhaps a bit slighter. It was a reminder he neither wanted nor needed.

They continued walking along the lip of the quay. After about thirty seconds he saw Saduq ever so slightly hesitate, cast an unobtrusive glance around, then resume his steady pace beside the other man without giving them another look.

Kealey drew Abby closer and appeared to nuzzle her cheek, brushing her ear with his lips. He could feel the small bulk of his ammunition rig between them. "You see him check us out?" he murmured without slowing down.

She nodded. "What do you think?"

"We're fine," he said, giving her a lover's gentle and affectionate smile.

"So, Yasir, I trust all is quiet on the waterfront?" Saduq asked one of the two guards on the quay in Arabic.

Puffing on a Djarum Black, the guard gave an affirmative nod. "*Na'am, sayyidi,*" he replied. Behind him the yacht's sea stairs had been firmly secured to its starboard side and lowered to the dock.

Saduq stood in the warm breeze drifting off the bay, the spicy aroma of the clove cigarette mingling with the salt air. "A beautiful night is always to be savored," he said and tilted his head toward the man and woman strolling up the street behind them. "Too bad the best of it is reserved for young lovers rather than men of our restless ambition, eh, Nicolas?"

Nicolas Barre glanced in their direction. "I hadn't noticed them behind us."

"Perhaps it's because your thoughts have lingered on the blond songstress—we're not immune to romantic impulses, after all," Saduq said with a laugh. "Come. . . . Let's get aboard before you're irresistibly drawn back to the hotel and her vocal charms."

Barre turned from the couple. Saduq motioned for Barre to precede him onto the quay, and he did so, climbing the sea stairs to the deck of the *Yemaja*. A moment later Saduq followed, leaving only the strollers and his guards behind in the dimness along the dock.

As Saduq and his companion mounted the sea stairs, Kealey gave Abby's arm a soft tug, pausing under the pale silver glow of the half-moon to motion toward the bay. A casual observer might have thought he was pointing out a harbor beacon in the near distance, or possibly one of the constellations visible above the low horizon, its stars spilling across the sky as countless tiny sequins of light.

"You've killed before," he whispered. It was not so much a question as confirmation.

She stood looking out over the water, her features becoming almost imperceptibly tighter. "Yes."

Kealey couldn't have articulated how he'd known. To say it was something he'd seen in her eyes was oversimplistic, although that was part of it, and he paid close attention to what he intuited. But he supposed another part was realizing she wouldn't have gone along with his plan if she hadn't, because killing was essential to its success. He decided to leave it alone.

"Those guards on the dock will be armed," he said. "I can take them. But I'll need you to distract the one with the cigarette."

She nodded her head. "Okay, let's get on with it."

Arm in arm, they walked the rest of the way up the dock, past the bobbing recreational boats, to the *Yemaja*.

"Excuse me," Abby said. "Might I trouble you for a cig?"

Saduq's guards had been aware of the couple even before their employer and Barre turned to board the yacht, but their attention had turned up a notch as they'd come within a yard or two of the berthing area.

His Djarum between his lips, Yasir looked at her in stony silence. He had understood her question perfectly but was interested only in seeing the pair move on.

Abby slipped her arm out from Kealey's and mimed

holding a smoke to her lips. "Cigarette?" she said, tilting her head back in the direction of the Bonny Bight. "I must have left mine back there in the lounge." She sniffed the breeze. "Did you know clove cigarettes were banned in the States? It's been a problem since I moved there. . . ."

Yasir continued to ignore her with visibly growing impatience. Kealey could see a concealed weapon bunching the fabric on the right side of his sport jacket and, while looking at him peripherally, noted how his partner's jacket fell over a holster in the small of his back. Having the weapon in that spot would add at least a fraction of a second to his draw time.

Kealey turned to face the second guard, keeping his hand loose near his hip. "Sorry if we've bothered you, but—"

The Muela combat knife came out from under Kealey's Windbreaker in a blur, his right fist around its lightweight rubber grip even as he grabbed the man's wrist with his free hand, locking his fingers around it, pulling him forward and off balance an instant before he tried reaching back for his firearm. The black blade plunged deep into the man's throat, Kealey giving it a sudden twist, dragging it through the flesh as bright, warm carotid blood came out in a spurt. Then he shoved the man back hard with his forearm, plunging him into the dark water between the yacht and quay.

A pulse beat later Kealey spun toward the one with the cigarette, the MP9 appearing from under his jacket. He jammed the forward end of its cylindrical sound suppressor between the second man's ribs and then moved between him and Abby and squeezed the trigger. The *flump* of the discharging weapon was louder than Kealey would have wanted, its removable tube not nearly as effective as what an integrated can would have done, and he knew the sound would echo across the water. But there was the slap of the current and the soft creaking of wooden planks and the openness around him—and, most of all, an element of surprise, which he hoped would buy him the small amount of time he needed.

The lighted cigarette spinning out of his hand, the guard went limp and collapsed around the barrel of the gun as the 9-mil round's kinetic energy burst his heart in his chest. Kealey bodied into him with his entire weight, pushing *hard,* forcing him off the dock and into the bay seconds after the first man had toppled into it with a dull splash.

Soft, swift footsteps came now from the direction of the parking area—Etienne Brun sprinting light-footedly toward him as they'd arranged, a B&T MP9 identical to Kealey's against his thigh.

Kealey made eye contact with him, sheathed his knife, glanced around to see Abby staring down at the water, her hair blowing about her face. Her posture was wooden, the tendons of her neck bulging out in tight, strained cords.

"Come on, let's move!" he said, placing his hand firmly around her arm to snap her out of it.

She took a breath, nodded. And then the three of them were bounding off the dock and up the sea stairs onto the deck of Hassan al-Saduq's yacht.

"Hell, *look,*" Martin said in the SUV's backseat.

Steiner saw him motion toward the Bonny Bight, flicked his eyes toward his window, and instantly spotted three large men trotting toward the dock through the tall, columnar trunks of the royal palms. Hurrying along Avenue de la Marina, they ran abreast with furious purpose . . . and there was no mistaking them for ordinary guests of the hotel.

"You think they're with Saduq or the pirate?" Martin asked.

"I don't know—but it's only important that we stop them." Steiner slapped a clip into his submachine gun with the ball of his palm and heard Martin doing the same, his magazine locking into place with a metallic click. Then he set the gun down beside him on his seat and keyed the ignition. *"Hang on!"*

He stepped on the gas, shot out of the parking space with a jolt, then swung the steering wheel to the right and pulled from the lot onto the pavement, his front end facing the curb. Gripping his door handle, he braked to a sudden stop between the men and the dock, grabbed his compact assault rifle, and lunged out of the SUV, keeping its armored body between himself and the trio. He had his ID holder in one hand, the rifle in the other.

"Halt! *Halte!*" He waved the ID holder at them. "Europol!"

The men held in their tracks, one slightly ahead of his comrades. Steiner kept his identification in clear view as Martin exited the right side of the vehicle. Using his partially open door as a shield, Martin angled his weapon at them over the top of its laminar glass window.

"What do you want from us?" one of the men said in English. "Let us through—"

"I'm afraid we cannot," Martin said.

"What are you talking about?" The man motioned past him toward the yacht. "We have to get over there. Our employer is expecting us to—"

"That's enough bullshit," Martin said. "Put your hands over your heads. All three of you."

The men just glared at him.

"*Merde,* are you deaf?" Martin jerked his weapon upward. "Let's see your hands in the air *now.*"

The lead man's eyes continued boring into Martin as he finally frowned and raised his arms with slow reluctance. The other two followed suit a moment later.

Alert for any sudden move, Martin slid around his side of the car, his left hand around the assault gun's barrel, his right on the pistol grip, the back of its stock pressed into the hollow between his shoulder and chest. Out the tail of his eye he saw the sparse traffic on the street slowing down at the scene as drivers in both directions began to rubberneck. Then he became aware of something else—the warble of police sirens in the near distance. At least one of those gawkers must have phoned for the gendarmes.

Which, Martin thought, was not the worst thing for him and Steiner. The key was to play the situation to their advantage. The Interpol-EU antipiracy task force was under no obligation to coordinate its efforts with local authorities. A little finesse, then, and their actions here might be explained as falling inside the bounds of a covert investigation. But Hassan al-Saduq had not been charged with any crimes. The task force could not violate the law, and hijacking Saduq's yacht crossed lines Martin didn't wish to contemplate. Or explain.

He would have ample opportunity to consider that later, though. Right now he needed to buy Kealey and the others more time—and make sure these men stayed right where they were.

He glanced at Steiner, nodded for him to frisk the three while he covered him with his MP9. Steiner moved quickly from the SUV to where they stood, found a holstered Beretta under the lead man's jacket, and shoved it into his pocket. The second man had the same weapon at his side—and a Walther PPK in an ankle holster. He handed off both to Martin, who tossed them back into the SUV while keeping his rifle leveled.

"Who do you work for?" Martin asked them. "Is it Saduq or his sailing companion?"

Cold stares in return.

"We already have a good idea why they came here," Martin said. "Tell us the truth and it might help you in the long run."

The lead man snorted loudly, then spat in Martin's direction. Martin just smiled—it was more or less the response he'd expected. His greater concern was that a hurried glance over his shoulder had disclosed that the arms trader's yacht still remained berthed at the quay. He did not know if it meant the American's mad plan— if it truly could be considered one—had led to trouble for Abby and Brun, or if they simply needed more time. But he was hoping he wouldn't have to find ways to buy it for them and stall the gendarmes from going aboard.

Steiner, meanwhile, had disarmed the third man, producing a Ruger semiautomatic from under his blazer. He backed toward the SUV with it as the sirens in the night got louder and closer. Within seconds the police cars appeared, their roof lights flashing, shooting past Saduq's yacht as they arrived from the direction of the harbor.

It had not taken them very long, Martin thought, his back to the vehicles. But he had known their precinct house was close. Limbe was a small city, with its wealthiest citizens and visitors—and therefore those the police most diligently protected—concentrated here at the shore.

The patrol cars pulled up, their doors flying open, uniformed officers pouring out with their guns drawn. There might have been four or five vehicles. Martin was unsure of the exact number. He would neither lower his own weapon nor take his attention off the men on whom it was pointed to count them.

"Drop your gun!" one of the uniforms shouted.

Martin held out his identification in one hand. "To whom do I have the pleasure of speaking?"

"Captain Justine," the gendarme barked. "Your weapon."

Martin spared the gendarme a glance. Tall and husky, he was holding his regulation Beretta out in front of him, aiming it at Martin in a two-handed police grip.

Martin tossed his ID holder at him, heard it hit the ground. "I'm with Interpol, Captain. Léonard Martin. Since you couldn't manage to see my goddamned identification while I held it, feel free to pick it up for a better look."

Justine bent to lift the holder from where it had landed near his feet, eyes quickly moving over it, then shifting to Steiner and the three men still standing with their hands up in the air.

"What's going on here?" Justine barked.

Martin took a long, deep breath and held it, wishing he had the vaguest notion of how to explain.

Aboard the *Yemaja,* the two deckhands had been raising fenders and pulling in lines when they heard the scuffling below on the quay.

Leading the way up onto the boat, Abby and Brun behind him, Kealey came off the stairs to see one of the hands turning from the rail toward the master cabin. His MP9 holstered, Kealey took one running stride after him, another, and then grabbed him before he could run in under the tail of the flybridge, clamping his right arm around his throat and hauling him backward while jamming a knee into the base of his spine.

The deckhand groaned in pain but managed to take a decent swing at Kealey as he was unwillingly spun in a circle. Kealey easily ducked the blow, bounced up on his knees, and punched him hard in the face, smashing his nose with his fist. As the man's legs folded, Kealey moved in to hit him again, taking no chances, delivering a second blow across his jaw, feeling it give at the hinge, then grabbing his sleeve and tossing him against the rail. The man slammed back into it before he crumpled to his knees, spitting and coughing up blood.

Kealey looked around to check on his teammates. He did not see Abby anywhere, but picked up Brun in close pursuit of the deckhand who'd been hauling the lines. The crewman ran aft outside the master cabin toward the stern and, to Kealey's surprise, revealed himself to be armed, stopping in the main cabin just inside the entrance to pull a gun on the Interpol agent.

His assault rifle already in his grip, Brun pumped a short burst into the crewman's midsection. Staggering backward, he somehow remained on his feet long enough to return fire, the round he had triggered catching Brun above the elbow, before he turned in a swoony half circle and dropped to the floorboards in a heap.

Kealey dashed back toward the rear deck. Enclosed by a paneled curve of glass, the main cabin ran the full beam of the yacht to form a luxury suite with leather chaise lounges and teak floors and furnishings. Hassan al-Saduq was on the other side of the window panels amidships, his gaze momentarily meeting Kealey's before he hastened down a hatchway beside the cockpit to the lower deck. But Kealey saw no sign of the man he'd met at the hotel. And Abby? Where was *she?*

Kealey hooked through the cabin entrance to Brun, who stood just inside it, clutching his arm, bracing himself against a ladder running up to the flybridge.

"Shit," Kealey said, eyeing his left shirtsleeve. "That doesn't look good."

"Just a nick," Brun said through gritted teeth.

"You're losing blood." Kealey shook his head. "It won't stop by itself."

Brun waved him off with his right hand—the one still holding his assault gun. "I'm all right," he said. "You'd better get on with things."

Kealey expelled a breath. "Where's Abby?"

Brun angled his chin at the ladder to the flybridge. "Up top," he said. "She went after Saduq's friend and—"

The yacht abruptly jolted as its engines thrummed to life belowdecks, almost throwing Kealey off his feet. He simultaneously grabbed the rail of the ladder and reached out to steady Brun, then stole a glance at the cockpit. It remained unoccupied.

The captain, then, was also up on the flybridge. The boat would have a second pilot's station up there. Kealey drew his submachine gun, gave Brun a nod, and scrambled up the ladder.

He was pulling his way up off its final rung behind an open-air banquette seat when he heard the crack of a gunshot, the bullet whistling past his ear less than an inch to his right. Raising his head slightly above the back of the seat, Kealey took in everything at once: The pilot's station was up toward the bow on the port side of the sundeck, the captain at the throttles. His quarry standing behind it with a pistol in his hand and a brown rucksack over his shoulder. Farther toward the rear,

Abby had taken cover behind a fixed stowage container near the starboard rail.

The pirate got off another shot at Kealey, but it missed by a slightly greater distance than the first. Instead of dropping down behind the banquette, Kealey heaved himself up over the ledge of the flybridge without a moment's indecision, then squeezed a burst of fire over the seat back and scurried to his left. With Abby behind the single stowage container on the right side of the deck, and just the banquette between him and the gunfire, he would have far less protection here. But Kealey wanted to divide the pirate's attention—and aim—by giving him widely separated targets.

"You have a large enough catch down below," the pirate shouted. "Leave me and be satisfied with it."

Kealey did not answer . . . but given their situation, it was hard to see what he meant. *Leave me.* Did the pirate think he could toss them Saduq in exchange for command of the boat? What good would that do him if they were all stuck on it together? Unless . . .

Kealey realized what was happening all at once. The yacht was clipping along over the water now, its captain pushing thirty knots at the helm, and it was obvious the pirate hadn't ordered him to pour on the speed without good reason. He was not taking flight—there was no one in pursuit—and to Kealey that could only mean one thing.

He did not intend to remain on the *Yemaja*, but intended to meet up with another vessel somewhere out on the bay.

The pirates in the motor launch wore head scarves, military-style khakis with swim vests over them, and lightweight tactical combat boots. They were armed with fully automatic rifles and shoulder-mounted rocket launchers, with several wearing daggers or machetes in scabbards at their waists. Like their leader, Nicolas Barre, they had scorpion tattoos on their necks as symbols of their brotherhood.

In the vessel's otherwise blacked-out wheelhouse, the maritime GPS unit presently casting a muted glow over the pilot's face had guided them to the exact coordinates Barre had set for their rendezvous. But having reached it well ahead of the scheduled meet time, they had anticipated there would be little for them to do for the next twenty minutes or so but await the yacht's arrival.

Now, however, the man behind the wheel saw the unexpected brightness of a bow light pierce the darkness no more than 50 or 60 meters off to starboard. Listening, too, he could hear the throb of a powerful engine grow louder by the moment.

Turning quickly from the wheelhouse, he leaned forward against his craft's low gunwale and peered in the direction of the oncoming vessel with his night vision binoculars.

"Asad . . . what is it?"

The pilot looked at the man who'd come up beside him, passed him the glasses, and took notice of the stunned, puzzled expression on his face.

"It must be the yacht," the man said. "But for it to approach at that speed without Nicolas signaling ahead—"

"We'd better hurry up and prepare, Guleed," the pilot said.

On his haunches behind the banquette, Kealey lined his gun sight on the pirate as the yacht raced over the black water of the bay. He did not want to get into a shoot-out here on the flybridge. He wanted the man for information, and that meant he did *not* want him dead. But he had no intention of letting him escape with the unknown contents of the rucksack—a bag he had not carried with him from the Hotel Bonny Bight, and that he therefore had picked up on the yacht. He wanted to know what was in it.

Kealey was fairly confident he could squeeze off an accurate volley even with the vibrating movement of the boat. Aim for the man's legs, with a short three-round burst, and it would cut them out from under him. Miss his target, on the other hand, and all kinds of chaos would erupt. But the alternative was to remain at an impasse until they reached whatever was waiting for the pirate out in the night. If Kealey was going to do it, he couldn't wait.

He inhaled deeply, then held his breath, preparing to pull the trigger on his exhale, the old sniper's technique. . . .

He never had the chance to get off his salvo. An instant before he would have fired, the pirate's weapon abruptly produced a loud report, then a second and third, the bullets slamming into the banquette in front of him. Kealey barely had time to wonder what had prompted his shots before the yacht veered sharply to starboard, throwing him off balance. Then he angrily realized he'd waited too long—they had reached the meet point.

He tried to spring to his feet to return the fire, and the yacht careered again, this time turning even more sharply in the water, the violent motion flinging him onto his side and knocking the assault rifle from his grasp. As it skittered across the deck, he saw Abby clinging to the fixed stowage container, struggling to hang on to it so she wouldn't tumble across the flybridge.

Kealey heard his own furious snarl as he again tried to right himself and saw the pirate holding tightly onto the rail, peering down over the side of the boat. *God damn, God damn!* They'd been taken for idiots, suckered. . . .

The yacht kicked to a halt, its mainframe shuddering, throwing Kealey back onto the deck. Cursing under his breath, he grabbed hold of the banquette in front of him and launched to his feet, but by then the pirate had already leaped down from the pilot's station and was on his way over the side.

Kealey ran forward, grabbing up his rifle as he hurtled toward the rail just in time to see the launch speeding away from the yacht ahead of a churning wake of foam, vanishing in the pitch darkness, taking the pirate and the rucksack with it.

Expelling a disgusted breath, he turned to the pilot's station, grabbed the boat's captain by his collar, and tossed him off his seat.

"Stay away from those controls, you stupid bastard," he said, pushing the bore of his gun against the man's temple with such force, it bent his head back. "You move this boat an inch—a fucking inch—and I swear I'll blow your useless brains out."

Rushing down the ladder from the flybridge now, past Brun to the hatchway and down again, and then through a passage on the lower deck, Kealey reached the master cabin amidships, where Saduq had holed up behind his locked door.

He stood outside the door, inhaled, and then kicked it below the handle so that it went flying inward with a loud bang, the frame buckling around it, partially torn away from the side of the passage.

Saduq stood staring at him from the middle of the cabin, his eyes wide in his face.

"Who are you?" he said. "What is it you want?"

Kealey stormed into the cabin and pushed him so hard that Saduq went flying backward over a chair into the wall, the breath woofing from his lips.

"Who I am doesn't matter," Kealey said. "All that does is that you're going to talk."

CHAPTER 16

GULF OF GUINEA, CAMEROON

"This isn't complicated, Mr. al-Saduq," Kealey said. "We know how you earn your living. We know you came to Limbe to broker an arms and equipment deal between Ishmael Mirghani and the man who jumped overboard with what is presumably a considerable sum of money. We have a good idea about the merchandise on the selling block—"

"If you already know so much, then what more do you hope to learn from me?" Saduq said.

Kealey looked down at him, the assault rifle in his hand pointed down at the floor. They were in the *Yemaja*'s master cabin minutes after he had slammed in its door, Saduq on a cushioned teakwood armchair against the wall, Brun sitting on the bed with his own MP9 on his lap and a pressure bandage around his arm—the wrap having come from a first aid kit they had gotten the boat's captain to provide. Abby, meanwhile, had brought the captain down off the flybridge to the interior pilot's station, where she was presently standing guard over him.

Kealey's dark gray eyes regarded Saduq with an almost casual detachment. "I hate to repeat myself," he said. "But the key here for everyone really comes down to keeping things simple. What we want from you are answers to the questions we *don't* know. There are only a handful that matter."

"And they are . . . ?"

"The identity of the person who made off with the rucksack. And what you think he's going to do with the money now that he almost certainly realizes you've been captured." Kealey paused. "Most of all, Mr. Saduq, we're interested in Mirghani's plans for the shipment, should he get his hands on it . . . meaning the name of its end user. That information would take us all a good way toward getting off this boat. In fact, I can almost guarantee it will eventually get you back to shore alive and in one piece."

Saduq stared up at him from his chair. "Who are you?" he asked. "By what authority do you seize my vessel with impunity and try to intimidate—"

Kealey didn't wait for him to finish his sentence. He took a lunging step forward, clamped his hand under Saduq's chin, and pushed his head back against the cabin wall. Saduq grunted out in surprise.

"You are out of your mind," he said.

"Maybe that's true," Kealey said. "It even might be one of the reasons I'm here. But there's one thing you've got absolutely right—no maybes. I am in command of your ship. My people have boarded her, and from this point on we control where she goes. And decide what happens to you."

Saduq regarded him, quickly summoning up his composure. "Are you CIA?"

"I'm asking the questions."

"Maybe so, but I can tell you are an American," Saduq said. "I have many long-standing and high-placed relationships within your country. If you are CIA, I can promise your brutish tactics will not be taken lightly by those who sent you."

Kealey looked at him. "You seriously believe that's true?"

Saduq nodded. "I am an international businessman, not someone to be treated like a cheap criminal."

Kealey looked at him another moment, then grabbed him under the chin again and smashed him back with greater force than before, keeping his fingers locked around his throat.

"I want answers," Kealey said. "We're staying on this boat together until I get them, do you understand?"

Saduq said nothing. Staring at him, Kealey was struck with an odd sense of dissociation; it was as if he'd been watching the scene in the cabin unfold from some significant remove and taken cold recognition of two things. The first was that he once might have felt a mixture of anger and admiration for Saduq's unfaltering composure. The second was the complete and utter absence of any feelings or compunctions within him at all. It was exactly as he had told Abby before. He just wanted to get the job done.

"I asked if you understood," he said and slammed the arms merchant back into the wall a third time.

Saduq remained silent. Kealey's upper and lower molars clicked together. *All right, have it your way.* He raised his gun and pressed its bore into the middle of his captive's forehead, tightening his grip around his neck, clamping off his windpipe.

"Let's try again," he said in a flat, mechanical tone, looking directly into Saduq's eyes. "Do you understand me? Yes or no?"

Saduq swallowed and took a thin, wheezing breath, his Adam's apple a hard, straining lump against the rigid vise of Kealey's hand. Not letting up, Kealey dug his fingers in deeper, bringing the gun barrel to bear against his forehead with a pressure that made the skin pale around it in a small circle.

"Yes or no?"

Saduq produced a strangled, gurgling sound, his tongue writhing thickly in his mouth, the veins of his temples pulsating, his eyes bulging in their sockets. "*Yeesss,*" he croaked at last.

Kealey unlocked his fingers from Saduq's throat without moving his gun from his forehead. At almost the same instant, he heard Brun shift on the bed, shot him a quick glance, and detected a measure of discomfort in the Interpol agent that had nothing to do with the physical pain of his gunshot wound. This registered in Kealey's awareness with no more emotion than anything else about his situation. It was just another factor to be inventoried should it enter into play.

"The man who came aboard with you," Kealey said, his eyes darting back to Saduq. "Who was he?"

The arms dealer swooped air into his lungs, his chest heaving up and down. "A Somali brigand," he sputtered.

"Does he have a name?"

"He . . . he calls himself Ali."

"What do you mean 'calls himself'?"

"I cannot . . . cannot tell you . . . whether it is . . . his true identity." Saduq pulled in another rapid series of breaths. "He is . . . a lieutenant. Nothing more. I have dealt with his group in the past."

"Its leader, then," Kealey said. "Give me *his* name."

"He goes by many aliases. . . . I know him as Dafo," Saduq said, massaging his throat. "They say he is based in Puntland . . . Boosaaso, Haradheere, or Eyl. But he communicates only via telephone and e-mail, and it's uncertain whether he even resides on the continent."

"And that's the best you can do?"

"As far as what you have asked to this point," Saduq said, looking him squarely in the eye. "I am prepared to tell you whatever else I might know about him . . . and can help with other information you wish to know."

"I'm sure," Kealey said. "Except you're full of shit."

"What?"

"You heard me."

Shaking his head in denial, Saduq began to respond, but before his lips could shape another word, Kealey bunched his collar in his fist and yanked him up off his chair, hauling him forward so he left his feet. He threw him to the cabin floor on his belly, the armchair momentarily getting tangled between his legs and clattering over sideways. As Saduq tried gathering himself, Kealey came up behind him, grabbed the back his shirt, and half dragged, half lifted him to his feet.

"What are you doing?" Saduq wheezed.

Kealey pushed the barrel of his gun rifle into Saduq's back. "We're going up top."

"Why . . . I don't see what reason there is for—"

"Upstairs," Kealey grunted, prodding him with the rifle. "Come on, let's go."

Saduq went into the stairwell and then climbed to the glass-enclosed main cabin, coming up beside the cockpit, where Abby Liu stood with her weapon trained on the captain. At a near standstill in the bay, the *Yemaja* drifted slightly leeward beneath the partial moon, the glimmer of the harbor lights visible far off behind to port.

"Everything copacetic?" Kealey asked Abby.

She nodded and gave him an inquisitive look. But before she could ask what he intended to do, Kealey had already turned away, shoving Saduq down the length of the cabin toward the entrance at the stern.

"Keep walking," he said.

The deckhand Brun had shot lay in a fetal position in the main cabin, a wide pool of blood around his dead body. Kealey skirted the dark red puddle as he followed the arms dealer into the open air, then steered him around to the narrow span of deck between the main cabin and the starboard rail. After a second he grabbed his shoulder and wrenched him around so they were facing one another.

"I want you to back toward the rail," he said. "Do it slowly."

His eyes on Kealey's face, Saduq obeyed his orders, taking one step, another . . . and then coming to an abrupt halt.

Kealey waved his gun. "I didn't tell you to stop."

"I'm getting close to the rail."

"No kidding." Kealey shrugged. "Go on. . . . Back up some more."

"What are you going to do to me?"

"It depends," Kealey said. "But if you don't pay attention, I promise you're going to end up like your deckhand in the main cabin. This isn't a bluff."

Saduq gazed at him in disbelief and resumed edging his way back toward the rail until he was flat up against it. He could go no farther without falling over the side.

"Okay," Kealey said. "Hold it right there."

Kealey noted the flicker of relief on Saduq's face as

he realized he was not going overboard . . . at least not yet. It was precisely the reaction he'd sought from the arms dealer. Let him feel he had a chance, give him a modicum of hope, and he would cling to it however he could.

Kealey took a quick stride forward and shoved the MP9 into Saduq's chest cavity. "You have balls, I'll give you that much. But for a deal maker you don't seem to be a great judge of people."

Saduq tensed. "What are you talking about?"

"Look into my face," Kealey said. "And then tell me if you believe I'd think twice about blowing you away. Right here and now."

Saduq tensed. "How would you explain it to whoever sent you?"

"I wouldn't," Kealey said. "I'm not CIA. I'm not anything. Consider me a walking ghost—I can pass through whatever walls I please." Kealey grinned. "If you and your captain don't return to shore, the local authorities would be the only ones asking questions. And I'm betting they could be convinced it was pirates."

Saduq was silent for a long moment. "I cannot believe you would kill me in cold blood. *Someone* sent you here, and it must have been for a reason. . . ."

"I told you to *look* at me." Kealey slugged him hard in his mouth, pushing the rifle into his middle with one hand. "Talk, Saduq. Talk, or I'll blow your guts out and dump you overboard like a barrel of trash. But I promise it won't be before I make you feel a whole world of hurt."

"*Ya Allah,*" Saduq rasped, blood trickling from his mouth. "What do you want?"

"The truth. All of it. Starting with what I asked you down below." He moved closer—so close Saduq was forced to lean back against the rail's upper horizontal bar. "That means the name of the man who came aboard with you. And who you were buying those weapons for. And whether your friend still intends to deliver the goods now that he's made off on a launch with their money."

Saduq dragged the back of his hand across his lips and chin, glanced down at his red-smeared knuckles. "If I do cooperate with you . . . I will be a hunted man."

"Better hunted than dead."

Saduq stared into his face. "I'm going to need protection."

Kealey shrugged. "We can worry about that later," he said. "First let's hear what you have to tell me."

Saduq hesitated for another moment before he finally expelled a long, trembling breath.

"The pirate's name is Nicolas Barre," he said.

"And?"

"As you'd surmised, the payment he took with him was from Ishmael Mirghani and another man . . . an American like yourself. I received it at my home in Darfur."

Something flashed in Kealey's eyes. "This American," he said. "Who's he?"

Saduq hawked up a mat of blood and saliva and spit it onto the deck. "He was introduced to me as White," he said. "Cullen White."

Kealey nodded. He was sure his features had revealed none of his satisfaction—or curiosity.

"Okay," he said. "I think we might be getting somewhere."

When Kealey was finished with Saduq on the deck, he brought him back down below to a guest cabin and had him locked inside with the *Yemaja's* captain, posting Brun on guard out in the passage.

"How's the arm?" he asked.

"Still attached," Brun said with a wan smile.

"Give it to me straight," Kealey said. He had thought the bullet had hit muscle and passed through cleanly, but wasn't looking for bravado. "I need to know if you'll be okay down here for a while."

Brun looked at him. "I'm fine," he said. "We packed the wound well enough. . . . There isn't much bleeding."

Kealey nodded, went upstairs to the main cabin. Abby Liu was in the cockpit, monitoring the yacht's basic positional data on its dashboard screens, and he squatted in the aisle beside her.

"How do we stand with the coast guard?" he asked.

She pointed to two numerically coded ship icons on the GPS tracker display. "Those are maritime patrol boats. They're on standby in case we need them. Thanks to Dirk and Leo, who apparently had quite an adventure after we left."

Kealey studied the display, grunted. "I got Saduq to open up," he said.

"I saw," she said coolly.

He looked at her. "Something wrong?"

"I told you," she said, nodding her head at the cabin's wraparound windows. "I saw how you obtained your information. What term shall we give to your interrogative tactics? Coercion? Intimidation? Or prisoner abuse? You see, Kealey, I'm trying to stay away from the word *torture* because that might be a little too strong."

Kealey sat quietly for a moment, shrugged. "Use whatever definition you want," he said. "I don't see what difference it makes."

"You threatened to kill Saduq. Would you really have done it?"

"Things never got to where it was something I needed to consider."

"Which ignores my question."

"No," Kealey said. "It's the most truthful answer I can give you. We don't have time for proper bows and curtsies. I thought it was something you understood."

"It was . . . and is," she said. "But I don't have to like watching you work, and don't know that I'm too proud of my participation." She stared into his face. "I'm also not sure I know what kind of man Harper sent me."

More silence. Kealey raised his eyes to hers, held them. "The truth is that I'm not sure, either," he said. "Let's leave it alone, okay? Just leave it be and stick to discussing our little assignment."

She frowned. Then after a second gave him a small, reluctant nod.

"Does the name Barre mean anything to you?" Kealey asked.

"Nicolas Barre?"

"That's it."

"He's head of the *Hangarihi* . . . the Scorpion gang," Abby said. "The Somali pirate organizations you hear about are the Marka Group, the Puntland Group, the Somali Marines, and the National Volunteer Coast Guard. But this is based on outdated intelligence. There are more than those four major bands. I'd estimate between seven and a dozen, some with active alliances, others in competition, and all affiliated with one or more warlords. Barre's group is relatively new, but it's one of the most sophisticated—a breakaway from the marines, who are known for their military-type chain of command and technology."

"And their politics?"

"Money and greed," she said.

Kealey grunted. "According to al-Saduq, he's going to fulfill his end of their bargain. What's your take?"

"I'd be surprised if he didn't."

"Why? Our bandit's already made off with his cash. If you're right, that would make him more trustworthy than Saduq." Kealey massaged the back of his neck. "Think about it. He brokers the original arms deal between Russia and the Egyptian government, then turns around and arranges for it to be taken by Barre's men."

"Quite a spin on what you Americans call regifting, I know," Abby said. "Still, Hassan al-Saduq has built up considerable international cachet—and deniability, since there's no firm link between him and Barre's capture of the shipment."

"So you're saying Barre realizes he can't hide behind a reputation of legitimacy."

"Or quasi legitimacy, I suppose. He's an upstart on the scene."

"And by that logic his goal is what? To prove there can be honor among thieves?"

She shrugged. "It's good business. The success of this deal would mark Barre as a player on a large regional scale. Especially when word gets around that he could have easily taken his bundle and run."

"And then resold . . . *regifted* . . . the shipment a third time," Kealey said.

She nodded.

Kealey was thoughtful a moment. "Saduq insists the details of the arms delivery weren't worked out. He says it was something they'd meant to discuss aboard the yacht before we rudely interrupted."

"My turn to ask, then," Abby said. "Do you believe him?"

Kealey tried to choose his words carefully. He did not want their conversation doubling back to where it had started out. "I think he realized it would be in his best interests to tell me the truth."

She gave him a glance that said his bit of verbal finesse hadn't made his methods any easier to tolerate. "Which means there's going to be direct contact between Saduq and Mirghani."

"There'll have to be," he said. "The delivery needs to happen soon."

"Is this something else Saduq told you?"

"He didn't need to," Kealey said. "Back in Yaoundé, you told me the merchandise was initially loaded aboard a Ukrainian ship bound for Egypt and was then meant to be transported into Sudan. . . . Is that accurate?"

"That was our intelligence, yes."

Kealey looked at her. "Think about the difficulty of it for a minute. Guns and artillery would be one thing—the Egyptians could have piled them aboard a C-One-thirty Hercules or two and airlifted them over the border. But you talked about thirty-odd tanks, a dozen attack birds. . . . They're too heavy to be flown in without a fleet of air transports bigger than anything Egypt could muster. Unless you're talking about a whole lot of very conspicuous trips."

"They would have been moved overland, then," Abby said. "At least for part of the distance."

Kealey was nodding in the affirmative. "I guess the easiest way would have been for the ship to pull into Port Sudan via the Red Sea, off-load its cargo, then rail it east to Khartoum. That entire route's controlled by Omar al-Bashir, so his forces could've kept a tight lid on things. You figure from there the tanks and choppers might have been divvied into small groups, warehoused at stopover points, and then slowly integrated into Sudanese army units. The biggest hurdle would have been surveillance by Israeli patrol boats out of Eilat *before* the ships reached harbor." He paused. "Israel wouldn't intercede unless the consignment got it really edgy—but it would have damn well made sure intel satellites were keeping tabs on its composition and movement from the docks."

Abby considered that. "The fact is, Kealey, all of this has become moot, hasn't it? The shipment never made it to Egypt. And if it's going to Mirghani's *opposition* forces, there's the double obstacle of needing to slip it past Bashir's security. Even if the Scorpion band made a transfer along their water route and moved the matériel from the Ukrainian vessel to some rusty barge or barges, no amount of bribes could have gotten it past Bashir's harbor agents in Port Sudan. They simply wouldn't bring it that far north."

"That's right," he said. "But any way you cut it, a haul of this magnitude would be tough to keep under wraps. It's what I meant about the delivery needing to get done before too long. The seizure took place in the Gulf of Aden, down near Yemen. I think we need to be looking at the quickest and likeliest routes into Sudan from there."

Abby reached for her sat phone and keyed up a map. "So what do you think? If the merchandise is coming in from the south, does it travel *up* by land from Ethiopia or Eritrea?"

"Eritrea would be my pick," Kealey said. "It's actually just right. The bribes are cheaper and tracking the shipment's harder. You can barge the merch to Massawa, then probably rail or truck it west to the border on the old nomad trails, where the outposts are lightly manned . . . except maybe at Kassala." He thought for a moment. "The territorial line with Eritrea runs, what, something like two hundred kilometers?"

"Closer to three," Abby said, studying the map.

"That's a lot of barren terrain unless you're an archeologist," Kealey said. "And if you do get noticed, there are going to be fewer hands held out."

Abby tapped a key to zoom in on Sudan. "The railway at Kassala has stops to the southwest in Shobak and Gederef. It runs from coast to coast, with spurs into South Darfur, and north into Port Sudan, Khartoum, and Egypt."

"In other words it can take you almost anywhere in the country."

She was nodding. "Did Saduq have any idea where the munitions are being brought? Or what they're to be used for?"

"I don't think he knows or wants to know," Kealey said, shaking his head. "I suppose I could push him harder to be positive. But I wouldn't want to make you upset at me again."

Abby did not look amused. "What's next? If we can't learn the shipment's destination, the best we can do is try and have it interdicted while it's being smuggled over the border into Sudan—"

"No," Kealey said. "You're wrong."

"How is that?"

"We can find out where the arms are headed from Ishmael Mirghani. We *need* to find out. Because that's the first step toward finding out his objective."

"Kealey . . . how do you plan to go about that?"

He adjusted himself in the aisle, still crouching beside Abby. "Saduq told me two men brought him the cash for tonight's handoff. They flew it from Khartoum to his home in Darfur. One of them was Mirghani. The other was an American named Cullen White."

She gave him a perceptive look. "You sound like you know a bit about him."

"I can give you the full lowdown later," Kealey said. "The important thing for you to know now is that he's an operator. Former CIA, smart, and connected."

"Connected to whom?"

"Long story . . . and like I told you, it can wait," Kealey said. "You've been at this game awhile, Abby. It was you who gave John Harper the dossier on Simon Nusairi . . . aka David Khadir. You know as well as I do that it's always about following the money. And White having brought it to Saduq is big."

"It tells us he's bankrolling Mirghani," she agreed. "Or that whoever's behind him is doing it, since he doesn't sound like the sort who'd have that kind of funding in his piggy bank."

Kealey nodded, his brow creased in thought. "Here's what we need to consider right now. Barre is going to tell Mirghani we've got Saduq . . . that's if he hasn't already . . . and then Mirghani will relay the news to White. But for all he knows, this was strictly an antipiracy raid, and our interest was on the shipment and the people who stole it. He might wonder if it goes beyond that, but there'll be no proof, nothing concrete. He'll be on the alert, though. And he'll pass the word about what happened along to his backer."

"Do you think that will stop whatever they plan to do with the armaments?"

"No," Kealey said. "My guess would be the exact opposite. If anything, their plans could be stepped up. They're in too deep to quit based on White's suspicions.

Because they don't know who we are, won't know I'm involved, won't know the scope of our operation . . ."

Abby held up her hand to interrupt him. "Before you get too far ahead of yourself, you might want to consider that *I* don't know its scope, either—or my role in it going forward," she said. "Yes, I shared some information about Khadir with John Harper. But if your Mr. White's connections are the sort I think they might be . . . Interpol will *not* become involved in an investigation of your internal government affairs. Particularly, if I may be frank, if it leads to its highest offices—"

Kealey was shaking his head, his features suddenly darkening. "What if it isn't really that complicated?" he said. "If it leads back to a massacre at a refugee camp in Darfur six months ago, and an innocent young woman that somebody had raped, beaten, and murdered so they could dangle her dead body in front of someone like bait on a hook? What if I told you that's the only reason *I'm* involved?"

Abby stared at him for a long minute, her expression bordering on astonishment, looking completely taken off guard by the intensity in his eyes, the emphatic emotion in his voice. She opened her mouth to answer, then closed it, at a loss for words. Finally she seemed to distill all the questions inside her to a single brief, almost preposterously bland sentence.

"What do you intend to do next?" she said.

Kealey looked at her. "First bring this yacht ashore and dump Saduq somewhere your people can keep him out of sight and sound for a while," he said. "Then contact Harper and have him get the two of us into Sudan."

CHAPTER 17

WASHINGTON, D.C. • ASWÂN, EGYPT • KHARTOUM

It was six o'clock in the evening in Washington, D.C., when the waiter arrived at the small corner table Harper had reserved for his dinner with Robert Andrews at the crowded Dubliner Pub on North Capitol Street. He'd ordered a Jameson's on the rocks and a corned beef sandwich as an afterthought; the food would help preserve the appearance that he had an appetite for something that was both solid and did not have an alcoholic proof measure.

Andrews, who'd arrived shortly after Harper, had gotten a Philly cheesesteak and a Sam Adams. The DCI was a native Philadelphian and seemed to relish being identified with the city. He'd also played college baseball and secretly harbored a dream that he'd be drafted by his hometown team. After a World Series game he'd attended at Yankee Stadium in 2009, he had been thrown into a weeklong funk because the New York Yankees rallied late to defeat his beloved Phillies. What

had added insult to injury was that some wiseass in the
control booth had put a clip from the movie *Rocky Bal-
boa* up on the Diamond Vision screen to pump up the
local fans. *It ain't about how hard you hit. It's about how
hard you can get hit and keep moving forward.* In jumbo
high-definition, no less.

In Andrews's often stated opinion, it had been unprincipled, unsportsmanlike thievery for the Yanks to
appropriate Rocky, as iconic to Philadelphia as the Lib-
erty Bell, for their ballpark. Never mind that Stallone
the actor hailed from Hell's Kitchen in New York,
Rocky the *character* was from the tough streets of Kensington, in South Philly. What could the Phillies have
done to counter that move? Neither De Niro's "You
talkin' to me?" line nor Pacino's "Attica!" had seemed
effective rallying cries when his beloved hometown
team fell behind by a few runs. With that one low-down
coup, he had lamented, it became a fait accompli that
the damned Yankees would wind up drinking the victory champagne.

Wishing they had nothing more serious to discuss
now than ill-gotten Yankee supremacy, Harper eyed his
tumbler and made himself reach for his sandwich, reluctant to seem too anxious for the former. Opposite
him, Andrews prepared to take a bite of his dinner,
carefully using his knife and fork to fold an ample wad
of onions and melted provolone around a slice of steak.
Unlike his boss, Harper had never been much of a professional sports fan. As a boy he had envisioned himself
in daring exploits on faraway shores, and as a young
man he'd gotten to live out his share. He had never felt
any of their outcomes turned on rallying cries, although in hindsight he thought it possible he had
sometimes partially gotten through on dumb luck.

He wondered why all this was passing through his mind right now. None of it had anything to do with anything, or at least he didn't think it did. Unless it was to show that when you were in the thick of exceptional situations, there sometimes seemed no discernible way to sequence the cause and effect of how they'd developed or know whether your attempts to seize control of them were anything but self-deceptive, if not altogether delusory. Still, you kept on plugging away; the alternative was a concession Harper did not have it within himself to ever make.

He chewed his sandwich without tasting it, estimating it would be appropriate to start on his whiskey in a minute.

"John, you look like you haven't slept for a week," Andrews said.

"Thank you," Harper said. "Considering it's been months since I've actually gotten a decent night's shut-eye, I'll take that as encouragement that I'm holding my own under pressure."

Andrews gave a small smile. "It's nice to enjoy the food and atmosphere here after a long day of White House briefings, particularly when they involve Stralen, Fitzgerald, and POTUS all but showing me the door midway through . . . which you may recall is what they did that day back in April at Camp David," he said. "I got the sense from your call, though, that you had something urgent to talk about."

Harper nodded slowly. "I weighed having this conversation over the phone," he said. "I hate to sound paranoid. . . . A secure line falls within my comfort zone under most circumstances."

"Don't sweat it, John. When push comes to shove, I'll always take a noisy tavern over SCIP encryption. The

NSA developed the damn protocols, and who the hell can trust *them* to keep their ears out of our business?"

Harper chuckled. He supposed paranoia was a professional hazard.

The two men sat without saying anything for a while. Around them the tavern, with its paneled walls and polished horseshoe bar, was becoming jammed with the usual Capitol Hill end-of-the-day office crowd—politicians, lobbyists, aides, secretaries.

"So," Andrews said, "where do things stand?"

"Ryan Kealey contacted me about an hour ago—he was aboard Hassan al-Saduq's play boat in Limbe," Harper said in a low voice. "It was eleven o'clock at night there, and al-Saduq was about to be handed over into the custody of the EU antipiracy task force."

"From aboard the yacht?"

"That's correct. Kealey and his team aboard were apparently waiting for a launch."

"Are there legitimate grounds for holding him?"

"One could make a reasonable argument." Harper shrugged. "I'm not sure the evidentiary case would persuade a judge, particularly in Cameroon . . . but it isn't too important. Saduq gave Kealey whatever he could of importance. I'll have a complete report on your desk in the morning."

"This sounds positive."

"Yes."

"But you didn't ask to meet here just to tell me about it."

"No."

"So I gather there's a negative you haven't mentioned yet."

"More than one." Harper picked up his whiskey, took a long swallow, felt the smooth warmth spread from his throat to his chest. Then he put down the tumbler, leaned slightly forward, and spoke in a voice only Andrews could have heard over the hubbub of the crowd and the rhythmic pop music thumping from the juke. "Cullen White and the leader of the Darfur People's Army met with Saduq approximately forty-eight hours ago. They'd flown from Khartoum to his ranch in Quaila . . . White apparently as a money courier."

Andrews heard his fork clink against the rim of his plate and realized he'd almost dropped it. "Goddamn," he said, glancing quickly around to make sure no one was in earshot. "This links him right up to that captured boatful of Russian and Libyan hardware."

Harper nodded. "White and whoever put him on the ground in Sudan," he said, his voice hushed. "I won't say the name of the person I suspect that is. Won't even whisper it. But I don't really think it's necessary."

"No, not at all—we know whose protégé he's always been." Andrews was shaking his head. "Okay, let's have the rest."

"Kealey wasn't able to keep the deal from getting done," he said. "The Somali Blackbeard made off with the payment. He's an up-and-comer on the scene, and Kealey and the EU task force people are convinced he means to keep his end of the bargain . . . meaning we've got the equivalent of two tactical tank and fighter helo squadrons and an unknown amount of ordnance about to fall into unknown hands in Sudan." He paused, seeing the question on the DCI's face. "For purposes equally unknown."

Andrews frowned. "John, we can't target our spy birds in on their movement without State and the DOD getting wind of it."

"And the DIA by extension," Harper said. *The ten-ton gorilla in the room.* "If we're going to track them, it will

have to be done old school. From the ground. You mentioned the scene at Camp David, and you and I might as
well be right there now in that truck, discussing Ryan
Kealey being our man. We need to put him and a member of his team in Sudan, and there isn't any time to
waste."

Several seconds elapsed. Andrews massaged his temples, his dinner no longer commanding a sliver of attention. "Our problem is that this isn't April anymore.
The way the rhetoric's heated up, we're lucky our exist-
ing embassy staff in Khartoum hasn't already been told
to pack their luggage."

Harper sighed. "Speaking of which . . . our man
there's Seth Holland," Harper said. "He's experienced
and can provide support. But he'll have to work around
the chief of mission, Walter Reynolds."

Andrews gave a nod of tacit acknowledgment.
Reynolds and Brynn Fitzgerald had a long-standing
friendship, and putting him in the loop would be potentially no less compromising than a request to jog the
orbit of a Keyhole sat.

"I've got no doubts about Holland," he said. "But it
comes back around to what I told you about the difficulty of getting anyone into the country."

Harper had some more of his whiskey but deliberately refrained from emptying the tumbler. Somewhere
in the back of his mind, he wondered what Julie—and
Allison Dearborn—would think of both his impulse to
slug it down and his calculated moderation in the presence of his boss. Wasn't that supposed to be the telltale
sign of a problem? "The intended route for the Russki
shipment was through Egypt," he said. "That obviously
doesn't happen without full Egyptian complicity . . .
from the president down to *Mukhabarat al-Amma*."

Andrews nodded, the concentration on his face signaling that he'd again immediately registered Harper's unspoken communication. *Mukhabarat al-Amma* was Egypt's name for its General Intelligence Service, a rough equivalent to the CIA. The agencies had been involved in numerous cooperative efforts, several ongoing, to keep tabs on several antigovernment factions with ties to Hamas and other militant Islamists. Over the past year alone intel provided by the CIA had thwarted a major terrorist bombing in Cairo and a conspiracy against President Mubarak's life.

Harper and Andrews sat in a thoughtful pocket of silence amid the swells of dinnertime pub noise around them. It seemed that a long period elapsed before the DCI at last lifted his fork and knife, used them to skillfully form another amalgam of steak, onions, and cheese, and took his next bite. Swallowing, then, he glanced at his wristwatch.

"Let's finish up and ask for the check," he said. "It's damn near two o'clock in the morning in Cairo, and I don't want the person I need to call there feeling too cranky when I get him out of bed."

"Asser, how are you this morning?" Andrews said over his sat phone.

He waited, listening to his counterpart at *Mukhabarat al-Amma* produce a sequence of phlegmy rumbling sounds as he shook off sleep at the other end of the line. The DCI was in his study in the two-bedroom Tenth Street apartment he had recently bought for over three-quarters of a million dollars, a canny real estate agent having persuaded him it would be cheaper and easier to maintain than the spacious old two-story, four-bedroom home across the Potomac in which he and his wife had raised their four children. Thus far the verdict was out; although Andrews appreciated the lower maintenance costs, the concierge, and private elevator, he had nearly broken his neck twice slipping on the too-slick tiles of the building's marble lobby on rainy days and missed staring wistfully into the bedroom his youngest daughter had vacated when she went off to college.

"At this hour, Robert, it is only technically morning, and I have a poor mind for technicalities even when wide awake," Asser Kassab replied with a snorting yawn. "That said, I assume you would not have gotten me out of bed for an inconsequential reason."

Andrews went right for it. "Asser," he said, "I need to get two people into the Sudanese capital."

"May I ask who they are?"

"Employees of an Egyptian chemical company."

"Though not Egyptian nationals, I assume."

"A technicality," Andrews said with a wry smile. "Though you're correct. They're Westerners."

A sigh. "And which of our companies employs them?"

"That's your pick and choose," Andrews said. "They'll have proper identification and international work permits. But I'll need your assistance with their specific professional affiliation."

Kassab's negative reaction was almost palpable across the vast distance between them. "This cannot be done," he said.

"Of course it can. Your government just opened that huge new Products Marketing Center in Khartoum. On Al-Steen Street. Nice-looking place—I've got aerial photos going back to when the foundation was laid."

"I do not doubt it," Kassab said. "Or your general inquisitiveness."

Andrews admittedly enjoyed his displeasure, however much a token it might be. "How many corporations have their export offices there? Must be dozens of them, selling everything from petrochemicals to paints."

"I tell you it cannot be done," Kassab repeated emphatically. "We . . . my country, that is . . . respects America's position regarding Omar al-Bashir. But we share a geographic border and have vital economic ties with the Sudanese."

"Unfortunately that's part of the problem," Andrews said, deciding to play his trump card. "And it's why you're going to help me."

"What are you suggesting?"

"That your *country* was prepared to assist in the cross-border transport of a massive armaments shipment to the Sudanese army, presumably from Aswân down to Wadi Halfa, in violation of the United Nations arms embargo," Andrews said. "This is before it was captured by pirates at the Horn."

"I know nothing of it."

"Of course you don't, Asser. I wouldn't figure head of Egyptian intelligence would have a clue."

"It is perhaps good for our friendship that I am too drowsy to have noticed your sarcasm," Kassab said. "Moreover, if what you tell me is correct, this movement of weapons would not have been sanctioned by my government. There are many outlaws in the south, and their network is well organized."

"No thanks to your agency providing support," Andrews said.

Silence. "I think, Robert, that I would rather not continue our chat right now. I will happily return your call from my office tomorrow—"

"I think you'd better hang on the phone until I've

finished my piece," Andrews said. "Whether or not you believe it, we're on the same page here. Or does your government *not* want Omar al-Bashir to stay comfortably nestled in the presidential palace?"

"A gross mischaracterization," Kassab said. "I must remind you that, like the United States, we are not a signatory to the ICC. As I have also made clear, this no more makes us supporters of his regime than it does your government or the others that abstained. We simply contend that acting on the warrant for his arrest would throw his already destabilized nation into anarchy. Whatever new issues may have arisen to aggravate the already dangerous tensions between America and Sudan . . . presumably they would include this arms sale you've mentioned . . . I would recommend pursuing a remedy through diplomatic channels."

Andrews scowled with growing anger and impatience. He was good at keeping his temper in check; if he wasn't, the bureaucracy through which he'd steered for his entire career would have long since spat him out. But when the dam broke, it came down with a crash.

"Look, Asser, it's time to cut the bullshit," he said. "I called you from my home instead of the office for a reason. And tired as you are from standing around with your head in the desert sand, I think that tells you something about the delicacy of my own situation."

"Robert, listen to me—"

"No. Now *you* listen. The GIS owns at least half the petrochemical companies headquartered in that Products Marketing Center."

"Robert . . ."

"It controls and coordinates the smuggling operations down at the borders and would have been instru-

mental in running that illegal weapons shipment down
into Sudan," Andrews said. "If that information somehow leaked out to various House and Senate sub-
committees, there could be repercussions. For example, my agency might have to pull its support of the
GIS's efforts to keep your president from getting his
head blown off by hard-core extremists on a daily basis."
He paused, took a deep breath. "Asser, you talked about
what's building between the United States and Sudan.
Man to man, I'm telling you the situation's on the verge
of exploding, and I'm trying to stop that, even if it
means Bashir stays in power, which falls right in line
with your own government's preference. I'm also going
to tell you that the damned shipment is still heading
into Sudan—just not to its original buyer."

Kassab hesitated. "To whom, then, *is* it going?"

"That's frankly something I might not share with you
if I knew," Andrews said. "But I will advise that you do
yourself a favor and cooperate."

There was silence at the other end of the line. Then,
finally, a heavy, resigned sigh. "Where are your chemical
workers presently located?"

"Cameroon," Harper said. "They can be out of
Yaoundé and on their way to Cairo within twenty-four
hours."

"Very well," Kassab said. "Please send me their photographs immediately so the corporate identifications can
be readied. When they arrive here, I will see to it they
are met at the airport and accompanied to Aswân with a
special escort. The Nile River Ferry Company runs a
daily boat into Wadi Halfa. Although an air shuttle
would be faster, the ferry would probably be best as I
have personal influence with its ownership."

"Got it."

"Also, I would suggest you make sure your people have ample funds to cover their travel expenses—including those that may arise without prior notice. These are lean budgetary times, and a bit extra might be of use here and there."

"Right. Anything else?"

"Only that I might return to my sleep and dream peaceful, uninterrupted dreams."

Andrews grinned. "Asser, if you're very fortunate, it might happen after you retire," he said. "Men like us, though . . . I'm guessing we've seen too much of what makes the world tick to ever enjoy that luxury again."

The ferry from Aswân to Wadi Halfa was a crowded, rackety metal steamer that ostensibly left at noon every Monday from a sand-blown pier at Aswân High Dam—or El Sadd el Ali—on the large manmade body of water known as Lake Nasser. Bound by a system of three massive dikes on the Egyptian side of the Nile, the reservoir was the product of a major construction effort in the 1970s, its southern edge lapping up on the pebbled Sudanese shoreline, where the preference was to call it Buhayrat Nubiya.

Kealey and Abby had landed in Cairo Sunday morning, after an uneventful five-hour flight, their embarkation of the plane at Yaoundé airport having been a successful first test of their cover documents. These had arrived separately at the United States and Egyptian consulates in sealed diplomatic pouches, then had been couriered over to Kealey at the Hilton on Boulevard du 20 Mai, where they were directly handed off to him in his room. The pouch from the U.S. consulate had also included envelopes containing several thousand dollars in mixed American bills and an equivalent sum in euros.

The name printed alongside Kealey's U.S. passport photograph was Ryan Harner. Abby, whose passport declared her to be of French citizenship, was identified as Abigail Leung Evart. In addition to the CIA-fabricated passports, both had received, through the swift efforts of Asser Kassab, a variety of credentials establishing them as employees of the Boutros Advanced Packaging Corporation in Alexandria, a developer of biodegradable and recyclable shipping materials for food, pharmaceuticals, and other commercially transported goods. A note in the Egyptian packet explained that someone named Yusuf would await them at the Cairo International arrivals terminal.

A dark-eyed and alacritous young man who spoke fluent English, Yusuf was there as arranged, his car waiting in the parking lot. Within minutes of their arrival, Yusuf was driving them over the bridge to the train station at El Giza, explaining that the minor detour was necessitated by expansion work at the Cairo station on the east bank of the Nile.

With its elaborate façade of limestone building blocks and classic colonnades, the El Giza railway station was an impressive, vaulting structure teeming with humanity, the travelers passing through its entrance doors and lined up at the ticket windows scrutinized by white-uniformed security personnel. Although Kealey and Abby's tickets had been purchased in advance, Yusuf discreetly asked Kealey for four hundred dollars inside the station, nodding in the direction of two guards standing near the gate for their train to Aswân.

"It will ensure that your papers are given quick inspections," he explained. "And viewed in the most favorable light."

Which they were with accepting nods.

"*Rihlah muwaffaqah*," Yusuf said in colloquial Arabic, wishing the pair well as they were waved onto the platform. "The ferry's booking agent in Aswân is a Mr. Ferran. Your crossing to Sudan will be in his very capable hands. Should you encounter any problems, however, mention my name."

A short while later the sleek, air-conditioned *Abela* express had pulled from the station, leaving on schedule for the country's southernmost border town . . . an overnight journey of somewhat under 900 kilometers. Yusuf had reserved a two-berth sleeper compartment, and both Kealey and Abby, leaving their cots folded, managed to doze off intermittently in their seats en route to Aswân.

It was half past eleven the next morning when they reached the village center—and just thirty minutes before their boat was supposed to set sail. There was a row of cabs waiting outside the station, and they hurriedly took one to the ferry line's ticket office, which was tucked away amid a ramshackle outdoor mall consisting of a fruit and vegetable stand, the local tourist center, and a spice market that sold powdered laundry detergent in unmarked baskets alongside its ground, dried edibles.

The office itself was a small, unadorned, somewhat shabby storefront with a counter at the rear. Wearing a traditional Muslim robe and embroidered *taqiyah* on his head, the man on the stool behind it provided a stark, immediate contrast to his surroundings. He was perfectly shaven and manicured, with gleaming diamond rings on several fingers of each hand. Entering the door, Kealey could at once smell his expensive oriental cologne—its blend of musk and agarwood, dabbed on judiciously so as not to overwhelm, accenting an overall air of fastidiousness that approached, but did not quite reach, the threshold of excess or ostentation.

"Mr. Ferran?" Kealey said.

The man rose from his stool, nodded. His expression, such as it was, seemed indicative of a mild strain of boredom.

Kealey took Abby's documents from her hand, moved to the counter, produced his own identification from the carryall on his shoulder, and set them all down in front of Ferran. "We need to get aboard the next ferry to Wadi Halfa," he said.

Ferran glanced at the wall clock on his side of the counter, shook his head. "The boat is departing in fifteen minutes," he said. "If you left here this minute, it would be too late."

"We've come all the way from Cairo," Kealey said, looking at him. "It's very important that we get across."

"Impossible." Ferran's tone was disinterested. "I can look at your documents and issue tickets, but they will be inspected a second time at the dock. That alone might take an hour . . . or more if there is a backup." He paused. "We have a barge leaving tomorrow afternoon. It is meant for vehicles and items of freight. I can find room aboard on occasion, but the cost of passage would be high, and there is no seating for passengers."

Abby had come up to stand beside Kealey. "Yusuf assured us we could count on you, Mr. Ferran," she said.

Ferran turned to her. "Yusuf."

"That's right," she said. "I expect you know who he is?"

Ferran's eyes had narrowed. "Yes," he said. "Full well."

"Then don't play games with us," Kealey said. "We need to be on that boat when it leaves today. Tell me what it's going to take."

Ferran had returned his attention to Kealey. "One thousand dollars," he said.

Kealey nodded, started opening the flap of his carry-all.

"For each of you," Ferran said.

Kealey snapped a glance at Ferran's face, kept it there a moment before reaching into the carryall for one of the envelopes he'd gotten from the courier pouch. He counted out two thousand dollars in hundreds, doing it slowly enough for Ferran to watch. Then he held the money over the counter. "Here," he said. "Let's get it done."

Ferran took the money from him, slid open a drawer beneath the countertop, deposited it inside, and pushed the drawer shut. Then he reached into a pocket of his robe for a cell phone and fingered a speed-dial key.

"Gamal," he said, "inform the passengers aboard the ferry there is to be a slight delay . . . for minor repairs, yes? In the meantime, I have two additional fares who will be seeing you at the dock shortly. . . ."

In the garden behind Ishmael Mirghani's home in Khartoum's upscale Bahri section—his chair near the very spot where he had once watched a late-afternoon breeze scatter cinders of his Harold Traylor identity beyond recovery—Cullen White sat opposite Mirghani in the shade of a guava tree laden with ripe yellow fruit, his satellite phone in hand, the hand lowered to his lap. His face sober, his jaw set, he glanced down at the phone, then up at Mirghani.

"This isn't going to be pleasant," he said. For either of them, he thought, but most of all for him. "You know that."

Mirghani nodded. He looked, if not quite as nervous as he had during the flight to Darfur less than a week ago, then close to it.

"I would place the call myself if it were possible," he said, his frank gaze taking White a bit by surprise. Damned if he didn't seem to mean it; the man deserved credit for his accountability. "Unfortunately, I do not believe it would be the wisest of proposals."

White could have almost managed a grin. "No, it wouldn't," he said. "I appreciate the thought, Ishmael. I'm serious. Like I told you, though, his anger is something I can accept. I don't know whether you can understand, but it's his disappointment that will be most difficult. He entrusted me with an operation of enormous magnitude and the upshot . . ."

He let the sentence trail off. What exactly would the upshot be? He didn't, *couldn't* know, and supposed that uncertainty, translated as possibility, might yet be his saving grace. Yes, if he had it to do over again, he would have accompanied Hassan al-Saduq to Cameroon for his meet with the bloody pirate. Would have accompanied him aboard the yacht, overseen the entire money transfer. And whoever had boarded the boat and captured him would have had much more to handle than Saduq's cheap, amateurish excuse for a security team. *Yes,* he thought, *a great deal more.*

But that was behind him, an error that could not be undone—but whose damage still might be limited. One of the most vital lessons he had learned in his day was that survival often hinged on untethering the past before its weight dragged you down into the muck of failure. The thing was just to stay on track.

He lifted the phone to his ear, thumbed in a number in America. He didn't have long to wait; none to his surprise, it took only two rings before his party answered. Some version of the news, however, sketchy, would have reached him by now.

"Yes?" he asked over the phone's encrypted channel. "Condor, this is—"

"I know who it is. I also know the reason for your call. I've been expecting it."

White could almost picture his baleful glare. "Sir, I don't want to rehash whatever you already might have heard. It's clear we have a problem. . . ."

"We have a problem, all right. A fucking monster of a problem. Who were those people in Limbe? Can you tell me that?"

"No, sir. The question's been with me every waking minute since it happened. They're saying in the media it was an EU antipiracy team that was conducting a probe into our man's activities—"

"And you believe it?"

White inhaled, exhaled. He was thinking he could lie here, make it easier. Except he couldn't, not to the man at the other end of the line. "No. Or only partially. It makes for a good blind."

"The cover story should be true in its own right. Like that search for the *Titanic,* the glory hound that dove on her wants to go waltzing through her grand ballroom and show movies on television. But first he's got to find a submarine the Russians sunk in the Cold War. Office of Naval Intelligence pays his way, but he never tells the frog scientists aboard his research ship his real mission."

"Yes, sir. Exactly."

"So you believe somebody here at home was working with the EU task force?"

"I'm inclined to think so, yes. The timing doesn't seem a coincidence—"

"And your shit antennae probably tell you there's more than we're sniffing on the surface."

"Yessir," White said. "A standoff on the street near the marina, the seizure of the yacht, and most of all our man being kept under tight wraps . . . does have a feel about it."

"Have you spoken to the Exile?"

"Not yet, sir. He's been out of phone and radio contact. But I expect to be in touch with him within the next few hours—"

"*Listen* to me," Condor interrupted. "You damn well better get in touch with him. You can send a carrier pigeon, or you can sprout wings. You can do whatever the hell it takes under the sun, moon, and stars. But we aren't going to be passive. I want this operation's timetable ramped up."

"Yes, I don't see that we have any alternative. But there are eventualities we can't altogether control. The delivery, for example—"

"Those thugs took our money and we have to be concerned with delivery?"

"Sir—"

"No. I understand contingencies. But I'm not hanging on them. I refuse to accept that, and I refuse to be advised about them. . . . Am I making myself clear?"

"Yessir."

"Good. Then get this moving. It doesn't matter who's onto it. You stay two steps ahead of them. I know you're capable. I'm counting on you, White. Get it moving *now*."

White nodded with the phone still against his ear, staring across at Mirghani, meeting his gaze with his own even as he realized the line had gone silent, leaving only the odd echoing silence particular to Satcom links.

He sat motionless for a while, immersed in his thoughts.

"Well?" Mirghani asked. "How did you fare?"

White gave a slow shrug, lowered the phone.

"As I'd expected," he said finally.

CHAPTER 18

SUDAN

Navigating under cover of night's darkness with their sophisticated GPS systems, the pirates had pulled their long, flat cargo barges to shore at Zula on the Bay of Arafali, some 50 kilometers south of the far busier port of Massawa, with its commercial dhow and tourist boat traffic, American naval base, police stations, and railway line. Thousands of years in the past this tiny Eritrean village had been an extension of Adulis, a major center of trade within the vast and influential Kingdom of Aksum, later to be known as Ethiopia. In the modern era, with the great empires fractured and degraded, their glory crumbled into sand, it was a sparsely populated belt of semiarid Sahel, with the thatch huts of its native tribesmen dotting the land near occasional springs and wadis, and stretches of feature-less dun-colored terrain, over which archeologists would bump along in their 4x4s while heading toward the ancient ruins and excavations a stone's throw to the north.

Standing very straight in his desert camouflage uniform, his hands planted on his hips above a nylon web
belt—its pistol holster on the right, an ammunition
pack on the left—the commander moved his gaze
along the dockside, where half the total consignment of
Zolfaqar MBTs and ANSAT/Sharaf combat helos had
been discharged onto waiting heavy equipment transports. He would have preferred receiving the arms and
equipment in a single delivery, and expedience was
hardly his principal reason. It would be a sufficient
challenge to get the trucks across the border without
detection even once; twice invited complications and
escalated the already considerable risks. But the pirates
had wisely transferred the shipment from its original
Ukrainian freighter onto a pair of smaller barges, and
there had been restrictions on the size and weight of
the loads those aging vessels could carry. That aside,
the commander himself had corresponding practical
and logistical limits. Seventy-five feet long from end to
end, his giant tractor trailers could travel between 400
and 600 miles cross-country at a fair enough clip given
the inhospitable desert landscape, their 500-horse-
power diesel engines fueled by massive driver- and
passenger-side gasoline tanks. Still, it would take two
trips to move all the matériel to the staging ground,
whatever quantity the pirates were able to bring with
them tonight. The bottom line was that he had just so
many available trucks.

Now he reached for the canteen strapped over his
shoulder, removed its cap, and took a drink of tepid
water, swishing it around his mouth before he gulped it
down. It was now almost two o'clock in the morning, six
hours since the *Hangarihi* had guided the barges ashore
and deployed their off-load ramps. His men had since
driven the Zolfaqars onto the trailers and put their

backs into manually rolling the helicopters from the barges on metal tow carts, grunting and sweating as they hastened to complete their arduous work so the convoy could set out with many hours of darkness still ahead.

Lined along the gunwales of the barges, the *Hangar-ihi* had watched the laborious effort as if it were a relaxing diversion, smoking and drinking whiskey from tin flasks, the tips of their cigarettes glowing like orange fireflies in the night. They had offered no assistance after their cargo had been unlashed from its pallets, and the commander and his men had expected nothing else from them. In delivering his plunder without delay, their leader had stuck to his end of the bargain when he could have simply made off with the loot, using the raid on the yacht of Hassan al-Saduq as justification to go into hiding. That alone had earned him a large quantum of respect. With its easily defended coves and grottos, the Somali coast was a rabbit warren where he could have laid low indefinitely . . . not that it would have been his single best recourse. In the pirate boomtowns that were the underpinnings of the country's new economy, Nicolas Barre would be treated as a king in his stronghold, and the people there would go to any lengths to shelter and protect them from legal authorities or any other threats.

The commander heard the growl of powerful engines coming to life, twisted the cap back onto his canteen with long, graceful fingers as he saw his chief lieutenant, Mabuir, striding toward him from the line of HETs. Although Mabuir had not shied from assisting in the off-load, it did not escape the commander's notice that he looked crisp in his beret and field uniform. A great deal had changed about his fighters since the events at Camp Hadith—or the best of them, at any rate.

The reason was no mystery, and the commander credited himself for recognizing that the first step in preparing his force for what lay ahead would be to alter its composition. He had winnowed out the incorrigible brutes, the ones who were addicted to the adrenal highs of unbridled destruction and its spoils . . . who knew only the way of the gang and were incapable of restraint and strict obedience to his authority. Although the rest had lost none of their ferocity, it was as if their basest urges had been expunged, seared away in the cauldron of that blood-soaked raid. The commander himself had no qualms about what he had done in retrospect, and would have been surprised if any of his followers, to a man, recalled their actions that night with the faintest tinge of regret . . . not the killing, not the burning, not what they had done to the young American woman. But he managed to instill them with a discipline and purpose that went beyond the primal lust for combat, a sense of larger mission, which would be imperative for all that was to occur next. His goal, his driving motivation, was to reclaim for Africa what was African—its very lifeblood, a source of unsurpassed power that outsiders had drawn from its sand through conquest and subjugation and had used to further their own global dominance.

The Americans, the Russians, and recently the Chinese . . . their empires had risen as those on this continent had fallen into stagnation and decay. Risen to unthinkable heights on their broken souls and spines. But the reality they took for granted was about to be struck by the thunder and lightning of change, the geopolitical puzzle they had pieced together swept from the table at which they sat, its pieces scattered helter-skelter around them. With the commander leading a charge none of them could foresee, a new Pan-Africanism would be born.

Oil—it was the lifeblood of the earth, pulsing through the heart and veins of every contemporary superpower. Control its flow and you controlled them. Control them and you quite simply became supreme.

Some called him the Exile, and he did not object to that term in the least—in fact, its sublime irony amused him. When in times past had the visionary achieved recognition before the products of his imagination, his revolutionary dreams and ambitions, were actualized?

Simon Nusairi felt as if the entire arcing trajectory of his life—the fall from privilege to ignominy and disgrace for his refusal to accept complacency, his family's rejection and ultimate denial of his rightful heritage, his embracing the role of pariah and outcast as a form of liberation, and finally his regenesis as a master gamesman and warrior—had been preparation for the great redemptive achievement that lay ahead of him.

He would soon shake the world in his fist. Grab it by the throat and *shake* it. And he would not release it from his choke hold until they acquiesced to his demands. . . .

"Sir, we are ready to get under way on your orders," Mabuir said, tearing him from his thoughts.

The commander nodded, glanced at the tarpaulin-covered equipment. "Give everything a last inspection. . . . I want to be doubly certain the tanks and helicopters are well secured for the trip. The tarps as well. Everything. It's best we take precautions now to avoid delays than have to proceed in fits and starts."

Mabuir gave a brisk military salute. Nusairi gave no outward display of satisfaction, but for him it was yet another affirmative sign that the ragtag band of fighters he'd pieced together had been tightened into a legitimate armed force. He returned his lieutenant's gesture and then reached into his field jacket for his satellite phone.

"Hello?" On the first ring.

Nusairi gave a thin smile. The leader of the so-called Darfur People's Army was another of those in for a surprise. There would soon be no more room for his breed of minor insurgents; they would fall into step or else. But that was still something for the future.

"Ishmael," he said. "I take it you have been waiting for my call."

"Yes," Mirghani said. "How could it be otherwise?"

"And the American?"

"He has retired to my guest room. Whether he sleeps or not is another story. But I confess to envying how he manages to be calm under most circumstances . . . or act as if he is, at any rate."

"Well, he has substantial cause to relax," Nusairi said.

"The shipment came as arranged?"

"Precisely." Nusairi was gazing at the assembly of transport vehicles. "It is already aboard our trucks and set to move west over the border."

"This is the most encouraging word I could have gotten tonight, my friend," Mirghani said, breathing an audible sigh of relief. "After the news from Cameroon several days ago . . ."

"Put it out of your mind," Nusairi said. "It was of trifling consequence in the broader scheme of things." He paused in thought. "I would recommend that you knock on the American's door and pass on your recovered optimism. It's my expectation that he will in turn want to convey it to his puppeteer in the United States."

Mirghani's chuckle was slightly uncomfortable. "I don't believe he would appreciate your characterization of him . . . or the one to whom he answers."

"It makes no difference," Nusairi said. "For all his bluster, he is a hand puppet to be waggled on his master's fingers. A pawn who does as he is told. Let him reassure the one who makes him twitch and jerk that we arc on course."

"I will update him immediately," Mirghani said. "*Allah ma'ak,* may God be with you on your journey."

Nusairi pocketed the phone without a word of farewell. Mirghani was a fool. Another narrow-minded separatist warlord, one of dozens used to firing potshots at Omar Bashir and one another while crouched out of sight behind rocks or inside burrows. If the opportunity arose, he would resort to licking the soles of Western boots in exchange for a fiefdom through which he could parade at will, lording over his flatterers and subjects, strutting about like a peacock with his tail feathers outspread for their admiration.

Grunting to himself, Nusairi walked toward the convoy, gave it a quick once-over, then climbed into the passenger seat of the second truck and radioed the order to move.

A minute later its oversized wheels began to roll.

Playing with her sat phone to kill time aboard the cramped, grimy train from the railway junction at Atbara to Port Sudan, Abby Liu had found a Google search result that read, "The Road from Wadi Halfa to Khartoum." When she'd clicked on the link, she'd come upon a color photograph of a young man standing thigh-deep in an infinite vista of powdery gray sand, a set of barely distinguishable tire treads running between him and the camera lens. Besides the blue screen of sky overhead, and those old, faded tracks, nothing disturbed the barrenness of the near or far horizons.

She'd smiled thinly at the online snapshot, then nudged Kealey in the seat next to her, holding the phone out to show him the image, thinking whoever had posted it had a caustic sense of humor . . . and that it might help break the silence in which he'd sat staring out the window for hours.

He had glanced down at it expressionlessly, shrugged her off, then turned back toward the dust-filmed window.

"My apologies, Ryan," she said. "I won't do it again."

He looked at her. "What?"

"Interrupt the grinding monotony of this ride," she said. "I mistakenly thought you might appreciate it."

Kealey said nothing for a long moment. Then he shook his head. "We need to get to where we're going," he said. "This is like, I don't know. . . ."

"Being stuck in sand?"

He studied her face. And this time a smile ghosted at his lips. "Yeah," he said. "I suppose that's as good a way of putting it as any."

She nodded, a gleam in her slanted brown eyes.

"Something else you find amusing?" Kealey asked.

It was her turn to shrug. "We can only do what we can do," Abby said quietly. "That doesn't include shrinking the desert or laying highways across it—so where's the use in brooding over our situation?" She took her voice down another notch so the local travelers packing the aisles couldn't hear it. "I count us damned fortunate to have gotten this far without any snags."

He grunted. In fact, she was right. Ferran's arrangements had gone beyond holding the ferry's departure for them; Gamal, his fixer at the Aswân pier, had gotten them past the Egyptian customs and immigration officers and onto the boat without a single one of them so much as glancing at their documents. Gamal had assured Kealey there likewise would be no hitch at all when they reached Wadi Halfa the next day, and true to his word, things had gone smoothly, the blue-uniformed Sudanese customs men moving them from the ferry onto the waiting train with alacrity. In that sense, the two thousand dollars Kealey had used to grease Ferran's palm had seemed an absolute bargain.

The problem was that he had not considered that the railway trip to Khartoum aboard the antiquated, slow-moving Sudanese train would take over two days. It had been an oversight that had little bearing on things, since there had been no faster means of transport available to them. The only remedy, using the word loosely, had been to alter their planned route and switch to the Port Sudan line at the Atbara junction. In the port city, they would have the option of hopping a plane to Khartoum or motoring down a paved road—and after a phone call to Seth Holland, the Agency man at the embassy, it had been determined that he would dispatch one of his staff there to meet and drive them down into the capital, once again staying away from the unwanted scrutiny of air security personnel. Which was all well and good. But still . . .

"I have to remind you about Cullen White," Kealey said, looking at Abby. "The man is calculating, and quick on his feet. Once he hears about Saduq being in custody, he's going to put two and two together."

"He can't possibly know you're involved."

"He doesn't have to," Kealey said. "All he does have to do is get a whiff that something about the raid on Saduq's yacht—or his being held out of sight—deviated from what's SOP with Interpol or the EU task force. I think that's already happened, and I'm pretty sure the same thought must have crossed John Harper's mind more than once. I guarantee White won't be waiting around for the sky to fall on his head. Whatever he's been working on, we can expect he'll very quickly start looking at contingencies. And that means ways to shift into high gear." He shook his head. "This holdup is about the last thing we needed. Doesn't matter if we were stuck with it from the get-go . . . I wish I'd at least seen it coming."

Her features serious, Abby sat beside Kealey in private thought as the train clanked along over obsolete wooden railroad ties, the blackness outside its windows no more uniform than the sandy landscape visible by day. Around her, passengers rustled in their sleep amid heaps of shabby-looking baggage and loosely packed cartons.

"We're in far from an ideal spot. I won't quibble with you there," she said at length. And then hesitated, still looking contemplative. "Ryan, this probably doesn't need stating, but we're very different. I don't *work* like you. I'm used to careful planning, gathering of evidence, adherence to rules and process. . . ."

"And you're wondering what happens when we do reach Khartoum," Kealey said.

She simply looked at him, and he all at once recognized something in her expression that he had not seen there before, a kind of vulnerability that caught him off guard.

"I wish I could tell you," he said, whispering now. "But I won't lie, Abby. I have no idea beyond what I said in Limbe. We're going after Ishmael Mirghani. We came into the game late . . . and I get the feeling that we're close to being out of time. All I know is we're at the stage where we'll have to wing it again, and it means we'll have to hit the ground running—"

"And do whatever's necessary," she said, finishing the sentence.

Kealey gave her a long glance, studying her face, and was surprised to find himself wishing he could say something to relieve the unsettled look that continued lingering over it.

But he could not give that much of himself. Try as he might, he could not. And instead he turned away from her, his eyes returning to the window and the black emptiness into which it seemed he'd been staring for an unendurable eternity.

Jacoby Phillips had spent almost an hour tailing Ishmael Mirghani through Khartoum in his ten-year-old blue Saab SPG, having picked him up when he'd exited his suburban home in the northern section of Bahri, leaving a short while after the man who had once introduced himself to the American chargé d'affaires as James Landis slipped out a back entrance and then turned onto a side street from the rear garden.

Phillips had watched Landis hasten down the street from Mirghani's yard, then climb into a waiting Ford Escort, which had promptly driven off toward the highway, heading in the general direction of the Kober Bridge, or Armed Forces Bridge—which, he'd realized, was the most direct route to the airport. Although Landis was not Phillips's assignment, the CIA agent had taken a video capture of him entering the black sedan with his DVR cell phone, making sure to get a close-up shot of its plates. He'd then relayed the encrypted file to his colleague Bruce Mackenzie, whose job *was* to stay on Landis, using the Agency's secure Intelink-SCI wireless intranet, and continued cooped up about a half block from Mirghani's house.

After about ten minutes Mirghani emerged from his front door, carrying a hard-shell briefcase, strode a few blocks to the bus station, and got on the express shuttle to the downtown area. Staying close to him, Phillips slowed down as he boarded, and then eased along three car lengths behind the bus, following it past the Kober Bridge, which Landis's vehicle had taken, and then over the old Blue Nile suspension bridge for the short ride across the river.

Mackenzie had spotted the black Escort within minutes of receiving Phillips's e-mail and video attachment, having waited just a few blocks away from Mirghani's home, outside an area of landscaped trees and lawn along the riverside. The CIA agents had known it was just a matter of time before one, the other, or both of their birds flew the coop, and their assumption had been that they would do so separately. It would have been a source of intensely curious attention had the Muslim radical and his unlikely Western visitor left there together at the peak of U.S.-Sudanese relations; for them to do so now in plain sight was incomprehensible.

In fact, Mackenzie had thought, the same could be said about their relationship, *period*. Whatever link had formed between those two could mean nothing but trouble.

As he'd borne west from Mirghani's neighborhood, the Escort had gotten on the highway belting the Nile and then swung onto the Kober Bridge's wide concrete span. Mackenzie, driving a Honda, had followed it past Al Salaam Park and then the Burrii Cemetery to the traffic circle, where it had turned right onto Buri Road toward the turnoff to the airport.

Moments after the Escort made the turn, however, its driver unexpectedly hit his left signal, slowed, and then pulled onto the shoulder of the two-lane access road and came to a complete halt with his flashers on. Caught by surprise two cars behind it, Mackenzie saw no recourse but to continue straight ahead toward the airport. What else was he supposed to do? Stop behind the Escort? Of course, that was out of the question and just underscored the realization that anything *besides* driving on past the car would have been an outrageous giveaway. But what the hell had happened? There'd been no sign that the Escort was having car trouble. No sign it had gotten a flat tire. And he had been careful to stay far enough behind so that Landis and his driver would not suspect they had anybody on them.

Mackenzie sighed in disgust and resignation. Whatever reason the Escort had for stopping, the real problem was that there was nobody available to take his place on its ass; Phillips was the only other man on the job, and his gig was to stay with Mirghani. He figured the least conspicuous thing he could do now would be to go on to the security checkpoint up ahead, show his diplomatic ID to the guards, then turn toward the arrivals terminal as if he was picking someone up there and simply leave the airport through an alternate route. The only excuse they would have for busting his chops would be that he wasn't in a car with official plates, but he had a registration certificate to show this was his personal vehicle . . . which happened to be the absolute truth.

As he approached the checkpoint, Mackenzie reached across the dash to get his documents out of the glove

box, simultaneously glancing into his rearview mirror
just to see what was up with the Escort.

And then his eyebrows lifted in surprise. Landis's car
had doubled back around the way it had come after
making a U-turn on the access road. And its blinkers
were no longer flashing.

Mackenzie cursed aloud behind the steering wheel.
What in fucking hell was going on? All he could figure
was that Landis had decided to return to Mirghani's
home for some reason—unless, of course, he'd actually,
and inexplicably, realized he was being followed in spite
of every precaution Mackenzie had taken. It was hard
to imagine . . . though he couldn't think of a third explanation that held the slightest bit of water.

He tapped his brakes, slowing for one of the guards
as he left his booth at the lowered barriers. Mackenzie's
preferred explanation for what had occurred would be
that Landis *had* in fact returned to his point of origin
for a reason having nothing to do with his being followed . . . and obviously so, since it would mean he hadn't
caught on to it and would allow Phillips to resume keeping a lookout on him—perhaps even long enough for
Mackenzie to get back on the job.

A minute after passing through the checkpoint under
the leery eyeballs of the security guards, he reached for
his sat phone and punched in Phillips's number, hoping
the Escort had reappeared at Mirghani's place.

The word from his partner, unfortunately, wasn't
close to what he'd wanted to hear.

"Bruce, what's up?" Phillips asked, answering his sat
phone.

Mackenzie gave him an aggravated, profanity-laced
rundown of what had happened on the airport road
and asked if the Escort had gone back across the river
to Bahri.

"No," Phillips said. "Or not to Mirghani's, anyway. He's already left. I'm behind him on the Blue Nile, near the southbound exit ramp."

"Shit on ice," Mackenzie said. "How am I supposed to fucking break this to Holland?"

"Any way you want . . . as long as you do it," Phillips said. "It's one thing if Landis knows somebody's on him. There are candidates galore—for all he knows, it could be the Sudanese. But if he realizes it's *us,* or even suspects it, we could have bigger problems."

Mackenzie grunted in his ear. "Okay, got you," he said.

"Another thought," Phillips said. He'd left the bridge and gotten onto El Geish Avenue, the main thoroughfare into the middle of Khartoum. "You might want to run some traces on the Escort and see what turns up. You got that vid I sent, right?"

"Yeah," Mackenzie said. "I did."

"We have the car's plate numbers, then," Phillips said. "You never know, they might lead to something."

"Or someone," Mackenzie said. He sighed. "Guess I ought to abort the tail."

"May as well, unless you intend on hanging around the arrivals or departures terminal all day and hoping your man eventually crosses your path, which sounds like a crapshoot to me. Even if he heads back to the airport and you're lucky and wind up in the right place . . . if he made you once, he'll be on the lookout for you again."

Mackenzie expelled another breath. "I'm heading toward the exit now," he said. "Goddamn, Jake, where's this leave us?"

Phillips looked out his windshield. The road here in the city proper was already crowded with *bakassi,* or unlicensed minibuses run by private operators, and he

had to be careful not to lose the bus he'd been shadow-
ing as they weaved in and out of the lanes between
them. "With Mirghani, for the moment," he said.
"Look, traffic's getting heavy and I want to stay on the
ball. I'll be in touch later. Out."

"Out," Mackenzie said. He signed off, then turned
toward Ebed Khatim Street on the western side of the
airport. "And fuck Landis and his whore of a mother, assuming the scumbag *has* a mother," he added into the
silence of the car.

"We should be in the clear, Bakri," Cullen White told
the driver, glancing at his wristwatch. "But let's make it
quick now. I don't want to miss my flight."

The man behind the wheel nodded and then pulled
out from the parking area on the University of Juba
campus, near Africa Street. From there an access road
led directly to the airport, approaching it from the east
rather than the north, where White had been when
he'd noticed the Honda behind him.

He had always considered his photographic memory
as much a curse as a gift. Once he saw a face or heard a
name, he would not forget it. He never needed directions to a location—or around it—after paying it even
the briefest visit. He'd always learned easily in school,
not just because he could remember the contents of
what he read, but because he could call to mind how
the words had appeared on the page or computer
screen. In a flash, he could go back to the experience of
making love to a woman decades before—the sensa-
tions he'd felt, the look in her eyes, the sounds and
whispers of their mounting pleasure. He was equally
able to savor the taste of revenge long after it had been
taken on an enemy.

These were some of the blessings.

The curse was remembering—no, *reliving*—in totality his mistakes, his failures, and the pain of embarrassment, dishonor, and ostracism. He understood the value of taking one's lessons from the past. But having to carry it with him like some sort of ghost whose essence dwelled within his very cellular material—that was too often an unwanted burden.

Today, however, White was not about to complain about his eidetic memory. Were it not for the vivid accuracy of his memory, he might not have recognized the gray Honda sedan that had been following him from the greenbelt across the Blue Nile near the entrance to the Kober Bridge. Recognized the car or its driver. For he had seen both for no more than two or three seconds weeks ago, when he had been entering the U.S. embassy in Khartoum for a sit-down with Walter Reynolds. As he'd turned from the street to the embassy steps, the car had been swinging from the avenue in front into the curb cut on his right, which in turn led to the ramp that went down to the facility's underground parking garage.

There had been nothing exceptional about that moment. Nothing he could quantify about why it was imprinted on his synapses. But when he'd noticed the car behind him today, he had recognized it—its plate number, its minor dents, the fact that only three of its four tires were whitewalls, and that the all-black tire also had a slightly different type of hub. He couldn't explain why he remembered. It was just that way for him.

The man in the Honda was a worker at the embassy. His nominal post wasn't of any importance. As far as White was concerned, it only mattered that he had been put on his tail—and that he was almost certainly a

CIA plant within the embassy staff. The question was . . . what did it mean in the broad scope of things?

The press had attributed the Limbe raid on Hassan al-Saduq's yacht to an Interpol-EU antipiracy operation. It had directed its questions and criticisms about the arms merchant's unexplained, and seemingly extra-judicial, disappearance while in custody at the investigative task force and the Cameroonian authorities. The coverage about the motive behind the attack, and its legality, centered on civil liberties issues.

There was no mention of Agency involvement, no reason anyone in the press would suspect it . . . but the press didn't know what White knew about the deal that had been taking place aboard the boat.

His suspicions had been right all along. His and Stralen's. Somebody in Washington had sniffed out what was going on. That meant a schism had arisen between DCI Andrews on one side and POTUS, Stralen, and Fitzgerald on the other—and not just in terms of foreign policy. If the details of their plan were uncovered, there would be more, much more, for the press to write about than the questionable legalities of a weapons peddler's arrest in Cameroon. It would be the biggest political story to hit the international headlines in years and would likely topple everyone involved. Most especially General Stralen.

Stralen . . . if what he'd done was fully uncovered, he would be labeled a traitor. A conspirator to a crime many would find reprehensible. There would be no debate over extenuating circumstances, as with the planners of Iran-Contra. No chance of redemption. Historians would cast him with the likes of Benedict Arnold, Lee Harvey Oswald, and John Wilkes Booth. His name would go down in *infamy*.

White cut free of his thoughts as Bakri slowed to a halt at the first airport checkpoint, fishing his papers out of his travel bag, then reaching over to hand them to the driver. A minute later the guard passed them back through the Escort's lowered window and waved the vehicle through.

"Bakri, you've done your job well while I've been here," White said as the driver returned his documents to him. "There's no higher compliment I can offer."

Bakri thanked him with an appreciative nod and swung to the left, following the signs to the Sudan Airways departure terminal.

As they neared the drop-off area, Cullen White took hold of his bag and slid over toward his door, waiting for the car to stop. The time for reflection was over. History could shine whatever light it might on the legacy of someone like Joel Stralen. But White knew only one thing—he owed nothing to anyone *but* the general. He himself had no moral constraints. He didn't care a whit how the world remembered him, or if it remembered him at all. Posterity was outside his realm of consideration. He was a role player, a man who worked out of sight in the interstices of power and politics, who lubricated the gears of machinery others saw the need to construct, who did whatever it took to see a mission through from inception to execution. That was it.

You've done your job well. . . . There's no higher compliment I can offer.

White had sincerely meant what he said to his driver. And soon he would be on his way to Kassala to meet up with Simon Nusairi's strike force, where he intended to at last finish the job General Stralen had entrusted him to do.

He hoped that he, too, would prove worthy in the final accounting.

* * *

The third most senior of Seth Holland's handful of Agency personnel, Jacoby Phillips was the only member of his staff who did not reside at the embassy, but rather occupied an apartment suite at the sprawling and elegant Hotel Granville on the banks of the Nile, where he held the titular position of resort manager. Owned by the Brits since its establishment, the Granville had been Winston Churchill's preferred choice of room and board on his trips to the country during the colonial era, and it had continued to accommodate international businessmen in the many decades since Sudan gained its constitutional independence.

When Holland had requested an operative for placement outside the embassy's confines in the late nineties, Phillips had been an ideal candidate for the assignment. Much of it had to do with his background. Of mixed cultural descent, he had inherited his Ethiopian mother's gingery brown skin and was born and partially raised in London, where his white-as-crumpet-dough father had run a large air transport firm before the family's eventual relocation to New York. Even before the current flare-up between the United States and Sudan, Caucasian foreigners, especially from the U.S. of A., had been regarded with heavy suspicion and hostility by many locals, whose anti-Western fervor had been on the rise for decades. However, if you were black—or *looked* black like Phillips, who resisted defining himself according to race, being equally proud of both sides of his heritage—there was at least a chance you would receive more civil treatment than people with white faces, although it could sometimes contrarily provoke an antagonistic backlash among elements of the population who regarded black Americans as sellouts to Western culture and ideology.

Phillips figured you could never totally win at the race game no matter what country you were in, but being a black man still beat the hell out of being white in Khartoum, and how was *that* for a turnaround? As he had learned soon after accepting the post here, his skin color and multiethnic background made it a challenge for the ignoramuses on the street to figure out what particular slurs to hurl at him, and, more significantly, for radical Islamic terrorists—among them members of al-Qaeda, which had been a major player in the neighborhood before Omar al-Bashir had fallen into its disfavor for expelling certain rabble-rousing mujahideen—to decide whether they ought to attempt to rob him, take him hostage, and/or murder him for the sheer sport of it.

But Phillips had other things to think about now. The bus carrying his man had reached the city center and had stopped to discharge its passengers about five blocks west of the *Souq Arabi.* Phillips stayed on Mirghani as he walked in the general direction of the city's commercial hub, saw an open parking space along the curb, and pulled in while he had the chance. The traffic here remained tolerable, but he knew the streets and avenues would grow exponentially more congested as they got closer to the *souq,* with its businesses and outdoor markets. From here on out it would be easier to follow him on foot.

Phillips exited the car and started up the busy sidewalk, remaining 10 yards or so behind the political leader. He was wearing a navy sport jacket, tan slacks, and a white shirt with what appeared to be his credit-card-sized Hotel Granville photo identification clipped to its breast pocket. The card was outwardly indistinguishable from his usual ID unless examined closely by a discerning eye, at which point it indeed might be possible to see the photographic lens in front camouflaged by the hotel's logo. While Phillips wasn't nearly as in love with gadgets as many of his colleagues, he would have admitted to finding the eight-gigabyte digital video recorder a clever and useful spy tool, particularly when coupled with the cell phone digital recorder he'd used earlier in his surveillance.

After three blocks Mirghani came to the Al Shamal Islamic Bank and turned inside. Phillips found this somewhat serendipitous, since the Granville's employee accounts—including his own, since he drew an income from the hotel in addition to his CIA paycheck—were at the same institution. He could therefore find a legit reason for being inside the place while keeping tabs on his mark.

Once inside the bank, Phillips was quick to observe a couple of things that were interesting enough to make him finger the tiny record button on his ID card cam. The first was that there were three men waiting for Mirghani just past the door. All wore traditional Muslim garb and had the wary demeanor of trained bodyguards. The second was that after briefly conferring with them, Mirghani had gone right over to the carpeted area alongside the banking floor, where the officers sat at their desks. A guard had immediately shown him to one of the officers, while the guards who'd met up with him hung back on the banking floor . . . their watchfulness convincing Phillips his initial impression of them had been accurate.

Phillips found a customer counter that gave him a good vantage of the officer's desk, parked himself there, and took his DVR phone out of his pocket. He preferred it to the ID card cam for this situation, since he would not have to conspicuously stand facing Mirghani to record his images, but could position himself—and the phone—at different angles while pretending to have a conversation.

Mirghani and the officer wasted no time commencing with their transaction. After a courteous exchange at his desk, the bank officer gave him some papers to fill out and then led him off down a short hall behind the tellers' stations—Mirghani bringing his attaché case with him. Waiting for him to reappear, Phillips put away his phone contraption, took a withdrawal slip from a rack, and began filling it out. The trio of guards just stuck around near the officers' area, making no attempt to look like anything but what they were.

Phillips, who in contrast to the guards very *much* wanted to blend into the woodwork, then got on the longest teller's queue he could find. When he was better than two-thirds of the way to the window and Mirghani still hadn't reappeared, he glanced down at his withdrawal slip, feigned realizing he'd made an error on it, then went back to the customer counter for a replacement and begun writing out another. That gave him several extra minutes of waiting around without being noticed.

It was all he needed. Less than half an hour after entering the bank, Mirghani and the officer emerged from the hall into which they'd gone off together and shook hands, the officer going back to his desk, Mirghani rejoining his bodyguards with his attaché.

As the four men left the bank, Phillips tore up his withdrawal slip, deposited it in a trash receptacle, and trailed them out to the street. Mirghani and his escorts did not return to the bus station but went the opposite way, toward the gold market. As Mirghani and two of the men entered one of the exchanges lined along the sidewalk, a third went on up the street and disappeared around the corner. Phillips remained outside the exchange, his phone in hand.

The third guard returned about ten minutes later in a white minivan, double-parking outside the gold exchange. Shortly afterward, Mirghani left the exchange with the other guards and entered the minivan. Though he was still carrying his attaché case, the guards who'd entered the gold exchange with him were now toting a pair of larger metal cases that looked fairly hefty in their grasps. Phillips didn't think it would take a deductive genius to figure out what was inside them, considering where they'd come from.

He took more videos as the foursome drove off, wishing he'd been in his car so he could stay on them, or that he could phone somebody else to pick them up. But with Bruce Mackenzie likely still out near the airport after being given the shake by Landis, and George Swanson in Port Sudan to meet and greet the new arrivals, there was no one to do it. To say the team in Khartoum was undermanned was putting it mildly; the truth was that Holland had been making do here for years with nothing more than a skeleton crew.

He left the gold market to head back the way he had come, hoofing through the city center toward his parked Saab. He was going to work on a hunch and try to shortcut it back to Bahri. If his instincts proved correct—and he trusted they would—Ishmael Mirghani would be returning there as well.

The thing the CIA man mostly found himself wondering was how long he meant to stick around . . . and whether it would be possible to keep him from flying the coop.

*   *   *

"Mr. Harner, Ms. Evart, I'm very pleased to welcome you to Sudan on behalf of the Boutros Corporation," George Swanson said outside the railway station, using not only their aliases but also the cover he'd been given for his drive between Khartoum and Port Sudan.

Abby was shaking his hand. "It's fine to use my first name," she said with a wry little smile. "I've been Abby to everyone my entire life. Call me anything else, and I might not know who you're talking to."

Swanson's own smile was accompanied by a knowing glance. "Certainly, Abby," he said. And then nodded to his right. "The parking area's over there. . . . My vehicle's the white Jeep Cherokee off the center aisle. If you'd like, we can get some refreshments before hitting the road—"

Feeling stiff and disheveled after the long, cramped train ride from Atbara, Kealey stood beside Abby and looked at him. Behind them, passengers were leaving the station in groups, carrying their bags and bundles from the railroad cars. Some were being greeted by friends and relatives as others haggled over fares with the drivers of beaten-up gypsy cabs outside the station.

"We aren't driving to Khartoum," Kealey said. He did not have to turn in Abby's direction to feel her eyes on him.

Swanson's face, meanwhile, had become a question mark. "I'm not exactly sure I understand. . . ."

"It's seven hundred and fifty miles from here to there," Kealey said. "What does that make the drive time on the local roads? Twelve, fifteen hours?"

"About that, yes," Swanson replied.

"And a flight from the airport here to Khartoum International? How long would it take?"

"I see what you're getting at," Swanson said. "But we've made arrangements—"

"How long?"

Swanson hesitated. "An hour or so if we're able to catch a flight without too much waiting around," he said. He lowered his voice. "The airport security's tighter at both ends. That's the reason Holland decided the roads were our safest bet."

Kealey shrugged. "He's probably right. But we've killed too much time traveling to worry about what's safe right now," he said. "Whatever's been on the burner in Khartoum has to be reaching a boil. Our papers have to be good enough, because we're flying in."

Swanson regarded him steadily for a full thirty seconds, then turned to Abby. "You're with him on this?"

She frowned. "I suppose," she said, then cast a prickly look at Kealey. "Although it would have been nice if I'd had a chance to consider it beforehand."

Kealey kept his eyes on Swanson, saying nothing. Finally the CIA man produced a relenting sigh. "Any idea what I'm supposed to do with the Cherokee?"

Kealey shrugged. "Leave it in the airport parking lot," he said.

Swanson didn't bother replying that he could have figured that out all by himself.

CHAPTER 19

KHARTOUM

"Are we able to talk openly?" Kealey asked. "I mean, without prying eyes and ears."

He was in the station chief's office at the embassy on Ali Abdel Latif Street, less than an hour after his thankfully uneventful flight from Port Sudan had alighted on the tarmac at Khartoum International.

"I think we can feel at ease," Holland replied from across his desk. Placing a hush-hush request to Sergeant Sadowski, he had seen to it that his office at the embassy was swept by a suitcase-sized broad spectrum countersurveillance device consisting of radio, audio, infrared, and acoustic correlation scanners. Simply put, the advanced microcomputer-controlled detection suite could detect everything from passive and active microphone bugs in phones and light fixtures to the low-freq oscillations created by the tiny motors in concealed spy cameras. "As much as is possible anywhere these days."

Kealey nodded. With him in the room besides the CIA station chief were Abby Liu and agents Phillips and Swanson. Mackenzie had switched up with Phillips and was across the river, monitoring the activities at Ishmael Mirghani's house.

"What about Walter Reynolds?" Phillips asked.

"What about him?" Holland said. "I'm having a closed-door personnel meeting that's none of his business."

Phillips gave Abby and Kealey inclusive nods. "With a couple of staffers he's never seen before."

Holland shrugged. "I'm through tiptoeing around him. We've got the head of the DIA's personal reclamation project, Cullen White, teamed up with Hassan al-Saduq, Somali pirates, and Ishmael Mirghani, the founder of a Sudanese militant group that may be more anti-American than the current regime." He glanced at Abby. "Thanks to our esteemed colleagues at Interpol, we've got evidence that Saduq first cut a major illegal arms and equipment deal with Omar al-Bashir's government—in cahoots with Egypt, no less—and then arranged for the shipment to be hijacked so he could resell the merchandise to a third party allied with Mirghani's Darfur People's Army . . . or possibly in command and control of it. Finally, we have an almost ironclad case that Stralen, directly or through White, provided the cash that Mirghani and company used to pay for the shipment, which is literally enough to equip a small army, using smurfed Department of Defense funds." Holland paused. "I'll shut up in a second, Jake. But to finish answering your question . . . Reynolds may not realize it, but what he knows or doesn't know isn't important anymore. He's provided secret assistance to White, and that puts him waist-deep in shit. If he wants to keep from sinking in to his nose and mouth, he can't do anything to obstruct our work that won't further compromise him and God knows who else in Washington. His best recourse is to keep out of our way and think about ducking for cover."

"Then let's forget him and concentrate on Mirghani," Kealey said. He nodded toward Abby. "He might not be the whole reason we've been jumping back and forth across the African continent, but he's a big part of it. We need to get our hands on him."

"And time might be running out after this morning," Phillips said. "The sequence of events speaks for itself. After meeting with White at his home, he busses into the city, makes what appears to be a large bank withdrawal, then walks over to the gold market with his bodyguards and leaves there with two large, heavy-looking security briefcases—driving off in a minivan. To me that can only indicate one thing. . . ."

"He's getting ready to leave the country," Swanson said. "Gold is universal currency, and right now it's trading at a high, going for almost eight hundred dollars per troy ounce. From Jake's description, those briefcases would have held quite a few cast bars."

"It certainly doesn't sound as if he's just going on holiday," Abby said. "What's the latest on him?"

"Swanson says he's cleaning house," Holland said. "No question, Kealey, we have to move. But one thing we cannot afford is a repeat of Limbe."

Kealey shot him a glance. "Meaning?"

"I've got less than six months left to my hitch in North Africa," Holland said. "I have a wife and son in Florida that I miss terribly, and I've been told that my next assignment will be in the States. When I leave here, I'm not looking back, Kealey. I won't fuck up, and

I won't be sent to any more foreign boondocks as punishment for anyone else fucking up."

Kealey shrugged. "If you're going to send Mirghani a formal invitation to join us for coffee, we'd better sign it fast and messenger it over to him, because I doubt the local mail service will deliver it before he books."

The station chief bristled, straightened in his chair. "I would appreciate it if you could rein in the sarcasm."

"And I've had my fill of hearing about Limbe," Kealey said. "I was asked to make the calls there, and I did, and all things considered, we were successful pulling off what we intended. If you're setting the operational guidelines now, fine, tell me what they are. But for Christ's sake let's get on with it before everything becomes moot."

Silence. After a moment Holland's posture relaxed. "I'm not going to tie your hands, Kealey. We're taking Mirghani into custody, and I don't expect he'll volunteer with a smile. But Omar al-Bashir won't be sorry to be rid of him. He can have somebody else do the dirty work and not lose face or alienate the Muslim fringes. It's likely he won't interfere with us either pre or post factum."

"So, I repeat, what are the ground rules?" Kealey said.

"Just that you recognize we're in a hostile environment," Holland said. "We're better off doing this peacefully. . . . If there's a chance, then take it, so we can at least say we tried."

"That's it?"

Holland nodded. "Yes, Kealey," he said. "Besides wishing you Godspeed."

*   *   *

It was almost dusk when George Swanson drove the pair of newcomers across the river to Bahri, Kealey beside him in the passenger seat of a Jeep Cherokee 4x4, Abby in the rear. Requisitioned from the embassy's fleet, the vehicle was identical to the one in which he'd ridden to Port Sudan . . . and that was now being babysat at the U.S. consular office there.

Phillips was behind them in his Saab, followed by Mackenzie in a freshly req-slipped Subaru. The thinking had been that if White-slash-Landis had identified the Honda as a surveillance vehicle that morning, there was a fair chance he'd passed along the information to Mirghani. It was just good sense, then, that Mackenzie use a different car as a precaution against easy identification . . . although subtlety would not be a vital component of the team's approach.

"We're all through here in Khartoum after tonight," Swanson mused aloud to his passengers, turning left off the Blue Nile Bridge. "Phillips, Mac, myself . . . Our covers are going to be blown."

"You sound almost sorry about the prospect of moving on," Abby said. She turned from the window to look at him. "I'd think you'd welcome the change."

"We've been together for a while," Swanson said. "Four years for me, almost as long for Mac. Phillips was the newbie, came over to us maybe two years ago. Holland wanted a man who worked outside the embassy and got creative with him. Jake manages an old Brit hotel called the Granville, but it looks like they're about to have a job vacancy." He shrugged. "People get used to working as a team, what can I say? I guess when you're stuck in hell, the heat just strengthens the bonds."

Abby gave a smile. "I've been there," she said. "Several times."

Swanson glanced in the rearview. "What about you, Kealey? Word is you've been around."

"Enough to figure out it doesn't pay getting attached to anyone or anything," Kealey said tersely. "How close are we to Mirghani's house?"

Swanson's eyes had returned to the windshield. "It's under a mile up ahead," he said.

"We need somebody ready in case he tries to break for it," Kealey said. "Who's best? Phillips or Mackenzie?"

Swanson shrugged. "Mackenzie was a counterterrorist in Afghanistan right after nine-eleven, one of the first to hook up with the Northern Alliance."

"Jawbreaker?" asked Kealey.

Swanson made a zipping gesture across his lips. "You'd have to ask him the details," he said. "We can all handle ourselves. But if you want my opinion, Mac's got the quals for any situation."

Kealey nodded. "Buzz him on the cell," he said. "I want him out back of the house."

Swanson nodded, reached for his sat phone, passed along Kealey's instructions as he drove on for several minutes. The sun was sinking low now, its glow staining the sky to the west shades of red and violet, casting orange embers on the slow-moving Nile waters to their right. Flat-roofed homes the color of sandstone lined the street to their left, ranging from single-story buildings to some that rose three stories high. Many had trees and iron gates in front.

"This used to be Osama bin Laden's neighborhood before he got Tomahawked, did you know?" Swanson jabbed a finger at one of the taller houses. "There's Mirghani's place just up ahead . . . but I guess you might have figured it out for yourself."

Kealey looked out his window. There were several vehicles parked in front—three cars and a minivan, which he took to be the one Phillips had seen Mirghani climb into outside the gold exchange in the *Souq Arabi*. A group of men were on the sidewalk, some standing vigilantly near the vehicles, others gathered near Mirghani's door. He took a quick head count. "Bodyguards," he said. "Five of them."

"Compared to four of us . . . and that's just from what we can see," Swanson said. "What do you think of our odds if we have to tangle?"

"I never bet against myself," Kealey said. "Does Mirghani always have that kind of protection?"

"Exactly the opposite," Swanson said with a shake of his head. "This is unusual. He keeps a low profile, never flaunts his clout. It's partly why Bashir tolerates him."

"What's the other part?" Kealey asked.

"His supporters make up a large political and religious base," Swanson said. "With all the pressure coming at him from outside the country, Bashir needs to unify the political factions inside it, especially here in the northern part of the country. There've been some deep divisions over Darfur, and then over the new hydroelectric plant to the east, which provides most of the power to the capital. Whole villages were wiped out to make room for it, which didn't do much for Bashir's popularity in those areas. And no wonder, since it was already damned low."

"Any particular reason?"

"Thousands of people were already displaced by Chinese and Russian petroleum refineries that process the crude oil drilled in the south. They pipeline it up here and then ship the barrels out of Port Sudan."

Kealey grunted thoughtfully, still watching the men on the sidewalk. "Okay, slow down," he said. "Let's stop across the street from them. I mean *right* across. Phillips too."

"I suppose you want them to notice us," said Swanson.

Kealey nodded in the affirmative. "And to know we don't care about it."

"Do you mind if I ask what comes after that?" Swanson asked.

"Holland wanted us to try the peaceful approach," Kealey said. "We're going to have a talk with them."

Kealey, Abby, and Swanson exited the Cherokee together, Phillips leaving his car and hastening over to them as they crossed to where Mirghani's bodyguards watched curiously from the sidewalk. Although Kealey had taken a quick shower and changed clothes at the embassy, he hadn't shaved since leaving Cameroon, and his cheeks showed almost a week's dark growth of beard. He was wearing a lightweight black field jacket over a Glock 35 9mm that Seth Holland had provided on loan, the jacket halfway unbuttoned so he could have rapid access to the gun.

He went straight toward the largest of the bodyguards, a tall, blockish, square-shouldered man in loose trousers and a traditional thigh-length tunic with a holstered pistol bulging underneath it. He was leaning against the front of the parked minivan, studying the Westerners with the intensity of a raptor perched on a ledge.

"You speak English?" Kealey said. He'd stepped onto the pavement to face the bodyguard, aware Abby and the others had moved in slightly behind him.

The bodyguard fixed him in a long stare. "What are you doing here?"

"We want to talk," Kealey said.

"Who sent you?"

"I already answered one question," Kealey said. "It's your turn."

The man kept looking at him. "Go ahead," he said then. "Talk."

"Not to you," Kealey said. "We have some questions for Ishmael Mirghani."

"He cannot see anyone now."

"He'll be willing to see us," Kealey said. "If he's smart."

The bodyguard's stare hardened. "Whoever you are, this is not your country," he said. "You do not belong here. And you must leave at once."

"Like Mirghani's leaving?" Kealey said. He tilted his head toward the minivan. "Somebody's going somewhere, and I assume he's the man. But I propose you do him a favor. Phone inside the house, or have one of your men do it. Let him know I'd like to talk to him."

The bodyguard studied his features for another long moment. "Who are you?"

"You can tell him my name is Ryan Kealey," he said. "And that I know Cullen White."

The bodyguard shot one of the others a glance. "Ahzir," he said, extending his hand. "Give me your phone."

Ahzir took his cell phone out of his pocket and handed it to him. He thumbed a key, spoke into the phone in Arabic. Kealey heard his name mentioned, and then White's, but the rest was unintelligible to him. After a moment the bodyguard paused, dropped his voice, added something too quiet for Kealey to hear. Finally he looked at Kealey again, shaking his head.

"It is as I told you," he said, the phone still raised to his ear. "He cannot speak—"

Kealey lunged at him, simultaneously drawing his 9mm, knowing he'd have to take him by surprise. He jammed the gun into the big man's solar plexus and shoved him back against the side of the minivan, snatching the cell phone from his grasp before he could recover his balance.

Behind him, Abby, Phillips, and Swanson had pulled their sidearms on the other bodyguards and were holding them out in two-handed grips.

"Stay where you are!" Swanson barked, motioning with his gun. "One move, you're dead! *Mat!* Understand?"

Kealey, meanwhile, pressed the cell against his own cheek, keeping the Glock buried in the tall bodyguard's ribs. "Mirghani, you there?" he shouted into the phone.

Silence. But Kealey could hear him breathing into the mouthpiece.

"Come on, Mirghani, *talk*," he said. "There's no point pretending you can't hear me."

More audible breaths over the phone. Then: "Why are you here, Mr. Kealey?"

"I want information," Kealey said. "You can leave the city, keep your gold, bring whatever else you want out with you. But first you'll have to answer some questions—"

Kealey was interrupted by a sudden, startling crack of gunfire behind him and to his right. There was one shot, another, then Abby shouting, "*No!*" And three more rapid bursts.

His attention diverted by the chaotic sounds, Kealey flicked a glance over his shoulder and saw Phillips on his knees, clutching the middle of his chest, blood slicking his fingers as it gushed out between them to puddle on the sidewalk around his sagging form. Standing over him as he sunk to the pavement, his eyes wide, Swanson was still covering his man, who'd kept his hands up above his head. But one of the other bodyguards lay sprawled on his back nearby, Abby standing over him with her own semiautomatic pistol. The right side of his head had been blown apart, reduced to a horrible amalgam of bone, brains, and bits of ragged, bloody flesh.

Kealey realized what had happened in an instant. The bodyguard had reached for his gun despite Swanson's warning, and Abby had taken him out. But not before he'd caught Phillips in the chest, maybe more than once. And the rhythmic spurts of blood through his hands made it clear the field agent had been struck in his heart or a connected blood vessel.

It was with Kealey's attention momentarily divided that Ahzir seized the chance to whip a concealed gun out from under his flowing tunic. At the same time, the big man he'd backed against the minivan chopped an enormous hand up under Kealey's arm, knocking the snout of his 9mm away from his body. The brawny bodyguard locked his fingers around Kealey's wrist, digging them into it like pistons, twisting it, trying to wrest the weapon from his grip.

Kealey's reaction was automatic, his years of combat training kicking in as muscle memory—all of him, his mind and body, his entire *being*, pulled into focus. His mind stripped of conscious thought, he brought his knee up between the big man's legs, heard a guttural exclamation of pain as the breath rushed from his mouth. Kealey, unrelenting, smashed a fist hard into his jaw, hit him a second time in the face, and then the man staggered backward, his fingers loosening around Kealey's wrist. Tearing free of his grasp, Kealey spun on Ahzir, raised his pistol and squeezed the trigger, firing twice into him at close range. The front of Ahzir's tunic puffed out where the bullets struck, red splotches appearing

on the white cotton fabric. Then his legs went soft and
he crumpled lifelessly to the ground.

Even as he fell, Kealey had pivoted back around toward the big man—and none too soon. The man had
sufficiently recovered to lunge at him, shoving a hand
under his jacket to pull his own gun from its holster.

Kealey took cold aim before the weapon could appear and shot him once in the middle of the forehead.
The big man looked at him with what might have been
a mute expression of astonishment and disbelief, the
bullet hole ringed by an aureole of seared flesh, his
mouth gaping open as a thin rill of blood slid down between his eyes and over his nose. Then he produced a
kind of belching croak and dropped hard onto his face.

Kealey was peripherally aware of what was going on
around him on the street—cars slowing, people's heads
briefly appearing from doors and windows, the sound
of their keyed-up voices exchanging fearful words before they retreated inside. It was a sure thing the authorities would show before long.

He turned back toward where Phillips had been
shot, saw that he was lying on the ground, with Abby
and Swanson huddled over his supine body. Abby had
taken off the Windbreaker she'd been wearing and
bunched it over the wound in his chest, trying to
staunch the flow of blood, but it was completely soaked
through, and Phillips was neither moving nor, to all ap-
pearances, breathing.

Kealey hurried over, pressed two fingers against
Phillips's neck, then slid one finger down the side of his
jaw.

Abby stared at him. "Ryan, is he—"

"*Shhh!*" Nothing from the carotid or facial arteries.
Kealey lifted Phillips's wrist, felt for a pulse there, didn't

detect one. And the pinkish red foam on his lips and chin was a bad sign—it meant a lung had been punctured and would have been filling with blood as he tried to draw in air. Kealey looked up, shook his head. "He's gone," he said, snapping his eyes to Swanson's stunned face. "Where'd your guy go?"

Swanson nodded behind him. "Ran off in that direction, I think."

"No way to tell if he's bolted or gone for reinforcements," Kealey said, shaking his head. He motioned toward Phillips's body. "Take him back to the Jeep."

The field op swallowed hard. "What about you?"

"I'm going in," Kealey said, nodding toward the house. "Abby . . . get Mackenzie on the phone. Tell him to stay put out back."

"And then what?" Her voice was trembling. "You can't go in alone."

"Listen to me, Abby. Somebody's sure to have called the police by now. We have to get this done before they show. And I'll need you on the lookout," Kealey replied.

"But Mirghani might have more guards inside—"

"I can handle them." Kealey sprang to his feet. "I've got my cell. When you two hear the sirens, warn me if you can and get out of here. I'll meet you back at the embassy."

He turned toward Mirghani's house, leapfrogged the low iron fence, and raced over a tiled outer court to its front door, trying the knob. As expected, it was unlocked; his men had been in the process of clearing the place out when Kealey's team arrived.

He pushed the door open, went through, and assayed his surroundings, the Glock extended in his grip. He was in an entry foyer that broadened out into a spacious, cleanly furnished oval parlor or living room with a polished hardwood floor, wide archways on two sides, and light organdy curtains over its rear windows. Kealey peered through the arch to his right, saw it gave way to another open parlor with some damask chairs and pillows, an inlaid coffee table on an oriental rug, and a number of packed and half-packed cartons on the floor. A hasty inspection revealed that another arch on the far side of that room led to a kitchen.

There was nobody in any of the rooms.

Cautiously, Kealey stepped deeper into the main parlor, moving along its left wall. Then he pivoted on his heel to look past its second archway and saw a flight of runnered stairs climbing up to the home's second story.

His gun still pointed out in front of him, he turned through the arch and streaked up the steps, taking them two at a time. On the second floor he passed two bedrooms, a bathroom, a hallway with a large walk-in closet on the right wall. Still no sign anyone was present.

He reached into a pocket for his cell. "Mackenzie, it's Kealey. I'm inside the house."

"Roger," the agent said. "I . . . I heard what happened to Phillips—"

"We can't afford to think about that now," Kealey said. "You see anybody leave through a back door?"

"No."

"You're positive? Not out the door, the garden, a window . . . ?"

"Nobody left the house," Mackenzie said. "Not through any entrance but the front. I'd have seen him."

"Then Mirghani has to be in here someplace." His eyes swept the hallway. "Where the hell—"

"Kealey? You all right?"

"Yeah," Kealey said. He'd settled his gaze on the

walk-in closet with its closed sliding door. "Stay where you are, Mackenzie. I'm going to need you to be there, copy?"

"Roger that."

Kealey pocketed the phone, moved across to the right side of the hallway, flattened his back against the wall, and then sidled along to the edge of the closet's door. His 9mm in his right fist, he reached his free hand across the wall for the closet door's finger pull handle and tugged the door open on its tracks. Finally he heaved himself off the wall with a half turn so he'd end up looking directly into the closet.

There was the loud discharge of a gun inside it, and a bullet shrieked past his ear. The bodyguard hidden among the row of hanging garments had no chance to get off a second shot; Kealey, reflexively down in a squat, pumped three shots into his heart and watched him droop backward into a corner of the closet, one leg bent underneath him, the other sticking straight out across its floor.

Entering, Kealey crouched over the dead man and took the gun from his slackened grasp. It was a 9mm semiautomatic Caracal, the ammo usable for his own weapon. Depressing the catch, he ejected its magazine and shoved it into a cargo pocket on his trousers. Then he stepped over the guard's outstretched leg and pushed aside the clothes on the hanger pole—traditional Arabic robes and shawls as well as Western-style suits.

There on the back wall of the closet were the telltale seams of a safe-room door . . . and the camouflaged digital peephole lens above it. Kealey moved deeper inside, stood in front of the steel-reinforced panel, and rapped it with his fist. The solid thud he heard was reminiscent of when he'd tested the door of the EU team's armored BMW in Yaoundé.

Kealey heard his phone trill in his pocket. Abby probably. She must have heard the shots. But there was no time to answer.

"Mirghani, I know you can hear me!" he shouted. Exactly how much time *did* he have before the police stormed in? Not much, it couldn't be much at all, though he guessed he'd been in the house less than five minutes. "I'm telling you right now, you're coming *out*."

No answer. Kealey hadn't figured he'd get one.

"My people have the back entrance to the house covered!" he yelled. "Either you leave with me or you aren't going anywhere."

Nothing. Kealey's mind raced. Mirghani would know the police were on the way. Figure he could wait things out till they got here. Unless . . .

Whirling in a circle, Kealey holstered his gun, then sprinted over to the stairs and down to the first floor. He couldn't afford to lose a second.

In the main parlor now, he turned, ran through the foyer, and a heartbeat later was out in the courtyard. Abby was standing there inside the fence. Her cell phone in her hand, she was looking at him with tense, agitated features.

"Kealey, what's going on? I heard the gunfire inside, and when you didn't answer—"

"Just wait here," he said. "Don't move."

And then he went loping across the street, zigzagging past rubberneckers toward the Cherokee, where Swanson sat tensely behind the wheel, Phillips's body covered with a blanket in the cargo section. He hurried around back without a word, yanked open the hatch, looked around for a jerrican, knowing there had to be one. This was an Agency vehicle, and here in Sudan, where you never knew when you'd be traveling hundreds of damned miles through the desert, it would be as standard as a tire wrench.

Kealey found the plastic container almost right away, reached inside to grab it from a storage slot in the rear compartment, then slammed the hatch shut and deliberately sloshed its contents around. It was three-quarters full, maybe better, meaning there had to be almost five gallons of gasoline inside.

He returned to the driver's door. "Swanson, listen," he said through its lowered window. "The second the cops get close, I mean the *second,* you and Abby take off without looking back . . . and make sure they see you. I'm going to need a deke, got it? We'll have the embassy take care of the rest. These sons of bitches are going to find out soon enough we're trying to save their president's miserable ass."

Swanson stared at him. "Kealey . . . what the hell are you doing?"

Kealey didn't stop to answer now, but instead dashed back across to the house with the jerrican, pausing only to motion Abby toward the Jeep before he plunged inside, this time hooking sharply right through the two downstairs parlors into the kitchen. He looked around for matches, pulled open a drawer, still didn't see any, decided to quit searching, and grabbed a dishrag from a countertop near the sink.

He wound the rag tightly into a makeshift torch, uncapped the jerrican, poured gasoline over one end. Next he went to the range, turned on a burner, and held the saturated end of the dishrag in the flame. It immediately caught fire.

Kealey went bounding to the second floor with the

fiery rag in one hand and the open jerrican in the other. He'd need water in a minute, but the rag was really ablaze now, and he again jogged on past the bathroom to the walk-in closet.

"Mirghani!" He held the rag and jerrican up to the safe room's peephole now. "See this? I'm setting fire to the closet—and if you think the police are coming, you're wrong. I've got them fooled. Same if you think the firemen can get here before the smoke kills you. You watch, Mirghani. *Watch!*"

And with that Kealey began dousing the closet with gasoline, splashing it over the clothes draped over the hangers, the walls, even the body of the guard he'd shot. When he'd emptied the container, he stepped back from the door panel and tossed the burning rag into the closet.

The gas-soaked clothes and body burst into flame with a *whuuuump* of displaced air, orange-yellow tongues of fire fiercely leaping upward over everything, climbing the walls to lick at the ceiling.

Kealey had time to hear an alarm go off before he ran back down the hall to the bathroom, snatching a large bath towel from a rack, then going to the tub and opening the cold water tap. He soaked the towel under the faucet, threw it over his head like a shawl, and returned to the walk-in closet.

It was already filled with churning, acrid smoke, gray blobs of it spewing into the hall, making his eyes water and his throat involuntarily clench. He hadn't lied to Mirghani; while the door and walls of the safe room were bound to be fire resistant, possibly saving every material possession he might have stashed in there, it would not keep the carbon monoxide smoke from seeping through. He would die of asphyxiation if he stayed put.

The cold, dripping towel still covering his head and shoulders, Kealey thrust himself inside through the searing flames.

"Come out of there, you stupid bastard," he said, almost overcome by smoke. The towel was sizzling around his head, steam coiling off it; it would not keep him from the fire's clutches for very long. He could already feel the hair on his arms singeing from the heat. "Come on out! I told you I just want to talk—"

The door suddenly burst open, a man Kealey identified from photos as Ishmael Mirghani pushing into the closet, wheezing and gagging. "You're a lunatic," he gasped and hacked out a series of sputtering coughs. "Whoever you are, you will kill us both. . . ."

"*Shut up!*" Kealey hollered and yanked him from the closet. The smoke had gotten so thick around him, it was hard to see, but he had no problem hearing the jangle of household fire alarms and, underneath it, the more troublesome howl of oncoming sirens. He had to get out of the place, toot sweet, and could only hope Swanson and Abby would provide a diversion if he needed it.

Grabbing Mirghani by his arm, he towed him downstairs into the main parlor, then outside through the door into the back garden. Outside its low hedge, Mackenzie sat parked against the curb in his Subaru.

"Let's move," Kealey said, hustling Mirghani along toward the car. The sirens were close now—too close for anything that remotely passed for comfort.

"Where are you taking me?" The opposition leader was sweating profusely, and Kealey didn't think it was from exertion.

"You'll find out when we get there," he said and then wrenched open the Subaru's back door, shoved Mirghani through it, and followed him inside.

A split second later Mackenzie went screeching off into the gathering dusk.

CHAPTER 20

WASHINGTON, D.C. • SUDAN

David Brenneman had always felt something special sitting behind the *Resolute* desk in the Executive Office. Inspiration was probably the best word for it, but there was also a certain assurance imparted by its impressive size and solidity, its sturdy design fashioned from the timbers of a nineteenth-century British expeditionary vessel that had braved and survived the Arctic wastes to return intact. FDR and Truman had sat behind it in times of peril and momentous decision. John F. Kennedy, whose solitary ponderings had often run deep into the night, must have gathered his will and inner fortitude at that very desk when the Russians and Cubans threatened nuclear war in the summer of 1962. Brenneman, who as a young man was an enthusiastic member of Kennedy's Peace Corps and was originally moved toward public service by his early admiration of the murdered president, liked to think the desk was infused by that which was best about the men who had preceded him as occupants of the Oval Office—their strength of purpose and higher ideals, regardless of political affiliation.

This morning, however, he felt like an exposed impostor, unworthy of the place he occupied behind the *Resolute*. A pressed-wood desk might better suit him . . . some less than authentic material, wood shavings and flimsy veneers held together with glue.

How had he allowed himself to be so badly led by the nose? When had he become such a *fool?* He thought of his pigheadedness, his unwillingness to listen to trusted advisors, his dismissal of men who had his best interests—and the best interests of the nation—at heart. He thought of his faulty judgment, colored by some amok inner wrath rather than anything that approached wisdom, intelligence, and a calm examination of information. He thought of his refusal to probe and question, his eagerness to lash out in vengeance . . . and he looked across a desk that now seemed a reminder of his unworthiness at John Harper and Bob Andrews, two of the men he'd ignored, and then at the troubled face of the woman he'd dragged along with him, Brynn Fitzgerald, who had been as susceptible to manipulation as he himself.

"I've blown this terribly," he said. "I want you all to know that I will own up to my mistakes, whatever the consequences from this point forward. That I will do what I can to rectify them. And I also want to apologize to each of you for actions that damned well might be inexcusable. . . ."

He fell silent, his hands balling into fists on the desk. He could feel his fingernails digging into his palm.

"Sir, thanks to the capture of Ishmael Mirghani, we're in a position to do what you say—prevent this whole thing from exploding on us and the rest of the world," Andrews said from across the room. "We are still in a position to stop Simon Nusairi. He's acquired the necessary weapons and equipment, and I won't diminish the imminent threat of an attack in northern Sudan. But let's remember he hasn't yet launched it—"

"No," Brenneman interrupted. "He did with great success in Darfur, though, most relevantly for us against the refugees at Camp Hadith." His voice sounded almost self-pitying to his own ears, and that had been far from his intent. "He and his people, disguised as regular Sudanese army, raped and killed my niece, and I took the bait. I *bit* like a fish going for the hook."

"It isn't as if Omar al-Bashir is an innocent," Harper said. "In fairness, the man's earned his reputation for genocidal brutality and then some. . . ."

Brenneman shook his head vehemently. "Don't massage me here. For all the ass kissing he gets from the Russians, Chinese, and his neighborhood friends in the Arab world, Bashir is a wanted criminal. An international outcast. We'd gone a long way toward isolating him without a shooting war that could result in more people dying . . . potentially tens of thousands of people. But I botched it. I authorized the misappropriation of millions of dollars of taxpayer funds at a time when our national economy is stretched to the limit. And before you stop me again, John, we can split hairs about what constitutes a legitimate CINC discretionary project, but the head of the Senate Armed Services Committee won't when it comes time for midterm elections, and he'll be completely justified in lining us up like targets in a firing range. We . . . no, *I* . . . could have listened to you and Bob. I could have paid attention back at Camp David. Instead, I dismissed you from my presence. I sanctioned Stralen's plan to deal with Somali pirates and get stolen tanks and helicopters into the hands of Sudanese rebels. I armed, equipped, and financed a small army led by Simon Nusairi, who may be a worse devil than the one we hoped to unseat, and is certainly shrewder and more calculating in his ability to manipulate us."

The secretary of state produced a long sigh, her face worn despite a careful application of makeup, her mouth and eyes surrounded by radial lines, which seemed to have stamped the skin around them in an almost inconceivably short time. "Mr. President, with all due respect, we now have two choices. We can beat ourselves up about this, or we can do what you and Bob have explicitly and implicitly suggested today. Which is to act quickly and use the small window of opportunity that remains to take charge of the situation . . . *rehabilitate* it, if you will . . . before it deteriorates beyond repair."

"Brynn's absolutely right," Andrews said. "The capture of Ishmael Mirghani was more than an intelligence score. It could be an achievement that has lasting positive ramifications. And I don't mean in terms of politics, but real benefits for the Sudanese people."

Harper was nodding. "When I met with Ryan Kealey in South Africa, I recall that we spent a few minutes pondering Mirghani's reasons for splintering off from a couple of known rebel factions . . . particularly the Sudanese Liberation Army," he said. "But here's where the Agency takes some of the blame for what's developed—it turns out it's something that should have been assessed with organized, targeted intelligence analysis." He paused. "Based on his questioning at the embassy in Khartoum, Mirghani is a far more politically and socially moderate alternative to Bashir than any other opposition leader in the country. That is why he parted ways with the SLA. When he first joined the organization, it was supposed to be a nonreligious coalition of Darfurian peoples who were under oppression from Bashir. But it's turned out to be highly polarized along tribal lines . . . and over time its reprisals against civilians who aren't members of the cause have grown as barbaric as Bashir's. Mirghani, on the other hand, split with them over those coercive tactics and has a record of vocal opposition to human rights abuses—"

"Unless it happened to be the bloodbath at Camp Hadith," Brenneman said. "He *knew* Nusairi was responsible. How am I supposed to see him as anything but a run-of-the-mill opportunist when he's allied himself with that murderer?"

"It's a good point," Harper said. "I'm not trying to paint a portrait of Mirghani with a halo and wings . . . or tell you he'll become a champion of democratic rule in Sudan. He closed his eyes to an unpardonable atrocity. But he did not participate in its planning or commit any of his guerrilla forces to it. And his cousin Hassan Saduq has independently, and without knowledge of Mirghani's capture, told Interpol that his linkage with Nusairi was formed out of desperation. Rightly or wrongly, he'd become convinced there was no other way to unseat the Bashir regime and end the civil war."

"And I came to the same conclusion," Fitzgerald said. "Let's be honest. We are sitting here right now because of our willingness to enter into a moral compromise. We knew Nusairi had an unstable personality. We were well aware he'd provoked antigovernment riots that left hundreds dead or imprisoned, and then egged on more protests based on those deaths—a cynical, manipulative way to keep stoking hostilities against Bashir. And that was fine with us. . . . So why hold Mirghani to a higher standard?"

Brenneman was shaking his head. "There's a difference. We had no evidence Nusairi was guilty of butchery. In some cases with his own hands . . . as we now know all too well."

"Mr. President, that's the trap General Stralen and I fell into," Fitzgerald said. "You can close one eye or the other to ugliness, or just squint so what you're seeing is enough of a blur that you can stomach it. It's still deliberately choosing not to see what's right there in front of you." She sighed. "But let's take a step back. I shouldn't have brought up the possibility of Mirghani as a future ally in Sudan. We can evaluate that, or not, at a later date—it's a digression we don't need at this stage. I want to get back to what Bob said at the start of this meeting. If we move fast, we can prevent what is about to happen on the ground there *now*. That, and that alone, is of the essence."

Brenneman looked thoughtful, just vaguely aware his hands had begun to unclench on the desktop. "What's our present objective?" he asked simply.

Fitzgerald glanced at Andrews, deferring to him.

"It's twofold," he said. "Nusairi played us. He claimed he intended to use the tanks and choppers against Bashir's troops in Darfur, at the southern end of the country, and instead moved them into the *north* right under our noses."

"That's if Mirghani is to be believed," Brenneman said. "How is it the spy sats can't tell us anything?"

"They can," Andrews said. "But it takes time to deflect them from orbit, and Nusairi's known it all along. He also knows it takes time to deploy our surveillance drones. That's why he moved the tanks and choppers to the staging grounds so quickly. But thanks to Mirghani—and I do believe he can be trusted—*we* now know his goal is to invade the petroleum refineries and pipelines outside Khartoum and seize control of their production. From a tactical standpoint there are only several possible staging grounds for a takeover of the area."

Brenneman shook his head in disgust. He'd been played, all right. Not only had the Chinese and Russians poured trillions into those refineries, but their current fuel demands required the uninterrupted production and shipment of oil out of Port Sudan. If Nusairi took control of the facilities, he would control the flow of oil to their shores—and gain a stranglehold on their economies. Whether they bowed to his demands or tried to retake the facilities, the destabilizing effect on global politics would be incalculable . . . and any military action against him would surely result in the refineries' destruction at his hands. In one swoop, that butcher would become one of the world's most powerful men, and it would be only a matter of time before it was revealed that the United States had given him that power.

He expelled a deep breath, pulling his thoughts together. "Okay, Bob," he said. "By a twofold goal, I assume you mean our first is to find out where Nusairi intends to launch his attack, and our second is to prevent him from getting away with it."

Andrews nodded. "Plainly stated, that's the position in which we've put ourselves. Though there are no assurances we can accomplish it."

"And where do you propose we start trying?" asked Brenneman.

Andrews looked at his assistant director, nodded for him to pick up the ball.

"With Omar al-Bashir, distasteful as that may be," Harper said. "And on the ground with Ryan Kealey."

"Simon," Mirghani said into his satellite phone. "I have some hard news to deliver."

"It has already reached me on *Talfazat*," Nusairi said.

Mirghani had expected it would. The Arabic Internet news service carried feeds from the Sudanese Radio and Television Corporation as well as Al-Jazeera.

"I have watched the images of your home burning," Nusairi said. "They say those who conducted the raid have not yet been identified, and that you somehow managed to elude them."

"Only by the grace of Allah," Mirghani said. "But 'elude' is not quite the word. I was fortunate enough to have been warned of the attack shortly before it occurred. A number of my loyal guards were killed. Had you heard?"

"Yes. The information being given is incomplete. There are reports of gunfire and several deaths, but the police have allowed no witnesses to speak." A pause. "How are you?"

"Well enough," Mirghani said. "I am in a safe place."

"And do you have any idea who was responsible?"

"It was *Mukhabarat*."

"Bashir's secret service?"

"Yes," Mirghani said. "I have expected such a move for weeks. Al-Bashir blames me for the unrest in the city. The protests and civil disobedience. The strike was in retaliation. . . . He seeks to intimidate me."

"So it had nothing to do with our immediate plans?"

"No."

"You're certain?"

"It was unrelated," Mirghani replied. "As I said, I was advised it might happen by informants within the service."

A pause. "Ishmael, I do not doubt you. But perhaps it would be best if you avoid the staging area."

"I would greatly regret that. Our day has been long awaited."

"I know. But under the circumstances, it is best to be cautious."

Mirghani was silent.

"My brother, listen to me," Nusairi said. "Let us not put in jeopardy everything toward which we have worked together."

Mirghani did not say anything for another several seconds. Then he produced a relenting sigh. "I cannot argue against prudence," he said at last. "The American, White, left the city well ahead of me. I expect he will be at the prearranged meeting place to taste the sweetness of our nation's fruit."

Nusairi laughed a little. "I am sure," he said. "And your fighters?"

"They are in position to join your forces. . . . There will be four hundred and more."

"Good," Nusairi said. "They will carry your spirit with them, Ishmael. And do not fear. We shall have adequate time to celebrate our victory."

"Yes," Mirghani said. "*Insha'Allah,* God willing, I have faith we will."

He thumbed the disconnect button on his phone, wiped a hand across his brow, and glanced up from his chair at Seth Holland and Ryan Kealey, who were standing to either side of him in the CIA station chief's fourth-floor embassy office.

"There," he said. "It is done."

Kealey looked at him stonily. "For you, anyway," he said.

In a traditional mud brick home near the defunct rail station at Kassala, a short distance from the city's famed outdoor markets and some 250 miles from Khartoum, Simon Nusairi sat looking across a simple wooden table at Cullen White. There was no electrical power in the dwelling, and an oil lamp burned between them to illuminate the room.

"It is as you suspected," Nusairi said. His features showed a kind of simmering anger. "The CIA has taken Mirghani into custody, and he has likely told them everything."

White mulled that a second. "How soon can you roll?"

"The second convoy of tanks and helicopters will not reach the outskirts of the city until tomorrow," Nusairi said. "I can have my men stand by for action, but it would be the next day before we are properly organized."

"Then the next day is when it has to be," White said.

Another silence. Nusairi watched the shadows hurled off by the lamp's burning wick cavort across the rough brown walls of the brick house.

"Mirghani went out of his way to mention our rendezvous," he said. "I think we should go through with it. As if we haven't yet met."

"A setup?"

"Yes," Nusairi said. "Clearly a net has been cast."

White sat for a moment, nodded.

"We'll have to see who gets snagged," he said.

CHAPTER 21

SUDAN

Enriched by the fertile soil of the Gash River delta, Kassala was known for the fruit groves and grape fields spread out for miles around the city proper, where its low, flat-roofed homes were laid out in a rectangle around a spacious open-air *souq*. There the crops were brought by donkey, truck, and camel train and sold from dawn to dusk, the citrus fruits, mangoes, pomegranates, and melons arranged around the market's ruler-straight borders, where they overflowed their baskets among the woven goods of Beja artisans and the silver bracelets, necklaces, and charms crafted by women of Rashaida origin.

The prevailing religion in Kassala was Islam; the ethnic mix varied. Brown jute waistcoats over their long white robes, turbans wrapped around their *taqiyahs,* steel longswords at their waists, and wooden boomerangs across their backs, the Beja clansmen, who composed the majority of the village's population, would often mill about the *souq* to trade for the superior livestock of the more colorfully dressed Rashaida nomads, whose sheep and goats were herded on seasonal migrations between the village and the Eritrean lowlands.

Kealey, Abby, and Mackenzie had driven from Khartoum in the crepuscular gloom before sunrise, Mackenzie at the wheel of the Jeep, their route following the main road out of the city southeast along the Blue Nile to Wad Medani, then turning due east across 150 miles of irrigated grain fields and parched sandy expanses to Gedaref, where the terrain gradually transitioned to rolling green hills.

Mackenzie drove mostly in dour silence. Just the day before he had helped lift the bloody remains of Jacoby Phillips from the rear section of the very Cherokee that he was now navigating toward Kassala. He and Phillips had been pretty good friends. They had often exchanged war stories—Mackenzie sharing some of his exploits in Afghanistan, Phillips speaking of his time disrupting Saddam's communications infrastructure in the Persian Gulf. They had talked, on occasion, of getting together when they finished with their hitches in Sudan. Mackenzie, who'd inherited a family home on the Tennessee River at the Kentucky border, had told Phillips of the catfish traps they would lay in the morning from his outboard, and had explained how they would go out on the boat that same evening and bring in a haul for the community fish fry. Phillips had laughed about it. *Community fry? We can catch that many fish in a single day?* Mackenzie had explained you didn't need to, not if you brought along plenty of bourbon to keep everyone happy.

The trio inside the Cherokee rolled on through the sunrise and early morning. By full daylight the uneven macadam beneath their tires had swung back north into flat plains and desert, clinging to the old British railway tracks near the Ethiopian and Eritrean borders as it took them first to the little village of Shobak, then under the loom of the twisted, humped Taka Mountains.

They had not been concerned with military checkpoints. Nor would they have to be as they neared their destination. The U.S. secretary of state and the foreign minister of Sudan had had a back-channel chat during the night and had arranged for a subsequent top secret conversation between their respective presidents. And when Omar al-Bashir and David Brenneman had spoken, Brenneman had advised Bashir of intelligence he'd received that vindicated him as far as having staged the assault on Camp Hadith and the murder of Lily Durant. While vague on many details, he had made it unequivocally clear that the United States, and indeed the world, had been deceived by subversive elements within Sudan who had planned to undermine the Bashir government, seeing that it was held responsible for the blatant atrocities committed against Camp Hadith's starved, sick refugees and the U.S. president's beloved niece. Finally, Brenneman had suggested that their mutual cooperation in bringing the conspirators to justice could lead to more than just a temporary thaw in relations between the two nations, but perhaps to a relaxing of trade embargoes and other long-term improvements in their relationship—including a U.S. reevaluation of its stance on Bashir's international criminal status. And naturally Bashir had jumped at the deal.

Kealey hated that his government was now accommodating one bloody monster in order to stop another that it had given fangs and claws. He hated the facile blurring of moral lines and, most of all, hated feeling that he was being used as a pawn in a dirty political game.

But he had gotten involved with the Agency again for one and only one reason. For him it began and ended with the photograph that John Harper had shown him in that Pretoria bar, the snapshot of a plain, dark-haired woman in her midtwenties, an aid worker surrounded by starved-looking African children, her infectious smile somehow managing to catch hold on their gaunt, hollow-eyed faces.

He wanted the man who killed Lily Durant. He wanted him more now than ever. Call it justice; call it revenge; it didn't matter. He could taste his desire for it at the back of his tongue, as he had tasted it every moment since he'd seen that picture. . . .

And it was bitter. Unbearably bitter.

"That's Jebel Atweila, about a mile east of us," Mackenzie said. He pointed out the right side of his windshield. After passing through the main checkpoint into Kassala, he had crossed the Gash River over the bridge spanning its narrows and looped around the eastern edge of town, leaving the rutted blacktop behind for dirt and gravel tracks, then swinging completely off road toward the heaving escarpments. "The other two mountains are Taka and Totil."

Kealey looked at his chronograph. "Almost noon," he said. "Mirghani's people should be there about now."

Mackenzie steered toward Atweila and was soon bumping over the pebbly deposits spread out around the slope, glancing repeatedly at his GPS unit to check his coordinates against those that had been preset for their meet. Sticking close to the base of Atweila, he continued around it until he spotted a rock-strewn switchback in the shadow of a large, anvil-shaped spur. When he got there, he swung onto it, twisted up the mountain for about 50 yards, jounced to a halt, and cut the ignition.

Kealey glanced around at their surroundings, reached for his door handle, and got out, Mackenzie and Abby exiting with him. Seth Holland's Glock 35 was in a sidearm holster under his Windbreaker, which also concealed the Muela combat blade he'd bought back in Yaoundé and carried in a sheath at his waist.

They had hiked 30 or 40 feet up along the switchback, taking several winding turns, when a group of fighters appeared from behind a knobby granite outcrop . . . almost all of them in khakis, head scarves, and combat boots, standing openly in the baking sun. All had rifles on their shoulders—M14s, AK-47s, Steyr and FAMAS bullpups.

Kealey and his companions stopped, waited as a wiry man with a short, dark beard on his tanned face approached.

"*A s'amaa zarqaa,*" Mackenzie said.

The bearded man gave his response to the code phrase. "*Wa quul id-diir.*"

They shook hands, had a brief exchange in Arabic. Then Mackenzie turned to Kealey. "This is Tariq . . . Ishmael Mirghani's second in command," he said, making their introductions. "Tariq, Ryan Kealey. And Abby Liu."

The fighter extended his hand to Kealey and gave Abby a polite nod in keeping with traditional Islamic custom toward women. Then he returned his gaze to Mackenzie.

"Your trip has been without difficulty?" he said, speaking English now.

"Happily so." Mackenzie gave a nod. "We are grateful for the invention of the GPS."

Tariq grinned. But Kealey had noticed that not all the men were quite as demonstrative in their welcomes—quite a few of them eyeing the Westerners with narrow mistrust.

"Our camp is around the mountain in a . . . how do you say . . . kerf?" Tariq touched the fingers of his hands together to form a kind of wedge.

"A notch," Mackenzie said.

Tariq nodded. "It is a short distance from here."

"How many of your men have come?" Kealey asked.

"Half again the number you see with me now," Tariq said. "We hope more will arrive before the day ends. The rest go north but will not take arms with Commander Nusairi."

Kealey considered that. Mirghani had not wanted to arouse Nusairi's suspicions by holding back his guerrillas from the attack and so had sent them along as if to join his forces. But they would experience convenient delays that would keep them from sharing the same fate as the raiders—if things went as planned.

"Do you know where Nusairi is right now?" Kealey asked after a moment.

"He arrived in the city with some men yesterday and stayed overnight in Sikka Hadiid," Tariq said. "That is where he met the other. There are still many *buyut*—"

"The other?" Kealey interrupted.

"A Westerner like yourself," replied Tariq.

"About the same age and height? Brown hair?" Kealey asked.

"Yes." Tariq touched his own eyes. "He wears *naddaaraat*."

"Glasses?"

"Yes," said Tariq.

Kealey turned to Mackenzie. "Cullen White," he said.

"So the son-of-a-bitch bastard flew out of Khartoum after he shook me," Mackenzie said, nodding. "The Sikka Hadiid is Kassala's old railway quarter. . . . I'd guess it's three, four kilometers west of these mountains and across the Gash. I've been there before. Tell you about it later." He briefly raised his eyes to Kealey's to indicate it was something he wanted to discuss in private. "The British railway station was built right around the turn of the last century. It was abandoned a long time ago, but most of the structures are intact. When you walk around the area, you see some big colonial buildings where the Brit administrators lived, and then rows and rows of round huts built for the workers and their families. . . . They're spread out pretty good. Some are modernized inside, kind of like bungalow hostels, but a whole lot of them have hardly changed in a hundred years—there's no electricity or running water. The locals have short-term rentals for travelers. Student backpackers, different types." He gave Kealey another confidential glance. "They're what Tariq called *buyut.*"

The rebel was nodding.

Kealey stood rubbing his chin in thought.

"What about the tanks and helicopters?" Abby said, breaking her attentive silence. "Have you seen them?"

"See, no," Tariq said. "But I know they came ashore at Zula in Eritrea and were brought across the border by truck. And I know they are to strike in two places. Some go toward the Nile between Khartoum and Ed Damer . . . perhaps two hundred fifty kilometers to the west of us."

"Where the oil pipeline from the fields down south follows the bend of the river to the Suakim oil terminal outside Port Sudan," Mackenzie said. "It runs for almost a thousand miles and delivers three or four hundred thousand barrels of crude a day."

"And the rest of the attack force?" Abby asked.

"It goes north."

"To the Suakim terminal—and the nearby refineries," Abby said.

Tariq's head went up and down.

"All right," Kealey said. He looked at Tariq. "I assume you have men keeping watch on Nusairi?"

"Yes, of course," Tariq said. "He remains for now in Sikka Hadiid . . . and I do not believe he will try to leave until after nightfall."

Kealey grunted, massaging his chin some more. "I think you'd better lead us to your camp so we can talk about making sure that doesn't happen," he said.

"Brynn, hello. I'm sorry I wasn't able to return your call earlier," said Israeli prime minister Avram Kessler over his secure line. He was staring out the window of his study at Bet Agion, his official residence in Rehavia, Jerusalem, watching night settle over the ancient city. "I'm afraid it's been one of those days. . . ."

"It's like old times at Northwestern, isn't it?" Brynn Fitzgerald said from her White House office. "Some things never change, Avi. You and I were always trying to make arrangements and going back and forth with our voice messages until it was too late. And then, of course, Lee would try to join in and further complicate things."

Kessler had heard her tone suddenly grow subdued. Kessler, whose parents were American Jews, had done his undergraduate studies at Northwestern University along with Fitzgerald and their mutual friend Lee Patterson, the U.S. ambassador who had been killed riding alongside Fitzgerald when her motorcade was attacked in Pakistan the year before.

"I suppose the only difference is our game of phone tag's just gone international," he said. "What's going on, Brynn? Your message sounded urgent, and I had a strange premonition it meant your esteemed commander in chief had decided on taking overt military action against Omar al-Bashir."

Silence.

Kessler's face drew taut. "Brynn . . . I was right, wasn't I?"

"Let's say your psychic receptors were well tuned but the signals hit interference somewhere over the Atlantic," she said. "Avi, we need your help."

"If you mean insofar as providing a staging area for an attack, I'll need to bring the Defense Ministry into this conversation—"

"I don't, but he'll need to be brought in, anyway," Fitzgerald said. "And probably several other members of your cabinet. Internal Affairs, Internal Security . . . but these talks will have to be brief."

Kessler's thoughts suddenly did a double take. It was something she'd said a moment ago. He had had a long day meeting with heads of the Knesset, and he was feeling laggy. "What kind of 'interference'?"

"I was thinking back to February oh-nine, when your planes hit that arms convoy in Sudan."

"Reportedly," Kessler said.

"Right, I stand corrected. When a squadron of F-sixteens reportedly hit seventeen trucks full of illegal Libyan arms in the Hala'ib Triangle. This occurred as they were reportedly being driven toward the Egyptian border by smugglers from Sudan, Ethiopia, and Eritrea, who intended to slip them through tunnels in Gaza to Hamas."

"I do recall the stories in the press," Kessler said.

"They followed reports that you'd knocked out a small convoy the month before with Hermes four-fifty drones out of Palmachim Air Base, though a little chirping birdie told me you'd moved them to Navatim. My recollection of the February story is that you'd made several passes and used the drones to assess the success of each one—"

"Brynn?"

"Yes?"

"Did that birdie happen to be wearing a yarmulke?"

A sober laugh. "Avi, you're moments from receiving a classified intelligence packet via e-mail. It will tell you about a strike force equipped with two convoys of tanks and support helicopters that is preparing to invade or possibly destroy the northern oil pipeline and refineries. We do not have real-time intel about their current position, but we know they are close to their staging ground and that the siege is imminent."

Kessler gripped the phone more tightly in his hand. "Who's behind this?"

"An alliance of rebels led by Simon Nusairi," Fitzgerald said. "I suspect your Mossad has exhaustive dossiers on him, but we'll share all our own information."

"It doesn't sound like he has your backing."

"He absolutely does not," Fitzgerald said. "This attack must be stopped. But given the immediacy of the situation, the United States does not have sufficient resources in place, or time to move those resources to do so. And we are asking a favor of your nation that, if granted, will be something I promise you will not regret."

Kessler inhaled. "You want us to launch a mission on *behalf* of Omar al-Bashir?"

"It isn't that simple. We are cooperating with Bashir to defuse a situation with dangerous global ramifications. Should you opt to assist us, he will lift the no-fly zone over certain sections of his country to allow your aircraft total operational latitude." She paused for a good ten seconds. "I will be up front with you, Avi. There may be diplomatic compromises forthcoming between my government and the Sudanese concerning Bashir's status. But you have my assurance we will in no way remain passive if his regime commits further acts of blatant ethnic violence inside its borders . . . or attempts any aggression beyond them."

Kessler thought he'd taken another breath, but wasn't sure, and consciously told himself to do it. Then he tapped his computer out of its idle mode, opened his e-mail program, and noted the new message in the queue.

"I see your packet's arrived," he said.

"Read it and get back to me," Fitzgerald said. "Don't worry about another round of phone tag, either. . . . I'll be standing by for your call."

It was shortly before sunset when they took the bridge over the Gash to Sikka Hadiid, having left the east side of town and gone around and past the souq in a motley procession of vehicles. Kealey, Mackenzie, and Abby kept their Cherokee behind Tariq, who was in a battered Outback with several of his fighters. The rest of their group—its head count had grown to two dozen men as they filtered into the mountain camp through-

out the day—rode in a dusty Jeep Wrangler, a Volkswagen hatchback, a Hyundai wagon, and an aging Ford
sedan.

On the west bank of the river the Hyundai split off
from the line and pulled under the trees outside a cul-
tivated patch of farmland. Behind the wheel of the
Cherokee, Mackenzie glanced briefly in the rearview
mirror.

"Wish we had more men to cover that area," he said.

Kealey looked at him. Back in the mountains,
Mackenzie had walked from camp with him and made
good on his promise to expand on his familiarity with
Kassala and the Sikka Hadiid. For forty years, he'd explained, fugitives from persecution during the endless
civil wars in Eritrea and Ethiopia had crossed the border plateau into Sudan, many entering through treach-
erous passes in the Taka range. On his assumption of
power, Omar al-Bashir had attempted to crack down on
the flow of refugees, since many had ancestral ties to
antigovernment factions within Kassala's Beja and
Rashaida clans.

"Bashir's problem was that he had his hands full with
the secessionists in the south and couldn't commit
enough forces to keep a tight fist on this area," Mackenzie had said. "What you should know is that Mirghani
hasn't just gotten more tolerance than other opponents
because he's from the north and not an avowed separatist. It's racial. . . . He's Arabic, and the divisions in
this country are really between Arabic and black Muslims."

"Like the refugees that came through the mountains," Kealey had said.

Mackenzie had nodded. "It wasn't so far back histor-
ically that the Arabs were making slave raids on the

south. And there hasn't been much progress in the way of attitude among the people who rule this country," he said. "What you need to know is that the majority of refugees are black, and some are aligned with the opposition in Darfur. Over the past decade we—the Agency—did some things to assist their entering the country. That included helping them dig a tunnel between the west side of the river and some of those huts in Sikka Hadiid. They'd take temporary shelter there and get out of the city. For them it was a lifesaver while their own countrymen were burning down their villages. For us it was building another segment of the population that was hostile to Bashir . . . completely win-win."

Kealey had taken a long moment to digest all that, standing in the hot sun beating down on the craggy slope. "We're going to have to keep the tunnel's entrance covered tonight," he'd said. "In case Nusairi and White try using it to make a getaway."

"Yup."

"That means you're going to have to let Tariq know about it."

"If he doesn't already. There isn't much that gets past Mirghani or his headmen."

"That isn't my point," Kealey said. "It's one thing for them to be aware the tunnels exist. Another to find out the Agency had a role in digging them. Or that it chose to support a particular group—ethnic, political, whatever—over theirs."

Mackenzie had shrugged his shoulders. "Them's the breaks," he'd said. "This is a complicated world. Now we need them, and they need us. A whole new codependency is born. We can't worry about Tariq feeling slighted."

All of which was true, Kealey thought now as they

rolled by the decayed, sun-bleached railway station with its merging of Arabian and British architecture—the simple curve of the entry arch overlooked by Victorian gables with elaborate moldings and the remnants of a high clock tower, its dial and workings long ago removed by thieves or vandals.

With the station and its splintered, torn-up tracks at their rear, they doused their headlamps in the deepening night, then passed the buildings that had housed the British officials and finally saw the long rows of workers' huts ahead of them in the dimness.

"We'll be there in a couple minutes," Mackenzie said to his passengers. "Better get ready."

Kealey took three sets of thermal night vision goggles on headsets from a compartment under the dash, passed one back to Abby, and put the other between himself and Mackenzie. A moment later he heard Abby palm a 30-round clip into her Sig 552 5.56mm assault rifle and reached for the 552 in his seat well, setting it across his lap. Seth Holland's knee-jerk admonition to treat the weapons with care back at the embassy had been almost the same as when he'd handed Kealey his Glock 9mm pistol before they headed out to Bahri.

Under very different circumstances, the recollection might have struck Kealey as humorous. But he found nothing remotely amusing about what was about to go down tonight, just as he could find nothing to like about the rapidly shifting political expedients and allegiances around him. On the other hand, he thought, it was worth reminding himself that his own objective was neither complicated nor ambiguous.

He wanted Simon Nusairi; it really couldn't have been simpler, or more serious, than that.

* * *

"The commander is in the *beyt* there . . . the last in this line," Tariq said, pointing. He had braked to a halt in front of the Cherokee, gotten out, and hastened over to speak with Mac through the driver's side window. "There are three or four of his men in the one next to it."

Mackenzie nodded, gazed out into the night. He could see what appeared to be firelight in the windows. "No chance he could've left the lamps burning to trick us and snuck off while the cats were away?"

Tariq angled his head slightly toward one of the tall, vacant officers' buildings behind them. "My cats have had their eyes on him from the rooftops," he said. "He and the American remain within."

Kealey looked across the seat at Tariq. "Okay," he said. "Let's move in."

Tariq nodded and hurriedly returned to the Outback.

The plan was to hit hard and fast, using the element of surprise to their best advantage, and to keep their targets from scattering into the night.

Tariq sped up to the farthest hut, the one occupied by Nusairi and White, jolting to a halt directly behind it. His wheels spinning up dirt and pebbles, Mackenzie simultaneously sheered up in front so no one could rabbit through the entrance, the Cherokee's doors flying open even as it stopped, Kealey and Abby springing from inside with their night vision goggles down over their eyes, Mackenzie following an instant later.

Behind them, Tariq's fighters in the Wrangler and Volkswagen stuck to the same execution, the Wrangler shooting around back of the second hut, the VW screaming up to its front door, its occupants spilling from both vehicles. The Hyundai wagon took up a rear position, its men doubling as lookouts and backups in case anyone managed to escape from either of the two huts.

Semiautomatic gunfire tore from inside the huts at once, the staccato bursts shattering their windowpanes amid explosive sprays of glass. Kealey rushed over to the first hut in a crouch, flattened his back against it to one side of a broken window, peered inside. And then he saw them in shades of gray through the lenses of his NVGs—Cullen White and Simon Nusairi. White held what appeared to be a Kalashnikov in his hands and had ducked behind a table with an oil lamp on it. Nusairi was scrambling through a door on the far side of the room, an identical weapon in his fist spitting bullets ahead of his path.

Kealey pivoted on the ball of his foot and returned fire, the Sig 552 quivering in his hand. Then he went flat alongside the window again. He heard guns answering Nusairi's volley out back—Tariq and his men. Abby, meanwhile, had shuffled up next to him even as Mackenzie backed against the opposite side of the window frame and triggered a salvo of his own into the hut.

A dozen yards away the second hut was also caught in a storm of semiauto fire, the salvos blowing out its windows, bullets pecking splinters from its wooden door. Kealey heard an extended peal from one of the guns inside the hut and then saw one of Tariq's fighters go down to the ground with a howl of pain, clutching his stomach as he curled into a semifetal position.

He zoned in on his goal, looked across at MacKenzie and Abby.

"*Cover me!*" he called, motioning toward the door.

A brisk nod from Mackenzie, then Abby. Mackenzie edged from the window to the door along the outer wall of the house, stayed there to the right of the entrance. Abby, head tucked low, raced around the Cherokee, using it as a shield as she put herself to the left of the door.

Kealey looked over at Mackenzie, held up three fingers, ticked off a visual countdown. *Three, two, one . . .*

And then Mackenzie backed up a step, directed his fire at the lock plate, almost tearing it free of the door itself. He released the AK's trigger, sent the door crashing inward with a high leg kick to the twisted remnants of the flimsy metal plate, and poured more rounds into the hut, Abby joining him now with a rippling burst from her rifle.

"*Now!*" Kealey shouted, and they momentarily ceased fire as he went in low, the stock of his weapon against his arm, his fist around the grip, finger squeezing the trigger.

Bullets streamed from his gun into the hut as he laid out a side-to-side firing pattern, sweeping the room, his eyes seeking out White through the goggles.

He was still kneeling behind the table, having shuffled behind a chair. Incredibly, the oil lamp on the tabletop remained unbroken, throwing its pallid orange light around the room. Not wanting to be a stationary target, Kealey dove to one side, swung the rifle in White's direction, prepared to fire—and suddenly the chair was thrown across the room at him, flying through the air, nearly hitting him smack in the chest. He managed to avoid it on reflex and had some vague, marginal awareness of it hitting the wall directly behind where he'd stood as he arced the snout of his gun toward the oil lamp and blew it to bits and pieces.

Oil spilled from the disintegrated lamp onto the table and chairs, igniting instantly, bathing them in fire. Burning puddles formed on the floor. White was caught in a shower of burning droplets, snaps of flame erupting on his sleeves and trousers. As he stood, trying to slap them out with his hands, Kealey ran across the room and tackled him across the waist, the momentum of his lunge sending both men down amid the spreading blaze.

His clothes on fire, White hit the floor on his back, grunting out an expulsion of breath, Kealey landing atop him, his weapon over his shoulder on its strap. He saw White's hand come chopping up at his throat, blocked it with a muscular forearm, and then brought his elbow down on White's neck and punched him squarely in the middle of his face. Blood gushing from his broken nose, White somehow wrapped his fingers around Kealey's throat, his thumbs pressing up under his chin even as his shirt and trousers continued burning.

Kealey hit him again in the face, felt his fingers loosen around his windpipe, and tore them free. Suddenly, then, a gun muzzle came down against White's temple, pushing it sideways.

"Don't move, fucker!" Mackenzie, his legs planted wide, stood just to one side of the two men, the bore of his rifle steady against White's head. "I ought to goddamn let you lay here and burn!"

Kealey got to his feet, swooped in a breath. He could smell White's singed hair and flesh. He looked around, saw a field jacket on a wall hook to his right, tore it down off the hook, and used it to beat out the flames on White's clothes and the floor around him.

"I want this son of a bitch alive," he said. And then glanced at the doorway at the back of the room, where the hut had been partitioned with a plasterboard wall. Goggles on, Abby was just on the other side of the door in the darkness, holding her weapon across her body, looking down at the floor.

Knowing what to expect, Kealey swore under his breath, raced into the second room, and saw the oriental rug tossed back from the open wooden floor panel. Outside the hut the sound of gunfire had become light and sporadic.

He and Abby exchanged glances through the monocular lenses of their NVGs.

"Did you see Nusairi go down there?" he asked.

She shook her head no. "We can't head in after him. . . . If he's waiting, he could easily pick us off."

"He isn't waiting," Kealey said. "He intends to reach his forces at Suakim or Ed Damer. And he's got enough of a lead so we'd never chase him down on foot. I—"

The heavy tramp of boots now, coming through the hut from out front. Kealey jerked upright, swung his weapon around at the door to the room . . . and then felt the tension drain from his limbs. It was Tariq, a silhouette against the deeper darkness, squinting down at the tunnel entrance with his unaided eyes.

"We've finished those *ghabanat* in the other hut. . . . I lost Abdul, a good friend. And another, Mahzin, is badly wounded," he said, shaking his head. Then he snapped his cell phone from his pocket and looked at Kealey through the gloom. "I left my men at the other end of the tunnel, over by the Gash."

Kealey's molars ground together. Yes, Tariq had left his men there. But wouldn't Nusairi anticipate it? At any rate this would not be left up to them. Or anyone else.

Spinning toward the door without a word, he ran out to where Mackenzie stood with his gun still pointed down at White. A pair of Tariq's fighters were trussing his arms and legs with strips of rawhide cord.

"The car keys," he said, holding out his hand. *"Now!"*

Mackenzie got the key ring from his pocket and tossed it to him without asking questions . . . not that Kealey would have lost a moment pausing to answer before he raced from the hut into the night.

No longer wearing his goggles, Kealey white-knuckled the Cherokee's steering wheel, its high beams lancing the night, his foot hard to the gas pedal as he roared over the curving, potholed road toward the river. It was two miles to the mountains, just over a quarter that distance to the bridge. Head start or not, Nusairi was on foot. He would not be able to gain much distance on him.

The rail station behind him now, Kealey sped past square patches of farmland to the grove of trees at the river's edge, came to a short stop. Where *had* Tariq positioned his men?

He glanced over his left shoulder, then right at a copse of shrubs and trees. Yes, there.

Leaving the headlights on, he pushed out his door, hastened a yard or two through the screening brush . . . and then almost stumbled over something underfoot.

He knew what it was before looking down. The body lay sprawled faceup on the ground, a bullet hole in its forehead, the toe of its boot against its outstretched arm. The second of Tariq's men was on his side only inches from the first, blood oozing from what was left of his mouth and chin.

Their old Ford sedan was gone. A few feet away from where its tires had flattened the surrounding vegetation, Kealey saw the hinged trapdoor to the tunnel. It was thrown wide open, the packed sod and twigs that had camouflaged it flapped aside.

He turned back to the Cherokee, keyed it to life, and tore off for the river crossing.

Kealey was coming off the east side of the bridge when he spotted the wink of taillights up ahead of him to the right, on the street turning off toward the *souq* at the heart of Kassala. There were no other vehicles on the road, no people around; the town had rolled up whatever damned sidewalks it had. . . . He would have to take his chances that it was Nusairi.

He swung onto the narrow street, pouring on the gas. The taillights, where were they? The main part of town was a labyrinth of twists and turns, and he'd momentarily lost sight of them. . . .

Mouthing a string of profanities, Kealey whipped his head back and forth, then thankfully picked up the gleaming red lights around another sharp bend to his right. He swung into it, found himself on a relative straightaway, and accelerated, noticing the car ahead had sped up, too. He'd gambled correctly, then—it had to be Nusairi.

He bumped on over the cobbled street, his foot to the pedal, gaining on the Ford. It would be no match for his Cherokee, but Nusairi probably knew the city's layout better than he did, giving him that far from negligible advantage. Kealey was afraid he might yet reach another twisty section of town and shake him loose.

Reaching the next corner, the Ford took a sudden left, Kealey almost on its bumper now, able to see Nusairi hunched over the wheel. He swerved after him, realized they'd gotten to the wide-open central market— there were stalls and wagons all around, *everywhere,* some emptied out for the night, others with their wares covered with tarpaulins.

Kealey poured it on now, getting closer, closer, and then cutting his wheel to the left so he pulled directly alongside the Ford. He looked out his passenger window, briefly met Nusairi's gaze through double panes of glass, and swung the wheel hard to his right.

He felt the collision of their doors jar his back, heard the tortured, scraping grind of metal on metal. Then Nusairi's lighter vehicle half bounced, half skidded to the right and went plowing into a cart of woven textiles, knocking off its wheel so it spun wildly over the cobbles, the cart toppling onto its side, blankets and sheets of fabric spilling everywhere over the street.

Somehow, though, Nusairi managed to hang on to control of the Ford. Kealey swung hard into his flank again, this time almost lifting Nusairi's wheels off the ground to send him careening through a high stack of packing crates. The crates broke apart over his hood and windshield, wood flying, the burlap sacks of millet and corn inside them breaking open to disgorge their contents. Nusairi tailspun across the square into a vendor's stall and smashed into a long wooden table, upending it before he hit the back of the stall and brought its bare plank walls crashing down on him, demolishing the Ford's windshield.

Kealey stopped the Cherokee and exited it in a heartbeat, rushing across the square to the Ford as Nusairi pushed himself out of its scraped and beaten driver's door. Blood trickling from under his eye, cuts on his cheeks and forehead, Nusairi looked at him, turned away, and started to make a break for the shadows.

On him now, right *behind* him, Kealey took a running leap at Nusairi that almost knocked both men to the cobblestones, wrapping his arms around his back to try and catch hold of him. But Nusairi, staggering, managed to stay on his feet. He twisted around to face

Kealey, locking eyes with him, his features distorted with rage and malice—the rage showing above all else, completely overtaking him, his eyes flaring, his lips peeled back from his tightly clenched teeth in an almost bestial grimace.

And then he dove at Kealey, literally dove, giving Kealey little time to realize that the bottom of his shirt had pulled out from the waistband of his cargo pants and bunched up to reveal the handle of his combat knife.

Nusairi snatched hold of the knife, pulling it from its sheath, the blade flashing in his right hand as it came up. He took a vicious swipe at Kealey, barely missed carving a deep gash across his abdomen, and might have done so if Kealey hadn't feinted backward at the last instant. As Nusairi came charging at him with the blade again, Kealey recovered his balance, pivoted on the forward part of his left foot, and shot both hands out in front of him, his right clenching Nusairi's knife hand, his left grabbing the same elbow, twisting it around, yanking it up and back toward Nusairi.

They grappled like that for an endless minute, strength against strength, their faces inches apart. Kealey could feel Nusairi's breath, see his cheeks puffing with exertion, the blade suspended between them.

And then he felt something in Nusairi's grip give way, just for a split second. He moved forward into him, knowing it might be his one opportunity, bending the knife back toward Nusairi's chest, back so its point was directly under his rib cage . . . and, mustering everything he had, gave it a hard upward shove to bury it inside him to the handle.

Still on his feet, Nusairi produced a feral sound that was something between a grunt and a moan, his hands going to his chest, his blood pouring over them in crimson sheets. At last, after what seemed another long while, his legs began to sag.

Kealey pulled out the knife before Nusairi could fall, stepped back, and stood looking at him, looking into his eyes. . . .

Looking into his eyes, his gaze calm and unwavering as the life faded out of them.

"That was for Lily Durant," he said before the last spark was extinguished. Then, waiting for Nusairi's body to finally hit the ground, he bent over him to add something that had struck him almost as an afterthought. "And by the way, all your tanks and choppers are about to get blown to kingdom come."

True to Brynn Fitzgerald's "chirping birdie," the Israelis did indeed launch the Hermes "Ziq" 450s out of Navatim for their strikes at Sudan. Although the unmanned aerial vehicles were indeed a component of the 166th Squadron at Palmachim Air Base near Tel Aviv, moving them to the base outside Be'er Sheva in the southeastern part of the country—and closer to the Red Sea route to the Sudanese border—extended their tactical range both in terms of fuel usage and data communications.

Another tactical advantage to having the drones take off from Navatim, alternately known as Air Base 28, was that it put them at the same spot as the 116th "Defenders of the South" Squadron and the 140th "Golden Eagle" Squadron, both of which were home to the F-16 fighter jets that would be essential to destroying tanks and helicopters. The UAVs, with their respective payloads of two Rafael missiles, were formidable weapons against convoys bearing arms and missile launchers. But when it came to destroying thirty-three tanks and over a dozen choppers, they were best used in a support role, sending the Israelis real-time pictures, taking out a secondary target or two, and perhaps doing some cleanup.

Having Sudanese air space unrestricted to them, however, the F-16s left little to be cleaned up. Their massive array of air-to-ground missiles and laser-guided bombs took care of the convoy quite neatly in just three runs—the third precautionary.

It was not always the size of the strike force, but how it was used, that counted. Simon Nusairi's purchase barely got out of the box, however, rendering even that observation moot.

CHAPTER 22

SUDAN • WASHINGTON, D.C.

As the Cairo-bound Gulfstream 550 charter jet tax-ied left onto the runway at Khartoum Interna-tional, Ryan Kealey looked out his window and saw the Sudan People's Armed Forces troops that had escorted his group through the airport break into spontaneous applause, standing there ranked alongside the tarmac.

Abby Liu sat beside him, Mackenzie in the seat fac-ing her. Cullen White, in wrist and ankle cuffs, was next to Mackenzie and opposite Kealey. The rest of the char-ter jet's cabin was occupied by a contingent of six dark-suited Agency men who had flown in from Egypt the day before.

"Well, Kealey, it seems you're a local hero," White said in a quiet voice. His eyes had fixed on him through his wire-frame glasses. "The man who saved the com-passionate and lawful regime of Omar al-Bashir from scheming rebels . . . and their infidel coconspirator."

Stone-faced, Kealey ignored him and stared out at

the clapping soldiers in their dress regalia. He was glad when the plane angled off so they were out of sight.

"You should be proud," White said. "You even bagged the Western devil alive. Here I sit, flying back to America in shackles. Shame on me, right?"

"Shut up," Mackenzie said.

White glanced over at him. "What?"

"You heard me." Mackenzie met White's gaze with his own. "I don't want to hear your fucking mouth."

"Are you going to gag me?" White said with a small acid smile. "Or maybe just shoot me in my seat. If you're careful, there's very little risk of puncturing the side of the cabin. Though I know you all want me back in Washington so I can sing from my cage."

Mackenzie just looked at him for a long moment, then slowly turned his head away.

"You'd might as well have killed me back in Kassala," White said, facing Kealey again. "It's what you wanted, isn't it?"

Kealey stared out at the runway without response.

"I've no stories to share," White said. "Nothing to tell anyone. I was just a freelancer for Simon Nusairi. Hired help. Kind of like you were for a while, Kealey. Was it Blackwater . . . or Xe, as it calls itself now? I hear the company wanted to clean up its gunslinger image after your little exploit in South Africa."

Kealey turned from the window without speaking a word, not so much looking at White as past him. Abby, meanwhile, had shifted around in her seat.

"We have more than one bird in hand," she said. "I think you know that, Mr. White."

"Hassan Saduq? An arms peddler? Who'd tell you anything to save his neck? Is he going to be believed?" White said.

"Don't pretend to be naïve," she said. "There is a money trail."

"You might want to mention Walter Reynolds, the senior diplomat at the U.S. embassy in Khartoum," Mackenzie said. "Plus embassy staffers confirming this guy's visits there, security videos . . ."

"Thank you, Mac." Her almond-shaped brown eyes had settled on White again. "You see, no one needs to hear your song. There are others, enough for an opus. And your name and Nusairi's will be in every refrain."

"Your personal savior's too," Kealey said, breaking his silence. "We wouldn't want to forget the man who's as responsible for Lily Durant's death as Nusairi."

White's eyes narrowed on him. "I don't know who you mean."

"Sure, you don't," Kealey said. "Keep on saying it. But your time's running out and so is your line of bull-shit."

The two men looked at each other a moment, their silence only underscored by the loud whine of turbines as the plane accelerated for takeoff. Kealey felt the usual lurch inside him as it bucked against gravity and went wheels up into the air.

"It was Jonathan Harper who once demanded I leave the CIA," White finally said. "The *legendary* Harper. Did you know he called me to his office at Langley to request my departure in person?"

Kealey shrugged. "Guess he probably didn't think it was worth the cost of a phone call."

"Good one. I didn't realize you had a sense of humor." White chuckled automatically, kept staring at Kealey through his metal rims. "I only bring up his name for one reason. And that's to ask . . . without Harper, where would you be?"

"What's your point?" said Kealey.

"It's no secret he had faith in you when others didn't. That he's been your guardian angel at the Agency," White said. "What would you do if he needed, absolutely *required* you for a task he could entrust to no one else? An assignment that had certain vital elements you found . . . objectionable? Would you refuse? Or do it, anyway, because of everything you owed him?"

Kealey shook his head. "I don't believe in guardian angels," he said.

"Ah . . . but there is one who's believed in you," White replied.

Kealey was quiet for a while before he gave another shrug. "His problem," he said.

And he returned his eyes to his window as the jet banked to the right, leaving the African coastline behind for the Red Sea, then climbing gradually through a blue haze to cruising altitude and the greater part of its flight north to Egypt.

"I've just received word that Cullen White has been placed aboard a direct flight from Cairo to New York," President Brenneman said. He was at his desk in the Oval Office, talking to Brynn Fitzgerald, his back to the large bay windows looking out on the South Lawn. "He remains in the Agency's custody."

"And once he lands?" Fitzgerald asked.

"He'll be air-shuttled to D.C. and brought to a safe house for preliminary interrogation," Brenneman said. "I'm not sure a decision's been made as to where he'll be held after that."

Fitzgerald nodded. It was gusty outside, and as she sat facing the windows, she could see the breeze rustling the magnolias on the South Lawn. "Have you put in a call to the DIA?"

"Yes." Brenneman rubbed the bottom of his chin with his index finger. "Joel Stralen requested that his personnel have a role in White's questioning. His preference was that it be active, but he would have settled for having one or more people there as observers."

"And your response to him was . . . ?"

"Exactly what you would expect."

"And how did General Stralen react to being refused outright?"

"He's on his way over from the Pentagon right now. I suppose he intends to argue his case." Brenneman shrugged. "You know, Brynn . . . as a kind of mental exercise, or way of getting a handle on a person, I try to imagine their thoughts in terms of printed typestyles. Been doing it since my early teens. I've known the general for a long time and have always imagined him thinking in boldface."

"A large font, I'd guess."

"Very large," Brenneman said with a grim smile. "Joel Stralen is a hard-liner, and I wanted that perspective among my core advisors. We've all gotten so used to sticking our thumbs in the wind here in D.C., I felt it important."

"You weren't mistaken," Fitzgerald said. "Our error was in letting ourselves be swayed too far by his point of view." She hesitated. "May I speak personally of something? It's a difficult subject."

He nodded his head and sat there waiting.

"I've done a lot of soul-searching over the past several days," Fitzgerald said. "In fact, I've turned my soul inside out and shaken it to see what falls loose. And I realized I wasn't nearly as recovered from the trauma of my kidnapping as I'd believed. As a woman in the capital . . . in any position of authority, I suppose . . . you have to present a tough façade. I felt that if I didn't appear to be over what happened to me in Pakistan, my effectiveness as an advisor and negotiator would be comprised. I won't second-guess myself now, not in that regard. But where I erred, and erred terribly, was in buying my own act. I was swayed by Stralen because I identified too closely with your niece. I let emotions throw me off balance, overtake my capacity for making rational decisions—"

Brenneman raised a hand to interrupt. "Don't beat yourself up," he said. "You and I share the same essential regrets. Our emotions colored how we saw things. The timing was horrific, which does not mitigate our responsibility for what was done. We own the results of our decisions. . . . We will always own them. But all we can do now is move on and deal with the consequences." He expanded his chest with air, slowly breathed out, his sober, weary eyes holding on her face. "Brynn . . . when I say General Stralen views things in terms of absolutes, it is not to imply he's simpleminded. He's a shrewd, calculating military man. A chess player. And what I've wondered, God help us all—"

Brenneman's intercom line flashed, and he pressed the speakerphone button to answer his personal secretary. "Yes?"

"Mr. President, General Stralen is here to see you."

"Right on cue," Brenneman observed.

"Excuse me?" asked the secretary.

"Nothing, Fran . . . sorry." Brenneman saw his secretary of state look at him, her eyes silently asking whether he preferred she stay or excuse herself from the office. He motioned for her to stay put. "Tell the general to come right in," he said over the intercom.

* *. *

"Joel, please have a seat." Brenneman motioned the DIA chief into a chair without rising from behind his desk. "Brynn and I were just wrapping up our conversation about Cullen White."

In his air force dress blues, his jacket buttoned almost to the collar, Stralen looked surprised to see Fitzgerald in the office. Quick to recover, he took her hand decorously but remained on his feet. "Sir," he said, facing the president, "White's the reason I'm here as well, and I intend to be brief. If you don't mind, though"—he glanced back at Fitzgerald—"and with no disrespect to Madam Secretary, I'd ask that we speak privately."

"I think it's best we all stay," Brenneman said. "There's nothing that needs hiding between the three of us."

Stralen nodded. "I don't wish to hide anything. But my issue is strictly of concern to the DIA—"

"No," Brenneman said. "If it relates to Cullen White's activities in Sudan, it's all our concern . . . mine, yours, and Brynn's. You can forget about trying to compartmentalize."

"Fine, sir," Stralen said. "That is fully understood. Indeed, I might agree with it. But then why isn't the DIA a participant in White's interrogation?"

Brenneman looked at him. "Are you serious?"

"Of course." The skin tightened over the well-defined planes and angles of Stralen's face. "Do I sound like I'm joking?"

"Joking, no," Brenneman said. "But in frankness, I don't see how you think the DIA *can* participate. Only the CIA has clean hands here. DOD, State, this very office—we've all compromised ourselves."

"How so? What precisely have we done *wrong?*"

"If you don't already know, Joel, you are in pronounced denial," replied Brenneman.

Stralen was shaking his head. "The worst we can be
accused of is misappropriation of funds. And even so,
the distribution of CINC discretionary resources has its
gray areas. As far as seeming to run against our own embargo, we could argue—"

"My God, we shipped arms to the very people who
killed my *niece*," Brenneman said sharply. He inhaled,
struggling to control himself. "Enough, Joel. You can
save your argument for other ears besides mine. But
while you're here, I do have a question for you. A blunt
one. And I would appreciate a direct response."

Stralen did not budge from the middle of the room
but simply met the president's gaze. "I'm listening, sir."

Brenneman felt his whole body tense. Every muscle,
every tendon. He had not wanted to ask this of the man
standing there in front of him, someone he had called a
friend for decades. Had not even wanted to consider it.

"When you funded Simon Nusairi . . . did you have
any inkling he'd been involved in Lily's death? I mean,
any knowledge he may have been responsible for what
happened to her?"

Silence fell over the office. Both Brenneman and
Fitzgerald were looking at Stralen now, but he kept his
own eyes on the president's face.

"Sir, I am heading to my Virginia retreat for the
weekend. It has been a long six months, and my objective is to gather stamina for the political battles to
come," Stralen said. "Should you still want to ask that
question on my return, I will answer fully and completely."

More silence, Brenneman felt its weight press down

on his shoulders, felt his very *heart* sinking underneath it.

"Very well," he said. "Do as you wish."

And continued to feel his heart sink like a rock as Stralen abruptly turned and left the room.

EPILOGUE

WASHINGTON, D.C. • VIRGINIA BEACH

The CIA safe house on Twelfth Street NW off Massachusetts Avenue was a very intentionally nondescript three-story redbrick building opposite Our Lady of Divinity Catholic Church and bookended by a pre–World War II apartment house on the corner of Massachusetts and another small walk-up heading toward the M Street intersection.

Stepping out into the fresh air after the preliminary debriefing that had taken just shy of four hours, Kealey looked down the short flight of stairs descending to the sidewalk and saw John Harper leaning against his double-parked black Suburban, hands in the pockets of the light raglan trench coat flapping around his knees.

"Ryan," he said. "Seems I'm right in the nick of time."

Kealey went downstairs, crossed the pavement, slid between the front and rear bumpers of two curbed vehicles. Harper took a hand out of his pocket and extended it as he approached.

"Same set of Agency wheels as ever," Kealey said, eyeing the vehicle as they shook.

Harper shrugged. "You know what they say about old habits."

"Yours or the Agency's?"

"Some would say there isn't a damn bit of difference."

Kealey grunted. "Don't you get a driver anymore?"

"My option. I'm on unofficial business today."

Kealey looked at him in silence.

"This is a far cry from where we last met in Pretoria," Harper said after a moment.

Kealey nodded. "No Springsteen music," he said.

"No." Harper smiled a little. "No jukebox either."

They stood regarding one another in the shade of an elm tree as traffic and pedestrians moved quietly by on the street.

Harper checked his watch. "Almost five o'clock," he said. "I'm wondering if you'd like to come over for dinner. Stay the night if you want."

"That's okay," Kealey said. "Your people booked me at Best Western. It has room service, a decent view."

"All the amenities one would desire for a visit to the capital."

"Just about," Kealey said. "I'm set there, anyway."

Harper looked at him. "Julie knows you're in D.C. and is hoping to see you," he said. "It's been a long time."

"I don't think so."

"Why not?"

"Things have happened," Kealey said. "A lot's changed. . . ."

"Nature of life," Harper said with a mild shrug. "That and getting older."

Kealey hesitated. "Listen, thanks for the offer. And regards to Julie. But there's no point in her going to the trouble."

"No trouble," Harper said. "She invited a few friends over, anyway. Some staffers from back when she worked at Mayo. One of them's a woman named Allison Dearborn. She hooked up with Julie through me . . . long story there . . . and they organized a little reunion." He shrugged his shoulders. "I'm going to be bored stiff listening to their hospital war stories and complaints, Ryan. It would be a real favor."

Kealey looked at him. "That's another habit you can't seem to shake."

"Asking favors of you?"

Kealey nodded, prompting a chuckle from Harper.

"This isn't quite as big or demanding as the last," Harper said, "and it comes with Julie's great cooking. Chicken Marsala tonight."

Kealey turned his head, gazed up the street awhile at nothing in particular, then finally looked back at Harper and shrugged. "What the hell, John. But just so you know, it's Julie, not you, that I've missed."

Harper grinned, reached for the handle of his passenger door. "I'll take that as a positive once removed," he said, opening it for Kealey.

General Joel Stralen stood on the balcony of his Hampton Roads condominium, looking out over the white sands of Virginia Beach from ten stories up, watching the blue Atlantic waves lap at the shoreline. He had always loved this place, with its contemplative silences and placid vistas . . . always felt his most whole here.

Holding the balcony's rail, he turned his face up at

the cloudless sky, closing his eyes to let the warm sunshine beat against them. He had been something of a sun worshipper his entire life, not the smartest of habits, soaking up all those UVs. On the other hand, it took a while before they got to you, and they hadn't gotten to him yet.

He sighed into the breeze. Cullen White was on his way to the United States with John Harper's man Ryan Kealey, someone who was not even Agency anymore. On his way across the land and sea to testify that the director of the Defense Intelligence Agency, and a friend of President Brenneman, had not only engineered an illegal arms trade with Sudanese militiamen but also . . .

His hands tightened on the rail. It had been done in the nation's best interests. The *world's* best interests. What else might it have been considered when you weighed one sacrifice against all the thousands that had stood to benefit from the removal of a dictator like Omar al-Bashir and the seizure of the oil refineries that were giving the Russians and Chinese economic dominance over the United States?

If the plan had been successful, all that would have been taken care of at once. Lily Durant would not have died in vain, but would have given her life for a greater purpose.

That said, he had told Simon Nusairi where she was, and had arranged for her death in order to jolt David Brenneman and Brynn Fitzgerald from their passivity. He had not counted on the brutality of the act. . . .

The rape.

The torture.

No, Stralen had not counted on that. But would he have changed what he'd done if he had?

He took a slow, deep breath, moving closer to the rail. Would he have changed what he'd done if he had known not only that Lily would die but also the manner of her death?

He opened his eyes now, staring up into the dazzling brightness of the sky, gradually turning them toward the full glare of the sun. It was alone up there above him, not a plane or bird in sight.

Just him and the sun, the sun and him. And, of course, the sand and water below.

Stralen looked up into the glaring orb as long as he could, his eyes at once burning and filling with moisture.

He jumped without ever looking down.

More Books From Your Favorite Thriller Authors

More Thrilling Suspense From Your Favorite Thriller Authors